BLACK AND DEEP DESIRES

BLACK AND DEEP DESIRES

A Gothic Vampire Romance

BONDS OF BLOOD
BOOK I

CLAIRE TRELLA HILL

Book Hoard Press

This book is a work of fiction. Names, characters, places, and incidents are the product of the author's imagination or are used fictitiously and are not to be construed as real. Any resemblance to actual events, locales, or persons, living or dead, is coincidental.

Black and Deep Desires

*For Mom and Dad
I love you
Sorry about the vampires*

"Tis now the very witching time of night,
    When churchyards yawn and hell itself breathes out
    Contagion to this world; now could I drink hot blood,
    And do such bitter business as the day
    Would quake to look on."
    Hamlet 3.2.380-384

"What man can live and not see death?
    Can he deliver his life from the power of the grave?"
    Psalm 89:48

Prologue

His abode was secret, known only to a very few. When the first footstep whispered on the stair, he knew who sought him.

"Why do you come, Etienne?" His voice rang in the silence.

"Salem, I had to speak to you. I—"

The visitor had brought no lamp—he did not need one. Even so, he stumbled over the obstruction at the foot of the chamber's entrance.

"Did you never build any bookshelves for this hoard, Salem?" Etienne stared in dismay at the stacks of books that lurched around the room.

"I like it this way."

Etienne's colorless gaze found him in the armchair in the corner, and his eyes widened in horror. "*Merde*, how old are those clothes? Don't you know what year it is?"

Etienne had always been a dandy, and Salem had not expected him to change. His friend wore a suit of an unfamiliar cut, and oddly, a pair of spectacles that Salem knew he didn't need perched on his thin nose. Other than that, Etienne looked exactly the same—lean, blond curling hair, and marble-like eyes.

Salem rolled his eyes and stuck his finger in the page of the book to mark his place. "No, I don't know what year it is, and don't tell me. I don't want to know. Time marches on in a long unending train of sameness and I don't care." He laughed. The sound echoed strangely with another person in the chamber. Salem was attuned to the rhythms of his home, accustomed to the aloneness. Etienne's intrusion upset his usual silences.

"They never tell you how insufferable time itself becomes— 'tomorrow and tomorrow and tomorrow creeps in this petty pace from day to day, to the last syllable of recorded time; and all our yesterdays have lighted fools the way to dusty death. Out, out, brief candle!'"

The lone taper by his elbow, the room's sole source of light, wavered accommodatingly.

Etienne stared at him, flabbergasted.

Salem stood and snapped the book shut. "Macbeth," he said flatly.

His friend gazed around the room. "Is that what you've been doing all this time? Reading Shakespeare, camped in this hole in the ground?"

"And why not? What else is there?"

"*Mon Dieu*," Etienne said, ignoring that, "what do you do for sustenance?"

"It's sheep country," Salem said in an extremely dry voice. "I make do."

Etienne stared. "You've heard absolutely nothing about the world?" he said in tones of pure horror.

"Exactly. I've been moldering in my cellar and growing out my fingernails since 1860." Salem rolled his eyes. "*No*, I noticed when the rail roads went out this way. And I do read a newspaper once in a while."

Still eyeing the chamber's furnishings, Etienne said, "We call them railways now."

"Does it matter? Silly question. It doesn't; nothing matters." At Etienne's shocked look, he continued, "I don't know why you look so scandalized. 'Meaningless! Meaningless! Everything is meaningless!'"

They stared at each other.

Etienne blinked first. "Er, Shakespeare again?"

Salem sighed. "No. That was Ecclesiastes."

At Etienne's even odder look, he said stiffly, "It's comforting. Now please get to the point and tell me why you're here so you can leave."

Etienne's expression grew serious. "We need your help, Salem."

His answer was flat, uncompromising. "No."

Etienne said defensively, "I have not come from *him*."

"I do not care."

"Our people are...disappearing. I can find no trail, no explanation. And *he* does nothing, offers no protection. You are stronger than he," Etienne pleaded. "You have to help us."

"I renounced the lot of them," came the firm reply. "You all know it. I don't *have* to do anything ever again."

"If you won't help us, then help *me*!"

"Ask Kendrick for help if you need it."

"Kendrick has been on the continent for the last twenty years; he left just after you did. There is *no one else* I trust who can stand against those in power."

"Etienne, I fought long and hard for my freedom, and now I have it. I will not go back," Salem said.

"Free to do what," Etienne said incredulously, "rot in a hole in the ground?"

It's hardly that, he thought defensively. "If I like," he sneered. "As I understand it, that's what freedom is." Salem resumed his seat and found his stopping place in the book. "Go away, Etienne."

"Salem," Etienne whispered. "It is *Addie*."

His fingers tightened on the book.

Seeing this opening, Etienne pressed his advantage. "She is missing. No one has seen her. *He* refuses to look for her. He claims that it is not his responsibility to keep track of all his wayward children."

Between one blink and the next, Salem was across the room, his hand around his friend's neck. Salem's lips pulled back in a snarl. "You *lost her?*"

"She disappeared between one night and the next!" Etienne protested. "I tried to convince her to stay with me, but you know her. She's stubborn. And now no one else can counteract *his* orders or do anything to investigate—he made it a direct order. I'm not you; I can't do this alone. I need *help*. You are the only one I know of not blood-bound to him. This is my last loophole. Salem, *please*."

Salem stared, unseeing, down at the book in his other hand. He had thought to spend the rest of his days here—however long he decided that span would stretch. He *deserved* it here, had sworn he'd never go back.

But his obligation to Addie was one he could never repay.

"Very well," he said at last, releasing Etienne. "For Addie."

Etienne clasped his hand. "*Merci, cher ami*. I have seen the train schedules—we can make the departing train if we run. But we need to get you a haircut." He eyed the black hair brushing Salem's shoulders.

"You're not touching my hair," Salem said automatically. It was an old argument between them. That was inches of hair he would never get back—and too much had already been taken from him.

"Then perhaps new clothes? No one wears fashions twenty years out of date," his friend said in longsuffering tones.

Salem stared at the empty glass decanter gathering dust in the corner. In the glass, the reflection shivered, changing to the old phantasm that haunted him.

What can you do for Addie, besides cause her pain? The old foe sneered at him.

Salem felt the old hunger rise to do battle with him again, clawing at his throat, never quenched, never sated. "Clothes are the least of my worries, Etienne."

Chapter One

ENGLAND, OCTOBER 1880.

"Is it selfish?" asked Ophelia as they stepped out into the sunlight.

"But of course not," Marie-Claire assured her, patting her last nephew on the head as he scampered past. They both waved goodbye to Marie-Claire's sister and the rest of her brood as they left the village church.

"I did pray about it," Ophelia said, casting a glance back into the nave where the rest of the congregation filed out. "Most of the sermon, actually."

"It was on First John chapter four," Marie-Claire said. "'Beloved, if God so loved us, we also ought to love one another.' There, I have summed it up for you."

"I wrote again a fortnight ago, asking," Ophelia admitted, and smoothed the front of her navy skirt.

"And you've heard nothing?"

Ophelia shook her head.

Marie-Claire's brown face made a sympathetic moue. "It is not selfish to want a London season," she said. "It is your father's obligation to take you. How else will you find a husband? The pickings, as Owen says, are slim this far out in Yorkshire. I set my cap for the last eligible bachelor in Hartley, and that was five years ago." She smoothed her gown over her rounded waist. "If I had known your father would put off his duties so shamefully, I would have taken you last year and sponsored you, but this year...."

"Of course, you must focus on the baby," Ophelia assured her. "And you must make sure Owen does not worry himself to a shade."

Marie-Claire's smile warmed. "He does hover, does he not."

Owen had ordered them not to stir a step while he brought the gig around to the churchyard. The village was small enough that the Glenwoods could have walked—if Marie-Claire was not in an interesting condition. But it also allowed them to take Ophelia home, so the coach would not have to come back for her.

"Have you thought of names?" Ophelia asked.

"Owen says he is happy with my choice."

"All men should become so agreeable when their wife is with child."

Marie-Claire flashed her an impish smile. "*Mais oui*. I had thought, maybe something French, to carry on the tradition. Although I shall be quite put out at Cecily for stealing *Mémère's* name for Claudette for at *least* another month." Marie-Claire's grandmother had been a French emigree, and *her* mother was from Haiti, or Saint-Domingue, as it had been called, and the French names had continued down the line.

"Lovely," Ophelia said as Owen pulled the gig as close to the steps as he could. "You know, there is a French version of Ophelia...."

Marie-Claire threw back her head and laughed.

Owen leaped down from the gig to assist Marie-Claire, then solicitously helped Ophelia up as well. Ophelia clambered in, ignoring the twinge from her lame leg. It always pained her when it was going to rain, and there were grey clouds on the horizon.

She sat with a sigh, thankful for the narrow skirts and small bustle pad. Marie-Claire had told her large bustles might be returning to fashion, but she heartily hoped it was not true. She did not want to manage half a bird cage under her clothes. Plus, the exorbitant expense of altering her whole wardrobe to accommodate a larger skirt or buying all new clothes made her wince.

"What were you ladies discussing?" Owen Glenwood asked as he resumed his seat and clucked to the horse to walk on.

"Baby names. Before that, Ophelia and whether her father will launch her upon the marriage mart this year," said Marie-Claire. "She does not have high hopes."

"Ah," Owen said tactfully.

"I even wrote to Ben," Ophelia said, her melancholic mood returning. "I told him that if he would just let me come to London, I could keep house for him."

"You could not live with an unmarried brother without a chaperone," Marie-Claire said with a start.

"I don't see why not; he's family."

"It isn't done," her friend said firmly. "Perhaps if you had a companion—"

"There would have to be money for a companion." It wasn't done to speak of money and expense in front of others, either, but Marie-Claire knew her situation—and what Marie-Claire knew, Owen knew too.

"It's shameful," Marie-Claire announced. "The way your father behaves. He gets paid for his scientific work and lecturing, does he not? He has no excuse not to look after you."

Ophelia stared at the oncoming rainclouds in the east and didn't respond. Her father, Doctor Isaiah Shaw, was a very busy man. So busy that she had not seen him or her brothers in nearly a year. He sent precious little funds, and when he did, they paid the servants' wages, with almost nothing left over for the upkeep for Renwick Hall or Ophelia.

She glanced down guiltily at her dress. In fact, Marie-Claire had been the one to take her to the dressmaker when she remained in short skirts far longer than proper or practical. Marie-Claire had waved away her protestations, saying she would take care of Ophelia's wardrobe and send the bill to her father. Ophelia did not know if the bill had ever been paid—or even sent. She did not like to ask.

"I suppose he thinks it a waste of time, since I cannot dance," Ophelia finally said.

"There is so much to do during a season besides dancing. You need to meet and converse with gentlemen, go driving in the park, get ices, see operas and plays." Marie-Claire waved her hand. "And you *can* dance."

"Not well," Ophelia said glumly. She had been to one of the village assemblies last year, and Owen had kindly stood up with her. A few other men had, but looked plainly embarrassed as she moved with her funny gait. As Owen's American friend Mr. Faber had said to her several years ago at Owen and Marie-Claire's wedding, after asking if she had injured her foot and needed to sit down: "You've got a hitch in your giddyup."

She smiled at the memory, her mouth twisting up wryly against her will. *That's it, exactly—I've got a hitch in my giddyup.* She surreptitiously stretched her bad leg.

She had not always. As a small child there had been nothing wrong with her legs. But when she was nearly five, something had happened. She couldn't remember—her memories were not clear from that time—but she had been ill and fevered and her mother had cried, and Ophelia had been kept in bed for a long, long time. And when she got up and tried to walk again, it had been there—a curious weakness in her right knee and lower leg. When she walked, she limped.

Owen turned down the lane towards Renwick Hall and entered the Dimsely Wood, or as Ophelia privately thought of it, the Dismal Wood. The great oaks closed in overhead, making the path gloomy and dim.

Ophelia sighed. Renwick Hall inspired gloominess. It was their ancestral family home dating back to what *felt* like William the Conqueror, though it was probably more like the Cavaliers and Roundheads.

Renwick Hall's original structure had been a standard Tudor construction based on the historical medieval precedent—a long rectangle with the great hall being the focus of the house and life, with family living areas and bedchambers to one side and the kitchen and servants' domain to the other side of the hall. However, an ancestor in possession of a great many children and dependents, a fervor for the Italianate renaissance style of architecture, and *far* too much optimism had extended both sides of the house into long wings, changing the shape into a 'U'. The entrance and original portion of the house faced north and the east and west wings trailed back towards the south.

However, Renwick never again achieved the family size of that ancestor, nor the visitors he hoped to attract. For one, the house was situated not on a picturesque parkland where one could perambulate and ride while taking in the scenery, but in the middle of a wood, and what cleared ground had been available to the house, the wings had absorbed the majority. What was left went to the flower and kitchen gardens, and then became the wood. The wood encroached closer every year, it seemed.

Over the years, as funds depleted and the cost of upkeep rose, Ophelia's grandfather and then her father had repurposed most of the north and east portions of the house to serve as the functional sections of Renwick. The west wing had slowly fallen into disuse and disrepair, and now was nearly unsound in many places. The east wing was mostly livable, but the wood shrouded it from much of the sun it would've received.

Renwick was the sort of house in which you'd expect to find ghosts or a dungeon. But it had neither priest hole nor oubliette, and no ghosts as far as Ophelia could tell. There *was* a secret passage of sorts—but Ophelia thought it likely some ancestor had just disguised the entrances to a servants' hallway and it had fallen into disuse over the years, and so had become "secret."

The gardens were as overgrown as the wood, but that was because Ophelia's mother and grandmother had been the ones with the green thumb, and now there was no money for gardeners. Ophelia didn't mind that as much—the gardens provided Blaze, her collie, with much opportunity to ramble and explore, and the herbs like mint and thyme and all the varieties of rosebushes seemed to thrive as they outgrew their beds.

As the gig emerged from the wood, Ophelia straightened at the sight of Renwick Hall's imposing, ruinous exterior—and the coach and wagon in front of it.

"Has he come?" She hardly dared to breathe as her heart leaped in her chest.

Renwick's two footmen and a group of what looked like hired men were unloading something from the wagon.

"Gently, gent—be careful, you clod!" her father, Doctor Isaiah Shaw, barked as one of the men nearly lost his grip on the huge wooden box. It took six men to lift, giving the unsettling impression of a casket with pallbearers, though the box was the wrong shape.

"Take it to the west wing. Where have you been?" he snapped, turning an eagle-eyed glare on Ophelia just as Owen helped her down from the gig. Her father looked very much the same as the last time she had seen him, a year ago—same dark hair and beard, same perpetually irritated expression when he looked at her.

"Church, Father," she said, taken aback. "It's Sunday."

Her father snorted derisively.

Ophelia's oldest brother Absalom, who strongly resembled their father in appearance, emerged from the hall in time to hear this exchange. He did not bother to hide his snide smile.

Ophelia's stomach sank, and she clenched her teeth. She would have to collect the cats directly.

Normally her cats had the run of the house, coming and going between Renwick and the stables via the kitchen door under Mrs. Lowell's sufferance. The cats would hate being corralled in her room and forced to use a sandbox, but Ophelia did not trust Absalom within ten feet of them.

As complicated as her feelings were towards her oft-absent family, Ophelia thought she might hate Absalom. She felt vaguely guilty for it, since the sermon on loving one another still rang in her ears, but she had grounds for the enmity. He had been a mean-spirited boy who delighted in the pain of others. There was teasing, and then there was deep-rooted cruelty, and Absalom had always leaned far towards the latter, especially since he was eight years older than she. All her childhood torments at his hands held a decidedly malicious edge. She had distinct memories of him pulling the wings off flies and insects just for the fun of it, not to mention what he had done to poor Tibby.

Ophelia chose not to greet him, saving her smile for Benjamin, who followed him from the hall.

Ben was closer to her in age, though the gap was still significant at six years, but he had taken the time to tell her stories and read to her from gothic novels. The tales had given her nightmares since their rambling home was remarkably akin to the spooky castles and haunted abodes that littered those books, but she had never told him. She had craved that closeness and found it so rarely after their mother died when she was ten.

"It's wonderful to see you," she told Ben.

"Good to see you too, sister," Ben said. "And you as well, Mr. and Mrs. Glenwood."

Owen and Marie-Claire greeted him and the rest of her relatives, and Owen tipped his hat.

Absalom's greeting sounded utterly bored. Her father ignored her friends entirely, and Ophelia swallowed the oily feeling of shame.

"Thank you for the ride home," Ophelia told Marie-Claire and Owen. "I will see you tomorrow."

Marie-Claire cast dark glares at her father and Absalom as Owen turned the gig towards their home.

Ophelia stared at the workers struggling to shoulder the strange box once more. "How long will you be here?"

"It depends on how long our experiments last," her father said shortly, watching the box's progress into the house.

As the men carried it up the steps, she heard a thump.

The box rocked in their grasp, and the men had to scramble to keep their grip.

"Pay it no mind," the doctor barked to them. "The west wing's cellar. Double quick."

Ophelia stared after them, a cold, sinking feeling filling her chest.

"Don't wait dinner for us, we'll be working. We don't wish to be disturbed. Oh, and girl," her father said, fixing his cold gaze on her, "keep away from the laboratory." He disappeared into the house.

Chapter Two

From a young age, Ophelia loved collecting pets. She would create terrariums for lizards and butterflies, she would put mice in a shoebox, she fed all the homeless cats and dogs she could find and put them all on her bed at night to sleep.

But her number of pets never remained constant. The homeless cats and dogs might've moved on or run away. The lizards and mice could've escaped the homes she had painstakingly crafted for them. It always worried and saddened her when something she had named and loved disappeared, but her mother told her that was sometimes just the nature of animals.

But when Ophelia was eight, she found a mutt she named Sparky, and Sparky was especially dear to her because he had a paw that was curled up by his chest, and he limped about on three legs. And with this dog, she felt a deep kinship. They had similar struggles, but Sparky gamboled about freely, uncaring about how he looked, which encouraged her to stretch her own legs to play with him. She grew stronger and more confident instead of sitting quietly and worrying that her weak leg might give way under her without warning. And Sparky loved her, would sleep on her bed, and wake her up by licking her face every morning. They were almost inseparable.

But one morning Ophelia woke, and Sparky wasn't there. She was confused but thought perhaps a maid had perhaps taken him out for his morning constitution in the garden if he had needed to go earlier than usual. She dressed and went outside and called for him. But he did not come. Ophelia spent every minute before breakfast calling him, but she had to come in when it started to rain. Her mother had tried to comfort her, saying perhaps he was on a ramble. "But it's cold and wet!" Ophelia had cried. "He always comes home!" She waited all that day, but he did not appear.

After crying herself to sleep, the next morning she resolved to search the house. Perhaps he had gotten stuck in a room, or some unstable part of the house had trapped him or hurt him. She took herself up to the east wing attics and worked her way down, limping through unused bedroom and closed off parlors, calling for Sparky. She finally searched the whole east wing.

Then she turned with trepidation towards the west.

Even at that time, it was not well kept, and what was worse, her father's laboratories resided in the cellar.

Ophelia did not like her father. He stared at her and her auburn hair like she was a bug or a puzzle to solve, when her brothers had brown hair like his and her mother's hair was blond. He thundered when he did not get his way and was grimly triumphant when he did, and he made her mother cry.

So Ophelia left his domain for last as she tiptoed through dark and silent rooms of water stained wallpaper and motheaten carpets, furniture shrouded like ghosts. She found several spots where the floor was not sound, rooms with doors jammed shut from the damp, but no Sparky.

So, she finally descended to her father's laboratory, as apprehension and dread swelled within her.

And when Ophelia saw the half-assembled dog skeleton with a deformed leg, she screamed the house down.

She had been so upset that her mother had had to dose her with laudanum to get her to sleep. She had had opium-tinged nightmares of Sparky dying over and over again scored to the absolute battle royal her parents had waged as she screamed and cried.

"How dare you?" her mother had shrieked. "Your daughter's pet! You *know* how much she loved that dog! How could you be such an unfeeling *beast*?"

"It's just a dog, Cornelia," he had said coldly.

"The dog belonged to Ophelia!"

"She'll find another."

"Will you kill that one, too? What's happened to the others—the ones that have gone missing, lost, run away? Was it just you, a horrible grim reaper?"

"Science demands—"

"Oh, the dark god science demands a sacrifice every full moon? No. This is *you*! No more!"

Ophelia's mother had wrung a concession from him that he would leave Ophelia's pets alone. But after that, Ophelia had limited her animals to the mammalian variety and capped their number to those she could keep safe. Her father had no scruples when it came to science. He forged ahead no matter the hurt or the cost.

And that's why Ophelia knew she was going to have to venture back into the west wing.

Chapter Three

When the strangers entered the house, Blaze arrived in a flurry of growls and barks, alerting all and sundry that strangers were invading. The workers cursed and kicked as Blaze danced in between them, but they missed him. They scrambled to keep a hold of their heavy load.

"Someone catch that dog!" her father commanded over the barking.

Before Ophelia could reach him, Thomas, the footman, grabbed his collar and pulled him back. Ophelia smiled at him gratefully. Thomas slipped her a small wink as she made her way to them and took hold of Blaze's collar.

"Sit! Hush, Blaze," she scolded. Blaze sat and hushed.

In the relative quiet as the workers readjusted their hold on the box, Ophelia heard it again. Something hitting wood with a dull echo distinctly audible in the great hall. A thump.

Blaze growled, plastering himself protectively against her weak leg as the workers disappeared down the hallway towards the west wing.

"May I take your coat, Miss?" Thomas asked.

"No, I believe I'll take Blaze out for a moment," Ophelia said, and proceeded to do so.

As Blaze foraged in the bushes along the drive, she took a deep breath of the bracing air and stared up into the dark, twisted trees that loomed around Renwick Hall. Their tangle of boughs always cast the house in deep shadow, encouraging Cimmerian mists to linger in the late evenings and early mornings until the Hall itself seemed cut off from the sunlit world of the village. Ophelia shivered.

The box had made a noise. Twice.

Something was in that box.

Something *alive*.

Ophelia corralled Blaze and brought him inside. The main entrance led directly into what used to be the long rectangular great hall, with the grand stair between it and the east wing, and a massive fireplace and many ugly ancestral portraits along the south wall. A medieval broadsword also hung over the fireplace, hidden in the shadows. Ophelia never knew what ancestor it had belonged to. She had spent many childhood days peering up at it, imagining what hand had swung it and for what cause before hanging it above the mantle. To her knowledge, no one had ever taken it down since.

Appropriate. Renwick's masters were not much known for their application of justice these days.

With the curtains drawn and the fireplace unlit, the great hall was full of shadow. As Ophelia directed Blaze to wipe his paws on the mat by the door, her father emerged from the righthand hallway and made his way to the grand stair. Ophelia silently moved herself and Blaze out of the way.

He instructed Ben in passing, "Pay the men, and tell them if the buyer finds any more specimens, to let us know directly."

Ben counted out the coin to the workers who had followed them and then mounted the stairs towards his own room. He hadn't seen her in the shadows. Ophelia didn't know where Absalom had gone.

Rivers, the butler, ushered the hired men out of the house, his back poker-stiff that they had been admitted via the front door. The rest of the limited staff clustered together in the doorway to the east wing, which led to the dining room and kitchens. They whispered as they stared across the great hall.

"What has he got in that awful crate?"

"It made a noise; I heard it!"

"Unnatural experiments. No God-fearing...."

"That's enough!" Rivers said with a voice like a razor. "There'll be no disrespectful talk about the Master." He cast a glance towards Ophelia, who began struggling out of her cloak with belated help from Thomas. "Or the family." With a gimlet stare, he moved smoothly to her side and took over, nudging Thomas out of the way. "Welcome home, Miss Ophelia. How was the service?"

"Very nice, thank you Mr. Rivers," Ophelia said vaguely, keeping her gaze carefully away from the west wing corridor.

Of all the servants at Renwick Hall, most of whom were locals, Rivers was decidedly her father's man.

༄

Ophelia took the stairs slowly, as she usually did, one step at a time, one hand always on the railing, and she brought Blaze to her room before calling for the cats. Bathsheba gave her usual 'mrrrp' and oozed forth from under the bed, but from Tibby and Nevada, Ophelia heard nothing. She made a note to tell the maids to keep the cats in her room and left to look for the other two. Blaze whined as she shut him in her room.

"Kitty kitty," she called, slowly moving down the second floor of the east wing. Beyond the drawing room, morning room, and parlor, the floor contained bedrooms, the first of which was hers, for closest proximity to the stairs. If the west wing were more habitable, she would've relocated to the main floor, but the few times she had tried to bring it up to Rivers, he had given her such a look that she had let the issue lie.

"Nevada? Tibby? Where are you?"

A howl of masculine fury echoed from the drawing room, followed by a cat's hiss. A streak of gray shot through the doorway and past her down the hall.

Absalom jerked through the doorway, gripping the doorframe. Blood dripped from the scratches on his hand. "That goddamn cat," he spat.

"You have no cause for complaint," Ophelia said, putting herself in his way as he attempted to follow, malevolence in his gaze.

"No cause? She scratched me!" he yelled with several more oaths, shaking his hand in her face.

Ophelia flinched. "And you pulled her whiskers out. She clearly still remembers." *To say nothing of whatever happened just now,* she thought. She could hear Tibby growling from down the hallway.

"Absalom. Language," Ben said, stepping out of his room in his shirtsleeves.

Absalom ignored him. He sucked the blood off his cut as he stared at Ophelia, his eyes angry and flat. "If that cat crosses my path again, I'll wring her neck."

"Don't you touch my cat," Ophelia said, lifting her chin.

"Then you know what you have to do, don't you?" He sneered over her head at Ben and went into his room.

"Sorry about him," Ben said as Ophelia gathered a still-righteously-angry Tibby into her arms and stroked her fur. "The carriage ride was long."

"We're attributing Absalom's behavior and attitude to the carriage ride now?" Ophelia said bitterly. She didn't understand how or why Ben could excuse his cruel, spiteful behavior.

"You're right. He shouldn't have spoken to you like that."

Ophelia stared at him. "I don't care about his language. I care that he threatened to kill my cat!"

"It was a figure of speech, Ophelia," Ben said impatiently. "Don't be so dramatic." He disappeared back into his room.

Ophelia looked down at the cat and said quite pleasantly, "Like hell it was."

⚜

Ophelia ate dinner alone, staring down the length of the table in the dim formal dining room. She had given in and dressed for dinner, descending to the dark and oppressive dining room in the faint hope that Ben might come and eat with her. Alas.

When she was the lone family member in the house, she often ate in the library or in the parlor on a tray, with no courses so the servants—Mrs. Lowell in particular, a strangely angular and bitter soul for a cook—did not have to put herself out. But as the Master and his sons were home, Rivers was very much on his dignity and had taken the opportunity to order a full course dinner, no matter that the male Shaws themselves were taking the meal on trays in the dark workshop-cum-laboratory. So the meal was served in courses by Thomas to Ophelia, stranded at the end of the vast table, all alone.

How was it, she wondered as her fork scraped against the plate, echoing in the room, that the house could feel even lonelier when more people resided in it? But it was true. She was hyper-aware of where the extra people were and what they were doing— her family as well as the personal servants they had brought with them. She did not have a comforting cat waiting for her, purring away at the fire in the parlor, or her dog's claws clicking on the floor. The very air felt stifling.

I shouldn't have to partition myself off and make myself small, she thought as Thomas took away her plate and brought out the next course. *It's my house too.*

But it wasn't. Not legally. Even though her grandmother's stamp was on the dining room in the form of fern-patterned wallpaper and her mother's furniture choices stood in the parlor, none of it had really been theirs. Even the servants obeyed her father's orders over Ophelia's—as evidenced by this ridiculous procession of dishes.

This was one of the times when Ophelia wished they could manage to keep a housekeeper on for more than a few months. Surely someone to oppose Rivers and bring household decisions to the de facto lady of the house couldn't be a bad thing. But alas, Renwick Hall was too immured in the country for most housekeepers with excellent references, and the state of the place was challenging at best. The few housekeepers sent to them via agencies left after a few weeks, not able to stand up to Rivers' high-handedness or too unnerved by the atmosphere.

Renwick Hall was a dreary, lonely place from the outside. The crumbling façade and the mists and the wind in the eaves did not endear it to outsiders. But it could be a place of comfort, too. Ophelia had found it so when her mother was alive, and in her vague memories of her grandmother when she was small. Renwick had not seemed so formidable and gloomy then.

Perhaps houses reflected the slow loss of love just like people.

Ophelia stared into her wine glass as Thomas endeavored to camouflage himself amongst the fern-patterned wallpaper. A little spitefully, she hoped the food was cold by the time the trays made it to the cellars. Knowing how little the maids cared for that area of the house, she thought it a distinct possibility. She smirked into her wine.

Something rasped against the window, and she jumped, spilling a few drops on the tablecloth.

Thomas jumped forward with a cloth to blot the spill. "It's all right, Miss, just one of the trees grown too close and tapping on the window, like. Did it a fair bit when we were laying the table." Then he remembered footmen were supposed to be furniture and faded back against the wall.

"Thank you, Thomas; how very ominous it sounds!" Ophelia remarked as the tree did it again. Her imagination conjured visions of grasping branches seeking to encroach into human spaces. "Perhaps you will mention to Mr. Rivers that some of the trees need trimming?"

"Yes, Miss," he murmured, and quiet descended again.

Ophelia looked at the soufflé Thomas placed in front of her with little enthusiasm. Mrs. Lowell did not excel at soufflés. She tended to bake them overlong and did not bring them out with the expediency that the dish demanded, which meant they almost always fell. This one had indeed fallen. Ophelia suspected Rivers at work again, thinking that a difficult dish would lend conse-quence to the meal. Mrs. Lowell would not thank him for his interference.

They were probably eating apple fritters below stairs. She sighed at the thought and took a bite. The soufflé stuck in her throat. She coughed and took another sip of wine.

The silence was getting to her. She kept thinking about the thump.

A shiver ran down her spine. She traced the wine stain on the tablecloth and wondered if the maids would be able to get it out. It looked uncomfortably like blood.

Ophelia surreptitiously touched the roll and slices of ham hidden in her napkin. Whatever animal was down in the cellars was probably hungry. She lifted her chin. Her father wasn't going to kill it. Not again—she wouldn't let it happen again. She didn't care what kind of science he touted.

She pushed her fork around, spreading the soufflé over the plate as she thought. But what sort of animal would he put in a *box*? A cage, maybe, but a box? How would it breathe?

Unless he was just trying to get around her. Her family knew how she felt about animals used in experiments. It made sense they wouldn't want her to see.

But why would it be so heavy? It had taken six men to bring into the house.

Ophelia forced down one last bite of the soufflé and then stood. Thomas leaped to pull the chair back all the way and didn't say anything as she furtively slid the napkin into her pocket. They were used to her sneaking things for the cats and Blaze. Thomas wouldn't mention it to anyone. Ophelia bid him a quiet good night and then went upstairs.

Later, in a nightgown with her hair down in a braid, Ophelia pulled back her bedcovers and settled in to wait. Blaze served as a foot warmer at the end of the bed, and the cats jumped up to claim their nightly spots.

Bathsheba immediately plopped down on the other pillow and began bathing her ears. Bathsheba was thus called because as a twelve-year-old Ophelia had thought it unspeakably clever—the longhaired tabby was always grooming herself fastidiously. Now Ophelia thought it a little silly, the way one does looking back at embarrassing young antics. These days she mostly shortened the name to Sheba.

Tibby scrambled up to the coverlet and then burrowed underneath, finding a pocket of warmth to doze in. Ophelia ran a hand over her fur and scratched behind her ears. She was a fat gray cat who lounged for long periods of time and then had to adjourn to nap. She was getting old—Tibby was the last animal Ophelia's mother had helped name. After her uncharacteristic bout of rage at meeting Absalom again, Tibby had slept for most of the afternoon.

Last but definitely not least, Nevada leaped up and immediately demanded petting. Ophelia picked her up and stroked her as the cat preened.

Only about four, Nevada was named for some of the stories Owen's friend Mr. Faber had told her about finding silver in the

American state. He had taken the time, during a trip where he had crossed the Atlantic to see his friend married, to tell the bride's young and shy friend stories when he didn't have to. Ophelia had had something of an infatuation with him at the time. He had been far too old for her, and a widower with children only a little younger than her besides, but it had been an odd mix of attraction and hero worship and paternal feeling, because he had liked her and been willing to spend time with her, unlike her own father.

And he was a cowboy, after all, Ophelia thought with a little rueful smile, with a lanky build and deep voice and an air of rugged edges about him, appearing a little larger than life to her who had never traveled beyond rural Yorkshire. So she had immortalized him in Nevada, who had appeared on the estate as a kitten shortly after all the wedding guests had returned home.

Nevada, purring like mad, shoved herself against Ophelia's hands, pointedly ignoring Blaze, with whom she had a detente for Ophelia's attentions. Ophelia scratched her under the chin, remembering Nevada's kittenhood and the rambunctious antics that had brought Ophelia out of her misery, missing a man she had only known for two weeks.

There is a particular sort of pain, Ophelia mused as she selected a book from the stack by her bedside, that comes at the hands of people who are supposed to love you. And don't.

She opened her book, one of Mrs. Radcliffe's gothic novels Ben had sent her for Christmas. She figured it would keep her awake, until... her gaze swung to the drawer where she had stashed the ham and roll.

She marked the time on the clock, and then began to read.

Chapter Four

After midnight, Ophelia slipped her lockpicks in her pocket and filled the oil in her dark lantern. It only shone in one direction, with a shutter that could rotate to open or block light from coming through the lens. Ben had given it to her two years ago on her birthday, though he had called it her "smuggler's lantern." She supposed that appealed more to his sense of gothic than "police lantern."

She had asked the village blacksmith to make the lockpicks as a gift for Ben, a joke in return for the lantern. But she had decided to send him a cigar case instead. Renwick was full of locked doors, and Rivers refused to give her the housekeeper's set of keys. Practicing with the lockpicks had become a hidden rebellion.

Once she lit the lantern's wick, she shut Blaze and the cats in her room and crept to her father and brothers' rooms. Under the doors, she could see the glow of lamps and candles still burning, awaiting their return. That meant they were still...occupied in the laboratory.

Ophelia traversed the north wing's hallway and descended the disused servant's stair. She settled down to wait on the bottom steps. It was very close to the entrance to the cellar and the laboratory within, close enough to hear the comings and goings in the nocturnal silence.

They had not had gas put in Renwick, though a few people in the village had been discussing it. Perhaps her father had had it installed in the house in London—but she didn't know, since she hadn't ever been there and none of the letters from Ben had mentioned it. People said you could hear the gas hissing in the walls. It sounded disturbing. How could you sleep like that?

But there were probably much louder distractions in London.

Ophelia waited for a long time as her eyes fluttered shut and her feet felt like ice in her slippers. She huddled inside her thick wool wrapper and blew on her hands. The tin lantern beside her —with the shutter closed—was a welcome source of warmth. Whenever her hands felt too icy, she held them over the lantern's top vent. Next time she would wear her cloak. She yawned again —a jaw-popping sound—and rubbed her face briskly before kneading the muscles in her weak leg.

What a lark I'd be at parties in town. I'm too used to country hours to stay up until dawn. I suppose the dancing helps keep you awake, though.

Then the large clock in the hall struck one. The lone toll rang through the house, sending a shiver down her spine. Was this what they called the witching hour?

A low moan echoed up from the depths of the cellar. Like an animal in pain.

Or something from the depths of hell.

Her fingers clenched convulsively around the lantern's handle. The metal bit into her palm.

What if by the time she got down there, the thing in the crate was no longer alive?

Her leg cramped. She rubbed the knotted muscles with aching fingers. She felt like she crouched on the stair for ages, listening for another moan of pain, or anything else. But over her thrumming nerves, she heard the creak of a door, the low murmur of voices.... Slow footfalls moved away from her position, heading towards the great hall and the grand stair.

Ophelia held still, barely daring to breathe as the faint sounds died away to nothingness. She waited, counting heartbeats. One hundred...two hundred....

She straightened and stretched to make sure her leg would hold her. Then she slid the lantern's shutter open a sliver and made her way down to the cellars.

She heard the moan again as she inched her way down the stairs. Or was it a growl? She could not pinpoint what sort of animal it came from.

But it was a low, pain-filled sound.

At the foot of the stair, she tried the door, feeling in her pocket for the lockpicks.

But it wasn't necessary. The handle turned easily.

The door opened with a low groan.

The ray of light from the dark lantern stretched across the floor, illuminating the pitch-black laboratory. A shudder snaked down her spine.

Inside her father's laboratory stretched racks of chemical compounds, tables of glassware, animal skeletons. Not Sparky, though. She had buried him in the garden. Shelves of books lined the walls, and an examination table stood in the center of the laboratory...with wet streaks on the surface. Ophelia lifted the lantern higher, widening the beam of light.

Manacles lay discarded on the table. They shone silver in the light, speckled with more wet.

Ophelia leaned in closer.

Red.

Blood.

Something in the darkness hissed.

Ophelia recoiled, swinging the lantern in a wild arc, the light careening around the cellar. She stumbled over a pile of boards and barely caught herself on the examination table. "Who's there?" she yelped instinctively.

Silence.

Stupid, she thought. Animals couldn't talk. And it was hurt and afraid, more afraid than she was.

With trembling fingers, she opened the lantern's shutter wide.

The beam of light reached further into the recesses of the cellar. At the back, in an open area where the ceiling dipped down, silver bars glinted in the light. A cage. And inside it—

Ophelia gasped.

A girl crouched inside the bars. Tangled curly hair spilled around her shoulders in an inky mass. Her face was thin and wan, skin pulled tight over her cheekbones and jaw, and she wore a soiled nightgown smudged with dirt and other stains Ophelia didn't like to contemplate. Her bare feet showed under the ragged hem—and as she clutched herself in a tighter ball in the cage, something clinked.

Shackles.

The girl stared with wide, oddly colorless eyes at Ophelia. She looked like she might cry any second.

Ophelia couldn't feel her feet anymore. It was as if the frigid cold had spread to every part of her, invading her heart.

A person. Whatever they were doing—the blood, the manacles—they were doing it to a *person*. A girl only a little younger than her, by the look of it.

"Are you all right?" Ophelia whispered, lifting the lantern higher.

What a foolish question. Of course she wasn't.

"My name is Ophelia." She took a few steps forward. "What are you doing here? What do they want with you?"

The girl didn't move. She didn't even look as though she were breathing.

Ophelia took another step and remembered the food in her

pocket. "Are you hungry?" She fished for the napkin. "I brought you some—"

Quicker than she could blink, the girl threw herself forward, thrusting her arm through the bars.

Ophelia's leg saved her.

The shock made her start, and her bad leg collapsed. She crumpled, the napkin of food dropping to the ground so she could catch herself. The girl's grasping, clawing hand was only a few inches from her face.

Then the girl yelped and recoiled from the bars, shrinking back into the center of her cage.

Ophelia stared in shock. The girl's eyes now shone brilliant garnet red, nearly glowing in the darkness. The girl shivered and shuddered, rocking herself back and forth in the cage. Then she opened her mouth, and with two sharp white fangs, bit down on the heel of her thumb.

And sucked. Like a child.

Red-tinged tear tracks trailed from her eyes as she cried.

She just tried to—

Ophelia twitched—and winced belatedly. The dark lantern's handle had pinched and cut her hand when she fell.

The girl lifted her head, her blood—dark, odd—coating her mouth. Those red eyes focused on Ophelia's hand like a hunting dog pointing towards quarry.

Slowly, Ophelia fished for her handkerchief, and wound it around her hand. Soaking up the blood from the small cut. Hiding it from view.

With a sob, the girl turned back to her hand, now nearly chewing on the flesh as she shrank into a small ball.

Horror swept through Ophelia...and pity. Something awful had happened to this girl—was still happening, since she was in a cage in the laboratory. The girl couldn't even stand up in it. Ophelia glanced behind at the stack of boards piled haphazardly, the ones she had nearly tripped over. She would bet the boards had been the crate that had transported this cage.

No matter what was wrong with this girl, she needed help.

"Don't do that," Ophelia said softly. "Don't hurt your poor hand. Here. I brought you a sandwich. Chew on that."

She picked up the fallen napkin. The girl tensed, tracking her movement.

But Ophelia wasn't a fool. She pushed herself to her feet, using the edge of the closest worktable. The girl flinched as Ophelia scrabbled among the instruments in the lab tray and found a ruler. Ophelia grabbed it and limped back over the cage before using it to push the napkin—slowly—close enough to the bars that the girl could reach.

The girl slowly uncurled, moving like a wary animal that prepares to bite or dodge a kick, whichever was needed. She reached through an opening in the cage, and as she retrieved the bundle, her arm grazed one of the silver bars. She jerked and hissed, wincing. The skin looked raw and red before fading to pale and bluish gray in places, as it had been before. She unwrapped the sandwich and stared at it with distaste before taking a tiny bite. She made a face, and another tear rolled down her face. She swiped her face and licked the moisture off her fingers before it went to waste.

The phrase "beggars can't be choosers" popped into Ophelia's mind and refused to leave. They stared at each other in silence as the girl pinched off tiny bites and choked them down. As she did, Ophelia caught a glimpse of the hand she had been gnawing on.

There was no wound.

A cold knot formed in Ophelia's stomach. She had *seen* the blood. It had been on the girl's lips. And there wasn't a cut or a scab or scrape or *anything*.

Ophelia dug her fingers into her bad leg and rubbed to try to get her mind off the refrain *"how is that possible?"* But it only helped her physical aches.

The girl watched her movements. She swallowed the bite she was chewing. "Did something bad happen to you, too?" Her voice sounded like the quiet rustle of dead leaves.

Ophelia chanced another look at her eyes. They no longer glowed red like some kind of—well, she didn't know what. They appeared colorless again, like marbles, or doll's eyes leached of color.

"No," Ophelia said, clearing her throat. "No, I got sick as a child, and I was in bed for a very long time. They told me the fever settled in my leg."

"Oh," the girl said.

"My name's Ophelia," she said again. "Do you have a name?"

"Of course," the girl said, nonplussed. "Everyone has a name."

Ophelia supposed that was true. Everyone—even extremely frightened girls trapped in her cellar—had names. "What is it?"

The girl opened her mouth, then closed it. "Not supposed to say."

Ophelia blinked. "I won't tell my father," she promised. "I'm not even supposed to be here. If he found out—" she shuddered to think. "Well anyway, I won't tell."

"Your father?"

Under the girl's curiously blank stare, Ophelia felt herself flush...with shame. "The older man with dark hair and a beard. The scientist. He's my father."

"I'm not supposed to speak to strangers," the girl said in an abrupt non-sequitur. "They might try to take advantage." She repeated this as if she had learned it by rote, pleating her night-gown and scowling at the ragged edge.

The pleating action lifted her hem enough that Ophelia finally got a good look at the shackles around her ankles. The links and cuffs were silver—but stuffed in between the silver and her skin was the missing frilled hem from her nightgown. The skin around the shackles was inflamed, raw and oozing with sores or deep wounds. *Those* injuries were not disappearing like magic.

"Is it the silver?" Ophelia asked, glancing at the bars. "Does it hurt you?"

The girl just stared at her.

I suppose I wouldn't tell my captor anything either, Ophelia thought, suddenly depressed. The poor girl didn't even have a safe place to curl up and rest her head. She had to sit up and accept what little protection her nightgown offered from the bars underneath her.

"I'm sorry that this has happened to you," Ophelia whispered. "I don't know what I can do to help, but I want to."

"Blood," the girl said immediately.

"I'm sorry?"

"Blood," she repeated. She tucked her clenched fists under her chin, creating an oddly supplicant image. "I'm hungry. So hungry. Haven't eaten in days. The silver sickens me. They waited ages before deciding where to take me...." She licked her lips, her eyes flickering—just a flash of that inhuman light before returning to flat emptiness.

A slow creeping suspicion spread over Ophelia. Her chest felt tight, like she couldn't get enough air.

The girl's skin. Those eyes. The cut. That—inhuman lunge. The silver.

She swallowed hard.

Her reasonable, rational, light of day brain protested that this wasn't a torrid gothic of Ben's with mad monks and skullduggery and women in the attic. It was Renwick Hall. Her home. It was her *father*, who made scathing noises at any hint of spirituality or myth or legend that could not be proved by cold hard scientific fact.

But it was Ben, too, the traitor part of her said, the part that was in the cellar with the dark lantern and the girl in the silver cage. Ben, who never knew when to leave things well enough alone, who was overly keen on digging up Egyptian tombs and faerie hills and Celtic burial mounds, not letting dead things stay buried.

The sound of Ophelia's heartbeat thundered in her ears. Her sharp breaths hissed through the air. But that was all she heard.

No sound came from the other girl. She just silently watched.

She didn't even *breathe*.

Except when she needed to speak. "Addie."

Ophelia jumped. "What?"

"Addie. My name is Addie. If you told me your name, Ophelia, you're not a stranger."

"It's a pleasure to meet you, Addie," Ophelia said automatically.

And Addie's face lit up. She smiled, a happy, hopeful smile, like the ones Ophelia saw on the faces of the village school children or the parish orphanage on the rare occasion when Rivers agreed to her visits, and she could pass out sweets. The expression felt so incongruous with Addie's appearance.

"Really? Is it?" Addie asked humbly.

Ophelia nodded, her throat too tight to speak.

"It's a pleasure to meet you too, Ophelia," Addie said, a perfect mimic of her inflection. She shifted her position slightly, and the chains clinked.

Ophelia cleared her throat. "Addie, forgive me for asking this, but...."

"What?"

Ophelia swallowed. "Are you dead?"

Addie stared at her, puzzled. "Of course."

And she didn't understand why Ophelia dissolved into tears.

❧

"But why were *you* crying?" Addie asked again as Ophelia wiped her wet face on the sleeve of her wrapper, her handkerchief still in service around her cut. "I'm the one who's dead. And it's been a long time. I don't think about it much."

"I suppose I was—mourning."

Addie blinked. "For me?"

Mourning many things—her father graduating to human experimentation, never mind that Addie was technically dead; Ben, knowingly complicit; and her own innocence—that a poor girl could die and still be trapped.

Mourning Addie too, and possibility. Her possibility. Snuffed.

"Yes," Ophelia said, her shoulders slumping. "I'm sorry you died."

A strange look came over Addie's face. "No one's ever said sorry before." Addie rubbed her chest, where a heartbeat would've been.

Far, far away, Ophelia heard the clock strike two, the dual tones somehow lonelier than the single toll for one.

"I should go to bed," Ophelia whispered. She would be catatonic in the morning if she didn't. And Blaze did insist on his morning constitutional before breakfast.

"Will you come again?" Addie whispered, her eyes huge in her face.

"Yes. I won't say anything if you won't." Ophelia unwound the handkerchief from her hand. The bleeding had stopped. The blood had all soaked into the cloth.

Addie stared at it, the red glow in her eyes sparking again.

Ophelia looked from her handkerchief to Addie. Then, with the ruler, slowly inched the cloth across the floor.

When it was close enough, Addie's hand shot out and snatched it, stuffing the bloodstained cloth into her mouth and sucking. She closed her eyes.

Ophelia could not repress a shudder. Addie was dead. And dangerous. And sad.

Finally, Addie opened her eyes and took the cloth out of her mouth. She pushed it and the napkin back through the bars. "Won't tell. Won't tell. Promise," she whispered.

The handkerchief came back clean.

Chapter Five

As dusk gave way to night over London, two men departed the King's Cross train station and stood on the street as the aroma of the city permeated their clothes.

"Ah, London," Salem said lightly. "I did not miss thee at all. You smell entirely unchanged, and yet time has moved on without asking."

Etienne said, "You can reminisce later, Salem. What now? Are we to go to the Court and petition the Draugadróttinn?" Etienne's hand twitched towards the pistol he carried under his coat. Salem thought it ridiculous, considering what they were, but Etienne had died during the French revolution, and liked to keep a weapon handy. As it was no longer *de rigueur* to wear a rapier openly, he settled for a pistol.

Salem judged his friend was *not* in favor of petitioning—wait.

His eyebrows shot up. "The which?"

Etienne shared a sardonic glance with him. "He calls himself Draugadróttinn now, and us Thanes."

Draugadróttinn—a name for Odin as lord of the undead from the *Heimskringla*, and Thanes being a lord's retainers. Salem drawled, "Rupert always did have a high opinion of himself. It seems I haven't been the only one doing a little reading over the years." He flicked a piece of lint from his cloak. "Well, I suppose it's a change from the clichéd Master and servant. What about the humans?"

"Thralls."

"How apt," Salem muttered, the corners of his mouth turning down in a saturnine expression. "Rather mixing his origins, though."

"I am sure Rupert shows interest in history that predates himself only when it serves him."

Salem permitted himself a small smile. Given his druthers, he'd leave Etienne here and go find Addie without interference—but they had no information. He needed a way to get that information, as well as a way to retrieve Addie safely. And that required others.

But *not* Rupert. And Kendrick was somewhere on the Continent, too far away to help.

He lifted his hand to hail a hackney. "No, we shall not be going to the Court. I'd rather no one know I am back in London if I can help it."

"Brompton, then?"

"No. For now, we go see if the Black Dog Tavern is standing."

Etienne raised an eyebrow. "*Quoi?*"

Salem grinned. "To see a man about a dog."

❦

Salem pushed open the door of the London waterfront tavern and walked in, Etienne behind him. The inside was dim and smoky, just the way he liked it. They took seats at an out of the way corner and waited. If the man he was looking for was here, he'd find them.

Salem closed his eyes and breathed in the ripe, putrid scent of humanity and bad beer. He could feel the vitality in the room, and it made him salivate. Too tempting. He shrugged further into his voluminous cloak and waited.

It was not long before the proprietor slid in across from them. "What are the likes of you doing in my pub?" he growled, with a trace of Irish in his voice.

The man was older than Salem remembered, with gray streaks in his red beard and hair, but still not as old as the passing of twenty years would warrant. He still held himself like a powerful fighter.

"You got old, Faelad," Salem said, pushing back his hood.

Faelad stilled, nose flaring. Then he leaned back in his seat. "You didn't."

Salem inclined his head at the hit. "I thought you'd be far away with your lady fair, living a bucolic life of harmony and bliss."

Faelad's face darkened, and he turned away. "She would not have me."

"Ah," he said quietly. "My condolences." *The course of true love never did run smooth,* he thought with some cynicism.

"Old news." Faelad's eyes narrowed. "Never thought I'd see you again once you were free of the old leech. You said you'd never set foot in London again." He frowned. "Come to think of it, how did you get here?"

"We took the train, like everybody else."

"Everybody else doesn't ride in the luggage compartment."

Salem shot him a flat look as the sound in the tavern rose, raucous laughter echoing from a table of young tradesmen who had just been treated to another round. The voices jangled across his nerves, unused to such bombardment. It made the itch inside him stronger. "Etienne has brought me grave news."

Faelad smiled evilly at the pun. "Oh really?"

"Our folk are disappearing. No one knows how or why."

"And why should I care?" Faelad put a fist on the table, prepared to stand. "Good riddance, says I."

Salem stared meaningfully at the fist and the white scar that circled around the wrist, ugly and thick. "I'm calling in my favor," Salem said in a voice as quiet as death.

Faelad worked his jaw. "So, it's like that, is it?"

"It is."

"And after this, we're square?"

"Square," Salem vowed. "My word on it."

He gave a short nod. "What do you need?"

"I need to find Addie. And I need to discover who is behind this. We cannot involve any of the usual resources because the *Draugadróttinn*," Salem's tone turned biting; *damn* Rupert and his theatrics, "has forbidden it. Hence your help."

Faelad crossed his arms over his chest. "Well, easiest way to do it would be to go to the scene of the crime, so to speak."

Etienne put in, "We have not yet gone to Addie's resting place."

"I could tell you how many men took her, whether they knew to chew garlic and daub on the holy water, and who had neglected their Sunday baths." Faelad raised an eyebrow.

"I'm glad we waited for you then, because I believe the question is, was this a crime of opportunity, or was it planned? Did they know what Addie was? How did they know where she rested?" Salem licked his lips.

"Opportunity for what?" Faelad snorted. "It's about fifty years too late for resurrectionists."

"Not in America," Etienne pointed out.

"This isn't America, boyo. If more than just Addie have gone missing, I'd say someone has been talking." Faelad gave them both a significant look.

Salem licked his lips again as the hunger rose within him, clawing. Demanding. "I'll be right back," he muttered, and slid out of the booth.

He wove his way through the crowd. People unconsciously parted for him—as if there was something about his demeanor that unnerved them. Something dangerous. He stepped out into the alley and breathed in the scent of London—coal smoke, rain, refuse, humanity. He had not missed it, but it awoke something within him all the same. After all, it had been his home for a long, long time—time out of mind.

A footstep in the alley and the smell of too much cheap perfume. A rustle of cloth. "Care for a spot of company, ducks?" A game girl, a newer one from the lack of layered scent upon her. The slight falter in her voice. "Cold night to be alone."

He turned, a mere shadow in the darkness. She wavered on the edge of the streetlamp's light, knowing what could happen to a girl in a dark alley. Unfortunately, her profession demanded she do much of her business there.

It was sad, what became of impecunious girls alone in the world. Though she might not be alone. Many men in London sent their children out to thieve or walk the streets without care. Either way, most girls were just trying to keep soul and body together.

Salem pulled his purse from his pocket and let her hear the heavy jingle of coin. "Come and warm me up, then," he said, filling his voice with charm.

Encouraged by the coin and the laughter in his voice, she ventured forward, a pretty enough face above an overflowing bodice and faded skirts. "How do you like it then? Katie will take care of you." She pressed herself against him invitingly and reached for his trousers.

She was so warm against him, even though her fingers and shoulders certainly felt the October chill. Salem stilled her hands, catching both her wrists in his long fingers. "I like good girls that do what I say." He chaffed her fingers a moment before his hand caressed her cheek and down her neck, gripping her gently by the nape. He kissed her, the movement of his lips a drugging sensation as she melted against him. He kissed her forehead, her eyebrow. "Are you going to be good for me, Katie?"

"Oh yes," she breathed.

"Excellent. Now be a good girl, and hold still."

⁂

Salem sat the girl down at a table in the tavern with her cloak drawn about her warmly as she blinked in a fuddled way at the light. He tipped a serving girl generously to bring her a hot beverage. When she came to her senses again, she'd have a nice fuzzy memory, warm hands, and two pounds in her bodice.

His body hummed, full of energy, hunger assuaged. The illusion of heat coursed through him. Salem sat back down in the booth and licked his lips. "Are we ready to go?"

"You have to do that here?" Faelad snarled.

"She's fine," Salem said with an edge to his smile and his tone. "And two pounds richer. 'If money go before, all ways do lie open.'"

Faelad exchanged a baffled look with Etienne.

"He has been doing that," Etienne said apologetically.

"I used my freedom to gain knowledge. It's Shakespeare, you uncultured swine. Let's go."

They stepped out of the Black Dog and waited for a passing hansom. A flicker in Salem's vision caused him to turn. A face in profile flashed by, only a second of perception before he turned a corner, but it was enough. Salem growled.

"What?" Faelad turned.

"I think I saw...." Damn, what did he go by now? He could not recall. "Andrew. I saw Andrew." Salem's lip curled.

Etienne paled. "He calls himself Julius now. Did he see you?"

"What do you think?" Salem had no doubt the little toady had seen them. Andrew was good at sneaking around, finding out secrets. Then betraying them for the right price. As he had betrayed Salem.

"He is going to tell tales."

Andrew. The old anger rose in Salem again. His teeth ached. The fresh blood in his veins burned and his vision reddened. "I don't care. Let him tell Rupert all the tales he wants; that's all he's good for, a tale teller. I have other things on my mind." *Addie*.

They had to find answers, and they had to do it tonight.

The night was dark and clear, the waxing moon shining down through the trees, silvering the ferns and wild cabbage that grew among the slabs of Brompton Cemetery. Salem, Etienne, and Faelad passed silently through the tombstones and graves, the tall crosses casting long shadows Etienne took pains to avoid.

Salem did not bother. He was watching the angels with covered faces crouched protectively above their plots.

Angels, guardians—why? The people under the headstones were dead.

Maybe they're guarding against me, he thought.

His cloak brushed against a large monument with impressive script, and he turned to read it.

"*Esther Coalridge, Beloved Daughter. 1855-1870. Do not let this mortal body see decay. Psalm 16:10.*"

He shook his head as they continued. The only bodies that did not see decay were like his own, and he would not wish that on anyone.

If my body is destroyed, will I become a ghost, my soul forever barred from heaven? Or will I be sent directly to hell?

Out of the darkness, a creature streaked across their path. Etienne jumped a foot and swore.

The gray cat, revealed in a puddle of moonlight, jumped on top of a monument and glared at the two of them, its shadow stretching larger than life from atop the plinth.

"I have always wondered about your kind and graveyards," Faelad laughed.

"Keep wondering; this is a cemetery. No church on the premises."

"And if there was?"

"You mean would we catch fire upon entering a holy place? No, but we do miss all the Sunday morning services," Salem said with a bitter twist to his mouth. "Etienne, would you calm yourself? It's just a cat." Salem held out his hand to it.

The cat arched and hissed at him before scampering off into the darkness.

He sighed in disappointment, slowly retracting his hand. This always happened, but he couldn't help trying. It was a habit that even two hundred years hadn't been able to break. "I come, Graymalkin," he murmured, moving through the shadows.

Etienne muttered a few more pithy phrases in French and brushed down the front of his coat, then called Salem back when he moved on in the wrong direction. "I thought you knew where Addie bides?"

"From twenty years ago? With all these new graves? I remember helping Addie find a new resting place, but I have no idea where anything is."

"This way; a bit further on."

"Faelad, I hope it goes without saying that if you do anything with the knowledge of Addie's resting place, I will tear your throat out," Salem said lightly.

"As unnatural as I find your kind's propensity to rest among the dead, I have no ill will towards the lass," Faelad said. "I will discharge my debt to you and all memory of what we do here will be wiped away."

Unnatural? Salem snorted. *You're one to talk.*

They went deeper into the cemetery before Etienne called, "Here," and pointed to a large family mausoleum cast into deep shadow by a tall evergreen. "I never understood why she didn't just stay in the catacombs the way I urged her to."

"Addie chose it because to her, it looks like a tiny house. A family's house." Salem touched the litany of names on the mausoleum door before he lifted the latch.

Inside the mausoleum, the urns and caskets lay quietly in the dark, but his keen eyes noticed subtle disturbances. There were scrapes and drag marks along the floor, and the casket that rested in the middle row looked battered in a few places around the lid. As if the lid had been pried up with a crowbar.

As Faelad paced around the room, Salem opened the lid to see the inside of the casket. It was, predictably, empty, but a few splotches stained the interior. He touched his fingers to the marks and tasted.

Dead blood.

"Where are her things?" he asked.

Etienne surveyed the interior of the mausoleum, inspecting the other caskets and doors. "Ah!" Behind one of the dusty urns, he pulled a small bag from the shadows.

Salem turned it out. Inside was a set of women's clothes, a book full of pressed flowers and plants within the pages, and a few cheap pieces of jewelry.

His jaw tightened. "She's in her nightie." He didn't know why that fact made him so inexplicably angry, except that the last time Addie had been vulnerable and scared and as a result, horribly damaged, she had been wearing a nightgown, too.

"Four men," Faelad said, completing his circuit of the room and ending by the casket. "Human. I can smell the sweat and tang of fear on them. But not as much fear as I'd expect. She bled here."

"You're sure it was Addie?" Salem said, testing him.

Faelad shot him an irritated look. "I can scent the difference between a man and a woman, even a dead woman."

"They stole her during the daylight, then," Etienne said. "She would've fought them harder, else. You taught her well." His friend shot him a sympathetic glance, but Salem pretended not to see.

"They had silver with them," Faelad said. "A lot of it. And if it was daylight, there must've been a way to take her out of here both unseen and shielded from the sun." He pointed to the scuff-marks and disturbances in the floor's dust and grime.

"Does the agreement with the London gravediggers and sextons still stand?" Salem asked abruptly. "Would they have seen anything?"

Etienne gave a gallic shrug. "Even if they had, I cannot ask them. Forbidden to investigate, by order of the Draugadróttinn, you remember. What else do you wish to see?"

"I'd like to scout the other disappearance sites, see if Faelad can scent the same men or discover where they've gone, question the ferrymen. And if all else fails, I'll do what Addie did. I'll take her resting place, and hope I get snatched. Then I'll find who's taken her and follow the trail to who's behind all this."

"It's not a good idea. You could disappear too, Salem," Etienne said urgently.

"That's rather the point, my dear Etienne," Salem said dryly. "To find out where Addie has gone. You two will keep watch—Etienne at night, and Faelad by day. I trust you to guard me and watch where I am taken."

"But we don't know what could happen to you!" Etienne insisted.

Salem waved his hand in the air. "'To die—to sleep, no more; and by a sleep to say we end the heart-ache and the thousand natural shocks that flesh is heir to.'"

Etienne and Faelad exchanged looks.

"Are you just going to let him keep going?" Faelad demanded.

Salem laughed, and then stopped abruptly. "Etienne, you don't have to worry." He smiled, but it held no humor, only a rictus of teeth. "I'm already dead."

Chapter Six

B laze woke Ophelia up in the morning with face licks and whines, peering over the edge of the mattress as if to ask what she was doing still abed. Ophelia dragged a hand over her face. She had slept later than she ought, due to her late night and the tossing and turning afterward.

Downstairs in her cellar was a creature her father was experimenting on.

No, she corrected herself. A girl. A scared girl. Who was terrifying, but also tugged at her heartstrings.

What was she going to do about Addie?

When Ophelia had gotten back to her room, she had thought and thought, mind running in circles, but she couldn't see a way out. She couldn't leave Addie a blanket or a pillow—her father would know she had been there. She couldn't sneak food to Addie either; that wasn't what she needed.

But she couldn't let her out—not yet. Not until she knew more. Addie was still dangerous.

The lunge replayed itself in her mind, and she shivered.

For the same reason, Ophelia couldn't even hold Addie's hand to comfort her. Ophelia knew just how badly creatures needed touch. All the abandoned or abused animals that found their way to her, after their initial fear and hesitancy, would press against her trembling as she gently petted them, as if begging her not to send them away, hoping for this tiny scrap of kindness not to be turned against them. It was a feeling she knew all too well.

But the creature had to be the one to decide to trust. A scared or angry wild animal would still bite and claw if they felt threatened.

A tear had soaked into her pillow, thinking of Addie down there alone and afraid. And dead. Ophelia's last thought before falling asleep had been to pray and ask how she might help Addie. *"And Lord,"* she had added, *"be with her."*

But in the light of morning, she still wasn't sure what she could do.

Blaze whined again.

"I'm getting up," Ophelia sighed, and threw off the covers. Nevada jumped down, irritated at the disturbance. Tibby simply moved and went back to sleep.

Ophelia kneaded the muscles in her weak leg for a few minutes to try to work out the stiffness before she drew off her nightgown and hurried into her combinations and her stockings. She had just tied her garters and was doing up her boot laces when Nancy came in to build up the fires.

"Good morning, Miss," Nancy, the upstairs maid said, bobbing a curtsy, her large wide eyes glancing at Ophelia's leg.

"Good morning, Nancy," Ophelia said, hiding a sigh. There wasn't enough money—or perhaps her father was just too parsi-monious—to pay for a lady's maid, so Nancy helped her dress and then went about her duties. Ophelia was rather self-sufficient anyway. Nancy was a good girl, but slightly cross-eyed and blessed with long teeth rather reminiscent of a horse. She also tended to stare at Ophelia's leg like there might be a visual indication of her limp, the bone twisted or bowed. There was not.

Nancy built up the fire as Ophelia put on her corset and did up the busk. Then the maid helped tighten the laces just a tad and threw the petticoat over Ophelia's head and fastened it before tying on the small bustle pad. Then came Ophelia's skirt and bodice.

Ophelia did up those hooks as Nancy eyed her critically. "Would you like help with your hair, Miss?"

"No, thank you Nancy, that will be all."

"Yes miss." She bobbed another curtsy and left.

Ophelia ran a brush through her hair and pinned it up in a knot in her head, and then took Blaze out to the garden.

As Blaze took his morning constitutional, sniffing all the trees and bushes just in case they had moved in the night, Ophelia slowly followed him through the foliage, stretching out her leg from the previous night spent curled up on the stairs.

"Ophelia!"

She turned at Ben's shout. Blaze loped back to her side and pressed against her leg, his demeanor watchful.

Ben walked into the garden in shirtsleeves and his waistcoat.

"I didn't think rakish bachelors woke before noon," she said, burying her fingers in Blaze's fur. *Ben knows who was in the crate*, she thought. *He warned me. Does he know what Father's doing to her, too?*

"I remember that country hours are different, though I will enjoy my coffee and sausages at breakfast."

"Anyone else awake yet?"

Ben shrugged, smiling. "I doubt it. Sleep well?"

Her heart skipped a beat. "Yes." She swallowed.

"I thought you got up with the sun."

She hid suddenly clammy hands in her skirts. "Things do change when you've been away almost a year."

He had the decency to look shamefaced. "I'm sorry about that."

"I haven't seen you since Christmas, and that only for a day, and you barely write." She glared at him. "Did you get my letters?"

Ben hesitated. "Yes."

"But your answer's no," she whispered.

"Ophelia, you must know you can't live with me; it isn't done."

She stared down at Blaze, fighting to swallow past the lump in her throat.

"Oh, sweetheart."

"What am I to do, Ben?" She said through gritted teeth. "Father will ignore me forever, given the chance! And why, just because I'm a woman?" She gestured to Renwick Hall. "Will I languish here forever? In a crumbling manor with no prospects? I know I am crippled, but—"

"You're not crippled," he objected.

"I limp," she said flatly.

"That doesn't make you crippled."

"No, it just makes my marriage prospects slim to none, coupled with my lack of funds and being buried in the country."

"What are you talking about?"

She gestured to herself and the surrounding environs of Renwick hopelessly.

"No, about the money."

"Getting money from Father is like squeezing blood from a turnip. Marie-Claire had to pay for my frocks when I let down my skirts. If bustles are gaining size again...." Ophelia flushed at bringing up underclothes to her brother but forged ahead. "I'm in danger of being extremely dowdy because I can't pay to have them altered, and I can't ask her for help again. I have no pin money. I rationed what you gave me for Christmas for months."

"But Mother left you a trust."

Ophelia stared at him blankly.

"She left her money from her side of the family in trust for you. It's yours when you marry or when you turn twenty-one.

Father wanted it for his experiments, that's—that's why he's bitter about it."

"All of this," she said numbly. "It's been about *money?*"

"Ophelia—"

But she was making for the house as quick as her limp could carry her.

⊱❦⊰

Ophelia shut herself in her room and cuddled Sheba, who was curled up in the chair that used to be in her mother's sitting room. She had moved it into her room after Mother died, along with everything else Ophelia could lay her hands on when it became clear that her father would raze or brick up everything that had been Cornelia Shaw's.

The few pieces of jewelry that were not "family jewels" and kept in the safe (or sold—who knew what had become of them) lay safely in Ophelia's jewelry box, and her mother's bottles of scent sat on her dressing table. She loved the beautiful shapes, and the smell of her mother always comforted her—cinnamon and orange blossoms.

When Sheba got tired of being squeezed, Ophelia let her go and stood, opening the scent bottle and closing her eyes. The scent surrounded her, filling her with bittersweet courage. *Mother, you gave me such a gift...but why didn't you tell me?*

If she hadn't known about the money, what *else* did Ophelia not know about?

She dabbed the scent on, feeling as if she had been given a hug from a ghostly embrace. If she could endure until she was twenty-one—two years—she would have the trust. How much was it? Enough for a season, even if she was long in the tooth at that point? Or perhaps she could set up her own household? Gain independence from her father... but that meant leaving Renwick.

Which, for all its gloom and disrepair, was the only home she'd ever known.

But a fresh start...her own household....

Of course, if she married, then she could have the money immediately.

She scoffed, the sharp noise startling Tibby out of her contented snooze. The cat shook herself and curled back up into a ball as Ophelia smoothed her fur. "Sorry," she whispered. "I'm right back to my original problem of no funds to go to London for husband-hunting, and no one presently in the village."

It wasn't as if she was *picky*. Marie-Claire was in some sense correct—she *did* snatch the last eligible bachelor in Hartley. The village population had only produced a surfeit of girls for several years during the 1850s and 60s, of which Ophelia was one. All other bachelors did not quite deserve the title yet, being several years younger than her and still in school. The older gentlemen had more incentive to pick other ladies for their wives—plus all the women in their area appeared hale and hearty, prodigiously fecund when it came to childbearing. There were not many lonely widowers to be had.

If any *unsuitable* of-age person had shown himself to have any interest in her (that could be strong enough to surpass the class barrier...and her lack of dowry...and probably family disapproval on both sides, though Ophelia found this very hypocritical that her father would deign to show interest in her once she was *leaving* his household, but he had proven himself attentive to anything that might besmirch his professional reputation and name), Ophelia probably would have snatched up this mythical person like a shot. She did not consider herself so puffed up in her own consequence to decline an earnest proposal from a working-class man genuine in his affections.

Alas, no such paragon existed. Not within Hartley, at least.

She wasn't sure if her willingness to take *anyone* was a good thing or a bad thing. She hated to think herself desperate, because she was *not*. But it was one thing to declare independence of men and society if you were an heiress with an income who could set up her own household and be charmingly eccentric. *Or a plucky American orphan who could go off on adventures and brave the Wild West,* she acknowledged, thinking of her dime novels.

But she was neither—and her mother's eventual inheritance would in no way elevate her to an heiress. Surely it could not be much, but something was more than nothing....

Ophelia groaned and flopped back onto the bed, covering her face. It was a moot point. Either she married, or she waited years for her own money. Or she remained at Renwick forever.

The house creaked, settling as it did when the weather changed.

"Poor house," Ophelia whispered. "Either way, I lose you. Or you lose me. Would he close you forever, if I left? But staying means being beholden to Father forever. Or worse, Absalom." Ophelia shuddered. If something happened to Father, Absalom would be the male inheritor. What a horrible fate.

Ophelia stared at the ceiling sightlessly before shaking her head. There was no beau, and it was unlikely there would be any time soon. All that 'what-if'-ing was two years away. It was enough for now to know that there was some hope, no matter how slim.

For now, there was a vampire in her cellar. A hungry, dangerous one.

She pushed herself up and went back to her dressing table, where she threw open the lid of her jewelry box and fished inside. Her fingers found the simple silver cross and chain that had been her mother's, a gift for something—Ophelia's baptism, perhaps. She recalled from Ben's gothics that vampires—vampyres?—were weakened by sunlight, and silver, and running water...or was it holy water? Other things as well. She couldn't remember. Ophelia made a note to hunt up the copies in the library. Who knew what was truth and what was fiction—there was a *vampire* in her *cellar*

—but the legends certainly seemed to have some truth when it came to silver.

Ophelia didn't believe Addie would harm her out of malice, but she might not be able to help her...instincts. Wearing the silver cross couldn't hurt. There was no harm in being prepared. She clasped the chain around her neck and tucked the cross inside her bodice.

She just wished she had someone to *speak to* about all of this. Someone she could trust.

She whistled to Blaze, who sat up and wagged his tail. "Fancy going to the village this morning, Blaze?"

❧

Ophelia wore her green carriage dress and had the groom hitch Arabella, the pony, up to the pony trap for her, and then set off to the Glenwoods' home. She wished she could just walk, but too long a tramp taxed her leg and made it ache like the devil. Calling out the carriage felt like such an undertaking, and it always faintly smelled of damp. The pony trap was an adequate solution. Arabella wasn't precisely fast, but she was steady, and Ophelia could manage her. The pony always got them to their destination safely.

Blaze sat obediently at her side, ignoring possible squirrel distractions. He knew how to behave, and Arabella didn't mind him. She was a very placid mare; Renwick did not have the money to keep prime goers in their stable.

Leaving the boundaries of Renwick lands felt a little like waking from a dream. Emerging from the thick overhanging oaks and into the sunlit world made Ophelia's worries feel almost unreal.

But it had happened. She had proof. She fingered the handkerchief in her pocket, and the rip in the corner, from what she suspected was a fang.

She desperately wanted to speak to someone about Addie, and what to do. She did not feel equipped for this.

Brain buzzing with all the things to talk to Marie-Claire about —a trust of money, her father's appearance, and *vampires*—she made good time and reached Larkspur Cottage, which wasn't really a cottage but a very lovely and cozy house, just as Dr. Snow was leaving in his gig.

Ophelia's heart leapt in her throat.

The footman saw her approaching and waited to assist her with stepping down from the trap. The groom took charge of Arabella, while Ophelia snapped on Blaze's lead and let the footman take him to the kitchen for a nice bone. They were used to Blaze at Larkspur Cottage.

The Glenwoods' butler showed her into Marie-Claire's sitting room, where Marie-Claire looked up from her embroidery. "Ophelia! Oh, good, you're here."

"What is the matter?" Ophelia said, dropping heavily into a chair and tugging off her gloves. Marie-Claire didn't *look* ill, but....

"The matter?" her friend said, confused.

"I saw Dr. Snow leaving...."

"Oh!" Her friend laughed. "Yes. These last few weeks, Owen has been as nervous as a cat in a room full of rocking chairs, as Mr. Faber would say. He makes a fuss over every little thing. He's called poor Dr. Snow out any number of times if I get so much as a sniffle, so the doctor has taken to paying a call whenever he is in the area. We humor Owen," Marie-Claire said with a fond smile, patting her stomach. "After all, after the last time...." she trailed off. "He wants everything to go as smoothly as possible, so nothing upsets me."

Marie-Claire and Owen had lost their first child. A miscarriage halfway through the pregnancy. It had gone hard with them, and Marie-Claire took a long time recovering. Ophelia didn't blame Owen for being nervous.

"Oh yes, of course, that make sense," Ophelia said, biting her lip.

Marie-Claire laughed. "Speaking of cats... hello, you."

Ophelia turned to see the massive ginger tom emerge from under the sofa and stretch mightily, his snaggletooth mouth opening in a yawn.

"I vow he heard your voice," Marie-Claire said.

Ophelia reached down and scratched the large head. "Hello, Morris." He pushed against her hand and purred as she tickled his chin.

Ophelia had found him sniffing about Renwick Hall a few years ago, and had dearly wished to keep him, but he and Sheba had displayed a strong preference for each other—Sheba's own *petit ami,* as Marie-Claire put it. Kittens would have been a complication, much as she would've loved them. So, she had kept her cats an all-female cadre, and gifted Morris to Marie-Claire. And at just the right time too.

Marie-Claire had told Ophelia privately, months after, that she had cried buckets of tears in Morris's fur after losing the baby, and he had been very patient with her. To his credit, Owen was very tolerant about keeping a cat in the house who endeavored to shed on everything he could and even tried to take up prime real estate on their bed.

"Were you sleeping?" Ophelia asked him, as the cat oozed from her to Marie-Claire. "Taking a morning nap?"

"Regular as clockwork, our Morris."

The cat hopped up beside Marie-Claire and mountaineered to the back of the settee to survey his territory.

"Speaking of Mr. Faber, what do you hear from him? How is he?"

"He is well! He has cut ties with Owen's uncle and has bought his own parcel of land and cattle. He sounds as if he is thriving in Texas. His recent letter is in my escritoire—that was what made me think of the phrase. He wrote of a social gathering he attended where a group of ladies besieged him with warm welcomes."

"Good." Ophelia pasted a smile on her face. "That's wonderful."

"But you didn't come to hear news of Mr. Faber. What has flung your father home after all this time, Ophelia? And with your brothers in tow?"

Ophelia bit her lip. *Well, you see, he's got a girl in a cage in the cellar, and I don't know what he wants, but the girl is dead. Yet she walks and talks and craves human blood....*

Marie-Claire waited expectantly.

Pregnant Marie-Claire, who shouldn't be upset or shocked. Who had already sustained a loss.

Ophelia twisted her gloves in her lap. "Whoever knows with him," she said vaguely. "Doing some sort of experiment with Absalom and Ben that they want privacy for. I spoke to Ben about...living in London." She bit her lip. "He did say it was impossible."

Marie-Claire reached out and took her hand. "Oh, my dear, I am sorry."

Ophelia shrugged. "I did know how unlikely it was. But here's something Ben did tell me." She squeezed Marie-Claire's hand. "He said Mother had set up a trust for me, one that Father can't touch, and it will come to me on my twenty-first birthday or if I get married. I don't know how much or any particulars—"

"But this is incredible! *Merveilleux!*" Marie-Claire exclaimed. "Why were you not told?"

"Ben seemed to think I already knew," Ophelia muttered, "although how he'd expect me to know I can't imagine, since I was a child when Mother died, and prying letters or any other type of information out of the males in my family requires almost an act of God." *And even if the Almighty did descend from on high in order to give them a talking to, most of them would undoubtedly scoff. If not spit in the Lord's face.*

"Ohhh, undoubtedly your wretch of a father—" Marie-Claire broke off as Owen entered the sitting room.

"Good morning, my dear; hello, Ophelia." He kissed Marie-Claire on the cheek.

"Owen darling, we were just discussing Ophelia's horrible father. Do you know she has an inheritance?"

Morris gave Owen a look of disapproval and kneaded his claws along the settee.

"Ah, ah, none of that, old man," Owen said. He lifted Morris off the furniture. After an initial yowl of protest, Morris gave up and went limp. Owen gathered up the dangling limbs and held him in his arms like a baby. Morris looked very put upon.

"Well, this is new," Ophelia laughed. "Usually, you and the cat mutually suffer each other."

"Owen's practicing," Marie-Claire said mischievously.

Owen made a face at his wife. "What's this about your father, Ophelia?"

"Ben said my mother left me money in trust. Apparently, everyone knew but me. And that's... certainly a contributing factor to Father's antipathy with me."

Owen muttered an oath under his breath, then winced. "Apologies."

"No, it's true," Marie-Claire said, flapping a hand. "What else can we say about him?"

"Bad cess to him," Owen said in an American drawl, shooting his wife an amused look. Morris had had enough and fought to get down. When Owen released him, the cat took him off to the windowsill to sulk about his injured dignity. Owen took a seat by his wife. "How did your brother come to mention it?"

Ophelia swallowed. "I was raking Ben over the coals about the neglect and my future, and he told me. So apparently a good portion of my father's indifference is just because of...." Her throat closed, and she struggled to swallow.

"Greed," Marie-Claire said flatly. "Plain, selfish greed."

Ophelia slumped back against the chair, deflated. "Yes."

And you don't know the rest, the worst, she thought. *You don't know what he plans...and I don't know either.*

But she couldn't tell Marie-Claire that. She glanced at her friend's rounded stomach. If anything happened to her or the child because of something Ophelia did, even inadvertently, she would never forgive herself.

That meant the only person who was able to help Addie and find out what her father was up to... was herself.

Marie-Claire grumbled, "They all deserve to be boiled in oil."

Ophelia cracked a smile. "Sadly, I don't think Renwick ever had the capacity to repel invaders that way."

"These later months have made you remarkably bloodthirsty, my love," Owen murmured.

Marie-Claire folded her hands over her stomach and told him, "All women are bloodthirsty; I simply cannot be bothered to disguise it when I am *enceinte*." She sniffed. "Ophelia, I think at least you should short sheet their beds or serve them haggis. Something to make them suffer."

Ophelia blinked, and then her eyebrows rose. "You know," she said, smiling slowly, "that's not a bad idea."

❦

"Hello Mr. Burns," Ophelia told the village butcher, smiling politely. "I hope you and Mrs. Burns are doing well."

The village butcher was a large man with an impressive shoulder width and a blond Prince Albert moustache. He beamed back at her over the counter. "Good day to you, lass. And good morning to you, Master Blaze," he told the dog who waited patiently at her side. "Can't complain, can't complain. The missus is looking forward to our first grandchild, knitting like mad."

"Oh, please pass on my congratulations!" Ophelia said, brightening.

"I will at that! What might you be seeking today?" he said, rubbing his hands together.

"Marie-Claire has promised to expand my recipe knowledge," Ophelia lied, explaining her carefully crafted story. "I want to try making some blood pudding recipes."

"Blood pudding?" Mr. Burns repeated.

"Yes, and I decided this would be a good time to experiment, what with my brothers recently come home. They can eat my failed experiments. Cast iron stomachs, you know." She smiled, banking on Mr. Burns, who had several sons as well as daughters, understanding how healthy sibling dynamics ought to work.

"Oh aye," he said, a smile creeping across his face. "Eager to help you, are they?"

"It's a surprise." She smiled angelically.

He threw back his head and laughed. "Happy to help! How much?"

"I'm thinking I'll need to practice a few times to get it right. I'll probably need a steady supply of blood for a little while," Ophelia said, biting her tongue at the side of her mouth.

He nodded. "No trouble at all, Miss Shaw."

"And I'll come pick the packages up," Ophelia said hurriedly. "I wouldn't want to test Mrs. Lowell's temper further than necessary." She smiled.

"Oh aye," Mr. Burns laid a finger against his nose and wrinkled slyly. "You won't get no guff from that dragon on my account, Miss. I'll go and wrap up a parcel now, hmm?"

Chapter Seven

When Ophelia arrived home, armed with supplies and the tenuous beginnings of a plan, the groom, Judson, appeared to hold Arabella while she dismounted from the trap. Her knee protested, and she had to pause for a moment before her leg agreed to bear her weight. Ophelia took hold of Blaze's collar and thanked Judson before ascending the stairs.

Rivers met her at the door, staring down his nose dourly as she made Blaze wipe his paws on the mat placed there just for that purpose. "Good afternoon, Rivers," she said, handing off her cloak. "Might I have tea in my room today?"

"The Master has ordered it be served in the parlor, Miss."

"They're taking tea in the parlor?" Ophelia repeated faintly, suddenly hyper aware of the bottle of blood among her purchases, as well as her horsehair-dusted carriage dress. "I'd better go and freshen up, then." She patted her leg for Blaze to follow her.

In her room she secreted the bottles into a safe place, away from the animals, who gave them odd looks—perhaps they could smell them?—and took off her hat and gloves, changing from her riding habit to an afternoon gown of blue she thought looked well with her hair. She touched the silver chain around her neck again and made sure it was under her collar. "Better face the music," she told Tibby, who just blinked at her from the window seat.

⁂

"Hello, Father. Would you like me to pour?" Ophelia asked, taking her customary place in the parlor. Her father's stare discomfited her. He had watched her walk in with a keen eye to her gait, which made her feel like bug under a microscope. Her limp had not changed from the last time he had seen her. Why did he stare so?

He ignored the question entirely and demanded, "Where were you?"

Ophelia lifted the teapot anyway. "I went into the village to pay a call on Marie-Claire."

"Who?"

"Marie-Claire Glenwood. The daughter of Mother's friend Mrs. Fontaine." *You saw her just yesterday*, she wanted to add, but Ben shot her a warning look and she subsided.

He grunted. "I don't want you running all over creation when I want you."

That's rich, she thought, but handed around the teacups without making a face. "I didn't know you were looking for me. I apologize."

"We're expecting a guest," her father said abruptly.

The teapot wavered in her grasp. "A guest?"

"A colleague of ours. From London. He'll be here tomorrow on the train."

"I'll let Nancy know to clean and air out a bedchamber," Ophelia said, mystified. "Is he arriving on business, or is it a social visit?"

"A bit of both," Absalom said with a smirk.

Addie, Ophelia thought, the realization hitting her like an anvil. She clasped her hands into fists within the folds of her dress. *He's coming about Addie.*

"Shall I speak to Cook about the menus?" she ventured.

Her father waved his hand dismissively. "Of course, just don't bother me with domestic matters."

She nodded, hiding the relief that she could make a variety of purchases—including more blood. "And tonight?"

He frowned. "Tonight?"

"Will you be working through dinner again, or shall I instruct Rivers to set places for you in the dining room?"

"No. Trays," her father said flatly.

"I'll eat with you, Ophelia," Ben said.

Somehow, that did not contain the same allure that it had the day before.

❧

"So, what is Father obsessed with these days?" Ophelia finally asked as the third course was served that evening. She could stand it no longer. She had to know.

"Didn't I tell you not to worry about it?" Ben asked as Thomas placed the plate of pike and cream sauce in front of him.

"I'm not asking for specifics," she said, as if it was of no import. "We don't want me troubling my pretty little head about great thoughts, after all." She narrowed her eyes at him. *Never mind that I've devoured every book in this library and everything Marie-Claire has lent me.*

Ben shot her a chiding look. "It's not that you couldn't understand, Ophelia. But you know how Father gets with his secrets. He's paranoid about his discoveries before they're finalized and published."

"Just the subject," she pressed, taking a bite of the fish. "What brought him to Renwick? He's never done any great work here before."

"He doesn't want anything leaking out. London servants gossiping between houses, that sort of thing."

She thought about this. "But he's inviting a colleague to visit? Why?"

"Lucas is actually my friend. We met at Oxford and kept in contact. He's coming down to consult for us," he said.

"Oh, there's something Father isn't a full expert in? Some knowledge outside his purview?" Ophelia made a face.

"We're making a deal to exchange information," Ben chuckled, as the footman cleared away the plates and brought out the roast beef. "But that's all I'm going to say on the matter. You'll want to keep Father on your good side."

"Will I? Why?" Ophelia asked suspiciously.

"I spoke to Father, about your wish."

"What wish?"

"To go to London. Have a season. Get married."

She started, then narrowed her eyes. "And he listened?"

"He seemed to. He said he would give it some thought. That's not a no, is it?"

She admitted that it was not a flat denial. *But what is there to think about?* She wondered. "Thank you, Ben."

"You're welcome. Don't say I never did anything for you."

She half-smiled as the familiar mix of fondness and exasperation washed over her. "I don't believe I've ever said that." Indeed, he had been the only male family member to even try. "Speaking of marriage...do you remember anything more about the details of Mother's trust?"

"It was a long time ago," Ben said, pulling his napkin from his lap and dabbing at his mouth.

"But the records must be with the solicitor. I could write and find out. Will you give me their direction?"

"Yes, but I don't see why you're so interested. You won't be of age for two more years."

Ophelia noticed he said nothing about her marriage prospects.

She bit her lip and resolved not to pin too many hopes on a season being forthcoming. "I want to know why she didn't tell me. Why she didn't even mention it."

"Well, you were young."

"But wouldn't it have been read at her funeral? If it was part of her will?"

"Do you really think something like that would've made you take notice through the grief, at eleven?"

If it concerned me, I'd like to think so, Ophelia thought, but kept the words behind her teeth. "All right. Do *you* remember?"

"Well, no," he admitted.

"So how did you find out about the trust?"

He opened his mouth, then paused. "I think it must've been one of Father's rants. You know the type. The world is against him, no one understands his genius. It probably fell under 'lack of support.'"

"And you really think he'll take me to London, after all that?" Ophelia murmured, inspecting the tines of her fork.

Ben waved a hand. "I'm sure he'll get over it."

"He's had almost ten years to get over it, Ben. If he was going to, I think he would have by now." She pushed her chair back from the table before poor Thomas could help her. "Would you like me to leave you to your port?"

"I don't like port," Ben said. "I'd rather have whisky."

"Mind if I join you?"

"Why not?" He laughed, pushed back his chair, and went to the sideboard. Uncorking the correct decanter, he poured and handed her the whisky glass with a smirk. "Here. See how you like it."

Ophelia swirled the glass meditatively and took a sip. Then another longer sip. "It's all right."

Ben blinked at her, oddly disappointed. "You don't think it's strong?"

"Not really." She threw the rest of the glass back as the peaty taste ran over her tongue.

Ben stared at her in shock.

"You seem to forget I live here full time, Ben. I've had plenty of time to taste all of the liquors we have in the house and see what's to my liking."

She set the glass down and limped out to her brother's astonished laughter.

❧

Ophelia did not head up to bed immediately. She detoured by the library to plunder the gothics shelf, pulling down every tome that might be remotely useful. Forewarned was forearmed, and she intended to know more about what she was getting into before descending to the underworld tonight.

She came away with a substantial stack of books and began to sort through them. A few were novels, but several were volumes of poetry she remembered alluding to themes of death and blood.

Ophelia walked through the nonfiction sections on a faint hope, but the shelves were all stuffed with the latest scientific volumes and treatises. Her father had a habit of purchasing the volumes, reading them, and then, since there was apparently no library in the London townhouse, shipping them to Renwick Hall. Rivers was clearly at his wit's end on where to put them all. The shelves were fairly creaking with the weight.

Ophelia could see no volumes that might say *Vampires and their Scientific Genus* anywhere, but once she had a better grasp of the situation, maybe an idea would come to her.

She also did not recall any volumes of folklore or legend dealing with the undead. Therefore, fiction was her only recourse. Disgruntled, she poured herself another glass of whisky from the library decanters and drained it before stacking her haul and going slowly up the stairs, favoring her bad leg. It ached after the long day.

⁂

The whisky made her sleepy.

Ophelia yawned and opened the next book. She had found most alcohol made her tired, except ratafia, which was just vile on principle. The one time she had imbibed enough alcohol to get truly drunk, she had chosen whisky. It was when she was fifteen and pretending to be a cowboy. Cowboys drank hard liquor, not beer or wine, Mr. Faber had told her, since it kept its taste and potency no matter the temperature, while beer went flat in hot weather. As a result, she had investigated the decanters that Rivers kept filled, even though none of the menfolk of her family were home, found the one that was scotch whisky, and proceeded to pour herself a glass. She had tasted all the liquors before, and knew that the cowboy moniker of "firewater" was apt. But, screwing up her face, she had forced glass after glass back until the room spun and she had to stagger to her room.

Ophelia had woken the next day feeling like death and had thrown it all up again, suffering with a splitting headache for the rest of the day. After that, Ophelia contented herself with the alcohol she found tolerable and stopped once the sleepy feeling started.

A miscalculation tonight, as it turned out, even though seeing Ben's shocked face had been gratifying. She couldn't afford to be sleepy tonight.

Most of the books she had found proved unhelpful. Only a few seemed to ring true to what she had observed the night before—a poem by Byron, *Giaour*, which made passing reference to drinking blood; the novel *The Vampyre* by John Polidori, who had some connection to Byron; and *Varney the Vampire*, an absolutely gargantuan tome that originated as a series of penny dreadfuls. Ben read this to her as a child.

Ophelia recalled being irritated by it more than anything, as the time period was not entirely consistent, and the author seemed unable to make up his mind if Varney was truly some supernatural creature or just a horrible man. From her desultory skimming tonight, she didn't think she was wrong in her opinion. But a few things did strike a chord here and there, and she made careful note of them at her writing desk—fangs, drinking blood, more than human strength. She thought she recalled vampires having a horror of the church and other items like garlic or rowan...or maybe that was fairies? She hadn't found a mention of silver yet, which she had firm evidence for....

Holding in another yawn, she jotted the question down and set aside *Varney* with a grateful sigh, picking up another. Blaze and the cats slept on the bed, a pile of warmth as the wind moaned outside and the trees whispered. She took to pinching herself as the evening wore on, which helped; but she would probably have a nice array of bruises in the morning.

When the clock struck eleven, she pulled her wool wrapper securely around her and gathered up the flask of blood from where she had hidden it. Under her nightgown she wore flannel combinations. She slipped a short dime novel into her pocket in case the wait was as long as the night before. Then, shutting Blaze in with a whine and a stern command to hush and behave, Ophelia lit her lantern and ventured once again down to the cold dark cellar.

It was less frightening this night, because she knew what awaited her down in the dark laboratory, but a different kind of fear lurked within her now—what had happened to Addie in the intervening hours? What had they done to her? Would she be all right?

Ophelia did not have to wait as long tonight. When the clock chimes struck midnight, she heard the cellar door open and the men leave to go up to bed by the main stairs. Someone was grumbling—probably Absalom.

Then the footsteps faded. All was quiet, except for the creaking that was intrinsic to Renwick.

She waited a moment, then stood, making sure that her leg had all the time it needed to find its equilibrium—and then descended.

❧

The door hinges creaked as the cellar door swung open into darkness. Ophelia ventured cautiously through the mysterious shadows her lantern created from her father's equipment.

"Addie?" she whispered, lifting the light higher. "Addie, are you there?"

There had been no sounds tonight. A knot of worry sunk in Ophelia stomach. She didn't know whether that was good or bad.

Something hiccupped.

Ophelia sidestepped the examination table. The light illuminated the silver cage. "Addie?"

The girl lay in the corner, clutching her head. "Hurtsss," she whimpered, barely audible.

"What hurts?"

"M'head. Hurtssoo much. Always," Addie mumbled. Her words slurred together, and she hissed when her eyes caught the light. She turned away, clapping a hand to her eyes.

Ophelia set the lantern down, closing the shutter until it emitted only a dim glow. "Did my father do something?"

The girl didn't respond.

Ophelia waited a minute. "Addie?"

"Issee comin back?" She breathed.

"No, he's gone to bed," she assured her. "And I've brought you something. Look."

"Hm?"

Ophelia pulled the flask out of her pocket.

Addie opened one eye, the pupil blown wide. It turned ruby red when she saw the bottle. In one fluid, neatly instantaneous movement, she sat up. Her skin was paper thin, drawn tight over her bones. She was far thinner tonight—nearly skeletal. Something had clearly happened.

Ophelia eyed the space between them. She set the bottle down and inched it slowly across the floor. "Here."

Addie's hand shot through the bars and latched onto the bottle's neck. Ophelia couldn't help but recoil. Addie dragged it back through the bars and had it uncorked and up to her mouth in nearly the same amount of time.

Ophelia chewed her lip and watched as Addie drank swallow after swallow of the blood. Some of the unsettling gray pallor receded from her skin, and her face filled out a little.

Finally, Addie upended the bottle. Addie licked her lips and stared sadly at the empty receptacle. "It was all cold. And tasted of animal."

"It was pig's blood, I think," Ophelia said. "I told the butcher I would be making a lot of blood pudding. Sorry. Did it help?"

Addie kept staring at the bottle.

"Addie?"

She blinked, slowly.

"Addie, did it help?"

"He didn't hurt me."

"What?" Ophelia said. Now she was confused.

"The scientist man. He didn't hurt me tonight. It was the other one."

Dread coiled in her stomach. "What other one?"

"He cut me with silver. It took so long to heal." She stared unseeing. "He laughed when I cried."

Absalom. "Addie, I'm so sorry," Ophelia whispered. She instinctively stretched out her hand but pulled it back. Her heart wrenched. "Is there something I can do to make it better?"

Addie watched the motion dully. "Silver makes me sick," she said. "I'm surrounded by it. It fills up my lungs. That necklace. I can smell it."

Ophelia instinctively grasped the silver cross around her neck. "Is it the silver, or the cross, or both?"

Addie gave her a patent look of patience, the way one did to small children. "Crosses only hurt if you're crucified."

"So, they don't bother you?" What was the polite way of asking *'do you consider yourself sundered from divine grace?'*

She shook her head, then winced. "I wasn't crucified. Theron was. But that doesn't matter; he's ash now."

"Who's Theron?" Ophelia asked, but Addie did not respond. She tried a different tack. "Does silver make your head hurt?"

She gestured vaguely to her temple, and the dark discoloration there. "I hit my head."

"On the bars?"

"Long time ago." Addie stared off meditatively into the dark, licking her lips. Then she said, "The blood does help, even if it's cold." She tipped the bottle over her palm and licked up what few droplets ran out.

Ophelia felt distinctly unsettled, looking at the dark blood that she lapped so eagerly. "How long have you been...drinking blood?" Ophelia asked, gathering her wrap tightly around her as a chilly draft skated across the floor.

"Since I turned," Addie said.

"When was that?"

"When I died," Addie said blankly.

"You had to die to become a...."

"Vampire. Yes." She shrugged a little. "But I would've died either way." Before Ophelia could comment on that, Addie twirled the bottle meditatively, then reluctantly recorked it. "Here. If it is here, they will know." She put it back through the bars and pushed it. "Thank you."

It rolled towards Ophelia, who picked it up, surprised. "You're welcome."

"Sorry for before," Addie said. "I was hungry. I know better. The silver makes it hard to think, and then my head." She made another vague motion.

Ophelia looked at her ankles. They still looked very angry and swollen. "I'll try to bring you something to pad your shackles tomorrow night." She took note of the fabric Addie had ripped up to stuff in between her skin and the silver. She'd have to match it well so no one would notice. The guilt smote her again, that Addie was a prisoner in her home.

"Addie, I would let you out if I could, but I...." *Can't*. Punishment from her father, danger from the captive herself. *But what sort of consequence if I don't?* Ophelia thought, worrying at her bottom lip. Then her other comment sunk in. "What do you mean, you know better?"

"He taught me not to hurt when I feed, to take only what I need. 'Don't be greedy,'" Addie said, like she was quoting. "'Don't be a glutton. You don't have to be so full you get a stomachache.'"

"Who?"

She didn't seem to hear. "They'll miss me," she whispered, chewing at her nail. "He told Etienne to watch out for me. He'll know I'm gone."

And then she smiled, a bright joyous grin that seems so incongruous with the dark and dank settings. In the candlelight, it made her eyes—which had receded back into colorless marbles—glow like stars. "He'll be coming for me," she said with conviction.

A chill ran down Ophelia's spine. *Who?*

Chapter Eight

Blaze tugged at his lead and Ophelia let herself be dragged through the misty and overcast morning. Her whole brain felt foggy from staying up with Addie the night before and the tossing and turning afterward. Addie had clammed up and refused to say any more about who she was talking about —who might be coming for her. "I don't think I'm supposed to say," she had repeated and then refused to elaborate. Ophelia hadn't known what else to ask her about, so she had pulled out her well-thumbed dime novel and read a few chapters to Addie. The girl had closed her eyes and listened, and when Ophelia's eyes began to swim across the cheap paper, Addie had asked, "You'll come tomorrow, won't you?"

Ophelia had said yes.

What am I going to do about Addie? Ophelia thought, as Blaze forged ahead in the fog-shrouded wood that surrounded Renwick. If someone—some*thing*— was coming for her, they would *not* be pleased to find her in a cage in the cellar. What would a thing like Addie do, if it was free...and angry?

But could she let Addie go? How dangerous *was* she? Could Ophelia trust her?

And what kind of wrath would she experience from her father if he found his experiment gone, and only one possible person to blame for it?

Her thoughts circled around the problem over and over again without coming to a suitable solution. After letting Blaze putter around the grounds longer than usual, Ophelia returned to Renwick with an aching leg and made for the breakfast room. Upon entry, she discovered she was the only occupant. She lifted a tray on the sideboard and frowned down at the cold food.

"Would you like me to reheat the trays, miss?" Thomas asked, breaking his silent demeanor.

"Cook will be very put out with you, Thomas," Ophelia said tonelessly. "With me, too."

"Mrs. Lowell will understand I am just doing my job, miss."

"If you would brave the dragon in the kitchen, I would be most appreciative, thank you." She cast him a grateful look. "How goes your courtship? I recall you were walking out with a village girl."

"Kind of you to remember, Miss. Yes, my Nan and I plan to marry in the spring. Her uncle has a brewery up in Middlesbrough and he's looking for help. I'm saving so I can set Nan up nice while I learn the business."

"Oh. So you will be leaving us in the spring."

Thomas coughed. "Yes, miss. I offered to put in a word for her with Mr. Rivers, but...being so far from her family makes her uneasy."

Translation: Renwick Hall made Nan uneasy.

Ophelia's heart sank. Thomas was one of the few servants who was generally cheerful and kind. It would be a wrench to lose him. "Ah. Well, that's understandable. It's important to be close to family. We will miss you, Thomas, but I wish you and Nan every happiness and success."

"Thank you miss. And I'm not leaving right away. Still some

time to spring. I'll be back in a jiffy with more breakfast." He carried the trays from the room.

Ophelia stared around the morning room, as the loneliness of the house sank into her bones. One less person to inject any kind of life or kindness into the house. It felt as if the shadows were deepening already. She didn't know how much longer she could be the lone candle flame of hope for Renwick in the face of ill winds and cold resentment and outright malice. Buffeted by such trials, eventually she would burn down... and gutter out.

⚜

Ophelia spent most of the morning away from Renwick. She did not want to see her father or brothers, not until she had decided what to do about poor Addie, and so slipped out quietly as possible.

She did not want to see Marie-Claire either, for fear she would blurt out something of her worries and either upset her friend unduly or set her off. Marie-Claire on a tear was an unpredictable thing. What would *she* do, put in such a situation? She was brave. Probably march right up to her father and....

There Ophelia's imagination failed her. It always did under the power of her father's withering stares.

Ophelia ended up browsing aimlessly in the village shops, making small purchases that could ostensibly be added to the Hall's housekeeping tabs, and then headed to the butcher's to pick up another flask of blood. The weight of it surprised her the same way it had the first time—heavy and ponderous. Outside the butcher's, by happenstance, she met Reverend Anscombe, the vicar.

"Oh, good morning, Miss Shaw," he said, and tipped his hat to her. Reverend Anscombe had been in Hartley's village all her life, and had been the one to baptize her. He was a nice old gentleman with a fine mustache and a head full of iron gray hair.

"Good morning, sir," she said, and had a tickle of an idea. "Actually sir, would you mind if I walked with you?"

"What, back to the vicarage? Of course, Mrs. Anscombe would be happy to see you."

"Oh, well of course I will say hello to Mrs. Anscombe," Ophelia said, "but I actually had a...a question I'd like to ask you."

"Oh?" He offered her his arm, and she took it. "Ask away, my dear. A personal question, is it?"

"Um, more...theological in nature."

"I'm equipped for those too," he said with a smile. "Fire away."

"Do you believe that some people are damned? I mean, we're all damned before salvation, of course, but do you think some people are unsavable?"

"Well, either from personal inclination or pure stubbornness, there are those who reject Christ, and we would consider them damned, yes. But the Lord can still do a mighty work in men's hearts, you know. It is never too late," he said, giving her a keen stare. "Even until the point of death." He laughed a little. "And perhaps further if the Catholics have the right of it. But it's not we who do the saving, my dear. That is God's job." He squeezed her hand.

"Oh, that's—I'm not—" Ophelia's words stumbled to a half, a bit mortified. *He thinks I'm worried about my atheist father and who-knows-what brothers.* "I know that," she finally said, a little lamely. "But what I wondered was—is there something that could bar you from that chance of grace? Is there something so bad...." she trailed off.

"Well, some do say that suicide makes one damned," the vicar mused. "A mortal sin, as they say. I'm not sure I believe that, though. The poor troubled souls are often so weary and burdened in this life, can anyone wonder that they long for the next? And while I'm certain that's not what our Lord desires, I do not believe He would withhold His grace from them."

Ophelia chewed her lip. "Anything else?"

"Hmmm." The vicar stroked his chin. "In my sermon notes on the next chapter of First John, I've run across a mention of a sin that *leads* to death."

Ophelia swallowed.

He continued, "But I believe that refers to what Jesus spoke of in the Gospels, a blasphemy against the Holy Spirit, attributing the works of the Spirit to those of Satan."

She bit her lip. "Nothing else?"

"If even murderers can receive God's grace and be made new, I don't think you have much to worry about my dear," the vicar said, patting her hand. Then they were at the vicarage, and she could press no further. "Ah, here's Mrs. Anscombe. My dear, look who it is! Miss Shaw has come to say hello."

In the darkness, Salem dreamed. He saw Renata melt to dust again and again, her heart in his hand.

No, not dream—he never dreamed anymore. Memory.

I created you, she whispered before breaking apart.

"You killed me. And I ended you," he said aloud, and felt the pain spike as he drew breath. It was the silver spikes in his chest. He was burning, inside. Eternally burning. Was this what hellfire felt like?

You deserve it, Andrew said in his memory, eyes blood red. *You killed our Mistress.*

"I don't regret it," Salem said to the darkness. He felt the phantom severing of the blood bond, just as it had broken so long ago. She had made him into this. He had unmade her, and avenged—

The pain spiked again, and his memory twisted.

Through the mist of time, Rupert took his chance and stabbed a stake through Theron, now without his consort to protect him. The strike landed just off-center of his heart. Rupert drove more stakes into him, so Theron was pinned to the wall like a butterfly, or like a crucifixion victim. As the blood drained from Renata's lover, Rupert intoned, *I am the Master now. Draugadróttinn I name myself.* He sat on a throne as flakes of dust drifted from Theron's body, and the Court toadied to him, Gisela and Cuthbert and Joseph and Titus and all. No love or loyalty lost among the dead.

"No master of mine," Salem rasped, even though the silver tried to choke him. No fealty to a master. Not ever. "I'm leaving. You'll never see me again."

You can't escape. It's your fate, Andrew said, accepting the cup of Rupert's blood and binding himself to the new master.

"Why would I listen to the word of a traitor?"

Andrew snarled and prepared to spring. Salem couldn't help but brace himself. But a jerk and change in motion broke apart the memory. Andrew's shade dissolved into darkness, and he was left alone, confined in a cramped box, burning from the inside out.

Salem tried to think past the silver poisoning. He had been stabbed through the casket while he was resting. More spikes and chains of silver to confine him. Then thrown into this box full of silver bars. And now...moving.

The silver and lead coffin he was entombed in was moving.

He would meet his captors soon.

Chapter Nine

"Where have you been?" Absalom demanded, confronting her the moment she drew Arabella to a halt.

"In the village, making calls, doing some shopping," Ophelia said, pressing her lips together. The bottle in her dress pocket felt very heavy against her leg. She hated when Absalom loomed over her, like some domineering vulture. *He looks like one too,* she thought uncharitably. His nose conquered his face in a way that was not complimentary.

She accepted the groom's help stepping down from the trap and prepared to make her way indoors.

"No more going out, Ophelia," Absalom said, barring her way.

She pulled up short. "What?"

"You heard me. Father doesn't want you to leave Renwick anymore."

"What are you talking about?"

Ben emerged from the house and scowled at Absalom. "Shut up, thickhead. It's not like that, Ophelia."

"Well, what is it like, then?"

"Our colleague has arrived, and Father wants you here to be hostess."

Ophelia swallowed hard. "Well, let me pass, then; I need to change and tidy my hair."

Absalom caught her arm as she moved past him and hissed, "Remember what I said—no more leaving."

She wrenched herself free of his hold but could not repress the shudder.

Blaze and the cats greeted her enthusiastically at her bedroom door, and she yanked the bell pull to summon Nancy. As much as she'd like to dawdle in her dressing, it would be unwise to antagonize her father further.

Nancy came in with a sappy smile on her face, uncharacteristic of her.

"What is it?" Ophelia asked curiously.

"Oh miss," she said as she assisted Ophelia with her tapes and fasteners. "The gentleman's here. He's ever so handsome."

"Really?" Ophelia said, startled. That's right, this colleague was an acquaintance of Ben's. "A young man?"

"Only a bit older than Mr. Absalom, I'd say." Nancy sighed heavily. "With a head full of thick blond hair and the bluest eyes, Miss. And very pretty manners."

"Gracious," Ophelia murmured, smoothing the striped taffeta overskirt before sitting before her dressing table mirror. She held Nancy's assessment with a grain of salt—after all, Renwick was very isolated, and few strangers made their way to Hartley.

Ophelia pulled the pins from her hair and ran a brush through it to catch the wind-blown auburn strands. Nancy helped her pile it up again and secure her coiffure.

I have so many more headaches now that I am old enough to put my hair up, she reflected idly. *In so many ways.*

"Thank you, Nancy, you've been a great help. Has anyone sent tea to—where are they?"

"The library, Miss. And I'll ask Cook. I'll bring some if they haven't!" Nancy offered, far more eager for this duty than any other task at Renwick.

"Wonderful," Ophelia said wryly. "Thank you." She stood, bracing her leg, and waited until it decided to take her weight. "Once more unto the breach, dear friends," she told the animals before straightening her shoulders and making for the library.

❧

Astonishingly, Nancy's assessment of the new arrival was correct. When Ophelia arrived in the library, Ben performed the introductions between her and a tall, strapping man with waving blond hair and cornflower blue eyes. He had a square jaw and an easy smile as he bowed over her hand. But the smile did not reach all the way to his sharp, assessing eyes. His name was Lucas Harding.

When Nancy arrived with the tea, Ophelia was ridiculously thankful: it gave her something to do besides twist her hands in her lap.

"Milk or sugar?" she asked, pouring.

"Sugar," Mr. Harding said with a smile. "I love all things sweet."

Ophelia gave him a polite, non-committal smile and handed him his cup. "What sort of science are you involved in, Mr. Harding?" she asked, handing around the other cups.

"Oh, a little of this, a little of that." He smiled again. There were a lot of teeth in his mouth. "I'm more of a businessman than a scientist, really. I dabble."

Ophelia slid a glance toward her father, who did not seem to be attending. "I am sure you are being modest, sir; I can think of few people my father would choose to consult with on matters of science."

He smiled again. "Indeed."

"How long will you be with us? As long as the work progresses, I assume?"

"Yes, things seem promising so far; I think we'll be able to double our returns."

She widened her smile. "And what is it you are investigating?"

"Ophelia," Ben said in a low voice.

She turned an innocent gaze on him. "Hmm?"

"Don't push. The matter is very hush-hush. I told you that."

"Well, what else am I supposed to talk about?" She muttered through clenched teeth.

Ben cleared his throat. "Harding, did you see the new play at the Lyceum? Irving has done it again!"

"*The Corsican Brothers*, was it? No, I'm afraid I haven't; *Hamlet* was the last I saw, but I suppose I should go 'round soon. Not much one for the more serious plays, but I'm always willing to watch Irving tread the boards," Mr. Harding said.

And with that, Ben firmly steered the conversational course to safer waters—but effectively cut Ophelia out of the conversation. Nettled enough to ignore her manners, Ophelia leaned back in her chair and sipped her tea.

She had never met any of Ben's school friends before, but this gentleman did not endear himself to her. He had too many teeth and too readily displayed them. After a while of looking at him, the handsome blondness of his appearance wilted as he continued to talk. She could not see much substance in him.

She also could not forget that he had come here for some darker purpose, something to do with Addie that she did not yet understand.

After about ten minutes of the delights of London entertainments, Ben seemed to realize he had left her in the conversational dust. "What do you think about the theater, Ophelia?" He asked.

"As I have never seen a London stage production, only amateur theatricals, I suppose I am not qualified to comment," she said, letting her spoon scrape around her cup in what she knew to be a very ill-bred way. Scrape. Rasp. "But I do like reading plays—I enjoy Shakespeare very much. I would like to see them performed sometime, as well as operas and other entertainments."

"Oh, right," Ben said. "Well, you can't help that."

"Well, maybe if you took me to London," she muttered, shooting him a dark glance.

Her father, who until this time had bent his head close to Absalom in one of the library alcoves and spoken in low tones, set his cup down with a decisive click and stood. "We've wasted enough time: must get back to work."

The men stood. Ophelia didn't bother. "What time would you like dinner, Father?"

"Eight," he said. "And not a long procession of courses either. I don't want to waste time." He strode out of the library without a backward glance. Mr. Harding bowed to her, smiling his over-toothy smile, and Absalom followed him out.

Ben helped her tidy the tea tray, but as he turned to go, Ophelia caught him by the sleeve and pulled him to a halt.

"Ben, what are you experimenting *on?*"

He pried his sleeve from her grasp. "Just leave it, Ophelia."

"You know Father; you can't let him run these experiments on living things! He hurts them!"

Ben pivoted and gave her the sternest look she had ever seen. "I forbid you to investigate, Ophelia. It's too dangerous."

"Why?" she demanded. She wanted to hear him say it.

"Curiosity killed the cat, Ophelia. Leave it alone, for your own safety. I'm working on Father to allow you your dreams. Don't make that work go to waste. Stay out of the cellars."

⚜

Dinner was tense. Absalom and Ben monopolized Mr. Harding for most of the meal as they discussed spiritualism and the scientific qualms to it, especially evolution. Her father kept silent after a few derisive snorts, eating steadily. She could tell he was itching to get back to his laboratory. That made her silent, as a lump of nerves settled in her stomach. She had to do something about Addie.

Ben kept shooting Ophelia guilty glances, or maybe they were warnings. She couldn't tell. He didn't hold her eye for long enough to see.

"But surely you see the cases that have come to light as mediums and spiritualists are accused of fraud," Absalom argued.

"Of course, there are some charlatans, but I don't think ghosts are too far out of the realm of possibility," Mr. Harding chuckled. "Just consider the work we're engaged in now."

Ben shot him a stern look. "Two very different circumstances," he said in quelling tones.

"Even if ghosts do exist," Ophelia said, speaking up for the first time, "why should we bother them on behalf of the living?"

"To learn great mysteries," Mr. Harding said, turning to her eagerly. "Secrets."

"Why do we suppose ghosts would know any? I think the story of the Witch of Endor is clear that one should not call up the dead," Ophelia said. "But also, why should poor souls be trapped here, when heaven and hell are waiting? Unless it's a sort of purgatory and the Catholics have it right," she said, thinking of the Vicar's statement from earlier in the day.

"Perhaps they wish to avoid hell," Mr. Harding chuckled in a humoring sort of way.

"Why should that be within their ability to do? How can one avoid divine judgement after death?"

"Have you thought a lot about this, Miss Shaw?" He put his chin in his hand and regarded her as if she was a mildly entertaining child.

Ophelia pressed her lips together to conceal her irritation. "No, I am merely thinking about it logically."

"What about demons?"

"What about them?"

"Do you believe in them?"

"I believe they exist, and angels too."

"And God?"

"Of course. Without God the whole argument falls apart. And yours too."

"Oh?"

"How can ghosts, the souls of the dead, remain after someone dies, if God did not imbue us with souls? If evolution happened without a Creator directing it, then we are just better animals and have no souls to speak of."

"Then how are we speaking now?"

"How does a dog let you know he's hungry? Communication isn't dependent on souls. Science can't answer everything," she said, shooting a hard look down the table. "Philosophy and theology work together towards that purpose, too."

"What about...monsters?"

Reluctantly, she turned back to him, trying to keep her face calm. "What about them?"

"Do you believe they exist?"

"I suppose it depends on what you mean by monster."

"An unnatural creature? One bent on malice?"

"Why, yes," Ophelia said blandly. "Many people in this world would fit that description. But if Father is right about his theories, all creatures are natural. Unnatural would only be an apt descriptor if someone—like God—made a decree on what should be and what should not."

Her father glared down the length of the table. "That will do very well, Ophelia." He snapped his fingers at Thomas imperiously to bring the next course.

Translation: be quiet.

Ophelia subsided, pressing her lips together tightly.

"I mean a *supernatural entity*, Miss Shaw," Mr. Harding pressed. "Do you believe in such a thing?" He ignored Ben's overloud exclamation over the chicken in an attempt to redirect the conversation.

A chill ran down Ophelia's spine. "I believe angels and demons fit under that umbrella, and we've already established that I believe in them," she said lightly, with a cautious look towards her father. Once subjects were closed by Dr. Shaw, he considered them closed, dead, and buried.

"No, not a spiritual being, a real, physical creature possessed of supernatural abilities." Mr. Harding pinned her to the spot with his eyes. "If presented with proof, would you accept its existence?"

Addie, she thought. The tension around the table squeezed her. "If the proof was sufficient, I suppose," she whispered.

Ben coughed loudly and said, "Did you know that monster comes from the Latin root *monstrum*? It means portent—like a messenger. A warning. In old myths when heroes encountered a monster, it was a harbinger of something worse coming."

Dr. Shaw put his glass down with an audible clank, his brows drawing low in a thundercloud expression that had Ophelia shrinking back in her chair. "Myths were the ancients' way of ordering their universe. Stories of the gods and religion told how the seasons progressed because they had no knowledge of modern science. With the advent of our breakthroughs in science in this century, as well as the rule of reason, we have largely rendered religion obsolete. Only small minds look to legends and folderol for any true understanding. I urge you both to keep that in the forefront of your minds."

Absalom smirked. Ben and Mr. Harding looked mutinous. Finally, Ben gave a short nod. "Yes, Father."

In the silence, Thomas collected the mostly untouched plates.

Mr. Harding caught Ophelia's eye. "Makes one wonder, does it not?" he murmured, raising a sly eyebrow.

Ophelia stared at her wineglass, full of the deep red vintage. She was no longer hungry.

The rest of the dinner was largely silent. As the lone female, by rights she should have left the dining table first after the dessert course, but the men stood and took their leave of her to smoke their cigars and partake of the port before disappearing into the depths of the west wing.

The last to depart, Ben pulled her to the side of the room and in a lowered voice said, "You shouldn't have antagonized Father like that."

"*Me?* Ben, your friend was the one who refused to stop talking. Perhaps you should inform him that Father dislikes anyone challenging his scientific theories and to heed your conversational safety nets."

Ben made a face. "Sadly, Father is going to have to broaden his horizons a bit."

Broaden his horizons? *Father?* They both knew how unlikely that would be. Ophelia frowned. Did this have something to do with Addie? "What do you—"

Her breath caught in her throat.

"Ophelia, what is it?"

She stood as if rooted to the spot, staring past him out the window into the darkness. Under the oaks, she could just perceive the dark outline of a figure, unmoving—fixed upon Renwick Hall. Fixed upon—she gulped—*her?*

"Ben," she said falteringly. She moved to the window and beckoned hastily. "Look—"

But it wasn't there. When she looked back through the glass, the shadowy visage had disappeared.

Or become fully one with the dark.

"What?" Ben peered over her shoulder.

"I thought I saw a man, out there. Staring at the house." She pointed at the spot where she had seen the dark figure.

"I don't see anyone," Ben said. "It must've been a trick of the light."

"I saw a man," she insisted. "Right there, under that tree."

"Ophelia, there is no one out there. Maybe Absalom went out to smoke."

"But why would he be out in the dark? And staring at the house?"

"Who knows? Absalom does all manner of queer things. He enjoys wandering around in the dark. Does it all the time."

"If it was Absalom smoking, I would've seen the glow of his cigar," Ophelia said stubbornly.

"You are overtired," Ben said. "Perhaps you should retire early."

Ophelia shot him a wounded look, but he did not notice.

I know I saw someone out there. But it couldn't have been Absalom, Ophelia thought as she ascended the stairs to her bedchamber. The build was all wrong. Too slight, and not tall enough. *It couldn't have been Rivers or the footmen; they're occupied with clearing the supper dishes. And I would've recognized the grooms.*

But I know I saw someone.

So that meant a total stranger had been on the property, watching the house from under the shadow of the trees.

Chapter Ten

The cellar door was locked.

Ophelia felt for the latch and lifted the dark lantern for a better look.

Yes, the bolt was shot, and the key was missing from the lock. But why lock the door now? Was someone suspicious of her nighttime agenda? Her heart seized. Had Ben's comment about retiring early been more than a passing remark?

But Mr. Harding was here now as well. Was Father worried about unsupervised experimentation? Intellectual poaching?

Or...she cast her mind uneasily to the stranger about on Renwick's grounds. The man...the thing in the trees....

She shivered and pushed the thought away. It wasn't important right now.

Her lockpicks were safely sequestered upstairs in the dummy bottom of her jewelry box. She had simply assumed she wouldn't need them. The thought of going back upstairs when her leg already ached like the devil made her wince. But maybe....

Ophelia set the lantern down and stretched up on her toes. Her fingers trailed over the wall before her fingertips found the correct brick with the barely tangible print of the Shaw seal. She wriggled it. With a few tugs, the brick came loose, sliding free from its surrounding fellows with only a slight scrape. Tongue poking out of the corner of her mouth, Ophelia turned the brick over and felt in the hollow inside for…yes, here it was! The iron key fell into her palm.

She smiled a little as she slid the brick back into place. Her family still believed they kept some secrets of Renwick from her, but they were wrong. This was her home, her domain, no matter what they tried to do to it.

She slipped the key into the lock and turned it. The bolt slid back with a satisfying *click*.

As she pushed open the door, she heard Addie call, "Ophelia?"

She lifted her lantern and picked her way across the lab as the candlelight reached into the shadows. "I'm here," she said. "I've brought more blood, and I've made you some cuffs—"

A voice murmured, "Soft you now! The fair Ophelia!"

A *stranger's* voice.

She gasped. The lantern spun wildly in her grip, the light bobbing over the cellar's south wall.

In the dim shadows, the lantern light illuminated a second silver cage. Inside it, a man with black hair that curled over his collar stared at her through the bars. He wore a dark suit of a very outdated cut, his collar unbuttoned to reveal the pale gray expanse of his throat. The lantern caught his colorless eyes and imbued them with a glittering spark of fire.

Ophelia gulped as her heart attempted to beat its way out of her chest.

He smiled slowly, his pale lips parting to reveal white teeth. He purred with dark amusement, "Nymph, in thy orisons be all my sins remembered."

Then he threw back his head and laughed in a kind of manic delight. As he did, the lantern light caught and illuminated his bright, wicked fangs.

"Ophelia, he came, he came to rescue me," Addie said, inching forward in her cage. "Didn't I tell you he'd come? I knew he would." She turned to the man, smiling.

"Of course I came," he said, turning his colorless eyes on Addie and sparing Ophelia the weight of his regard. Addie beamed at him as if he had hung the moon.

Ophelia struggled to catch her breath. The man appeared young—but that could mean anything, given his obviously vampiric features—fangs, colorless eyes, his distinct pallor.

"Who are you?" Ophelia whispered.

He tilted his head to the side. "You may call me Salem. And you are Ophelia...?"

"My name is Ophelia Shaw." She managed to keep any 'it's lovely to meet you' inanities behind her teeth.

He smiled crookedly. "Are you honest?"

She blinked. "I...yes?"

"Are you fair?"

She shook her head. "I don't know what you're talking about."

The smile stayed, but his eyes narrowed infinitesimally. "What are you doing down here, darling?"

"I'm bringing Addie blood," she said, and pulled the flask from her pocket.

He stared at the flask, then at her. "And why are you doing that?" he asked in a deceptively light voice.

"She was hungry," Ophelia said. She carefully set the bottle down, and Addie just as carefully reached through the bars to scoop up the bottle. Then her motions blurred as she uncorked it and lifted it to her mouth.

Ophelia shifted the lantern to her other hand, watching his eyes as they flicked from Addie back to her. "I'm sorry, I only brought enough blood for Addie. I didn't know you were...here."

"I can share." They both turned as Addie lowered the bottle from her mouth "I—I only drank half. You can have the rest, Salem." Addie licked the red tint from her lips. "Ophelia, will you give it to him?" She slid the bottle across the floor, and the quiet rasp filled the room.

"Of course," Ophelia said a little unsteadily. "Here, try these cuffs I made for you. See if they will fit." She passed the flannel cuffs she had fashioned from an old nightgown to Addie.

Addie exclaimed over them and stuffed them between the silver shackles and her ankles. "They're just the nicest," she sniffed. "My bones don't scrape anymore."

Your bones never should've scraped to begin with, Ophelia thought, swallowing guilt. She bent to carefully retrieve the bottle of blood and moved toward the second cage, hovering a few feet away. "I can make you some padding as well," she said hesitantly. He had stuffed his trouser cuffs into the shackles on his bare feet.

"How very kind of you." Salem watched her languidly, his eyelids drooping over his marble-like eyes. A lazy cat's pose. He reminded her of a predator—a thing of wonder, and wildness, and beauty. Such a thing should not be caged—but there was no way to guarantee her own safety should she let him out. Wild things behaved according to their natures, and to him, she must be prey.

Did he who made the Lamb make thee?

"You're going to have to come a little closer than that," he said dryly, pointing to the bottle.

Ophelia licked her lips and swayed forward, then back. His reach was longer than hers. She eyed the distance between them and took a small step forward.

"Well, that helped a great deal," he said, extending his hand carefully through the bars and beckoning.

"I'll just...put it on the ground," she said.

He shrugged a shoulder. "As you like."

Ophelia took another wary step forward, extending her arm to set the bottle on the floor.

In a flurry of movement, he pounced. The vampire flew forward, hand lashing out to grasp her wrist and jerk.

Ophelia fell against the cage. She tried to push backward

against the silver bars, but he twisted her arm so she could not pull away.

"There," Salem said in a voice rich with satisfaction, "That's better." He plucked the bottle from her grasp with his free hand and cracked his neck. Two burn lines slowly faded from his skin, his sacrifice to seize her through the bars.

"Stop it—let go," she said in an unsteady voice, pulling without success against his hold.

"No," he said flatly.

Ophelia dropped the lantern, which by some miracle landed on its base, throwing wild shadows over the two of them. Ophelia fumbled for the chain around her neck. Her pulse was hammering in her throat. Could he hear it?

"Ah, very pretty," he said politely. "A lovely bauble, to be sure, but I'm already in a great deal of pain, hemmed in behind and before with silver, not to mention shackled with the damned stuff, and I'm not planning to bite your neck." His lips parted in a very sharp smile.

"Salem!" Addie said frantically. "Don't bite my friend."

"Maybe I won't," Salem said, "If she answers my questions very carefully."

He increased the pressure on her wrist, and Ophelia winced. He was too close. She could see his eyes shining in the dark.

"Now, in no particular order, where are we, who were those men in the lab earlier, what do they want, and what are you really doing down here, Ophelia?"

⁂

She was so—alive.

Salem didn't need the lantern's glow to see her—one small positive of being what he was. Auburn hair rippled over the shoulders of her thick blue dressing gown, hiding what little he could see of her figure. Hazel eyes rounded at the sight of him, her lips a delicate shade of rose. The hitch in her breath and her swallow were as loud as gunshots to him, overly sensitized as he was by the silver and the pain.

He had seen those eyes in the young men earlier in the night.

And her name was Ophelia.

God, everything really did come back to Shakespeare.

"We're in Yorkshire," she blurted out. "Quite close to Hartley, in Ashdale."

"Ah. Delightful." He leaned closer. He could see the pulse beating rapidly in the long line of her throat, the veins flush with blood under her skin. "And?"

"The men were—were my father, Dr. Shaw, and my brothers, and a colleague of theirs. They—well, my father is a scientist. I don't know what they want, and I *am* here to feed Addie."

His laugh had a hard edge. "What kind of fool are you, to feed a vampire?"

She said defensively, "A compassionate one. She was scared and alone and hungry. I tried to do what I could to help."

"You're not reporting back to your father, so he can add this to his scientific observations?"

She stared at him. "No. Why would I?"

"You're not trying the old tactic of catching flies with honey... or vampires with blood?"

"No," she said firmly. "I was warned to stay away. I would be in significantly more trouble if they knew I was down here."

Salem's grip tightened around her wrist. "And you didn't think that was perhaps a smart thing to do, after seeing what sort of monster had taken up residence underneath the house, inside its very foundation?"

"I didn't see a monster. I saw Addie."

"Maybe you should look a little closer," he said mockingly. He forced her hand—so warm—against the cool skin of his cheek. "I spent a long journey locked in a box, stabbed with spikes, and now I'm in a silver cage, so believe me when I say my patience is at an end. You don't know how long it's been since I've felt the warmth of a woman's flesh."

A day or so, thanks to the lovely Katie, but she didn't need to know that.

He bent his head and stared down at her arm, the lovely blue veins leading away from her wrist. The girl tugged against his hold, but even in this silver prison, he was strong enough to hold her without effort.

"Salem, don't! She's been kind to me. Please." Addie tried to grasp the bars that surrounded her and yelped, jerking back.

The beast within him snarled at Addie's pain. "She's our captor," he snapped.

Addie sniffed and shook her head. "No, she's my friend!"

Ophelia lifted her chin, even as her voice wavered. "If you're trying to scare me, you'd be singularly stupid to scare away your chance of regular meals."

He yanked her flush against the bars. They were so close that if he wanted to brave the burn of silver, he could lean forward and press his lips to hers. As it was, her chest heaved against the bars, even as she tried to lean away from him. "Maybe I prefer *fresh*."

"Salem, *please*. Please," Addie begged.

Ophelia's swallow strangled in her throat. She couldn't look away from him. Couldn't even blink.

"Please," Addie said again in a tearful voice.

Salem glanced at Addie, and his face shifted. The anger drained away, or maybe he forced it back. "All right, Addie darling," he said in a very different voice. "All right. Don't cry. I was just jesting. Do you want the rest of this blood?"

Ophelia chanced a glance at Addie.

"No," Addie said, swiping the back of her hand across her eyes. "No, that's for you. Don't hurt Ophelia."

"All right. It was a very thoughtful gesture. Mmm," he said, uncorking the bottle one-handed and tipping it back into his mouth. Ophelia watched the line of his throat as he swallowed. He lowered the bottle and licked his lips meditatively. "Better than nothing, I suppose."

Ophelia subtly tugged against his hold, hoping to slip free before he noticed....

"Ah, ah." Salem upended the bottle over her arm and let the dregs of the cold blood fall on her skin. She flinched, but she couldn't do anything to stop him. "Waste not," he said, and winked.

Ophelia locked eyes with him as he lowered his mouth to her skin. Her eyes widened as far as they would go.

He licked up every cold drop. She felt his lips, his *tongue*, cold against her skin. The sensation sent a shudder up her spine, and she was certain he felt *that*, too. He paused at the pulse point of her wrist, the corner of his mouth turning up in a smile as a fang caught her flesh. She felt the sting of skin parting.

Her jaw clenched, but she didn't dare look away. Though her heart pounded, she took deliberately slow breaths to disguise as much fear as she could. He was *tasting* her *blood*.

Don't flinch. Don't scream. That's what he wants.

Ophelia glared instead.

Salem lifted his head from her wrist. His face set in an expressionless mask. He placed the empty bottle in her grasp, and then released his grip, letting her slip through his fingers.

Ophelia was proud she didn't fling herself backwards. She carefully pulled her hand back, cradling it close to her chest like a wounded bird, and snatched up the lantern. She took two wobbling steps back before she sucked in a shaky breath.

"I'll be back tomorrow," she murmured to Addie, and slowly moved away from their cages, bumping against an examination table before she swung her lantern ahead of her to light her retreat.

"Ophelia," Salem called after her, "I am very proud, revenge-ful, ambitious, with more offences at my beck and call than I have thoughts to put them in, imagination to give them shape, or time to act them in. If I discover that you've been lying, it will go ill with you."

She did not doubt him.

Halfway up the back stair, it struck her. She stumbled.

Hamlet. He had been quoting *Hamlet*.

Chapter Eleven

Ophelia wound her hands into Blaze's ruff as far below the clock chimed two. She still felt the cold clasp of Salem's hands on her, even here. She couldn't seem to warm, even after she had stoked her fire from the coal bucket, even after all three cats *and* Blaze had joined her on the bed, and she had piled on the covers. The chill bit deep into her soul.

The two tapers on her bedside table still burned. She couldn't bear to blow them out.

Ophelia's eyes ached, grainy and painful, longing for sleep—but how could she sleep? How *could* she, knowing that *he* was underneath her at that very moment?

"Well, not directly underneath," she mumbled. It was a very cold comfort. At least she did not check under the bed for monsters when she returned from the cellars, as she had when she was a child, but it was a near thing.

Nevada looked up as though Ophelia might've been talking to her. Ophelia stroked her fur absently, and she settled back down.

There were more monsters out there than one terrified Addie, and they were hungry, and angry, and—Ophelia swallowed—hurting.

Salem scared her. No doubt about that. He was purposefully *trying* to scare her, which was also different. And she did not doubt for one iota of a moment that he was dangerous.

But it was vile, to cage and terrify living creatures.

But are *they alive?* she wondered.

And if they weren't, did that make a difference?

Ophelia shuddered, his voice ringing in her ears still. *"If I discover that you've been lying, it will go ill with you."*

What did it mean to be alive? Did Salem and Addie have a pulse? Ophelia didn't think so. They breathed in order to speak, but it didn't seem like they needed to otherwise.

But they hungered. Oh yes, they hungered. She felt the spectral grasp of his cold fingers on her wrist again, his mouth on her skin, the line of his throat as he swallowed the pig's blood. She set her thumb against the pulse point of her wrist, where she found the cut—a small score along the bone. A promise of what more he could've done.

But Salem had listened to Addie, had not acted on base desire or out of anger. And Ophelia had stared him in the eye the whole time. She still couldn't believe it.

His eyes had not turned red, Ophelia recalled with a start. Not once.

Did it matter if they were human or not? Alive or not? It didn't preclude them from being *people*. They were thinking and feeling beings, whatever else they were!

Ophelia gave a last shuddering breath before marshaling her will to blow the candle out. She lay in the dark, tracing the cut on her wrist, trying not to worry. Nothing could happen to her from one little scratch.

Could it?

"Why did you do that?" Addie demanded, glaring at Salem.

"Are you all right?" he said. Addie never got angry.

"No! You bit my friend!"

"I did not bite her, I grazed her with a fang. And she's not your friend, she's the daughter of the man who abducted you."

"It does not mean she is like them," Addie enunciated clearly, her eyes flashing red. "I know I'm broken, but I'm not stupid! I've seen—*felt*—what they've done to me. Ophelia is...."

"You're *not* broken," he said, the old guilt rising in him again. He ruthlessly shoved it aside. It would not serve him here, not when he had to keep Addie safe, even from herself.

"I'm not right either, not like I was. But I'm not a child. Nor a fool," she said tightly. "You're an ass."

"So I am," Salem said soothingly.

"And horrible."

"Very true."

"And you made me lose my train of thought," Addie added petulantly.

"And I'll help you find it again. You were telling me what Ophelia is."

"Ophelia...is kind."

Salem did not believe that. Kindness was not offered to things like them. It was trained out of them by their masters and makers, torn out of them if need be. And he remained deeply suspicious about the girl's motives. Those big hazel eyes could hide a world of guile behind a sheen of innocence and the scent of...orange blossoms.

Salem had smelled her, and his mouth had watered, remembering the taste of real, true fruit. Oranges tasted sweet and tart on the tongue—a sensation to be savored, for it was a Christmas present, the one day his family could afford the extravagance of the fruit. The taste of oranges carried with it the scent of hot cider, cold snow...sunlight.

He thought every aspect of his human life had been buried under years of damp earth and stone and darkness. The picture in his head had faded to a pale imitation, as substantial as a spider's web, but Ophelia's scent had the power to unearth it. Her hazel eyes, her hair like flame in the lamplight, the heat under his mouth. She was so... alive.

The scent had awakened a craving in him. He had wanted to bury his face in her neck, in her hair, and breathe the scent in again. Did her skin carry the scent? Would her blood taste like oranges? He wanted to remember.

He had given in.

At the first drop of her blood, the flavor had washed over him with all the force of a siren's call. He wanted to take it all in. Wanted to devour.

You'll never be more than this, the voice inside him hissed. *You're nothing but a monster.*

Ophelia hadn't even flinched, his brave little mouse. Just glared at him defiantly from the other side of the bars.

As far from him as a mourner above a grave, a chasm too deep to cross. The crossing from the sunlit lands to the underworld only ever happened one way. He would do well to remember that.

"I will...reserve judgement. For now," Salem told Addie. "Are *you* all right?"

"You're here now," Addie said, which was no answer. She twisted her fingers in her dirty nightgown. "Salem, how long do we have to stay here?"

"Until I know who's really in charge and how they found out about our existence."

"But how are we going to get *out*?"

"We aren't alone. Etienne is waiting with another friend, and as soon as we discover their secrets, I'll signal them and we'll be free." Though friend was not really the word for Faelad, but it's what Addie would understand. Salem prodded the part of himself that could gauge how much foreign blood remained within himself. He had three to four days of Faelad's left to get a message to him. Surely that would be enough.

"And Ophelia."

He raised an eyebrow. "Hmm?"

"Ophelia is my friend. She's helping us."

He propped his elbows on his knees, remembering the look in her eyes when he took her blood. Scared, brave...defiant. "Yes, all right."

"She gave me blood."

"Yes, I know."

"It was on a hankie," she said vaguely.

Salem turned his head. "What do you mean, Addie?"

"The first night. When I was scared. She brought a...." She opened her hands and stacked them. "Bread."

"A sandwich?"

"It tasted like nothing. But I ate it, to be full of something. I was so hungry." She shot him a guilty look. "I sucked my thumb."

"I told you that's bad for you," Salem said sternly. Recycling blood didn't do any good and made more injuries to heal on a depleted reserve.

"I know," Addie said in a small voice, ducking her head. "But then she gave me the hankie and I felt better."

"What hankie?"

"It was wrapping her cut," she said vaguely, "and all dry, but it still helped a little. And then she came with the bottles," she said, perking up. "Nasty but better than nothing. Ophelia's my friend. I told her you'd come."

"You know I'll always come when you need me," he said, but his mind went into overdrive. Addie had had Ophelia's blood? The practical part of him wondered what kind of talent Addie could bring to bear on Ophelia, though she had shown no indication of having one yet.

The other part of him, the foolish, rage-filled part of him hissed, *Mine!*

He caged the impulse ruthlessly. The girl was nothing to him.

"When we leave, are we going back to London?"

"You will; I'll go home again."

Addie continued wistfully, "I don't see why I can't live with you."

"You wouldn't like country life," he said. "Stuck with only me to talk to. Like now. You're a city girl."

"But I miss you. Why do you leave me alone? If you had been there, maybe this wouldn't have happened."

"Wasn't Etienne looking out for you?" Salem demanded, coming alert.

"Of course he was," Addie said. "Etienne always looks out for me."

Salem sighed, exasperated. "Well, I'm not all powerful, Addie. There's no difference between what I could've done and Etienne has done to find you."

Yes there is, his inner voice said. *Everything you touch is ruined. What happened to Addie is your fault—it was your fault then, and it's your fault now.*

"I know, but you could live with me; Etienne can't live with me. That's not appropriate."

Salem stared. "Why not?"

"He's not family. You're family." Before Salem could delve into Addie's conception of vampire blood ties, she continued, "I get lonely. I have Etienne but I miss you. And you're not there."

"Addie."

She hung her head.

Everything in him shrieked that prolonged contact with him would only hurt her in the long run, that all he did was hurt, but he knew she spoke from a place of real emotion. "Addie, we will spend time together once we're free of this place. I promise. But the best thing you could do for me right now is tell me about these men. What happened before I arrived?"

She avoided his gaze.

"Addie."

"They have knives," she said in a brittle voice. "And silver poles they stick in you so you can't reach them when they open up the doors. And they sample and poke and cut and watch."

His stomach clenched. He'd rip their throats out.

"I never spoke. They never asked me anything, so I never spoke. They were strangers. I thought you would come rescue me, not get captured too."

"That was good, the exact right thing to do, and I *did* come to rescue you. I will get us both out of here."

"How?"

She had forgotten, or perhaps needed the reassurance. Salem repeated patiently, "I need to find out how they knew where you slept. Etienne said others have disappeared. There is a leak, somewhere. Someone has talked. I need to find out who."

"But then we'll leave?"

"Yes, I promise."

"All right. As long as you're nice to Ophelia."

"I can be very nice," Salem said mildly. He ran his tongue over his teeth.

He could still taste her blood on his lips.

Chapter Twelve

Ophelia stared blearily up at the ceiling as Blaze dragged on her sleeve, hind end waggling in a semblance of need. Just then, the door scraped open as Nancy hauled in the coal bucket with a clank. "Good morning, miss. Still abed?" she asked in owl-eyed surprise.

Ophelia threw off her covers and dragged her wrap towards her.

"Would you like me to help you dress?" Nancy said eagerly.

"In a while, Nancy—I must take Blaze out," Ophelia mumbled, as Blaze bounded for the door, barely waiting for her. She went down the back stairs to the garden and shivered in the morning's stiff breeze as Blaze anointed the ferns. Dark clouds gathered overhead, and the faint rumblings of thunder could be heard in the distance.

The collie padded back to her, tail waving happily now that his need was assuaged.

"I wish I was as blithely happy as you," she murmured, patting his head.

Blaze set off in a wide arc into the woods. With a groan, Ophelia resigned herself to following.

The night before had exhausted her. The fear and worry of the evening had eaten away at her and disturbed her sleep. Even in her dreams she had a sense of weariness as she had wandered through a dark and lonely Renwick Hall, searching for something in the shadows—or hiding from it, she had never been quite sure. Anxiety had clawed at her as she attempted to evade that hunting sensation.

She had tossed and turned in restless slumber as her dream-self trailed through Renwick's rooms out of order, trying to stay ahead of whatever-it-was. Finally, her dream-self had arrived in front of the door to her room. That was where the cats and Blaze were; that was the room with a lock on the door that she possessed the key to.

But instead of going in, she had turned to face the thing behind her.

She hadn't seen anything. Hadn't even seen the vague outline of the hallway. But in the darkness, a figure had hovered, hesitating. Strange that after looking so hard for her, it would pause now.

She had taken a step forward.

The darkness sighed in recognition. "There you are."

And then she woke up.

The odd thing was, Ophelia thought, staring up at the dark, overcast sky, after running so long from the darkness, she hadn't been alarmed. Some part of her, separate from the dreamscape, had wanted to see what had pursued her so ardently. She had turned around to see what wanted her so much.

And her stupid, traitorous heart had lifted a little at the thought.

"Foolish fancies," she told the dog. "No more whisky after dinner, I think." She paused, frowning at Blaze's odd stance. "What is it?"

The dog had paused before a broad oak and a pile of leaves. His back was stiff, and his fur stood up. He rumbled a warning.

"Blaze?" She took a step forward.

"Don't move, girl!"

Ophelia flinched.

A large man holding a stout walking stick lunged from the trees. He jabbed the stick into the leaf pile. Metal clanged.

Ophelia jumped back. Blaze retreated and pressed himself against her, whining with his tail firmly tucked between his legs.

The man straightened. "T'was a trap," he said, in a deep voice that carried a hint of Irish brogue. He was a great giant of a man, scruffy looking, with a red beard streaked with gray. He wrestled his walking stick from the jaws of the trap and stood in a wide stance with feet firmly planted. He was dressed like a laborer, a hat clapped firmly on his head. His expression was closed and foreboding.

What is he doing here in the wood? Ophelia thought blankly.

Never mind that, her more sensible self insisted. *He just kept Blaze from stepping into that thing's jaws!*

She cleared her suddenly dry throat. "I-I thank you, sir," she stammered, since she had to say something. "So does my dog; I don't know how that trap came to be there." Poachers, perhaps? But so close to the house? "Can I help you? What are you doing at Renwick?"

He made a noise, low in his throat. "Getting the lay of the land."

Blaze wagged his tail, even though it was still firmly clamped to his hindquarters.

"Are you a stranger?" she ventured. Her voice sounded a little high to her ears. What a stupid question; she knew most of the people in the village by sight, if not to speak to.

He didn't say anything in response, just stared at her in a distinctly unnerving fashion. His nostrils flared as he inhaled a large bracing gust of the chilly air.

Ophelia swallowed hard. Could *he* be the strange figure she had seen out the window the night before? But no, he was far too broad to fit that silhouette.

Funny that the unsettling presence outside the house had been so overshadowed by the night's revelations.

"Are you looking for work?"

His eyes scanned her up and down, narrowing when he got back to her face. "Something wrong with your leg, girl?" He rumbled. "Caught it in a trap before?"

She stared at him in astonishment. "It's an old problem, from an illness when I was a child," she said, a little irritated he'd bring it up so abruptly and impolitely. "I'm sure there's always odd jobs in the village, if you're looking."

He raised a sardonic eyebrow. "None at that big house, though."

"No...not usually. We don't have many servants." Conscience pricked her. "You could ask, though. Rivers finds it hard to keep staff. Not many people like it so far out here."

Blaze jerked at the leash. He wanted to go, away from the man who had so unnerved him.

He nodded slowly. "Rivers, ey?"

"Yes. The butler. I will speak to him for you, if you like. You did save Blaze from the trap, and I am very grateful."

His eyes narrowed. "Mmmm."

How had he known the trap was there?

Ophelia cleared her throat, feeling the chill of the morning through her wrapper. She blushed. She must look a fright, with her hair unbound around her shoulders and in such a state of undress.

Blaze heaved on his lead. "I must be going. Have a good day, sir."

The large man said nothing in return, but she felt his eyes follow her as she left. She felt strangely like she was being tracked, like a hunter tracks prey. She beat as fast a retreat as her leg would let her without it appearing like she was fleeing. *Now I know what a wounded deer or fox feels like,* she thought.

Cornered. And frightened.

As they left the woods and made their way through the overgrown gardens, Ophelia pulled up short with a muffled shriek.

Directly in front of her stood Mr. Harding, smiling his large smile, white teeth gleaming.

"Mr. Harding! I didn't know you were there," she gasped. She grasped her wrapper around the neck.

"I thought to take advantage of the country air." Mr. Harding took a deep breath. "Bracing! So different from the London smog."

"I wouldn't know," she murmured. Blaze pressed himself to her leg, a rumble starting in his chest that she could feel vibrating against her. Even the dog could sense something off-putting about the man.

"But you did say you wanted to see London," he said, smiling at her again. She could not say what she so disliked about it. It was at once overly ingratiating and threatening. The kind of smile a wolf might give a sheep he wanted to devour.

"Yes, one day." Ophelia took a step to the side.

"I would be honored to escort you about town one day soon."

"That is...very kind of you, sir," she said, edging around him. "Unfortunately, it does not appear it will be as soon as I would like. Pray excuse me. I must repair my appearance." She pulled Blaze back by his collar and beat a hasty retreat, nerves frayed beyond repair.

❧

Once correctly attired in a day dress, Ophelia found Rivers in the front hallway, lingering like a shadow beside the entrance to the great hall. "Good morning, Rivers," she said.

He bowed just the right amount. "Good morning, Miss Shaw."

"Rivers, when I was walking Blaze this morning, we encountered a trap in the woods, not far from the house. Blaze nearly walked into it. Do you know anything about this? Who has been setting traps on our land?"

"I'm sure I don't know, Miss, but I will endeavor to find out," Rivers said with no expression on his face. "I hope the dog was not hurt."

"No, he wasn't, because a stranger appeared and tripped the spring mechanism before any harm was done."

This made Rivers's implacable expression crack. "A stranger?"

"Yes. He said he was looking for work. I promised I would mention him to you. If he comes, I'd appreciate it if you'd hire him. Perhaps as a gamekeeper or some such, since that trap looked relatively new."

"Of course, Miss." The butler's expression smoothed into its normal dour mien. "What is his name?"

"I did not get his name, but he is a large man with red hair and a beard, graying a little."

Rivers inclined his head. "Very good, Miss Shaw. May I inquire as to your plans today?"

Ophelia froze in her half-turned-away position. "I had not decided yet."

"The master asked me to remind you that he desires you remain at home for the duration of Mr. Harding's visit."

Bitterness coated her tongue. "Thank you, Rivers."

Ophelia stepped into the great hall to get away from him. Her uneven footsteps took her to the vast fireplace, unlit. She placed a hand on the cold mantle as the loneliness of the house sank into her bones. She was not allowed to go out today. She was instructed to "play hostess."

She huffed. Ordered to keep to the house, like she was a child. When her brothers and father and the visitor would be ensconced in the laboratory all day.

She could go out anyway, but Rivers would undoubtedly report on her activities to her father. And it was not wise to antagonize him. Not when she had to do something about Addie...and Salem.

The great hall was full of shadows from the ominous clouds. She could barely see the sword above the mantle, and all the ancestors that lined the grand stair appeared disapproving and dour. Only the men were displayed so prominently upon entering the house. Any women and other cursory relatives were consigned to the long gallery at the top of the house, where she had played on many a rainy day.

But it was not raining yet, for all the thunder still rumbled ominously. She had a little time before she would be truly trapped in the house. Ophelia walked back out to the front hall. "My cloak, please, Rivers," she said. "I shall go and visit my mother."

⊱✦⊰

The Shaw family mausoleum was located at the edge of the grounds, the other direction from her sojourn this morning. It was an imposing rectangular edifice with a high pointed roof and all manner of curls and flourishes, as well as a bevy of angels that always looked as if they were huddling under the eaves, out of the rain. Her paternal grandmother, of the fern motifs and pteridology mania, was buried there, and Ophelia's mother was buried there too. Cornelia Shaw.

As Ophelia limped up to the stone structure, the wind disturbed the fallen autumn leaves strewn on the steps and bench close by. The rustling sent shivers skittering down her spine.

Ophelia dusted off a layer of dead leaves and sat on the small stone bench beside the mausoleum. "Hello, Mother." She stared up at the ivy that wound its way around two sides of the crypt. Most days it made her feel closer to her mother, since Ophelia's middle name was Ivy. But today, something about the light made the ivy appear dark, thick and choking, crawling over the water-stained stone.

"I have...so many questions. Why didn't you tell me about the trust?" she said as the wind scattered the leaves. "Or did you mean to, and someone—" *Father, Ben* "—neglected to tell me? It's at times like this I really wish that you were here."

A roll of thunder echoed, but Ophelia ignored it. "I feel like the walls are closing in on me. Thomas is leaving soon. He was the only one of the staff that smiles at me in a kind way. Nancy does, but her smiles are ingratiating and sly. And now Father has commanded that I can't leave Renwick! I must stay and play hostess to their visitor." Her voice dropped to a whisper. "I can't even tell Marie-Claire about the worst thing, because I'm worried about her being upset. Mother...they've brought *vampires* home to Renwick."

Ophelia stared at her hands. "I wish I could ask you the right thing to do about Addie and Salem. I know I need to do *something*. Something more than giving them blood, of course. I must find a way to help them without putting myself at risk. They're being hurt, and I don't know Father's plans for them. I trust Addie—nominally," she amended, "but Salem...." She shuddered. "I think he's dangerous. Truly dangerous. But something about him is so...." *Compelling*, her mind filled in. He was compelling. Even when he was threatening her life. "Is it the danger that makes my heart race, or something else...?"

She faltered, feeling a deep chill permeate her bones, more than just a cold fall day. The wind gusted suddenly, picking up the dead leaves and blowing them into the air in a billowing cloud. The frigid blast felt as if it had come directly from the mausoleum.

Ophelia stood, swaying. A feeling of darkness and terror filled the air. The mausoleum's shadows deepened, for the first time garnering a menacing, fearful air.

She took a step back. The air pulsed, full of horrible foreboding.

Where was the sun? Where had it gone, why was it so dark?

The ivy coating the stones wavered, a creeping parasite. Ophelia took another step back.

The ivy at the base of the edifice darkened, liquified, mixing with the fog edging around the back of the crypt. It would slither towards her over the dead leaves, consuming everything in its path. If it reached her, it would…what? What would it do?

The angels under the eaves held their hands up, not in blessing, but in warning. Something waited in the dark, a ghastly, awful thing. The angels covered their faces in dismay, crowding together to hide.

Ophelia cast a wild glance around her. The forest leaned in, the branches reaching for her in the dim light, their twigged fingers grasping, demanding.

She had to get away. It wasn't safe here. Was Mother warning her to run?

Thunder cracked overhead, a powerful echo of sound that rattled the tree limbs above her and shook her from her paralysis.

Ophelia spun around and ran from the mausoleum, gaining what speed she could in a skipping gait, picking up her skirts as the feeling intensified. She had to run! *Get away!* Terror nipped at her heels, and she pushed for more speed, ignoring the aches and twinges from her leg. She couldn't keep this pace for long before her leg would give out. She had to reach safety before then!

From the path ahead, Mr. Harding emerged, his mouth opening in another toothy smile as he spied her. "Good morning again, Miss—"

She didn't stop. Ophelia cast him a wild, panicked glance and kept running until she reached the gardens and the house. The heavens opened in a roll of thunder ten paces from the door, and rain pelted down in a deluge. She stumbled to her knees as her leg gave out. Force of will and unreasonable terror forced her back up. Ophelia limped the last few steps inside and slammed the door, leaning against it as she tried to get her breath back. The cold water in her hair and soaking through her cloak to her dress felt as cold as ice.

Blaze entered the hall in a skitter of nails along the floorboards.

"How did you get out of my room?" she mumbled through numb lips.

He skidded to a stop and sniffed her all over, the hair on his back bristling. "It's so silly," she whispered, but allowed him his fuss and patted his head.

As her heart slowed, she took a minute to breathe. What on earth had happened? What had given her such a feeling of unthinking, mindless terror? Where had it *come from?*

Had it been something she said? Was something threatening her?

Or was it something else? She gulped, remembering Mr. Harding's emergence only a few seconds later. If she had been slower—if that horrible fear had not overwhelmed her—he would've heard her talking about the vampires.

She shuddered again, but for an entirely different reason.

"Ophelia?"

She jolted and whirled. Ben frowned at her curiously from the library doorway. "What on earth are you doing?"

"Oh, I—I—it started to rain," she said, trying not to sound like she was gasping for air. She motioned to her hair and clothes limply. "I thought you were working downstairs?"

"I needed to do some research. Good grief, get in some dry clothes immediately, before you catch a chill," Ben said, eyes widening. "Have that cross-eyed girl of yours build up your fire."

"All right," she said a little blankly, puzzled by this sudden display of brotherly concern. "Save some of your mother hen-ing for Mr. Harding; I saw him outside as well."

He ignored that. "You need to take better care of yourself, Ophelia," Ben said sternly, and then disappeared back into the library again, leaving her staring at a closed door.

"All I did was get rained on," she told the door. The emotional whiplash of the morning, in so short a time, on so little sleep, left her fairly wrung out. Blaze at her heels, she trailed upstairs to dry by the fire.

❧

Nancy had cast her some sullen looks for getting herself drenched, but helped her change and dutifully carried away her soaked gown to dry it in the laundry. Ophelia brushed out her wet hair and patted it dry in towels before letting it hang loose as she sat by the fire in her room. She could not seem to get warm. Her gaze wandered aimlessly over her books and keepsakes. The Westerns held no allure for her now, and the penny dreadfuls made her shiver harder.

Ophelia's eyes finally snagged on the scent bottles on her dressing table. Slowly, she straightened.

She had taken the bottles from her mother's bedroom when it was clear the room would be shut up after her mother's death, locked tight, joining the rows of rooms locked against dust, age... or snooping. In waves of grief, she had seized only the items that had meant something to *her* at the time. She had done no searching for other items of import to her mother. Perhaps there would be something in her mother's room that would tell her about the trust—a journal, a letter, a copy of the will or other legal documents detailing something, anything. The trick would be getting the keys from Rivers.

❧

A trick she could not accomplish, at any rate. "Making a survey of the linen closet" did not count as an adequate excuse, it seemed. Or not enough of one that Rivers would let her do it unsupervised.

"Rivers, I'm sure it's very vexing to be pulled away from your duties to hand out your keys," Ophelia said. "I know we have more than one set of house keys—the housekeeper's, for one, is unused. I should like to desist troubling you when I wish to unlock a closet. Perhaps if I took charge of the housekeeper's keys—"

"Not a good idea, Miss," Rivers said repressively. "Too many dangerous places, too many weak floor supports."

"I assure you I would not wander into the west wing." *I do have the sense God gave me,* she wanted to say, but didn't.

"Very unwise."

"I hate to put you out," Ophelia said, trying to keep her teeth from clenching.

"No trouble at all, Miss," Rivers said, his wooden expression unchanging.

So consequently, she and Nancy and the downstairs girl, Heloise, were held hostage to the linens, counting the number of sheets and pillowcases, toweling and tablecloths, and inspecting their condition after so long shut away. This did not endear her to Nancy any further, and by the time they finished, all three of them were cross. Ophelia tried to keep possession of the keys afterwards, but shutting the linen closet must've acted as a summoning, for Rivers appeared like a silent specter, holding his hand out for them.

Ophelia only let her lip curl when she walked around the corner.

❧

"Round two," she told Tibby and Nevada, who peered down at her as she fished under her mattress. "I tried easy. Now we'll try hard." She retrieved the lockpicks from the false bottom of her jewelry box.

She had had them made by the village smith, originally as a novelty gift for Ben. She had wanted to be able to show her brother she knew how to use them upon their presentation, so she had asked for a few lessons from old Mr. Severn, who in his youth had been a minor cracksman—in York, not London, hence the minor, but he had never been caught at it—until he met his wife and went to the Methodist meetings with her and "found religion" as he put it. They had moved to the country years ago to get away from the more unsavory elements of his past.

But that was all a long time ago, and he took great delight in teaching young Miss Shaw the tricks of his former trade, his large bushy eyebrows waggling as he instructed her how to go about convincing the tumblers to move to the correct positions. Of course, he had taught her mostly on padlocks and the like, being portable. But Ophelia had had doors in plenty to practice on in Renwick. What started as a novelty gift became a rebellion, the only way to open what had been locked away from her.

Now, as it appeared increasingly obvious that she would not be permitted lady-of-the-house status in her own home, Ophelia was deeply thankful she had kept the lockpicks.

To test her fingers, Ophelia carefully lowered herself to the floor in front of the trunk at the foot of her bed. In theory, it held her trousseau, what little of that there was. However, it was the historic childhood equivalent of a protected vault that kept safe anything she didn't want stolen or ruined by Absalom from age six to sixteen. And even now, she kept valuable memories there, safe and sequestered. The actual key lived safely inside a hollow book in her bookshelf. But for a warmup, Ophelia inserted the lockpicks and felt for the tumblers, listening for the telltale click.

It took a moment for her to recall the correct technique, but soon the lid of the trunk sprang open, revealing the ragged stuffed animals and the two dolls in their faded dresses, the result of a great many washings, as well as a few very nicely embroidered pillowcases, handkerchiefs, and frothy nightgowns for "someday" with lace trimming.

"Success," she exclaimed.

Blaze wagged his tail, lifting his head from the rug in front of the fire.

"Time to try this out, hmm?" Ophelia shut the lid and pushed herself to her feet.

Ophelia did not have to worry about running into family or their guest. If the pattern held, the men would surely be occupied until dinner, though she kept one ear out for any footsteps—Ben returning to his room for something, perhaps. Based on this morning, he was the most likely to roam. But when she had inquired about luncheon from Rivers, he had indicated all the men would be occupied in the laboratory.

Ophelia sent up a prayer for Addie. And then, reluctantly, another for Salem. The real trick would be avoiding the domestic staff, whose movements were harder to predict now that the house was filled with new inhabitants, both family and their valets, which meant new routines, new demands, and new patterns for cleaning and tending fires.

Ophelia waited for a long time at the door of her room, listening hard to pinpoint any staff above stairs. Once she was nearly positive Rivers wouldn't appear from a convenient shadow, she picked her way along the hall to the master bedroom...and beside it, her mother's apartments. Her lockpicks manipulated the tumblers, her hands only slipping once from nerves as she tried to keep one ear alert to any noises. Finally, what felt like an eternity after, the lock clicked. Ophelia slipped through the door and quickly closed it behind her.

The room was dim, silent and musty. Ophelia carefully tiptoed through the cloth-shrouded furniture to the closed window drapes. She pulled them back to let in what light she could. Rain traced down the dusty glass in rivulets as the outside world continued to endure the deluge.

The light, washed out and diluted by the storm, struggled to reach the corners of the room. The shrouded furniture crouched together like ghosts hovering at the edge of the world. Ophelia dragged the sheet away from the most likely place to start, her mother's writing desk, and began her search.

The desk was relatively empty and revealed no clues, nor did the wardrobe, which only contained a few old sachets of lavender at the bottom. She closed the doors again and next picked the lock to the dressing room, but after a quick perusal deemed it too close to her father's room for it to be a likely place to hide secret things. "Someone must've packed up all her belongings," Ophelia murmured to the silence. The room felt shockingly empty compared to the throng of knickknacks and trinkets in the rest of Renwick. That meant either everything was gone for good or put in storage in Renwick's vast attic. Ophelia made note to investigate that very soon.

Finally, after pulling out mismatched gloves, a prayer book, a scattering of button hooks, and an empty inkwell from the nightstand's drawer, her fingers caught a faint indentation on the bottom of the drawer. Carefully tracing it, she pressed, and felt the drawer's bottom lift. She sucked in a breath, her nails scrabbling to lift this false section of drawer. When she gained purchase, she reached into the space underneath...and pulled forth a small, ragged-looking clothbound book. She opened it carefully and stared at the small feminine script that filled the pages. A diary. She clutched it to her chest. Surely in here, she would find some answers.

Carefully getting to her feet, wincing as she did as her leg threatened to seize up, she threw the sheets back over the furniture, letting the ghosts retake their abode. She moved to the window to close the curtains.

She froze, her hand on the drape. The strange man whose name she still did not know was standing in the garden in the rain, staring up at the house.

Why would he be doing that? Had Rivers hired him? But why would he stare at the house in the rain?

No, not at the house. At the windows. This *window.*

But why should he stare at this window? He didn't know whose room it belonged to. Even so, her heart pounded, and her hand trembled on the curtains. *Had he seen her?*

So what if he had? Why should he care?

You're just closing a curtain, nothing to be alarmed about. Who's to say he can even see me at this distance anyway? Ophelia thought.

But she got the impression he was riveted on her, and could see every detail, rain and distance be damned as her hand hauled the curtain shut.

☙❦❧

Luncheon interrupted Ophelia's burning desire to read her mother's diary, but she dutifully went down and ate, alone save for Thomas against the fern wallpaper, to avoid any suspicion over her activities, though she would've loved to ask for a tray in her room. But as soon as she could, she escaped back to her room and retrieved the diary, turning up her lamps so that she did not have to strain to read the small, looping script.

Her mother had not been a daily diarist. She wrote down shopping lists, household to-do items, and drawings of ferns and ivy in between sporadic journal entries and what appeared to be a few written prayers. Sometimes several days or weeks would pass between entries, and sometimes the entries were not dated at all. This also appeared to be only the most recent in a line of journals, because it began *"Thank goodness for new pages."* Since she was looking for information on the trust, Ophelia decided to read the journal backwards, hoping any messages or details would be towards the end.

Not many entries existed during the period of her mother's

illness and eventual death. *"Too painful to write,"* was all one page said. Another: *"No strength for anything. Constantly weary."*

Ophelia bit her lip and turned the page. Her mother's illness had been short from her childhood's point of view, but these pages seemed to suggest that her mother had been ill long before she had taken to her bed.

Since she was moving backwards in time, it took Ophelia time to puzzle out the lack of context surrounding certain entries, but a third of the way through the pages she finally hit upon a hint of a clue regarding the trust.

> *"I must meet with Messrs. Warburton and Rowe as soon as may be to ensure the legal tangles are all accounted for. Isaiah could never touch my portion because of the iron-clad marriage settlement Papa drew up (bless and keep you, Papa, in heaven where the angels are!) and now I must do the same for Ophelia to ensure her security and protection.*
>
> *Isaiah never met a grudge he would not carry to the grave, and I do not want his hatred to touch her. Not more than it already has.*
>
> *I have often wondered if this is punishment for my sins. God is not that cruel. Only men dole out such hurt for wrongs. And so I hope the Lord forgives me when I say I fervently hope Isaiah is eaten by worms and dies, like Herod, in as much pain as I endure now. A fitting end. Lord, watch out for my precious girl."*

Ophelia traced the words, swallowing past the lump in her throat. Had she known she was sick? And what was that about a sin?

Ben insinuated Father's enmity with her resulted from these funds kept from him, but her mother seemed to believe he was angry with *her*—still about the money? Or was Ophelia's original childhood belief true, that her father hated her because she was a girl?

Intellectually, she knew anyone prioritizing one child over

another was foolish. However, the world was full of plenty of fools. And it shouldn't matter that she was female—he already had two sons!

But here she held proof that her mother did mean for the money to be hers, did provide for her as best as she was able. She hugged the journal to her chest for a long time before resuming reading. After going through another third of the pages, she found an entry, not about the trust, but about her mother's illness.

"I was finally forced to see the physician. Dr. Collins has found evidence of a lump, a growth, beneath my breast...He says there is very little medicine can do, no matter what salves and rubs quacks try to tout, and suggests I write to Isaiah to bring me to London, where some surgeons have done procedures to remove growths, with varying degrees of success.

I cannot tell Isaiah. At best he will shrug and turn away. At worst he will decide to research and test and investigate, but not for my health and wellbeing. For his own dreams of glory. Too, there is the all-too-likely chance he will seize the opportunity to turn that scalpel upon me himself, to finally have a live subject to experiment on. It cannot be borne. I have done my own investigations. There is no guarantee this growth won't have spread throughout the body already. I fear it has already done so...there have been too many signs I have ignored.

I will not lower myself to that indignity, that horror of placing myself utterly in his power when I have resisted for so long, not even for the slimmest chance of being saved.

Desmond, forgive me. I should not have stayed."

Ophelia looked up from the journal. She turned to Blaze, who was chewing on his stag stick on the hearth rug, and asked, "Who is Desmond?"

Chapter Thirteen

❧

"Some sort of mutagen healing ability. Perhaps a side effect of an unknown virus," the scientist mused, stroking his beard.

"In a dead person?" the younger man asked incredulously. "Father, it is nothing short of uncanny."

"She is animated."

"She has no heartbeat!"

The father wrote something in his notebook as the others stood watching the long incision slowly knit back together.

"Do you think," the bloody-minded one who twirled the scalpel over and over in his hand, eyes fixed on the laboratory table, "if we cut a finger off, it would grow back?"

Addie, chained with silver to the table and surrounded by men with knives, stifled a sob.

Salem threw himself against the silver bars with a growl.

They were hurting Addie. Torturing her. Cutting her open like she was a cadaver on a slab with no care for her person, ogling her internal organs and ignoring her nakedness, except for the one who enjoyed her pain. Salem could see him licking his lips. If

Salem could get a hold of them, any of them, he'd rip their throats out. He'd pull out their hearts, coat himself in their blood.

But the bars held. The silver sapped his waning strength and burned him, but he tried again. And again.

The bars did not give.

The scientists ignored him and Addie both.

"Absalom, it's technically dead, it has no generative properties," the other son said.

"What do you call that?" Absalom waved to Addie's midsection which was currently knitting itself together.

"Performing repairs. I don't think it would grow another finger like a lizard regrowing a tail."

"Besides, you don't want to ruin your only test subject, Absalom," the man who shared no familiar features with the others said.

Absalom pointed back at Salem with the scalpel. "We have that one."

"That one is mine; we are only collaborating. And I only found that one because I got a special tip."

Salem stilled, even as the pain sunk its teeth into his bones and his flesh hissed. He had assumed whatever vampire locales they knew about were simply checked on a routine basis. Who had *told* the scientists about him? Who could've known where he was? No one had—none but Etienne. And Etienne had gone to fetch him. He would never betray him.

But Salem had been betrayed before.

You bring it on yourself, his dark self whispered. *Too trusting. You need to be pitiless in this world to survive. The only person that deserves your care or regard is yourself.*

Salem shook the voice away and listened. *Say more about your source,* he urged. *Say more about how you learned vampires existed. Who among us has betrayed Addie?*

But they did not.

Absalom did not look happy at being denied. Salem knew his

sort—a toady and a bully boy, a little too eager to reach for the dissection knife, but not for any scientific reasons. He was the sort that just wanted to watch you writhe while he played with your insides.

But the first brother said, "Lucas is right. And besides, we decided that one subject was for experimentation and the other we would use for the blood."

The father tsked, watching the inner workings of the body, and then watched Addie's insides slowly try to close the incisions. He was a cold customer, cataloguing all the parts of his subject without ever seeing Addie the girl.

"Father, we have two *vampires* in our possession; it would be *irresponsible* to not perform experiments."

"We have in no way determined whether these subjects are any sort of supernatural creature. You and your gothic fiction, Benjamin."

"Then how do you explain the silver?" Benjamin demanded.

"Don't all stories have a grain of truth? Isn't sifting through truth and fiction the duty of a scientist?" the one called Lucas asked persuasively.

"The table is yours," the doctor said abruptly, and set the scalpel back down on the instrument tray. He moved to a different table, pulled out a notebook, and began making notes.

Ah, so Benjamin was built from a more mythic mold. He did not view them as scientific aberrations or undead test subjects, but vampires of lore and legend. There was a healthier wariness to him because of that—he had stories to fall back on of the danger Salem and Addie presented, as well as an awareness that he was not dealing with merely reanimated tissue, but a creature with insatiable hungers and lusts. A threat.

Lucas, the colleague who had arrived with Salem in tow, was similar—though he also had the scientific acumen of Dr. Shaw. Salem would have to study on that one more.

Benjamin moved forward eagerly, as did Lucas, and they began pulling items out of a black satchel. "What is that, holy water?" Absalom laughed. "What do you expect that to do?"

"We'll find out," Benjamin said, placing the bottle on the tray.

Lucas paused and tilted his head. "What is that?"

Salem had been hearing the warmup chords for a few minutes, but now at its full volume, the piano notes began to filter through to the mortals.

Benjamin shrugged. "Ophelia practicing, I expect. The music room is nearest to this wing."

"Is that a hymn?" Lucas asked.

Benjamin nodded, holding a vial up to the light. "Get the pipette."

The notes began to make a recognizable melody. *"Holy, holy, holy, Lord God Almighty, early in the morning my song will rise to Thee,"* Salem's memory dredged up.

On the table, Addie hiccupped, her chest just barely rising and falling. The humans failed to notice.

"What a little puritan, your sister," Lucas laughed, rummaging through the equipment.

"What do you expect out here," Benjamin said distractedly, laying out bundles of herbs. The scent reached Salem's nose, and he closed his eyes so they would not sting.

"I'm going to have to do something about that. Introduce a little culture to her repertoire," Lucas said, shuddering theatrically.

"Would you put your mind to the matter at hand?" Benjamin insisted.

Salem ground his teeth and tried his waning strength against the cage again and again, welcoming the burn of the silver, the scent of his flesh searing against the bars, if only to somehow share in Addie's suffering. She endured the spackle of holy water, the garlic and wild rose and hawthorn with fists clenched, head tilted to listen to the music.

The songs went on and on. Salem found himself both hating it and grateful for it. The songs did not belong down here amidst the blood and the pain and the fear. The men went about recording observations and drawings in their journals concerning the efficacy of their substances instead of a testament to Addie's pain. But the songs gave something for Addie to focus on, something outside this tomb of horrors.

Ophelia, darling that she was, played through "Rock of Ages" and "Christ the Lord is Risen Today," and then played several songs Salem did not recognize. Maybe they were newer.

"What next?" Benjamin asked, setting the clove of garlic aside.

"Would you like to give the badger a try?" Lucas asked.

The men turned to the wire cage holding the trapped animal. Absalom had brought it in that morning. Its paw was mauled; Salem could smell the blood and the infection setting in. It growled and hissed from the pain.

"Yes," Benjamin decided. "Absalom, help us. We're switching them out."

Salem tensed.

They unchained Addie from the table, but to keep her from attacking them or escaping, the bloody-minded one shoved a silver spike into her and used it to thrust her back into her cage and slam the door. Addie crumpled to the floor, shivering.

Salem lifted his head and locked eyes on his target as it came towards him with the skewer. He braced himself for the pain.

One brother jabbed him with a skewer through the bars while the other unlocked the door. Salem clenched his teeth as the silver punctured his flesh and ate into him. Then the door swung open and another spike thrust into him as the first pulled away. They thought to maneuver him like a fish on a hook—a butterfly on a pin.

They were mistaken.

This is going to hurt, Salem thought. He bared his teeth.

He thrust himself forward on the skewer, feeling it pass through him as he impaled himself on it, lunging for its wielder.

The silver slowed him. The bastard managed to get a hand up in time to keep Salem from ripping his throat out, but Salem sank his fangs into the hand and bit down with all the strength he could manage.

The agonized shriek of pain made the wildness inside him jeer in victory, even as the other men converged on him, beating him with silver and rowan branches and anointed knives. When he started seeing double from the blows, Salem released the hand. The world tilted, and before he knew it, he was chained with silver to the operating table and the men were clustered around Absalom, cursing loud enough to interfere with Ophelia's music playing.

"It *bit* me! What will happen to me?" Absalom demanded.

"Wash it out," his father said dispassionately. "Clean it with carbolic soap."

"Try a little holy water too," Benjamin coaxed.

"Did it express venom?" Lucas asked curiously. "The fangs are not like those of a snake. If no venom reached you, you will be fine."

"We have no idea what diseases it may carry in the saliva," the father said. "As a dog may carry rabies."

The silver sizzled against his skin, eating away at him like acid. Salem could feel the anger, the rage, everything in him ebb as his body tried to perform repairs without success. Without respite.

Salem twitched as they produced a scalpel and basin but could do nothing as the men cut into his arm and proceeded to bleed him as doctors had done to patients for centuries to relieve the conflation of the humors. Since Salem's heart only pumped when he wanted it to, it would take some time to exsanguinate him, but fear still crawled up Salem's throat as his dark blood dripped into the basin.

They had to cut him over and over, as his body kept trying to seal the wound. Finally, the scientist tsked and inserted a hollow silver needle into his vein.

That kept the blood flowing, with a constant burn.

Salem made himself listen to the keys, the chord changes, learn the melodies of the hymns Ophelia played that filtered faintly down from the place above. Anything to keep him still and silent, enduring so they did not pull Addie out of her cage for more of this horror.

But soon the music ceased, and he was alone in the dark with no hope.

The rage awoke again. She'd left him! Left him down there in the dark! She'd taken the music away! His skin felt like dry parchment against his bones. Salem found himself reaching for her along the connection formed by her blood. Some anchor to keep him occupied, to keep the pain from taking over. Not that he could do anything with it now. But it was something to hold onto.

His dark self castigated him. *Fool. She's the enemy.*

Was she?

It was hard to think.

Fine, he thought. *I'll find out the truth from her, then. And then we'll know where we both stand.*

Then I'll know.

Then I'll know.

A quarter hour later, he felt her fall into a dreamless sleep. The scientists were still recording their observations. Absalom was prodding the badger who kept growling and swiping at him. They were not yet done draining him dry.

Salem took a chance, clasped the connection, and pulled.

Ophelia thought she swam to wakefulness because Blaze had crawled onto the bed. The mattress dipped under his weight. But Blaze always curled up at the foot of the bed. This weight was by her side. And the cats didn't have enough weight to do that....

She opened one eye and did not see her rain-streaked windowpane. Had Nancy come in and closed the curtains? She opened the other eye.

"Don't scream."

She inhaled so sharply she choked.

Leaning above her was a black shadow, but the voice, low and mocking—she knew it. It was Salem.

"Or go ahead, it's no never mind to me," he said lightly. "No one's going to hear you."

Ophelia seized the bedclothes, barely resisting the urge to pull them over her head. "What are you doing here?" she forced out. "How did you—"

"Mmm. It took me some time to find you—very surprising. But I searched you out in the end." He took hold of her right hand and without effort pried open her white-knuckled grip. Her resistance was almost nothing to him. He turned her hand over and rubbed his cold thumb over the scratch on her wrist. "Hello, my little love."

Her whole being felt like it had been plunged into ice. He had tasted her blood. Ophelia stared at him in horror.

Salem smiled. His skin pulled tight over his face like a mask, his color worse than the night before. "Don't worry," he said, reaching out to stroke her hair. "This is just a dream. You've conjured me, from the depths of your most secret dreams. Or horrid nightmares. Whichever suits you."

It did not feel like a dream. Ophelia felt his cold hands caress her hair, slip down to stroke her cheek, her neck. She was positive he could feel the hyperactive pulse that thrummed in her throat. But there was very little light surrounding them. She could see her bed, the wardrobe, the dressing table, but they floated in a sea of darkness. She saw no door, no walls. Somehow the lack of her comforting blue wallpaper, a symbol of her room's sanctuary, unnerved her more than anything else.

"If it's my dream, I would like to wake up now," she whispered.

"Not just yet, darling," Salem said, smiling widely enough that she could see his fangs. It was almost a vicious smile, joyless—just a baring of teeth in the faint light. "First, we're going to talk a little more, you and I, without the bothersome barriers in between."

"Do I have to be supine while this happens?" Ophelia said. "Or is you looming part of the whole...." her free hand twitched on the covers. "The whole thing."

"Oh, I find this position so...intimate," he crooned. "Do you not think so? You, cowering before me, so recently trapped in slumber of darkest dreams and nightmares."

"I am not cowering," Ophelia said pointedly, attempting to look dignified while flat on her back. "I am horizontal, there's a difference. One is usually horizontal when napping."

"Semantics," he said airily. "Now, why don't we—" he broke off, staring at her bedcovers.

Her eyes darted sideways to see Sheba next to her, stretching in her sleep. Her paws kneaded at the blankets before the tabby curled back up in a ball. How had she entered this dreamscape, too? Was she real, or just a figment of Ophelia's imagination, longing for something safe and familiar?

Very hesitantly, he reached out his free hand. She could feel the grip he still had on her wrist tremble.

The vampire very gently stroked Sheba's thick fur. The cat gave no sign that she knew he was there. But was he really? Was this a dream, an apparition, a manifestation? But *Ophelia* could feel him—and apparently, Salem could feel the cat. He exhaled— the first time she saw him do so separate from the necessity of speech.

Ophelia felt her racing heart begin to slow as he continued to pet her cat, wholly absorbed in the task. His face was blank—but it struck her that the vampire was in no way unmoved by what he did. The vampire had been quite animated with his feelings before—this mask told her just how much he cared that he was petting her cat, and how important it was he not let on.

"Her name is Sheba," Ophelia said quietly. "Well, really Bathsheba. She takes a lot of baths. I thought it was clever when I was a child. So...Sheba."

She wiggled her toes, ascertaining if the others were on the bed. She felt two furry weights at the foot of the bed. "Tibby and Nevada are down there."

"Nevada?" Salem murmured, gaze flickering in their direction. She wondered how much he could see in this strange, murky half-light.

"Long story," she whispered.

"Mmmm. Yes. And I don't know how long this connection will hold." He turned away from the cat slowly and focused his gaze back on her.

Ophelia took the opportunity to push herself to a sitting position, and then looked down at herself. "Well, this must be a dream. I didn't put on my nightgown to take a nap." She plucked at the fabric. "This isn't even mine." She was wearing a white frothy lace confection that bore little resemblance to her flannel nightgown.

"But it looks lovely on you," he purred.

She jerked the covers up to her chin. "What do you want? How did you even do this?"

"It's a particular talent of mine," Salem said. "I want to know about your father's plans."

"I don't know anything about his plans," Ophelia protested. "I'm not even supposed to know you and Addie exist. Will you let go?" He still held her wrist.

"You should know that I would burn this whole wretched dump to the ground if anything happens to Addie," he said conversationally, his grip tightening on her wrist. "Are you prepared to pay that price?"

She wet her lips, shivering under the regard of his colorless gaze. "You love her."

He tilted his head to the side. "She's my responsibility. If she comes to more harm than she already has, I won't hesitate to wring your neck."

Ophelia knew by the tension in his arms and the strength of his hands he was telling the truth. She swallowed back the words *"she's already dead"* as a frisson of fear overcame her again. Beyond their cruelty, it ignored the fact that both Salem and Addie felt pain and fear like any other creature.

"I've got more blood," she said. "I can bring it tonight. I don't want anything to happen to Addie, either. Or you."

He stared at her so strangely, his colorless eyes luminous in the dark. "I just threatened your life, stupid girl. This is the second time. Don't lie to me."

"I'm not lying," she snapped, pushing against his hand. "I may not like you, but that doesn't mean I want horrible things to happen to you. That would be wrong."

"And right and wrong are very important to you, hmm? Well, let me tell you something. In the dark, you can't tell the difference between what's wrong and what's right. All you can do is make the choices presented to you."

"All right," she said, jutting out her chin. "I'm making a choice presented to me. I'm helping you."

"Then you will find out what your father wants with us, and let us out."

"I don't trust you yet," she said pointedly. "Also, my father will know who let you out. I have to think how to go about it."

He traced the curve of her cheek mockingly. "You'll put your little mind to it, will you?"

"You don't have to be condescending."

"Little girl, I've lived five times or more your lifetime."

"That doesn't make you wise, it just makes you old," she snapped.

He reared back like she had smacked him on the nose, like a misbehaving puppy.

"You don't look that much older than me, anyway. Stop

assuming I'm foolish because of the way I look. And stop threatening me," she added. "I know you could kill me. So could anyone else. So could a lightning bolt. So could a runaway horse. You're not special."

"I don't believe I've ever seen such a foolish mixture of soft-heartedness and bravado," Salem said.

"So what if I am?" she muttered.

"I heard you playing," he whispered, leaning so close to her face that she reared back, bracing herself with her free hand lest she fall back against the pillows again. "You play a lovely tune, sweet. But strange how so many of them dealt with *blood*."

Ophelia whispered, "Not really."

"Did you know we could hear you, down there in the dark?"

"Well, no, but I was hoping you would."

The music room was in the north-west corner on the ground floor—the only used room in the west wing, purely because only she played any of the instruments and no one wanted to be bothered to move the piano and lap harp in the corner that had belonged to her paternal grandmother, as well as the smaller instruments—the flute and violin and the harmonica that Mr. Faber had given her, tucked in a drawer.

The only reason Ophelia was tolerable at the piano was that all her governesses—she had gone through as many governesses as they had housekeepers at Renwick, for similar reasons—had been firm on piano expertise. Perhaps, Ophelia thought cynically, they had all anticipated that she would be doing little to no dancing, and decided to make her indispensable at parties in a different way. In between governesses, Mrs. Anscombe, the vicar's wife, had been more than happy to give her lessons. Thus, her repertoire leaned away from classical pieces and more towards dance tunes and hymns.

She had been at a loss that afternoon, adrift after finding her mother's diary, her insides twisted in knots. She had paced until her leg had protested, and then found herself outside the music room. She had thought of Salem and Addie, separated from her by only a few feet of earth and stone, and realized that if she played the piano, there was a chance—especially with the way sound carried and rattled in the cavernous house—that they may hear it. And... and she wasn't sure. Maybe it would help. Maybe they would know she was thinking of them, and they were not alone.

The smile fell away from Salem's face. He cupped the curve of her jaw, his thumb stroking her cheek. "There it is," he whispered, so close to her face she could feel the brush of his breath against her skin.

"What?"

"That soft heart." He tsked softly. "You know, you really shouldn't have shown it to me. Now I know just where to place my fangs."

He placed one finger below her collarbone, tracing it through the cloth, which felt as thin as a spiderweb under his touch. She couldn't help the convulsive shiver, or the way her heart jumped as the sensation flooded her.

"You should never willingly place yourself at a predator's mercy, for we have none. Lord, what fools these mortals be!"

Salem lifted his head, as if listening to something she couldn't hear. "We'll have to continue this conversation at another time, darling." He flashed her another brilliant smile, wide enough to see his fangs. "Until tonight."

❧

"Miss!"

Ophelia jolted awake, throwing herself up off the bed. Nancy recoiled, jumping back from where she had been bent over the bed. They both yelped.

"What is it?" Ophelia asked breathlessly.

"I didn't want to wake you, miss, but you were tossing and turning so," Nancy bleated.

"Just a bad dream," Ophelia said, passing a hand over her face as her heart tried to regain its normal speed. Though it had been so real—so *tangible*—she doubted it had been anything of the kind. She looked down at herself, and she was still wearing her corset cover and petticoats that she had gone to sleep in.

Gracious, what if Salem had dreamed me up in this? She thought in some panic. Somehow her nightgown didn't feel quite so scandalous after all. "What time is it?"

"Half past, miss—if you wish to dress for dinner you'll want to start."

Ophelia stared out the window at the darkened landscape. Rain still pelted down outside. "It's that late?" she gulped.

"You must've been tired, miss," Nancy said, turning towards the wardrobe.

"I must've been," Ophelia said through numb lips. How long had she been trapped in that dream world with Salem?

"Miss Shaw, what is this?"

Ophelia turned to see Nancy with a puzzled expression on her face, holding her last bottle of blood.

"That's mine," she snapped automatically. "It's—it's for Blaze. Just leave it." She held out her hand for the bottle.

Nancy handed it over, her puzzled expression turning sly. "Aye, miss," she said, tapping the side of her nose.

Ophelia stared at her blankly. The liquid in the bottle moved as she took it.

Oh. Nancy thought she was tippling. Ophelia hastily shoved the bottle behind some of her books, sure her face was contorting from trying not to laugh—really, she could go into any of the rooms with decanters to drink—and mortification that she hadn't been able to think of a better excuse. For *Blaze? Really?* Ugh.

"I'll wear the green silk, Nancy," she said. "Will you help me with my hair?"

The maid brightened. "Oh aye!" That helped pull her attention from the mysterious bottle, but unfortunately left Ophelia with plenty of time to reflect on her waking dream with Salem as she dressed and then sat for Nancy to arrange her hair.

He had been entirely too free with her person, holding her wrist, touching her face, leaning in close, an intimate distance. Petting her cat. Uneasily, she glanced over her shoulder, but Sheba seemed fine, repositioning herself on the bed for a more comfortable snooze.

What did he mean by inserting himself into her dreams? Could he do that—was it because of the blood? A very private place to perform an interrogation, away from Addie's distressed eyes. But she didn't have any valuable information like Salem thought.

Well, if I don't want him invading my head again, I'd best change that, Ophelia decided.

Chapter Fourteen

S alem held in the hiss as the scientist's bully boy shoved him back in the cage and gritted his teeth for what he knew was coming. Ah, there it was. The silver pole currently lodged in his abdomen and piercing his lung, if he was not mistaken, twisted and yanked. The bully boy jerked it free of Salem's undead flesh and slammed the silver cage door shut.

Salem could not repress a low growl as he pressed his fist to the wound. He experimented at taking a breath—yes, definitely punctured. He felt fluid bubble. He coughed and didn't breathe again. He wouldn't talk for a while until his body had knit itself back together. But that wouldn't be for a while. His healing rate was sluggish, no surprise to anyone. Being chained and impaled with silver and then being tapped like an American maple tree would do that. Caged in silver and denied sustenance certainly didn't help.

How he hated cages. Salem had sworn that no one would put him in a cage again. That no one—not his maker, not Andrew, not anyone—would have mastery over him.

If it wasn't for Addie, he wouldn't be here.

But he had sworn no one would cage Addie ever again, too.

Salem eyed the humans as they conferred over the lab table, ignoring the blood that pooled here and there. They took the basin brimming with his dark blood and filled a syringe, hauling the badger out of his cage with the aid of huge, padded gloves and a muzzle. They had learned something from him, it seemed.

Salem permitted himself a grim, bloody smile. He could still taste Absalom's blood on his lips. He licked it, savored it, stored it away. He had hurt Addie. He would pay.

You won't want to close your eyes for a long, long time, Salem promised grimly.

The scientists shoved the syringe into the badger's mouth and forced it to swallow the cold blood. They got three syringes of blood down the creature's throat, and then Lucas gave a wordless exclamation.

Salem didn't have to see the badger to know what was happening. The paw was knitting itself back together.

All the men began scribbling in their notebooks, staring at the badger, watching the regeneration.

If only my flesh would do the same, Salem thought, palpitating his wounds with a wince.

Ophelia—dearest, darling dupe Ophelia—would return to feed them tonight, even after he invaded her dreams. It was a calculated risk—anyone flightier would have written them off as too big a danger—but not Ophelia.

Salem hadn't been able to resist pricking her wrist with his fang. Just one drop, just one. He had been careful. But it had taken some searching to find her slumbering mind through the new connection. She had been hiding from him, clever minx. He hadn't ever found a human who could do that. But he had broken in eventually.

God, she looked beautiful with her auburn hair spread across her pillow, staring up at him with hazel eyes that fairly glowed in his dreamscape. Plus that lace thing she had denied dreaming up, an unconscious lie. He could only bring himself to the dreamer's mind. He couldn't create or destroy there. Just speak, like a phantasm, and touch, when the connection was strong. And...pet cats?

He was still puzzling over that one. But he had felt the warmth, the softness, felt the purr vibrate under his hand as the creature had slept on, unaware. He could not have conjured that. It had been too many years. The cat had been there.

He had petted it. It hadn't run.

Then he had proceeded to threaten its mistress. No shrinking violet, his darling. He'd see her soon, be fed soon...*Ophelia, Ophelia, Ophelia....*

She had given her word, and so he'd trust that she would be true. He had no choice.

Salem slanted a glance at Addie, huddled in a bedraggled heap at the corner of her cage. He wanted to get her out as soon as possible, but he needed to know where the scientists had gotten their information, how they had known of their existence and how to acquire them.

Only then could he make Addie truly safe.

He hoped they might speak more freely in front of subjects they believed to be mute monsters. Subhuman. That's why he had kept his mouth shut, going along with Addie's ruse. If time went on, he could always begin to talk and try to finagle answers out of them. This also afforded him with opportunity to observe and gain the measure of these fleshmongers.

Salem had allowed himself to drift comfortably in the dreamscape with Ophelia for a time, but he had let her wake when they had returned to him. It had only been to take the needle out and return him to the cage, but still. It didn't feel safe to rest while they were near, knowing at any moment he could be pulled from his cage and taken apart.

At the sound of a knock and a soft murmur outside the laboratory door, the men broke ranks around the badger and began to clean up—irritably, in the doctor's case, though Salem suspected that was his natural mien. All except for Absalom. "We're going to leave it here?" he demanded.

"Yes, we'll do more tests after dinner. Chart any further observations, and—"

"There's one test we haven't tried yet," Absalom said, smile as sharp as a blade.

"Abs—"

Quicker than his brother, Absalom stabbed the badger and slit its throat.

Lucas and Benjamin swore, leaping towards him to wrestle the scalpel from his hand. The father just stepped out of range of the growing puddle of blood on the floor. The badger thrashed in its death throes.

"Observe!" Absalom called gleefully. "Record! That's what good scientists do."

With an oath, Benjamin released his brother's collar and turned back to the badger. The twists and wheezes grew slower, slower....then stopped.

Salem was not surprised. His blood could only do so much. Regeneration was not instant. It took time for the body to knit itself back together. And if the mortal wound outpaced the healing, if the heart stopped—that was it. Death.

"Damn it, Absalom," Lucas growled, calling more obscene assertions down on his parentage.

"Now we wait," Absalom said, no remorse on his face at all. "We shall see what occurs when something dies with vampire blood in it. We shall see if there is a grain of truth in *this*."

They would wait a long time. In a human, there was a chance that they would rise, heart silent, a new thirst instilled within them, frozen at the point that they died. That took a day and a night, as rigor mortis took over and then released the body to its new purpose. But animals were different. There was nothing to capture and hold to the dead body—no soul in the way humans had souls, perhaps.

With more oaths and threats, the men left the lab for their supper, leaving the cooling body of the badger and the pool of blood on the floor.

Salem felt his body waking up, more alert as the sun descended below the horizon and the moon rose. A time of secrets and haunting. If the established pattern held, the men would return after dinner and stay until the eleventh hour or later —only then would Ophelia appear.

They left no illumination in the laboratory for their specimens, but darkness was as familiar to Salem as a lover. He could pick out Addie perfectly as she stirred from her ball in the back of the cage and scooted towards him. "Are you all right?" she whispered.

He nodded. "Fine." He experimented with breathing again and found that at least the hole to his lung had closed. "What about you, Addie? Are you all right?"

She twisted her fingers in her dirty nightgown as she shook her head yes, then no.

"We don't have to talk about it," he said in a low voice. "What do you want to talk about, to take your mind off it?" Speaking was an effort, but he'd do it for her.

"Was it Ophelia playing the piano? Did you know all those songs?"

"I knew a few."

"What were they?"

"'Holy Holy Holy.' 'Rock of Ages.' 'Christ the Lord is Risen Today.' I didn't know the rest. Why?"

Addie mouthed the words, like she was trying to commit them to memory. "Do you think Ophelia will come again? Would she tell me the others?"

"Probably. You like music now, Addie?"

"Etienne likes music and poetry and things. I don't know anything about that. I've only been good at one thing, and it isn't even any use to me now," Addie said mournfully.

"Etienne talks to you about music?"

"He takes me to concert halls and sneaks us in to listen. But those songs don't have words, or they're all in another language." Her nose wrinkled. "I never know what to say. I want to remember to tell him. If I forget, you'll remind me so I can tell him, won't you?" she asked anxiously.

Sometimes not everything stuck as well as Addie would like because of her head injury. "Of course I will," Salem said soothingly. "I'm glad Etienne is good to you."

Addie brightened. "Oh, yes. I like Etienne." She fiddled with the edge of her nightgown. "Do you think Etienne would kiss me if you asked him to?" she asked a little wistfully.

Salem shot up in shock, making his injuries scream. Then he tried not to act like an anvil had just fallen on his head. "Has he tried?" He mentally penned a note to himself to decapitate Etienne. He'd told him to *look after* Addie, damn it!

"No," she sighed. "But it looks nice."

"Would you settle for a kiss from me?" Salem asked. "Once we've escaped."

"Oh, I won't want a kiss on the *cheek*," she said, like it was obvious. "I want a kiss on the lips."

"I could do that."

"But we're *family*!" Addie exclaimed, and he correctly interpreted that tone as feminine shock and horror.

"Ah," he said, "Of course. That makes sense." Salem refrained from explaining that some vampires did not view the sharing of bloodlines as such familial kinship. Frankly, he was relieved Addie had not harbored a *tendre* for him, though he suspected if she had, it would've surfaced long before now. Though he had never thought she held a *tendre* for *Etienne*!

"Besides," Addie went on, "You want to kiss Ophelia."

Salem choked, and felt a very unpleasant twinge in his chest wound. "*What?*"

"You kissed her arm."

"I did not."

"You licked it."

"I was trying to scare her."

"Your eyes never turned." Addie eyed him, and coaxed, "Don't you think she's pretty? Her hair's so red."

"Yes, I do think she's pretty, but that doesn't mean I want to kiss her." *Liar*, his thoughts betrayed him. *Liar, liar, liar.* "And her hair is auburn."

"The gentleman doth protest too much, methinks," Addie said, with a self-satisfied feminine smile.

Salem's mouth dropped open. "Where did you hear that?"

"I listen when you talk," Addie said smugly. "It's *Hamlet.* 'To thine own self be true.' 'To be or not to be, that is the question.' 'Country matters.' '*I loved Ophelia*—'"

"All right, all right," Salem said hastily. "That's wonderful Addie. I'm very proud of you."

She sat back and preened while he contemplated this abrupt betrayal at the Bard's hands. Had Addie really seen something in him that pointed to attraction, or had she simply connected Ophelia with the romantic lines from the play?

Addie said, "Etienne makes it look nice."

"Makes what look nice?" Salem said automatically. Had Addie pulled those quotes at random?

"Kissing."

Well, that made him attend. "Who have you been watching Etienne kiss?" he demanded. He resolved to twist Etienne's head off at first opportunity.

"Just some human." Addie smirked. "I spied on him."

"And he didn't know you were there?" *You found him when he presumably didn't want to be found?* Shocking, given Etienne's talent to pass unnoticed by even his own kind.

"No. I walked softly like you taught me," Addie said proudly.

Salem dragged a hand down his face. "Very good, Addie." Salem fervently hoped that's all Etienne had been doing.

"So will you ask him?"

"No."

"Why not?"

He very much wanted to say, '*because he'd better not get within twenty feet of my blood-sworn little sister with those kinds of thoughts in his mind,*' but didn't. In the first place, Addie was neither a child nor simple, before or after her turning, even though some days her injuries gave that impression, especially when she was under great stress.

In the second, he could not command Addie. He had promised her as much, that fateful night so long ago. For the third...he had to grudgingly admit that Etienne was honorable, as far as their kind understood the word. He had been the most trustworthy person Salem could think of to ask to watch over Addie after he left. Addie hadn't formed an attachment to someone completely unsuitable, thankfully. Salem could think of a fair few vampires off the top of his head that would've been disastrous. He contented himself with, "You will have to ask him yourself, Addie."

"All right," she said, smoothing her nightgown over her knees. "Will we leave soon?"

"Soon," Salem said, and tried to keep himself from banging his head against the wall.

◈

The lantern light illuminated a smear of blood on stone.

Ophelia gasped and lifted the lantern higher as she stepped into the cellar laboratory. "Addie? Salem?"

It looked as though someone had tried to mop up a pool of blood—and had only been marginally successful. Brown streaks covered the floor. She swung the light wildly towards the silver cages, heart in her throat.

"We're all right," Addie said in a thready voice. "It was the badger."

"What?" Ophelia demanded.

Dinner had been interminable. No one spoke about anything she could contribute to, and Mr. Harding kept making obsequious comments to her. The only saving grace was that Absalom had asked for a tray in his room, claiming to be indisposed.

After a freezing wait in the back stairway, Ophelia had resolved not to let Salem rattle her. After she had heard the men leave after midnight, she had retrieved the key from its hiding place and gone inside to find…this.

"Badger? What badger?" Ophelia asked.

Salem rasped, "They killed a badger. It's over there."

She followed Salem's pointing finger. In a wire cage the body of a badger lay crumpled, its throat sliced open. Ophelia pressed her free hand to her mouth. "Oh! Where—where did it come from? Why did they kill it?" she demanded. The poor, poor thing.

"Its paw was mangled. They probably trapped it."

Trapped it. The trap hidden in the pile of leaves gleamed in her memory. *They* had put out traps on Renwick's land—for *this*?

"But its paw isn't mangled," Ophelia said, her eyes sweeping the poor badger again.

"They gave it my blood."

"Your—" Ophelia swung the lantern and peered at Salem. He did not look well—in fact, he looked even worse than he had the night before. His skin was a deep gray, tight over his cheekbones and with a dry, ashy texture. He had looked unwell in her dream, but not this bad. "What were they doing?" she whispered, stepping towards them.

Salem fixed her with his colorless gaze. "Are you sure you want to know?"

Ophelia swallowed. If he had to live through it, she could stand to hear it. "Yes."

"Well, they had fun cutting Addie open and watching her put herself back together for a while," Salem said in a voice that dripped poison. "And I'm going to get my pound of flesh for that. Then they tested all the vampire myths they had heard on her, holy water and rowan branches and the like."

"Salem, don't," Addie begged, covering her ears.

"Then they swapped us out and drained me dry. Then they fed my blood to the badger and watched it heal. Then your bloody-minded brother slit its throat."

Ophelia blinked back tears. "I'm so sorry," she whispered. "Addie, I'm sorry." Her gaze crept back towards the badger. "Is it...will it...."

"Come back?" Salem shook his head. "Animals don't."

The poor thing must've been so scared. *Addie* and *Salem* must've been so scared.

"But we heard you playing the piano," Addie said. She wiped a hand over her face. "It was pretty. What were the songs I didn't know?"

"Better to say which you *did* recognize so Ophelia can tell you," Salem said.

"I know which ones she means. They're American hymns," Ophelia said, slowly sitting on the floor in front of the cages. *At least the songs were good for something. At least it gave Addie something to keep her mind on.* "My friend's husband spent time in America on a cattle ranch, and he brought back some hymnals to our Vicar. We have hymn sings two evenings a month where we sing other songs besides Church of England hymns, like American or Methodist. Our Vicar finds them livelier."

"How do they go?" Addie asked eagerly.

Ophelia rummaged in her pocket with a sideways look at Salem. "I can play them for you. I brought my harmonica." She produced both the bottle of blood and the instrument. She deliberately didn't think about how she'd get more blood now that she was confined to the house. Maybe she could send Thomas...he'd not ask if she gave him the rehearsed excuse, would he?

Addie's eyes lit up. "Oh!"

Ophelia tried to hand her the bottle through the bars, but Addie waved it away. "Salem first. I want to listen."

Salem took the bottle she inched towards him and swallowed. Ophelia watched the pale line of his throat ripple as his Adam's apple bobbed. The blood seemed to remove a little pallor of the grave from him, but not much.

Tearing her gaze away, Ophelia cupped her hands around the harmonica and quietly picked out the tune to "Blessed Assurance." She wasn't very good on a harmonica, but it was a gift from Mr. Faber, and she could play it anywhere, not just in the music room. It was a versatile instrument, happy and joyous or sad and mournful depending on the song or occasion.

"That's pretty," Addie said when she finished. "Can you sing it?"

"I'm not a very good singer," Ophelia confessed, keeping her gaze away from Salem. She could carry a tune, there was just nothing remarkable about her voice. Marie-Claire could *sing*, and she did so with gusto during the church services as well as the local musicales put on throughout the year. Ophelia much preferred her friend's nearly magical voice.

"Oh, *please*," Addie begged.

"Go on," Salem said. Ophelia couldn't help a startled look in his direction. His face was inscrutable. "For Addie."

Ophelia licked dry lips and coughed. "'Blessed assurance, Jesus is mine,'" she began in a thin voice, "'oh, what a foretaste of glory divine. Heir of salvation, purchase of God, born of his spirit, washed in his blood. This is my story, this is my song, praising my Savior all the day long; this is my story, this is my song, praising my Savior all the day long.'"

"You *can* sing, Ophelia; that was lovely," Addie said, and hummed a few of the bars, her voice, in Ophelia's opinion, much fuller and more musical. "The next one?"

Ophelia picked out "I Need Thee Every Hour" on the

harmonica before singing the verse and the chorus for Addie. She kept her gaze trained on the girl, avoiding Salem's eyes.

Addie's fingers moved, tracing the notes in the air. "I like that one." She hummed a few bars. "Slow and pretty. It was so nice to have something to listen to rather than worry to death when they were cutting on Salem," she said earnestly.

A cold shock passed through Ophelia.

Addie traced the music through the air as she hummed.

"Addie," Salem said, "Here." He held out the bottle of blood. He did not look improved.

Ophelia slowly pivoted to Salem, who had not moved from his place against the wall, his arms propped on his knees. "Are you all right?" she whispered.

His gaze flicked from her to the bottle, then back to her. "Oh, after my lung knitted itself back together and I could speak, everything else is minor."

Her hand froze as she reached for the bottle. "What?" Her voice cracked. "They did that to you?"

His long fingers gently pressed the bottle into her slack hand.

"Of course they did," he said, face blank. "They want to know what makes their monster tick."

Ophelia passed the bottle to Addie, who snatched it and gulped, even as she made a face at the taste.

Then it hit her. *He touched me. He had me in his grasp.*

He let me go.

"What is this torture for? To what end?" she whispered.

"To find out the truth beyond the myths," he said grimly. "I want to know who whispered in their ear that vampires exist at all."

Ophelia sat up straighter. "I could help. I could find out."

"You could, could you?" Salem said cynically.

"I can search their rooms. What should I look for?"

"Letters, papers, books. I need *evidence*."

"Of what?"

"Of who sold us out. Where did they get their information? And what do they plan to do with it, though I suspect I already know. It would be nice to have it in their own words, however."

"What do you mean, you know?"

Salem's pale eyes glittered at her through the bars. "I believe your mad scientist father and brothers are trying to determine what makes dead things live. But he won't find out."

"He won't?"

"No. Because it's not a question science can answer, is it? It's more philosophy. The field of that brother of yours. Or theology. Whichever you like better."

She frowned. "Absalom?"

"No. The other one."

Ophelia's heart sank, even though she knew Ben was as culpable as her father or Absalom.

He continued, "Because it's a question of what animates us, isn't it? The soul and spirit. What makes us human." His laugh had a wicked edge to it. "Can these dry bones live? Oh Lord, you know."

She stared at him, shocked. He smiled at her, the expression the most honest delight she had seen him express.

"That's another question. If the undead are ungodly, where is the heavenly smite? It gets tangled very quickly. Did you know Egyptians thought the brain a useless organ? That's why they pulled it out so quickly after death and discarded it, while preserving the other bodily organs in jars. Or that's what historians think, anyway." He laughed. "Why not ask someone who was actually there? I wonder if there are any ancient Egyptian vampires. I don't know that I would like to meet one."

He ran his hand through his hair. "But of course, chopping off a head makes it pretty damn important. Even vampires cease their existence if you do that. But I'm dead. I haven't got a heartbeat, unless I choose to do it for a while. I don't have to breathe unless I want to speak. I remember dying. But I came back still me.

Frankenstein's monster came back completely different. Although that was fiction. I had a lot of time to read the past twenty years. But have you seen a dead body? It's clear the indelible bit that is them, their soul or spirit—and what's the difference, by the way?—has passed on. It has moved somewhere—heaven or hell. So what am I? Do I still have a soul? Or am I the soulless monster your brother names me?"

"That's not true."

"Well, it's half true. I am a monster."

Ophelia shook her head. "You're not a monster."

"How would you know?"

"I grew up in the same house as Absalom, who tore all the tails off my lizards and pulled the whiskers off my cat and set tripwires outside my room because he thought it was funny to watch me fall. Just because he could. When I was eight, he was sixteen and doing these things. Intentionally. Maliciously."

He stilled. "Your brother didn't stop him."

"Ben is younger."

"But he knew?"

"Yes."

"But didn't stop him."

"I said he was younger."

"How much younger?"

"Two years."

"And he couldn't have stopped him or tried to teach him a lesson at fourteen?"

"He would've gotten hurt—"

His eyes flashed ruby. "You were getting hurt! He couldn't punch his brother to defend his eight-year-old sister?"

Ophelia had to blink back tears again. No one since her mother had ever defended her, but this man—this man whose heart did not beat—did.

Salem's eyes narrowed. "I'll tell you this," he said abruptly. "If you really believe we are not monsters, really want to help us, let me drink from you," he said, like he was throwing down a gaunt-let. Like he was sure that was a bridge too far.

Ophelia swallowed. Was it? He had already tasted her blood and appeared in her dreams. And he hadn't hurt her.

"Why do you want to drink from me?"

"Because then I'll know you are honest. And I need more than that pigswill to regain my strength." His smile twisted. "But it could be risky. The thirst could overpower me at any moment, and I might rip your throat out. If I was a monster, that is."

This was a test. Did she really believe he wouldn't harm her? Did she have enough faith to place herself in his power? Ophelia clasped her hands in her lap. "Really? Because Addie told me she knew how to avoid killing when she fed. Someone must have taught her that."

"And so you decide to hold this up as an example of my good-ness?" Salem shook his head. "The principle of 'waste not' is a flimsy thread to cling to in the face of something hungry."

"What will happen if I let you drink?"

"You might have two little punctures in your wrist—or a gaping hole." His colorless eyes glittered. The red flash had disappeared.

You don't get to think you can frighten me away or make me cower. "All right."

Ophelia lifted her chin, and said it again, just to see the poleaxed look on his face one more time. "*All right.*"

❦

Salem couldn't believe it. She had agreed. She had *agreed*. He would get to taste her blood again. His mouth watered as the scent of oranges overwhelmed him. "Are you certain?" he said. "Because—"

"I said *all right*," Ophelia snapped, and thrust her arm through the bars.

He seized it on instinct, but they both jumped. Her, for all the reasons one should not thrust one's arms through the cage of a predator. Him.... because she was so warm. The life was right there, under her skin, pumping through her veins. It would only take a little pressure. A little nick. And then he'd have her blood in his mouth. He could take and take and take....

You deserve it, his dark self insisted. *Her family has taken your blood, it is only fair you take compensation from her. They hurt you, tortured Addie. Take it all. Drain her dry, teach them all, take your vengeance....*

Salem clenched his jaw so hard his teeth ground together. *No.*

When he had been caged before, and all his choices but one taken from him, he had sworn to himself that no one would ever rule over him again. And that meant taming his thirst. As long as he was ruled by the bloodlust, his Maker Renata, their Master Theron, his false friend Andrew....they would all have power over him. Would all seek to control him, lead him by his throat wherever they wanted.

So Salem had turned his will into iron. He had forged chains called "control" and "restraint" and had put them on himself so that no one else's fetters would fit. And he *had* taught Addie the same. It was little enough he could do for her.

He seized those chains now. *You will not rule over me,* he told his desires. *You do not drag me along behind you like a thrown rider from a horse's stirrups. I hold the reins. I determine the course.*

I say stop, and I stop.

Ophelia pursed her lips in a tight line, waiting. She thought it would all be pain and unpleasantness. Well, that he could change her mind about.

Salem pressed his lips against the warmth of her wrist, the thud of her pulse. It jumped and sped up. He hid a smile. He dragged his lips over her wrist just as he had the night before, drugging her with sensation, before he let his lips part and press an open-mouthed kiss to the scabbed cut. He felt her shiver.

Salem bit down, sinking his fang into the artery of her wrist. Ophelia flinched. *It won't hurt, not for long,* he thought, and sucked. The taste of oranges filled his mouth, along with the coppery tang of blood. Nothing like her brother's.

He pulled the blood from her wrist, his eyes fixed on hers. She did not look away, her hazel eyes wide. He ran his free hand along the skin of her arm, where her wrap and nightgown had ridden up. She was so soft. Warm. Lovely. He swallowed, feeling the blood fill him, heal his wounds, put the hint of life back into him.

But that's all it is, a hint. A phantasm. You're dead and drinking from her like a leech. It will never be enough, never. Take it all. Take it, take it—

You will not rule me, Salem thought grimly, even as his grip on her wrist tightened.

Just one more taste. Just one more sip. Just one more—

He felt Ophelia's fingertips stroke the skin of his neck. Just a touch, feather-light. Two fingers traced up and down what little of his skin they could reach.

The touch seared him. Scared him. Stoked his need higher.

Salem ripped himself away from her, his mouth full of oranges.

A trickle of blood ran down the inside of her wrist. Salem jerked his eyes away from the red smear and pressed a handkerchief to the puncture.

He swallowed and ran his tongue along his teeth to make sure all the blood was gone before he cleared his throat and said, "Press with this. For several minutes, until the blood clots."

Ophelia took the handkerchief and applied the pressure, her eyes still wide. She licked her lips. "You look better," she said, the corners of her mouth turning up.

He stared at her. Looked better? And she was happy about this? Didn't she understand that he had *drunk her blood* to have this effect?

Monster. Alone. Damned. Deservedly so.

"Nothing is going to...happen, is it?" she whispered.

He scoffed. "You mean will you turn into a vampire? No. But you're a fool for not pressing me for better answers."

She drew back, stung. The hurt expression on her face felt like another silver knife to the gut. *Only I wielded it myself.*

"What does turning mean?"

"What do you *think* it means?" he demanded.

Her lips tightened, her expression closing. "I mean what does it *entail, professor*; I ken very well it refers to the change from mortal to vampire."

Salem pressed, "Do you really want to know?"

"Yes."

"To turn someone into a vampire, you must drain them to nearly the point of death, make them drink your blood, and then they have to die. The next night, they will wake, alert, aware, but with their hearts stopped, and an insatiable lust for blood. Very hard to do on accident." He smiled. Slowly.

"Did you...did you want to be a vampire?"

"Sweetheart, only power-mad fools *want* to be a vampire, and I am neither power mad nor a fool."

Her eyes softened. "So, you didn't want this."

He sneered. "Please, spare me."

"If a dog is made to fight, people say it's vicious, dangerous, but it's not the dog's fault—"

Salem shook his head. "Are you trying to insinuate I'm not a blood drinker, a killer, and instead some kind of victim? Oh no, I am all those things and more. If you're still trying to find a man instead of the monster, you've made a poor choice, darling. I *have* killed.

"I killed Addie."

Chapter Fifteen

"Ah. You've got a hitch in your giddyup," Mr. Faber said at the tea Marie-Claire was giving for Owen's American friends.

They had sailed across an ocean to see him get married—as well as take care of some business for Owen's uncle, who "couldn't come." Marie-Claire had whispered to Ophelia that it meant he hadn't approved of Owen marrying someone of African descent. She pretended it didn't hurt, but Ophelia knew her friend. That's why Marie-Claire had gone to such lengths to show hospitality to Owen's friends who did make the journey.

Ophelia stared down at her shoes—visible below her skirts because Marie-Claire had not taken her to get a new wardrobe. She was fifteen, and would be in short skirts for two more years. Everyone could watch her gait as she limped. And now this stranger knew that she was like this all the time.

"I shouldn't have said that, I guess. My daughters scold me about my rough cowboy manners. I apologize."

"It's only what everyone is thinking," Ophelia told her shoes.

Mr. Faber's warm drawl was like a smooth slide of melted caramel or honey. "You know, I had me a horse just like that, and sure enough if that wasn't the smartest horse I ever owned. The color of a new copper penny, too—just like your hair. Prettiest color I ever saw."

She looked up hesitantly into his sun-roughened face. A dimple appeared as he smiled down at her. His clothes were different than she was used to—unselfconscious working man's best but still not the highest state of fashion. His dark hair was just beginning to grey at the temples.

Ophelia was so startled by his kind smile she blurted out, "It's not good for horses to be lame."

"Oh, I never said he was lame," Mr. Faber assured her. "He was sound in his hooves, all right. I made sure of that. He just had the strangest gait I ever saw. Like to jog every rider he ever had out of the saddle." His smile grew. "I suspected he did it on purpose. I told you he was smart."

She whispered, "Are you really a cowboy?"

"Well, I've been a lot of things over the course of my life, but I reckon you could call me a cowboy. I pushed more beeves than I could count up the Sedalia trail on cattle drives, though now I'm the foreman for the H Bar G. How d'you do, Miss...?"

"Oh, I'm not supposed to...Owen or Marie-Claire need to introduce us." Ophelia twisted her hands in her skirts, suffering a belated attack of propriety. "Mr. Glenwood and Miss Fontaine, I mean. Before we can converse." She fumbled to a stop, her cheeks heating.

"What about chalking this up to my poor American manners?" he said. "We'll get Miss Fontaine or Mr. Glenwood to do the official introduction when she's not tied up with her in-laws." He nodded towards the group across the room. "I spoke first. How 'bout I go first again? My name's Clay Faber."

"Ophelia Shaw. I'm Marie-Claire's friend. Obviously." She flushed again. "Our mothers were friends, I mean. We grew up together. She's older, though." She mumbled to a stop, mortified.

Mr. Faber reached out and took her hand in one of his broad, work-roughened ones, shaking it briskly. "I'm very pleased to meet you, Miss Shaw. I've got a little girl a few years younger than you. She likes cowboy stories, too."

In real life, Marie-Claire had broken free of Owen's parents and had come over to coax them over to the tea tray, and Mr. Faber had asked Ophelia to explain English tea manners, teasing her out of her self-consciousness.

But in her dream, Mr. Faber handed Ophelia the dime novels he had sent her after returning home to America, saying, "I think you should start with this one." He tapped the one on top.

She opened the book. The story had been replaced with the words of his letter that had accompanied the package. She touched the pages softly, recalling with a pitying gentleness for her younger self how many times she had reread the few pages. She had been stuck in that awkward, desperate stage where she was aware of his masculine appeal but still wanted to receive his attention as one of his own children would. To gain his approval the way she never would her own father's.

Mr. Faber had written her a standard epistle thanking her for shepherding him around the village and introducing him to her animals and sitting with him at Owen's wedding, and he sent the dime novels in thanks, knowing the flimsy volumes weren't typical English readership. He also included a harmonica in the package. That, plus the stories he had told her in person of cattle drives and silver rushes and the wide-open landscape of the west, somehow totaled up to more than any man save Ben had given her, ever.

Ophelia rubbed her thumb over the 'Sincerely' above his signature and sighed for that lonely girl. For the loneliness that still gnawed at her bones.

Nevada meowed.

"Who is this?" Salem asked slowly, walking onstage from the darkness that surrounded the dream parlor.

Ophelia started at his appearance. "Nobody," slipped out her lips before she thought.

His colorless eyes narrowed in thought. "Liar. If you're dreaming about him, he must be a *somebody*." He rolled his sleeves up to his elbows, baring pale gray skin, and pointed at Mr. Faber. "Who is he?"

Her fingers tightened around the book. "People dream strange things all the time. Falling. An old acquaintance. Teeth falling out."

"Not when I'm in their dreams." Salem smiled, his fangs gleaming. "And an old acquaintance is still a someone."

Ophelia looked from him to Mr. Faber, who had frozen along with the rest of her dream landscape. Marie-Claire's parlor had partly morphed into her bedroom, a strange mismatch of stage sets. Her short dress had morphed back into the frothy nightgown.

"You've got no right to poke your nose into my private dreams."

"What is it that you don't want me to see?" he pressed, stepping forward. "Why is this memory worth hiding?"

She threw up her hands. "I'm going to help you! You don't need to follow me into my dreams. Why do you keep doing this?"

He snatched the dime novel from her hand.

"Give that back! It's mine!" She snatched for the book, but he evaded her, dancing away to flip through the pages. She lunged for Salem, finding a purchase on his arm and almost climbing up him as he held the book above his head.

His free arm snaked around her and pinned her to his chest, restraining her with no effort. She could feel him against her as she drew in an outraged breath. He of course did not breathe at all. She thrashed and bucked, trying to pry herself from his grip, but he was like stone, immovable. If she continued to fight, she would exhaust herself from battering against him, like a wave continuing to crash against a cliff.

Throat tightening, Ophelia went limp in his grasp, misery flooding her. "Fine!" she gulped. "You want to know who he is? When I was fifteen, my best friend got married, and her husband-to-be had spent time in America. His uncle lives there. His American friends came to the wedding. Mr. Faber was kind enough to take an interest in my gawky self. He *talked* to me. That's all. And then after two weeks he went home to his family and his daughters."

She laughed, but it sounded more like a sob. "Go on! Tell me I'm an idiot for forming a deep obsession with the American West because a man twice my age was nice to me for two weeks. Tell me it's foolish and ridiculous to have a silly crush on a man like that." She fisted her hand in his shirt and shouted, "Tell me I'm desperate for affection! Tell me that no one is going to love me as much as I want them to! It's nothing I haven't told myself!"

Her eyes stung, but she wouldn't spare a hand to swipe them away. Blinking rapidly, she glared at him, even as her vision swam. She wouldn't give him the satisfaction.

Slowly, Salem lowered the hand that held her dime novel, his expression shifting to one of extreme intensity. He set the book down on the bed and lifted his free hand towards her face.

Ophelia smacked his hand away. "No. You don't get to do that. Look at me, Salem. Look at me and tell me: am I honest?"

The vampire's jaw tightened. "Ophelia—"

"*Am. I. Honest?* Tell the truth and shame the devil!" she commanded.

He reared back as if she had laid a solid blow to his chin. He stared at her, unblinking, as still as—death. Then he spoke. "You are. You are honest, Ophelia. But you aren't foolish."

Softly, so softly, he wiped away the sheen of tears under her eyes. "'Every man under the sun is light of brain, all eyes and no wits or sight.' Because they cannot see that you are loveliness, and light, and everything I...."

She sniffed. "Hate?" she snapped flippantly.

"Crave," Salem whispered, and never did he look less mortal.

She leaned away from him, wide-eyed. "You don't mean that."

"You are so...alive. You have no idea...." He slowly released her from his hold, as if he only just realized he was doing it, and stepped back. He licked her tears off his fingers, and his eyes fluttered shut for a moment in bliss.

Crave.

Her heart stuttered in her chest.

His colorless eyes reopened and caught her in their gaze.

"Do you know I can't dream anymore?" he said conversationally. "Can't even sleep. It's my gift. Or my curse. Some vampires develop talents that can be a double-edged sword. I can walk in your dreams, but I have none of my own. I go slow and quiet during daylight. Like a snake. I shut my eyes, stop thinking for a while. But I don't dream. I can only join you in yours. You, so full of light. Hope. Warmth." He reached up slowly, so slowly, and ran the back of his fingers down her cheek, a cool whisper touch. "And that's dangerous."

"Why?" she said dumbly.

"For *you*."

She blinked at him. Salem's eyes glittered in the dark as the part of her dream from years past faded away. Ophelia felt unsteady—inwardly as well as outwardly.

He pressed his hand against her cheek, cupped her face. "Because *I want it*. So. Badly."

"Because you're a monster?" she whispered. "I refuse to believe it. You may be a boor and an unfeeling rogue and a varlet, but you're not a monster."

His eyebrows shot up. "Varlet?"

She glared. "Hush!"

"Really? Varlet?" The corner of his mouth lifted before he realized and smoothed his expression back into a neutral mask, but she had seen it—it had happened.

He stared at her with his colorless eyes, a somber intensity shrouding him. "Ophelia. I want to tell you a story, so you understand."

Ophelia suspected, just by the look on his face, that she wouldn't like it. But he was willingly sharing part of himself with her—the dark parts, the scary parts that she sensed he kept securely under lock and key. How many people did he ever open that door for? "All right," she whispered.

"Long, long ago, I was a young man—one with dreams, ambition. I was a bookbinder's apprentice, if you can believe it. On our half day a group of us apprentices from different crafts would get together and go out drinking. We met a woman. She asked us if we wanted to come with her for ...an enjoyable night. The rest of the boys were keen, but I—I said no. I wanted to go home and read." The corner of his mouth twisted into a bitter smile. "For all that I worked at a bookbinder, I had precious little time or books to read, but I had just bought myself another. One of my friends —Andrew—he both wheedled and jeered at me until I finally gave in. We went into her house. Drank her wine. The next thing we knew, we found ourselves in cages, down in the dark."

Ophelia sucked in a sharp breath.

"She and the people with her made us fight each other," he went on tonelessly. "Fight to kill, for their entertainment, and for our spilt blood. We could use nothing but our fists. They said the victor would be allowed to leave with his life and a gift. I fought my attackers off, but the rest—they brutalized each other, beat each other to death, until only Andrew and I were left. I gained the upper hand, but I refused to kill him. He was my friend." Salem's head drooped, and he looked at her from under his brows. "Then Andrew grabbed a piece of broken glass and slit my throat."

Ophelia's heart broke.

Salem smiled crookedly. "She found that funny—Renata, her name was. So she fed me her blood as I lay there dying on the floor, and did the same to Andrew. Then she snapped his neck. I died shortly after.

"After we woke changed, she delighted in pitting us against each other. I tried so hard to hold on, Ophelia, but Andrew did everything she asked. There was no loyalty for me, his friend. If we had ever really been friends. Any bit of goodness in me they stomped out a hundred years before you were born. Don't look for it. It's dead, just like me."

No, Salem, no, Ophelia's heart cried. *Don't you see what you are to Addie? What are you are to me?* "What happened to her? Renata?"

"I killed her," he said simply. "I waited for years, and when I saw my chance, I took it. She was powerful, and wily—but she wasn't the Master of us all—just my maker. She was consort to Theron, the old Master, his power behind the throne. When she turned to ash, someone else saw their chance to kill Theron and take his place. I gained my freedom. But I'll never be that man again."

"What's beaten down can grow again," Ophelia said.

Salem shook his head. "No. Not when I'm only this.... body of death."

Chapter Sixteen

"Broken?" Ophelia asked, as her heart sank like a stone. "What do you mean broken?"

The groom scratched his head and replaced his cap on his head. "Just what I said, miss. The wheel is stove in."

"But I just took it out Monday and it was fine." Blaze tugged at his leash, and she put a hand on his head.

"Don't know what happened, Miss. You can look at it if you like."

Ophelia followed the groom to the carriage house in the early morning fog as the air's harsh chill tore through her and stole her breath. She needed more blood for Salem and Addie, and she had letters to post—one for Messrs. Warburton and Rowe with an inquiry about her mother's trust, and the other a note for Marie-Claire, informing her of Mr. Harding's visit and Ophelia's inability to get away for a few days. She had left the missive light and brief because she knew if she tried to explain about the unease she felt around Mr. Harding and the strangeness that surrounded Renwick, who knew what she'd end up confessing.

And she couldn't upset Marie-Claire. She couldn't pay back

her dearest friend with hardship when she so needed solace and quiet now.

If Ophelia had thought she could get away with a longer time away, she would just go and visit Marie-Claire to explain, but with her father's edict in place, she didn't want to risk it. She had planned on just a quick trip to the village and back, a way to escape the suffocating atmosphere of Renwick and clear her head. She had gotten up early to accomplish it, too; she hadn't even bothered with breakfast in the hope that if she was speedy enough, no one would miss her.

But now the wheel to her trap was broken.

When Judson presented her with the wheel, a deep sense of foreboding washed over her. It was clearly not damage suffered on the road or from the wear and tear of age. Someone had smashed the spokes in. Deliberately. Blaze approached and sniffed all over the wheel, making a strange noise low in his throat.

"Do we have another wheel?" she asked when her voice was steady enough to speak.

"No'm. We'll have to put in an order with Mr. Sandleton the wheelwright. Could be a few days, miss."

"All right, Judson," Ophelia said. "Please do so this morning."

The groom tugged on his forelock.

"Oh, and Judson? Would you post these letters in town when you do?" She held out the two missives.

He hesitated. "Mr. Rivers handles most all correspondence, Miss."

"I know, but if you're going, I wouldn't want to bother him with a separate trip." She smiled as winsomely as she could.

"Yes, miss." The groom reluctantly took the letters and tucked them into his jacket.

"Thank you," she said.

Blaze stiffened and growled.

"Ophelia, are you sneaking out? Naughty." Absalom appeared

around the corner of the carriage house, a smirk on his face. He crossed his arms over his chest.

Ophelia lifted her chin as Blaze's growls increased. "I am not sneaking anywhere."

"I told you, you've been ordered to stay home."

Fancy that, she thought, staring at Absalom. He grinned at her unpleasantly.

Her gaze dropped to the hand tucked in the crook of his arm. It had been heavily bandaged. The poor badger flashed through her memory.

"It was you setting traps on Renwick land."

He blinked in surprise but raised a haughty eyebrow. "So what if it was? It's all going to be mine one day; I can set traps where I like."

"And that's where you got that bite, I suppose. Good! You deserve it," she said, pivoting towards the house.

"Deserve!" Absalom exploded. He followed hard on her heels.

Ophelia hated the way he made her feel—like prey running from a predator. But she couldn't run. Not for long, and not for very far. Blaze wanted to round on Absalom, put himself between her and the threat, but she kept the leash short and held to it tightly. Badgers could bite her brother—and good for them!—but she had no doubt that any move Blaze made would be met with immediate retaliation, if not an insistence to see the dog destroyed.

"Any trapped creature that's in pain will bite—it's a lesson you should learn right away if you plan to 'set traps where you like,'" she said, fists clenched tightly in her skirts and on Blaze's lead. She kept her eyes on the house. "That's *their* right."

"You high and mighty little bitch," Absalom growled. "I could teach you the meaning of pain—"

"Ophelia?" Ben called from the morning room door that opened onto the garden. "Come and get out of this wind; it's going to rain again any second." He shot a look past her at Absalom that Ophelia could not decipher.

Absalom growled behind her. "You can't run forever, little rabbit," he said.

Blaze made a low, ugly noise, but Ophelia managed to pull him up the steps.

Ben held the door open for her. "You're just in time for breakfast."

He did not ask what she had been doing outside.

❧

Ophelia waited until her family had gone to the cellars to begin her search in their rooms. She decided to start in her father's rooms and end in Ben's, as she could better manufacture a reason to be in his room if questioned. She had also been in his room before and knew where to look if pressed for time.

After picking the lock on the master bedroom, she stepped inside her father's bedroom. She checked his desk, bookcase, and bedside in quick succession. She found no papers or correspondence, but she did find a stack of very old manuscripts and leatherbound books that smelled of mold and were so old as to be crumbling. A page in Ben's handwriting with several notes— "*Codex Diaboli, p. 493;*" "*read the second chapter of the Striga Treatise, very enlightening;*" "*compelling hypothesis in Lamia Incantatum*"— topped the stack. They appeared to be books Ben wanted their father to read; they were far more Ben's area of expertise than her father's dry scientific journals.

She cautiously opened a few, but none were written in English. Once again, she cursed the classical education of Latin and Greek that boys received but which was not extended to girls. Her smattering of French from spotty governess lessons and exposure to Marie-Claire was no help. Some of the letters in the manuscripts even looked Cyrillic.

"What did you find?"

Ophelia's whole body seized. She whirled around, a shriek caught in her throat.

In the shadowy corner stood Salem—or his image. She could see through his wavering form to the room's wallpaper. Ophelia gulped hard. What was this? A hallucination? A *ghost*?

"Well?" he said impatiently.

"What are you doing here?" She hissed. "*How* are you here?"

"You gave me a lot of blood," he said. "I can view your daydreams if I try."

Ophelia stiffened. "I'll thank you to keep your nose out of all my dreams henceforth."

"I'm here to help," he said. "What did you find?"

"I can't read this," she admitted after a moment, showing him the pages.

He moved forward but did not bend his head to read.

She coughed. "Is it Russian, do you think?"

He tore his gaze away from the window and refocused on the book.

Ophelia looked from him to the pale, drizzly morning visible out her father's half-shrouded window and a jolt of realization shook her. It was light out. How long had it been since he had seen the sun?

Ophelia paged through the books for him carefully, feeling like the pages could crumble at any moment. One volume had drawings, deeply disturbing drawings—dark creatures with claws and fangs tearing other humans apart, with graphic depictions of viscera.

"Ugh!" she shuddered. "Are you finished?"

"Yes," he said distantly. "It's all a human's suppositions. A few kernels of truth, but not many."

Ophelia quickly shut the book.

She checked the clock. Twenty minutes had passed. Three more rooms to go.

"I couldn't find anything but these books," she said. "Unless you have more ideas, let's change rooms."

"Fine with me."

Ophelia listened at the door before she opened it and relocked her father's room. Salem followed her soundlessly. Was he an apparition? If she came upon one of the staff, would *they* see him, or did he only exist in her mind? Gracious, what a coil!

Ophelia tried Absalom's door. It was unlocked. She pushed the door open and steeled herself for the search.

She found nothing helpful. No books, no papers, no mention of vampires. Just bad drawings of what she assumed were ...dissections. Sketches of people with their bodies opened. Thank goodness Absalom was no artist. She slapped the sketchbook shut and prayed the images were too badly rendered to give her nightmares. She pressed the heel of her hand to her eyes.

Salem snarled. "Your brother is a bloody-minded knave unfit for any place but hell."

"You don't have to tell me that," Ophelia said faintly. "He's a vindictive little slime. Every time I think he can't get worse, he does."

Salem's eyes sharpened. "What's he done now?"

"Broken the wheel to my pony trap," Ophelia said, her shoulders slumping. "I thought to go to the village and pick up more blood for you and Addie, but he decided to enforce my father's edict that I stay home. I'm sorry. I don't know if I'll have anything for you tonight." She cast an anxious glance at him. "Are you all right?"

"He's trapped you here." Salem said.

"I can ride," Ophelia said, a little stung. "But mounting and dismounting are difficult without help."

"Would any of the servants help you? Or take you in the carriage if you needed it?"

"Well...no," Ophelia admitted. "They're all ruled by Rivers, and he takes his orders directly from my father. But I'm not trapped; this is my home, and...."

"And you don't think a home can become a prison?"

Ophelia bit her lip and didn't answer. She couldn't very well refute it when she'd had the same fearful thought herself over the last few days.

Putting the horrible drawings away, she left the room. She left Ben's room for last, choosing next to peer inside the crimson guest chamber, where Mr. Harding was staying. She was able to get into his luggage fairly easily, but there ran into a roadblock. He had a fair number of notebooks with him, but they all appeared to be in some sort of shorthand that neither she nor Salem could make neither heads nor tails of. She found nothing else of note in the belongings he brought with him.

With the knowledge that her luck was undoubtedly running short, she picked the lock on Ben's room.

"You're very good at that," Salem observed.

Ophelia smiled. "Thank you." When the lock clicked, she performed the same sweeps she had in the previous rooms, but found nothing until, at a loss, she checked the pigeonholes in the desk and found a neat bundle of letters. Not in her brother's hand, but rather a collection of Mr. Harding's correspondence addressed to Ben.

While these were not in the mysterious shorthand, she found them equally difficult to decipher because Mr. Harding's handwriting was firstly atrocious, and secondly, he tended to cross his lines. How Ben had puzzled it out, she had no idea. Perhaps men of scientific bent all had the skill of translating chicken scratch. However, Ophelia picked out a few sections here and there, and they all made her shiver.

> *"If such creatures exist, such qualities could be leveraged...."*
> *"The pernicious vitality of a 'vampire' could truly be the key...."*
> *"...Immortality within our grasp...."*

"I've been advised of a breakthrough. If you will send payment...."

"What do you think it means?" Ophelia asked.

"They want the secret to eternal life without paying the price for it," Salem said over her shoulder. "They think to circumvent what they believe is an unpleasant quirk of nature. But vampirism is nothing natural—rather, supernatural. And if they don't take care, they are in for an unpleasant surprise."

She turned. "What surprise?"

He swept a hand over himself, and then pointed a finger at her. "This is the price, Ophelia. You can't cheat death unless you steal life from the living. And the compulsion is not an easy thing to subsist with."

"Stop pointing at me," she said, pushing his hand aside. "I refuse to think you are merely some parasites, some sort of leech on humanity. And you *have* proven you can control it."

"Very few have cultivated the kind of control I have from sheer obstinance. And we're worse than leeches; they are at least living creatures. We're simply bodies of death, seeking who we can devour." He pointed at her again. "This is what you refuse to see when you look at Addie and me."

"I told you to stop pointing at me," she snapped. "Why are you lecturing *me* to stay away from *you*? You're the one following me around."

"You lack the healthy fear necessary when dealing with vampires."

Her eyes narrowed. "I am not, and will not be, afraid of you."

"You should be." Salem waved his finger under her nose again.

Incensed, Ophelia opened her mouth and bit down on his fingertip.

Salem jerked his hand back and stared at her, aghast.

She pursed her lips. "What, you think you have a monopoly in biting? Oh, *excuuuuse* me—"

Salem cupped his hands around the back of her neck and roughly brought his face down to hers.

He kissed her like something hungry, with none of the studied seduction he had displayed on her wrist the night before. This was desperation. Ophelia's heart pounded.

I am being kissed. This is my first kiss. With a hallucination. A vampire hallucination.

Before her breath could do more than hitch and her blood fizz at the sensation, Salem pulled back, a stunned look on his face. Like she was...a revelation.

Ophelia reached for him and opened her mouth—to say what, she did not know—but Salem flinched. "Someone's coming. Get out now."

Then he disappeared.

Ophelia's mouth hung open. "That was my first kiss," she whispered. "How dare you. Get back here!"

Salem didn't.

Then what he said registered.

Eyes widening, Ophelia hurriedly bundled the letters back together and stuffed them in the desk. Then she cracked the bedroom door and listened. No one.

She eased her way out and locked the door, shoulders slumping in relief. No one was coming. She would have *words* with Salem after—

"Miss Ophelia!"

She nearly jumped out of her skin.

"Yes, Nancy?" she said, hoping she appeared nonchalant as she turned.

Nancy hurried down the corridor. "Miss, where have you been? I've been looking for you all over, climbing every stair in the house."

"Here and there. What's amiss?"

"Cook asks you to come down to the kitchen. Says there's a delivery."

"A delivery?" Ophelia repeated, her mind working furiously.

"Yes, miss." Nancy eyed her, a funny look on her face.

"Lead on, then." Ophelia followed Nancy down to the back of the east wing where the kitchens were situated. The few servants in the kitchen were studiously bent over their tasks, but she could see their furtive glances. Mrs. Lowell was in one of her moods, it seemed.

"Good morning, Mrs. Lowell," Ophelia said, trying a smile.

"That butcher came," the cook said without preamble. "Told me 'twas for you, and not to look in the package." Mrs. Lowell pointed at the large table in the center of the kitchen and stared down her long nose at Ophelia. She was an oddly tall and angular woman, for a cook. She appeared to never eat her own food.

Ophelia looked at the opened brown paper around the bottles on the table. "But clearly you did anyway."

"And a good thing I did," she said triumphantly. "These bottles are full of blood!"

Ophelia felt the gasp of surprise flow around the room.

"What do you plan on doing with *blood*, missy?" the cook demanded, ruffling up like a chicken.

Ophelia's lips thinned, but she widened her eyes in innocence at the woman. "Why you are so overset, Mrs. Lowell? I would think you would be familiar with the substance, considering the cuts of meat that come through your kitchen. To say nothing of blood pudding, a fairly normal dish."

"You're not making no blood in my kitchen! I won't have it!" Mrs. Lowell declared, planting a fist on her hip.

Ophelia raised an eyebrow. "Well, of course not, Mrs. Lowell. I would never intrude on your domain without asking. I merely mentioned it to express my surprise. These bottles are for a prank against my brothers. When I did not come to pick up my order, Mr. Burns must've kindly delivered them here. How good of him. I shall have to remember to express my thanks when next I go to the village."

"A prank?" Mrs. Lowell said suspiciously.

"Surely you remember pranks, Mrs. Lowell. My brothers played them on me often enough. Now that they are both here, I felt it time for a little light recompense. And unlike *their* pranks, I will make sure it causes no extra work for the staff," she said in a louder voice, casting a significant look around the room. Few had seniority enough to remember the great Honey Incident and the Flour Bomb Episodes, among others, but one or two would, and would pass the stories along. They had indeed been very time-consuming to clean up. "So, I hope that this will stay between us." Ophelia inserted a thread of steel into her tone.

The maids and footmen murmured their assent. Mrs. Lowell sniffed.

Nancy gave her a narrow-eyed look. Ophelia held her breath, but the maid said nothing.

❧

If Salem had been alive, his heart would have been racing.

Her lips tasted like oranges. How could he taste her in her waking dreams? *I kissed Ophelia.*

When Ophelia bit his finger, the wanting had overwhelmed him. He just snapped. And it had left him shaken.

This is all Addie's fault, Salem thought irritably. *She was the one talking about kissing.*

She *bit* his *finger*. He could not have been more surprised if she had sprouted fur and fangs.

Salem scrubbed his hands over his face as the scientists finished up their notes and left the laboratory. Perhaps for lunch or afternoon tea. He hadn't been able to judge based on the light. It had been too long since he had seen daylight. Indeed, he could barely believe he had been able to gaze out the window into a rainstorm. It didn't seem real.

All the men filed out the door—except Absalom. Salem stiffened.

The scum picked up one of the silver prods. Addie shrank down, her eyes huge as she huddled behind her knees. Salem's lip curled.

Absalom stepped forward, casually swinging the prod, a smile on his face, but dark circles under his eyes.

If you don't put that down, tonight will make your previous nightmares seem like a sweet daydream.

After walking through Ophelia's dreams, he had taken a jaunt through her older brother's mind, making the most of the blood he had obtained from tearing into his hand. Salem amused himself with hunting the man through the corridors of his mind, enjoying the tang of fear he gave off. He stifled a smile, remembering how the man had shrieked and woken in a fit of fear, before falling back asleep into the same frightening dream.

Salem had enough blood left to ruin his sleep another night.

"Do men get taken in by those big eyes? Do they try to chuck you under the chin before you rip their throats open?" Absalom approached Addie's cage and stuck the prod through the bars. She avoided it, but he forced her into a corner, and Salem heard her whimper as her bare skin pressed into the silver bars.

"Are you as violent as the other one, or are you just going to weep and snivel at me?"

Pick on someone your own size, Salem thought. He snarled and let his eyes spark red.

Absalom turned towards Salem. "Jot this down, Father dearest," he laughed. "The male exhibits feelings of...protectiveness...? towards the female." He pressed Addie into the silver again and she bit her lips, squeezing her eyes shut as the smell of singed flesh filled Salem's senses.

Salem bared his teeth. *Come at me, you piece of filth.*

Absalom laughed and pulled the prod free, approaching Salem. "You know, I refuse to believe you can't talk. Father and Ben have their heads stuck so far up their own importance that they haven't even thought why such urban monsters would be devoid of speech. You're not mindless. You wear goddamn clothes. You're just stubborn. Come on. What do you say?" He clicked his tongue. "Just you and me."

Salem stared at him in silence.

His lip curled. "If I can't make you talk, I'll just have to make you scream."

As the prod came through the bars, Salem grabbed it with both hands, even as they burned. He used it to shove Absalom back as hard as he could, giving him just a taste of his strength. Absalom flew backwards and hit one of the lab tables, driving the breath from his lungs. The impact scattered papers and sent instruments flying. As specimen trays clattered on the ground, Absalom wheezed, trying to get his breath back.

Salem smiled.

Absalom scrabbled away, a bitter, angry look on his face. He didn't bother to clean up the lab as he left.

Just wait, Salem thought. *Your time will come, and I will pay back every bit of fear and blood you owe Addie.*

Just wait.

Chapter Seventeen

❧

Salem had not reappeared after luncheon, which meant that Ophelia had time for a side exploration. She took up her dark lantern and filled it with oil and lit the wick. "Do you want to come with me to the attics?" She asked Blaze. "Maybe there will be some fun mice smells." Blaze lifted his head. So did Nevada, who had been cooped up for days. "You can come too," Ophelia decided, opening the door and leaving the room.

The door to the east wing attics was at the very top of the house, where the old nursery and the partially filled servants' quarters were located. Ophelia picked this lock easily and opened the old, creaking door. She turned her lantern's shutter fully open and shone the light over the great cavernous space. The beam of light moved over the dusty furniture, the trunks and the covered paintings, all festooned with dust.

Blaze wagged his tail and began to sniff around the dusty trunks, on the hunt for interesting scent trails. Then he sneezed explosively.

Ophelia patted his head and wiped his nose. "There, there. Now what did we learn?"

Blaze went right back to sniffing.

"Nothing, I suppose," Ophelia muttered.

Nevada oozed into the shadows and was off on the hunt.

Ophelia began to inspect the trunks and boxes for any indication of who they belonged to, but it quickly became apparent that the clothes and belongings interred inside were from a century earlier, and this attic was quite full. She didn't see any storage from a more recent time.

To the animals, she said, "If Father is so in need of funds, he might do well to sell a portion of this. Who knows what is in this attic." Then she thought, *Never mind Father. I could sell it for money.* She wiped her face and probably left a smear of dust across her forehead.

"I really don't think Mother's things are up here," she told Blaze. "But that means they'd be in the west wing attics." She turned her mind uneasily to the west wing and its decaying soundness.

She sighed. "Nothing for it, I suppose. Nevada! Nevada, let's go!"

The cat didn't come.

"Come on Nevada. Mouse! Nevada, mouse!"

Nothing.

"Nevada, bacon! Bacon, Nevada!"

Nevada scampered from in between a table's legs and wound around her skirts, purring.

"Greedy thing," Ophelia said, picking her up and making her way out of the attics. "Fine. Maybe we will ask Cook very politely for some bacon." Mrs. Lowell tolerated the household animals because the cats did exert constant vigilance over the mouse population in the east wing, specifically the kitchen stores. It did not endear her to them, however.

On the way down, Nevada declared herself bored with the search, so Ophelia left her in her bedroom room as she and Blaze continued on. She moved uneasily from the east wing to the west, with no lit lamps and its unswept corridors littered with layers of dust and cobwebs in the corners.

She skirted suspect places in the floorboards and made her way to the access door for the west wing attics. It was not only locked but wedged shut. The door felt as if it had swollen from the damp. She was forced to shoo Blaze away after she turned the recalcitrant tumblers and heave her scant weight against the door several times before it finally gave.

"I was considering getting a lever. Or maybe a battering ram. Gracious," Ophelia told Blaze, who was intent upon the cracked door. "Wait for me," she cautioned as the dog nosed forward. She shone the dark lantern through the doorway at the stairs. The steep stair looked choked with dust, and splintery to boot. She cautiously tried the treads, and then took a few steps up. The door groaned ominously behind her as it swung closed.

Ophelia stopped and hastily grabbed for the handle. "Help me find something to prop the door open with," she told Blaze, who was of course no help, but eventually she found a small end table near enough she could drag it to the door and prop it open.

Blaze disappeared up the attic steps.

"Blaze!" she called, climbing as quickly as she dared. Her light bobbed and swung as she ascended into darkness.

The dog whuffed just as she came out at the top of the house. Ophelia swept a hand across her forehead and trained the light on the attic's contents. This attic was not nearly as full as the east wing. The furniture and trunks had a more modern appearance— within the last fifty years rather than century.

Somewhere in the attic, something rustled. Blaze's ears pricked up, and he froze.

"Probably mice," Ophelia said. "Or a squirrel." It smelled strongly of some type of rodent or animal. Some creature or family of creatures had no doubt invaded the attic through the roof. Setting the lantern on a desk that did not sit level, she began to open trunks and boxes.

The first few she found contained widows' weeds and matron's gowns. The inside of the camelback trunk bore the name of Wilhelmina Shaw, her grandmother, who had begun the fern motif all over the house and in the gardens. She made note of their location; if she couldn't find anything of her mother's, she'd try searching these trunks more thoroughly. She didn't remember her grandmother well; she had passed when Ophelia was still quite small, so she had no idea when her things had all been boxed up. It wouldn't be outside the realm of possibility for the belongings of the two deceased female Shaws to have been packed away at the same time.

But after a few more boxes, she found a locked trunk that bore the initials CFP—Cornelia Felicity Paxton, her mother's maiden name. When she picked the lock, she found row after row of cloth bound journals, filled with small, neat writing.

"Look, Blaze!" Ophelia exclaimed. The dog paid no notice as she plucked out the journals and opened them. No dates, no indication of order—unless the order in the trunk was significant. Maybe her mother had been the one to lock them away, since they were filled and her private thoughts. The thought of touching what her mother had once touched—had maybe been the last to touch—made her throat thick.

But she couldn't read them here by the light of her lantern. Ophelia busied herself by pulling the stack of notebooks out of the trunk and hunting for anything else from the trunk that looked important.

"Blaze! Time to go." She had no clue what time it was. There were no windows in the attics, and she had not brought a pocket watch.

Ophelia moved to the top of the stairs as something fluttered in the attic. She froze. What was that? She lifted the lantern— then covered her head and yelped as creatures flew past her. "Bats!"

She pelted down the stairs, journals under one arm and lantern in the other as what felt like a whole flock of the creatures flew after her, their leathery wings beating the air. Blaze barked, leaping into the air to try to catch them.

"Blaze! Come!" Ophelia commanded.

Juggling her finds, the lantern, and trying to pull Blaze along by his collar, Ophelia did not watch where she was stepping. Halfway along the hallway, she felt the floorboard give way under her leg. She shrieked and threw the journals to try to catch herself.

Ophelia hit the floor hard, her good leg dangling through the rotted board and her bad leg crumpled up under her. The broken boards gouged into her leg. The pain was so strong that she barely realized that the lantern had, once again, scored a wound into her hand.

Blaze whined, hovering over her anxiously, sniffing.

"Get back! Back!" Ophelia waved the dog away and gingerly tested the flooring around her. Only when she ascertained what sections felt reasonably sound did she let him come forward.

Ophelia pried her hand free of the lantern and set it carefully aside. "Here." She patted where she wanted him to stand. "You're going to have to help me," she told Blaze through gritted teeth. She grasped his ruff with both hands, attempting to get any leverage with her bad leg. "Pull, Blaze! Pull me out. Pull!"

The dog heaved, his feet scrabbling.

Ophelia heard the wood groan under her as she heaved her leg free. Her teeth chattered with the pain. She scrabbled away from the hole, sweeping the journals and the lantern along with her until she felt the flooring was a little more trustworthy. Then she let a few tears escape as she tentatively probed at her leg.

Her dress and petticoats were ripped horribly, but they had taken some of the impact. Unfortunately, she still had several very nasty scrapes through her stocking and her combinations. With a shaking hand, she wrapped her handkerchief around the slice in her palm, and then inspected her leg. She picked free two visible splinters from the gashes, wincing. Blaze pushed his face forward, trying to be helpful, but she pushed him away. "No licking, no licking. Good boy. Good boy, you got me out. Good boy." He had blood in his ruff from her hand. "You're going to have to help me up."

It didn't go well.

"Oww," she said weakly as both Blaze and the wall had to be employed to get her to her feet. It was hard to put weight on either leg. "Well, this isn't good."

It took Ophelia forever to gather up the notebooks and find something to put them in. She finally ripped off a swath of her skirt and tied the slim volumes together, bundling them under her arm. The gouged hand still had to hold the lantern, because the other rested on Blaze's broad back for support. Then she had to slowly limp her way back to the east wing.

She knew she looked a fright—dirty, bloody, and torn up. But she had to make it to her room without being seen and prompting too many questions about where she had been and what she had been doing. The minute she reached the right floor, she slipped into the faux secret passage, pressing the hidden piece of carved molding to swing the door open. "Shh now," she whispered to Blaze as the door swung open. "We're going behind most of the rooms in the north and east wings. Shh."

Slowly, she picked her way down the narrow hallway. It was still dusty, but it was thankfully sound and it didn't have the same level of grime as the west wing. She was halfway to her room, as far as she could calculate, before she heard a voice.

"I'd like to discuss the settlements." Mr. Harding's voice came through the wall clearly. Maybe he was just on the other side of it. Ophelia froze.

"I told you that you will get equal collaborator credit on any papers we write," her father said, his voice more muffled, further away.

She felt Blaze's chest rumble with the beginnings of a growl. She laid a calming hand on Blaze's neck and tried not to breathe as she inched along.

Mr. Harding clarified, "I meant the settlements that pertain to Ophelia."

Her gaze flew to the wall, as if she could see between the boards and wallpaper to the room within.

"What about Ophelia?" her father asked impatiently, his voice growing a little clearer.

"I *am* marrying her," Mr. Harding said dryly.

As best she could with shaking hands, Ophelia slowly closed the lantern's shutter, plunging her and Blaze into total darkness. She clutched Blaze's ruff, her heart in her throat, and tried to keep the air flowing through her lungs. In. Out. In. Out. Blaze pressed against her, sensing her anxiety. His body trembled with menace. She prayed that he would stay silent.

Professor Shaw scoffed. "Marriage is a business transaction of assets and property; the human element is incidental. When you marry Ophelia, her trust becomes accessible, and you will receive a portion of it. Is that what you wanted to know?"

"Somewhat. What about homes, living? Do you care where I house her?"

"Plant her in a hole in the ground for all I care."

A shudder wracked Ophelia, and the darkness suddenly felt like a blessing.

"I think a rabbit's warren would not be conducive for what I have in mind."

"The siring of heirs becomes tiresome. Only an heir and spare are needed, after all."

"Ouch." Ben's dry voice came through the wall clearly, nearly as close as Mr. Harding's.

The floor wavered under Ophelia's feet.

"All becomes moot if you have no accomplishments or lauds to pass on to them." A pointed silence followed her father's clipped words.

"I have plans," Harding said tightly.

"I have seen no evidence of them."

"Father, our plans depend on what conclusions we reach in our experiments. It is overhasty to write a scientific paper before one's hypothesis has even been proved. We have much ground to cover," Ben said soothingly.

Lucas cleared his throat. "I look forward to our continued partnership. When can I marry her?"

"If you had brought a special license from London, it could've been right away."

"I wanted to have a look at the girl first. I don't buy a cow before I see it, after all."

"Ophelia isn't a cow," Ben said. "More like a dog who never ceases begging. It makes her easy to please."

Ophelia bit her lip so hard she felt flesh part and tasted copper on her tongue.

"And so, now you'll have to wait for the banns or go back to London. A good scientist is always prepared for success or failure." Her father's words were censorious and unimpressed.

"I can take Ophelia with me to London and marry her there. Then the lawyers will be on hand to release the funds."

Ben said, "Ophelia can't travel alone with you."

"Do you really care about the proprieties? I was thinking Saturday," Harding mused. "Go down to London, marry, release funds, check with my contacts for more specimens, then return to finish working here."

Ophelia's father said, "It doesn't affect me. Ben will go along to chaperone."

Harding chuckled, his voice moving further away, growing less distinct. "To collect your share of the trust and make sure I don't abscond with it, you mean."

"Semantics," her father said. A door creaked. Then there was silence.

Mouth dry, hands numb, Ophelia shook in the darkness for several minutes before she worked up the courage to inch further down the passage and open the lantern's shutter. She petted Blaze, rubbing his head and ears fiercely, a silent praise for staying quiet.

Once she had regained some control over her limbs, Ophelia limped her way to the end of the passageway, Blaze an anxious presence at her side. She possessed enough presence of mind to check when she exited the passage, but prioritized speed as she limped to her room and locked the door.

Silently, she stripped out of the ruined dress and stuffed it under her mattress, then gave her face, hands, and leg a perfunctory wash before falling into bed and pulling the covers over her head. Her heart still beat a frantic tattoo. It wouldn't stop racing.

Tibby sniffed at her curiously, but Ophelia didn't even have the strength to respond. She didn't know how long she lay there before Nancy came in.

"Time to dress for dinner, Miss."

"Oh, Nancy," Ophelia said in a choked voice. "I don't feel well at all."

❧

Ben came to her door after dinner, all concern. Ophelia said, "Come in," making sure her dressing gown was fastened up to her throat.

Blaze rumbled in his throat as Ben crossed the threshold, his eyes fixed on him.

"He still doesn't care for me," Ben said ruefully. He approached her bed and kissed her forehead. "How are you feeling?"

"Not good," Ophelia said in a small voice. It was the truth.

Both her legs ached like the dickens. Her hand stung when she tried to flex it, and she kept it under the covers so he wouldn't see the bandage around it. But more than just her legs and torso felt bruised. "My throat is sore. I think I'm coming down with something."

He glanced towards the window where water continued to pour. "From being out in the rain perhaps?" He felt her forehead.

His fraternal condescension rankled, but she admitted, "Perhaps," in a weak voice. Anything was better than the truth.

How could you do it? How could you say those things? she inwardly railed. *You're my brother—the good one, the caring one!*

But he had trapped two people in cages. He had carved into one and bled the other nearly dry.

He was never good.

"You do feel warm," Ben said under his breath. "Well, Nancy said you were able to eat the soup Mrs. Lowell sent up." He eyed her, a funny look on his face. "Odd that it's struck you now and not when you got soaked yesterday."

Ophelia licked her lips. "I did go out—this morning. To walk Blaze. You remember." She struggled to seem shamefaced. "He's a big dog, he needs exercise."

Ben snorted, exasperated. "You didn't think to send him with a footman?"

"I'm sure it's just a little cold," she said. "After the first day, it's just a nuisance drip from the nose. I just need to sleep until then."

"All right," he said dubiously.

"You can say 'I told you so'," she mumbled.

He laughed. "I told you so. I hope you feel better soon. Lucas also wants to wish you good night, is that all right?"

Ophelia shot him a horrified glance. "I'm in bed in my dressing gown!"

"He can stand in the doorway. I'll remain so it's proper. He just wants to wish you well."

She swallowed. Hoping to forestall another odd look from him, she acquiesced.

Ben moved to the doorway and motioned. Mr. Harding appeared in the doorway moments later, smiling at her with his conniving, smarmy expression.

Why bother, she wondered, *if you believe I'm being served to you on a silver platter?*

Ophelia forced her face to remain placid and slightly drowsy. Blaze's head shot up and pinned Harding in his gaze, moving to put himself between Ophelia and danger.

"I'm sorry to hear you're under the weather, Miss Shaw. We missed you at dinner. Please accept my best wishes for a speedy recovery."

Was her paranoia putting an ominous inflection on those words? "Thank you. I hope to feel better after some rest."

"Sleep well."

"Thank you," she said, letting her voice go a little thready. She patted the bedspread and Blaze bounded up and turned in a circle to situate himself for the night.

"I'll let you get some rest, too," Ben said, pressing a kiss to her forehead. "Don't let the bedbugs bite."

You sold me in marriage to this horrible man in a ploy to get my inheritance, and now you pretend to care for me? she seethed. *Was it all a lie? Or are you just so unspeakably blind to how this would hurt me? How can anyone be so unfeeling?*

She held her anger in check and managed a weak smile for him, letting her eyelids droop as he turned down her lamp and closed her door with a click.

Then she took a deep breath and opened her eyes wide, staring at the ceiling. She swallowed back the bitter gall and nausea that wanted to rise.

There was no more time to waste, she decided. It would have to be tonight.

Chapter Eighteen

S he had to leave.

There was no way she was going to let her father marry her off to that man in exchange for her dowry—how *mercenary*! What a *thieving* thing to do! The money was hers. She would be—she would be *damned* if she let them steal one cent of her mother's legacy. They'd have to pry it from her cold dead fingers.

Marie-Claire would surely let her stay with her and help her stand up to her father. Ophelia still worried about upsetting her, but maybe she could stay in the vicarage with the Reverend and his wife after tonight—or maybe Marie-Claire would suggest staying with her mother. Mrs. Fontaine was a dragon, and her mother's old friend. That would be a way to keep Marie-Claire's stress down.

Maybe then, once she was away, she could.... Ophelia pushed away "reason with Ben"; *that* ship had sailed, but old habits died hard. She'd decide what to do once away and safe.

But before leaving she had to free Addie and Salem. She was their only hope.

She would dress carefully in a plain, dark blue dress, one she could don without help. Buttons in the front. She knew just the one and where it *was* in the wardrobe. When the night had advanced a bit, she'd go down, exact a promise that they'd do her or the house residents no harm, and then pick the locks of their restrains.

Oh, the blood. She couldn't forget that. Ophelia made a mental note. Then she'd let them out an exit in the west wing, away from people. Once that was done, she'd come back, pack up Blaze and the cats, and saddle her horse. With the aid of a mounting block, she could be away from Renwick well before sunup.

Ophelia pressed a hand to her heart at the pang of loss, stronger than she imagined. She shouldn't have to leave her home. It was more hers than the rest of the Shaws. *They* were the ones who brought the darkness to the house and made her spook at shadows. Their dark motivations and experiments and secrets. But if Ophelia didn't get away, she'd suffocate in the place she was supposed to feel safe.

Ophelia reached over and re-lit the candle by her bed. She used the old-fashioned trick of driving a nail into a candle over a metal candleholder instead of an alarm clock that would make a shrill ring. She lay back down and tried to sleep.

It didn't work. She spent most of the eternity watching the flame sway and dance.

It had occurred to her that it might be easier to sneak away in London; easier to disappear and find a position in a city full of people. There would be less risk that some well-meaning male who had known her all her life would return her to her father, sure that all had been a family tiff. But that wouldn't free Addie and Salem.

It was life or death for them.

Finally, the nail *tink-ed* in the candle holder.

Ophelia sat up and limped to the wardrobe, wincing as she dressed in the simple gown. She slipped her lockpicks deep in the pocket of her skirt behind her, where the bustle pad sat, just in case she couldn't find the shackle keys. She carefully refilled the oil in her lantern, making sure her hands didn't shake. Then she lifted it and picked up the bottle of blood with her other hand. "Stay. I'll be back soon," she told Blaze and the cats, and shut the door.

She heard no noises from the lab as the clock chimed one, the lonely note ringing through the empty hall. She slipped down the stairs and pulled free the hidden brick. She slid the key into the lock. *Click*.

Ophelia cautiously pushed the door open, sliding the lantern's shutter open wider. "Addie?" She swallowed. "Salem?"

"Ophelia!"

The glad whisper made her smile. She limped up to the cages and scooted the bottle of blood to Addie. She chanced a quick glance at Salem and paused. He was giving her *such* an odd look. Was—was he thinking about the kiss?

This is not the time to think about the kiss! She reminded herself, and said. "What?"

"Nothing," he breathed, his eyes shining in the candlelight. "What, no nightgown tonight, darling?"

"No," she said firmly. "Because I'm leaving."

"Leaving?" he demanded. His brows slammed down. "And why do you smell like blood?"

"I went searching in the west wing for some of my mother's things, and...Never mind that, it's nothing," she said.

"What do you mean, you're leaving?" Addie asked plaintively.

Her hand trembled on the lantern, and she set it down hastily on the lab table, widening the shutter so that she could see when she used her lockpicks. "As part of this whole...debacle, my father has bargained me away to Mr. Harding in exchange for my inheritance from my mother. So I'm going to go to my friend Marie-Claire's and try to...find a solution. But before that, I'm going to let you out."

Salem's eyes went hard as marble. "Really."

"But they take the keys," Addie said.

"I'm going to pick the lock."

Addie leaned forward, eyes wide. "You know how?"

Ophelia nodded. "But I want your word of honor you will cause no harm to anyone in the house if I do."

Salem slowly shook his head. "I'm afraid you don't know me very well, darling. I'm a *vampire*, and I take revenge *very seriously*."

"Not if I'm letting you out, you're not."

Salem seemed to uncoil, leaning forward through the bars as far as he could. "'Vengeance is in my heart, death in my hand, blood and revenge are hammering in my head.' I won't let this offense pass."

She shook her head decisively. "Not if I let you out. You'll give me your word."

"Ophelia." His eyes burned as red as rubies. "You know what your brothers are. They kidnapped Addie. They hurt her. I will make them pay with their blood. I'll have it in my mouth if I have to tear out their throats with my teeth." He smiled, hard and feral, but there was no pleasure in it. His fangs gleamed. "Open the door."

Addie's wide eyes flew back and forth between the two of them as she clutched the neck of the bottle.

Ophelia shook her head, her throat tight. "Only if you give your word."

"Why even ask for my word, darling? I could agree to anything and as soon as the lock clicks, murder the whole house in their beds. To say nothing of what I could do to you."

"You could," Ophelia acknowledged with a tip of her head as goosebumps traveled down her spine. "Which is why I'm asking for your word first."

"Salem," Addie said, "don't be stupid. Ophelia's going to free us. We know enough about their plans. I need you." She licked anxiously at the red ring around her mouth.

"I'm a *vampire*," he sneered.

Ophelia crossed her arms. "But not, I think, a liar or an oath-breaker."

His laugh sounded strained. "What the hell gave you that impression? You can't even comprehend the horrible things I've done."

"Was one of them breaking your word?"

Ophelia went on, even as he opened his mouth to reply. "So do it then. Give me your word. I'll let you out, and then you may do what you like."

"Salem," Addie called.

"Why are you doing this?" he said incredulously. "Why let us out at all?"

"Because I don't want to leave you here while they do God knows what to you!" Ophelia said. "Addie is my friend, and I…I care what happens to you. Please."

"Salem!"

"I want you safe!" Before she could stop herself, before she contemplated what might be the foolhardiest thing she'd ever done, she stepped forward and reached through the bars of his cage to touch his cheek. "I care about you, Salem."

He stared at her in flat incomprehension, some realization dawning behind his eyes. Could he see the desperate longing written on her face? His gaze dropped to her arm, extended to him. Slowly, he lifted his hand—

"Salem!" Addie shrieked, grasping the bars. She shrank back with a low moan when her flesh hissed. "Someone's *coming*!"

❦

In the deathly silence, Salem heard what Addie had—footsteps on the stairs.

He also heard Ophelia's heart stutter and spike. Saw her eyes widen in fright.

Salem swung his head towards the door and spat a foul oath. His face hardened into an impenetrable sheet of marble. "Either open this door now, or hide," he forced through gritted teeth.

Open the door, he wanted to cry. *Open the door. I can protect you. It's your only chance, don't you see?*

But he hadn't sworn. She wouldn't let him out.

Not even for her own sake.

Ophelia swung the lantern in a wild arc, light bobbing around the dark laboratory as she searched for a hiding place. Where *was* there to hide—a cabinet? Behind shelves and tables? She took the first limping step—

Salem cursed. "The blood!"

Addie rolled the bottle through the bars.

Scooping up the bottle, Ophelia hobbled towards the most likely hiding place, behind shelving next to a closed and locked cabinet. She crouched into a tiny ball and closed her lantern's shutter.

Darkness descended. The only sound was the rapid beat of her heart.

If she stayed quiet, if they were merely returning to fetch notes or a book they had forgotten, she might have a chance.

Only then did Salem realize, *the door. The door is* unlocked.

His heart froze.

The feet on the stair pounded down, paused briefly on the threshold, and then threw the door open. It slammed against the wall with a heavy thud.

The room flooded with light as the men entered, carrying lamps. With so much illumination, so many eyes, she didn't have a prayer.

Salem ground his teeth together, his hands opening and closing at his sides.

The men spread out across the cellar, clearly searching for something. The bloody minded one, Absalom, caught sight of

Ophelia huddled behind the cabinet. With an oath, he grabbed her by the arm and hauled her into the open.

"What are you doing down here?" the father demanded with icy ominousness.

Lie. Say something. Anything. Salem's teeth cut into his lips. Blood filled his mouth.

Ophelia exclaimed, "I wanted to know what it was you were hiding. I didn't know you were keeping *people* in *cages*!"

"Ophelia, why didn't you just do as you were told?" Benjamin hissed through his teeth.

"They're not people, they're monsters," Absalom said, spinning her to look at Salem and Addie. "They'd kill you as soon as look at you. You'd be a nice, tasty *snack* to a thing like that."

Addie tucked into a tight ball, her eyes huge in her face.

Ophelia's eyes met Salem's, full of desperate bravery.

No, don't, Salem wanted to tell her. *Just go along, agree with them, apologize! I can't reach you now....* He knew the kind of harm men could and would inflict in their anger. He knew it very well.

She shook her head, just the tiniest bit. "You mean they'd want to bleed me dry?" she snapped back at her brother. "How novel! How unlike everyone else in this family! I know what you were planning. Well, I won't let you. I'm never marrying *him*!" She leaned around Absalom to point at Lucas.

"Ophelia, I thought marriage was what you *wanted*," Ben said.

"Don't *lie* to me! I heard you all talking, planning to split up my inheritance! Selling me, like I was chattel! I was coming down here to find out what you'd been doing, and stop it before I left for good."

"When you marry, your money becomes your husband's," Ben said slowly, like he was explaining a concept to a child. "Of course Lucas and Father were discussing it."

"But in most cases the bride's family isn't given a cut," Ophelia snarled.

Harding scoffed. "She's lying. She's known the creatures were down here for some time." He stooped to pick up the bottle, lying forgotten on the floor. He opened it and sniffed. "You see? Blood. Just as I told you. That slattern maid wasn't lying."

Ophelia froze.

"She's been feeding them," Harding went on, twiddling the bottle in his hands. "The devil's handmaiden, as it were."

All four of them stared at her.

"How long has it been happening?" her father said stonily.

"We'll have to start over," Harding said to Benjamin. "If they were being fed, our conclusions are off. It will change healing rates, sanguinary regeneration periods...." He turned to the instruments on the table and reached for the long silver prod.

"All that ruined work...Ophelia, *why?*" Benjamin demanded, horrified.

Absalom shook her in his hold like a terrier shakes a rat. "Answer, you little bitch."

She recoiled, her eyes glancing from the wickedly sharp silver skewer to the vampires in the cages. She lifted her chin, her eyes finding Salem again. "'For I was hungry, and you gave me meat: I was thirsty, and you gave me drink: I was a stranger, and you took me in; naked, and you clothed me: I was sick, and you visited me: I was in prison, and you came to me. Verily I say unto you, inasmuch as you did it unto one of the least of these, you did it unto me.'"

Absalom let go of her arm and backhanded her.

Ophelia fell hard against the examination table, scrabbling to catch herself before she fell to the floor.

Salem recoiled as if he had been the one to take the blow. His blood ran hot, then cold as a guttural snarl escaped his lips.

"Little pious bitch," Absalom snarled. Ophelia couldn't avoid the fist that followed.

Salem threw himself against the bars as she fell to the ground, clutching her eye. He tested the integrity of the cage harder than he had when Addie had been on the table. He did his best to make the bars give, even as the silver burned welts into his skin, seared his flesh down to the muscle as it sapped his strength.

"Not the face," Harding commanded. "I don't want her looking like dog meat." He said in an aside, "I'll still marry her, but I expect a larger percentage of her trust. She's going to be a handful."

Ophelia lifted her eyes and looked past the four men standing in judgment over her.

What must she think of you, Salem's shadow thought scornfully, *scrabbling and snarling like an animal? Now she knows exactly what sort of fiend you are.*

Salem thrust his arm through the bars as far as it would go. If he could get a hold of one of them—if he could draw their attention away from her for just a moment—just a *moment*—

But they were too far. He could feel the silver leeching away the strength, just when he needed to be strong for her. If he couldn't defend, couldn't protect, what was the point of him? What was the use of this curse?

Couldn't stop Addie's torture. Couldn't stop the human girl's. Too weak, his shadow self spat. *This is your sentence. This is your recompense.*

Ophelia fingers twitched, stretched towards him. Then she pushed herself to her feet and stared at Harding, delivering her ultimatum like a queen. "I wouldn't marry you if you were the last man on earth."

He smiled nastily. "Feisty. I like that. I'll have the devil's own time making you mind." He licked his lips like he was looking forward to it. "But your willingness is neither wanted nor required."

"Reverend Anscombe would never perform a marriage—"

"Why would we marry in this backwater? We'll get a special license in London, and enough coin can grease any sticky wheels. There'll be some benefits to marrying me. I won't keep you in such a horrible house, for one."

"Ben! Please!" Ophelia begged.

"Ophelia, you've brought this on yourself," her brother said in a low voice. "If you hadn't interfered with these monsters—"

"They're not the monsters!" she yelled. "You are! All of you. I showed simple *compassion*—"

"A weakness inherent in women," the father said briskly. "I should've eradicated that from you years ago."

"That would require you to care. And you've never done that."

"You've been disloyal to the family!" Absalom snarled. He shoved her and sent her sprawling.

"The family has never been loyal to me!" Ophelia shrieked.

Absalom pulled back his foot and kicked.

Salem threw himself against the bars again. *That's it,* he swore. *Your death is mine.*

⊗

Harding finally made Absalom stop kicking Ophelia after she retched. The whole time during the beating she kept thinking, *praise God for the small mercy of my steel corset.* That was, when she could draw breath to think at all.

Ben had to carry her upstairs past servants hovering in their dressing gowns, having heard the shouting and screaming. Tears streamed down her face, but she couldn't sob. That hurt too badly.

At the door of her room, Blaze lunged at Ben, nearly getting a mouthful of trouser leg, and barked loudly at Nancy and everyone else that tried to help Ophelia undress. Ben finally slammed the door shut and locked it. She had to struggle out of her clothes alone.

Ophelia couldn't look at her face in the mirror. Neither could she meet her poor dog's eyes. Blaze kept pacing between her and the door, keeping a patrol for any intruders or those who wished her harm. But the harm had already occurred.

She peeled off everything down to her corset and chemise but had to pause and breathe and grit her teeth before she could manage the hooks. She eased herself down on the bed as she sought surcease from the pain in the darkness of dreams. The cats wound themselves around her and purred, and she let their fur soak up some of the tears as she fell into darkness. Every time her body would try to shift in sleep, Ophelia would wake up as the pain ascended, but the darkness always pulled her back under.

In dreams, Ophelia was young again, tossing and turning and crying out, trying to throw back the covers as her mother fought to keep them on as the fever raged and her leg ached, so heavy she couldn't move it, weighed down.

A cairn of rocks on her leg.

Her mother, shrieking at Ben *why weren't you watching her,* at Absalom *why would you do such a thing,* at her father *why won't you do something, anything!?* as Ophelia cried on the long gallery floor.

Absalom saying *watch this* as he twisted her leg wrong.

A heavy crunch on the bone.

She cried in her sleep at the memory.

Then she slid away from the horrible past, to a place that was soft and safe and quiet, except for someone cursing incoherently, but most of it was lost in the haze of pain.

"I'm going to make them pay," said the darkness, as a phantom hand stroked her hair. "I'm going to ruin them all. I'll have their blood for it, I swear to you. I'll make sure you're safe."

She turned her face into the hand as it tenderly touched her cheek, and the touch didn't hurt her eye. It didn't hurt at all. It was wondrously cool on her face, and she exhaled shakily, leaning into the sensation. She tried to reach for her comforter in turn, but her hand moved through the darkness without end, her phantom as ephemeral as cobwebs.

The last whispered words she heard echoed in the silence before the dream dissolved into shreds: "I'm not going to let him have you. You're mine."

Chapter Nineteen

❧

I t was a long day.

Her door was locked from the outside. Blaze lunged at anyone who tried to open her door, knowing instinctively that *someone* was responsible for her hurt, and it was his job to protect her. Nancy shrieked the first time she tried to bring a breakfast tray, and from the bed Ophelia heard the smash and clatter of crockery.

Finally, Ben had to call through the door for her to hold Blaze while he came in with the tray and to build up the fire. Since Ophelia knew she should eat, even though the thought of food made her stomach clench, she did it.

She sensed Ben standing there looking at her after he put the tray on her bedside table, but she kept her gaze—swollen and bruised as it was—trained on Blaze and the wall. "He shouldn't have done it," he finally said. "But you provoked him, Ophelia. And releasing the monsters—why? I don't think it's spite. Why?"

Eventually he went away. Ophelia's leg ached fiercely and so did her ribs and her face.... She slept fitfully. Sometimes she thought she felt vague impressions of a presence, someone trying to speak to her, stroking her hair, but it was through a long tunnel, or it was too hard to reach out.

In the midafternoon, after another silent tray delivery from Ben, she heard a carriage drive up to Renwick. But by the time she had clambered from bed and dragged herself to the window, the Glenwoods' gig was turning around in the downpour.

"Come back," she whispered, pressing her hand to the window.

But no one heard her.

Blaze pressed his nose to her knee and whined.

"It's...." The lie 'all right' stuck in her throat. She just hugged him instead. Her gaze fell on her trunk. Inside she had stashed the notebooks from the attics.

She hadn't read them yet.

Ophelia swept up the pile and staggered back to bed, rubbing her legs. Her bad leg ached, and the skin around the cuts and scrapes on her injured leg felt hot and tight. She opened the first journal to take her mind off the pain.

In the third journal she picked up, with a splitting spine and faded cloth bookmark pressed between the pages, she found a revelation.

> *Isaiah has thrown another volley of barbed accusations because of Ophelia Ivy's hair color. It has become a darling auburn in the months after her birth, unlike the boys' dark locks or my ash blonde. But I have said again that my Aunt Agnes was a redhead, and he is a scientist, he knows the hereditary traits better than I.... He has subsided again, but I do not like this.*
>
> *He eyes her with suspicion, trying to discern whether she is the cuckoo in his nest he believes. This is the third time. I worry it will not stop...I blame myself. I brought this on her, on us. I cannot deny there is a chance she is not Isaiah's daughter.*

The book fell from Ophelia's numb fingers, spine cracking

even further when it hit the floor. She had to scramble to find the right page as the words rang in her ears. *Not Isaiah's...?*

> *I can never speak the words aloud, for if I do, I will never stop searching her sweet face for more of his likeness. I do not want her to be Isaiah's. I want a last precious piece of him—something good.*
>
> *Absalom takes all his cues from his father, and even Ben is pulling away from me, aware of the tensions in the home that Isaiah always brings with him. And now Isaiah has hired Rivers, the new butler, who is entirely Isaiah's eyes and ears—I do not misunderstand. He is here to keep an eye on me when Isaiah returns to London.*
>
> *Wilhelmina understands, too. She has always known the man her son is—like her husband, an all-too-old-fashioned brute. Isaiah has found science an outlet for most of it. Most.*
>
> *She found me weeping over Ophelia's cradle after his hurtful words—I am not usually such a watering pot, but I still get attacks of the weeps, even now after her birth...far more than after Absalom and Benjamin's births. I am surrounded by a dark chasm that feels only a step away. But she put her hand on my shoulder and patted it. "I know you enjoy the running of the house, but we must endeavor to engage a housekeeper, and good sturdy nursemaids."*
>
> *She told me, when I asked why, that battlelines had been drawn, and we must make opening salvos to quickly stake claims on domains of women, and we needed good soldiers in the fight that would listen to my words, and not his.*
>
> *I think she knows. Or suspects. But all she did was wiggle one of the baby's plump feet.*

There the entry ended.

Ophelia reread the section three times, and then flipped through the rest of the journal, searching, searching—but she saw no other entries that alluded to her paternity.

Ophelia sat heavily at her vanity and stared into the mirror.

The auburn hair.... was this why her father had hated her? Not her gender, not the money, but that he believed she was not his?

Was she truly not his daughter?

She stared at the shape of her face, the color of her eyes in the mirror.

"Desmond, forgive me. I should not have stayed."

Was that her father's name?

If Isaiah Shaw was not her father, then she did not have to honor him. She didn't have to obey him. He did not deserve anything from her—not her inheritance, not her love, not her respect, nothing.

Through the ache in her leg, the pain in her heart, she smiled at Blaze and the cats. "Don't worry. We're leaving tonight."

Because her maybe-family didn't know about the lockpicks.

⁂

Salem was biding his time. Saving his strength. The men had not done any cutting today, too busy discussing what was to be done with Ophelia, what her thoughts had been upon traipsing down to the basement. Of course, they hadn't said this in the lab. But they were somewhere close, and he could pick out the gist of the conversation from the most strident voices.

Salem cursed himself for a fool repeatedly. He could not reach Ophelia, or not well, through the dreamscape. The connection had thinned, the blood link worn out. He had wasted it, even though he knew it was reckless, but he had wanted—*damn* it! He slammed his hand into the silver bars, regardless of the burn.

They had *dared*—they had *hurt* her—his thoughts shorted out in the wake of his incoherent rage. It was too much. She had wanted to set him free....

A shining beacon in the dark. So beautiful...so alive. And they had dared touch her.

No. no. she was his. His light. He would get them out of here, and he would take Ophelia, too. They had forfeited their claim on her. They wouldn't be able to harm her if he took her away.

He could keep her safe.

Addie was curled into a tight ball, silent and still. She had railed at him the night before, hiccupping with fear as the scent of blood lingered in the air. "Is Ophelia going to be all right? Is she dying? Do humans die from that?"

"She wasn't hurt badly enough for that. They won't let her die," he had told her.

"Salem, you should've listened! You should've promised!" she had said tearfully. "You could've helped her, protected her!"

"Don't you think I *know* that?" he had exclaimed.

It's your fault. You're to blame. You failed, his shadow self said.

I'll make them pay, he thought now. He'd exact recompense for this, cut for cut, drop for drop. He'd have their throats opened. Blood spilled covered all sins, did it not? He'd cover all their sins in their blood and drink the rest, and then Ophelia would be safe. With him.

Salem felt for his connection to Faelad. It had enough vitality for one more connection. To hell with more sleuthing. Once it was full dark, once they were asleep in their beds tonight—then would his vengeance reign. Every drop of blood, he'd measure out. They'd answer for all of them.

Chapter Twenty

"I'll be back later for your tray," Ben said, dropping off Ophelia's dinner as the sun set below the horizon.

She nodded listlessly, staring at the wall.

"You don't have to take it so hard," he said, hovering in the doorway. "You're getting what you wanted, Ophelia."

Blaze growled, low and ugly.

Ben's lips thinned. He pulled the door shut.

As soon as the key turned in the lock, Ophelia threw back the covers and rolled off the bed, her ribs protesting the motion. After taking a moment to catch her breath, she shook out the skirts of the brown frock she had hidden under covers pulled up to her chin (after painstakingly donning it in slow stages). She had loaded the pockets with all the necessities—extra handkerchiefs, lemon drops, money, and lockpicks. She stuffed a slice of beef into a roll and put that in as well, wrapped in a handkerchief. The small packed portmanteau she nudged out from under the bed with her foot.

Then she pulled the large picnic basket from its place atop her wardrobe and blew off the dust. This was typically what she used to ferry puppies or cats to new homes because the lid could be tied down. It would have to fit all three of her cats tonight. She sent up a prayer of thanks that they usually got along with each other, even if they would not be happy about being in the basket. She lined it with a blanket and tipped Tibby in first, the easiest. Then she put in Sheba. By that time, Nevada had had time to eye the situation and decide she was not happy, so Ophelia had to hobble around her room, wincing at the ache from her cuts and scrapes, because Nevada kept oozing away from her behind chairs and curtains.

Finally, Ophelia cornered her under her vanity and snatched her up. She put the protesting cat into the basket and latched the lid. She would have to walk fast to keep the cats from starting to scream and alerting servants.

No one had thought to confiscate her dark lantern. Ben had just left it on her desk with a shake of his head. It still had enough lamp oil in it for one more night.

She hoped.

Ophelia swiped her sleeve over her forehead, feeling hot and achy. She winced as she accidentally scraped her black eye and a bolt of pain went through her head.

She tested lifting the basket and groaned at the weight. She'd need both hands.

Quickly, she opened the portmanteau and emptied it onto the bed and threw everything in it that she had so carefully folded and packed into a drawstring sack and threaded that over one arm. Then she used a strip of cloth to tie the dark lantern around her waist. She wouldn't need it until she ventured into the dark. Then she gathered up Blaze's lead and applied her lockpicks to the door.

"Shhh," she whispered to Blaze and the cats as the lock clicked. She cautiously poked her head out the door and looked both ways down the hallway. She saw no one.

"Now don't you dare trip me." She heaved the basket up and

shut her door. Then she made for the grand staircase as quick as she could force her legs to move.

It wasn't her first choice. She had planned to make her way to the far end of the west wing to lower the chance of anyone hearing them exit, but it was clear her leg might not hold up that long. Plus, she'd need to get the cats out of the house as quickly as possible before they alerted anyone. She eased her way down the stairs, on the alert for any servants not serving in the dining room or below stairs having their own supper. She peered over the carved balustrade before venturing to the main floor. The ancestral portraits stared disapprovingly into her back as she descended. *Betraying the Shaws! Leaving Renwick!*

And so, what? Off with my head? Ophelia thought as she hefted her burden. The old broadsword was barely visible above the unlit fireplace. *I may not be a Shaw after all, so what business is it of yours?*

Her only regret was abandoning the house, which did not deserve its masters.

When she reached the bottom, she had to set the basket full of cats (who were starting to rumble ominously) down and hold onto the newel post for a minute until her legs stopped shaking. Blaze whined, looking at her confused.

"Just a minute," she forced through white lips as she forced her legs to move to the heavy front door and unlock it. She did not need the lockpicks for this door, thankfully; the key stayed in it. She heaved the door open and admitted a blast of frigid air.

Ophelia clicked her tongue and sent Blaze out the door, his lead dragging down the stairs, and hauled the basket out after him. She took the entrance stairs one teeth-gritted step at a time. She set the basket at the base of the shrubbery that surrounded the front of the house and then caught Blaze's lead up and tied it to the hedge. "Stay," she said through chattering teeth, dumping down her sack beside the basket. "I'll be right back, I've got to.... I'll be back. With my coat. And a horse. Stay quiet."

The cats' growls had subsided a little as they realized that in the cold, they did not mind huddling together. Blaze whined and barked a little as she turned away. She took hold of his muzzle and held his eye. "Sit. Stay. Shh. Quiet." He subsided, clearly not happy about it but obedient.

Ophelia pulled the door shut behind her and paused, listening. She didn't hear anything from the dining room or the servants' hall in the east wing. She untied the lantern from her waist and lit it with shaking hands, then began the familiar route to the west wing and the cellars.

The key was of course gone from its brick, but she opened the lantern's shutter wide and worked on the lock's tumblers with dogged determination until it clicked. The pain was eroding her fear and hyper-attention to noise; she dragged the door open and limped inside with only a minute of worry. She had felt cold outside, but now she felt hot all over.

"Ophelia?" Addie called when the lantern light illuminated the lab. "What are you doing down here? The sun just set. Are you all right?" Her eyes widened at the sight of her. "Oh, your poor eye!"

Salem stared at her intently, a light burning in his eyes. "Are you feverish?" he demanded.

"No," she said, blinking.

"You're flushed. And what's the matter with your leg?"

"I scraped it. I told you."

His eyes narrowed. "You said 'never mind about the blood.' Did you *do* anything about the scrape?"

"Yes," she said, waving the strange concern away. "Listen. I'm leaving Renwick. Like I said last night, I will let you out if—" she swayed on her feet and caught herself on the lab tables. Salem's hands twitched, and he balled them into fists. "If you promise not to harm anyone in the house," she finished in a rush.

"I promise," Addie said immediately. "We promise, don't we, Salem?"

Ophelia looked at him, waiting.

His brows drew down low over his eyes, as they swept over

her. He grimaced, but through gritted teeth said, "I give you my word I will harm no one in the house."

Ophelia let out a breath she hadn't know she was holding. "Good." She glanced around the lab. "I don't suppose you know where the keys are?"

"They took them when they left," Addie said.

Ophelia swallowed a groan. "All right. Let me see if I can pick the shackles first," she said. She wanted the time they were free under Renwick's roof to be as short as possible. To reduce temptation.

Addie obligingly brought her feet as close to the bars as she could. Ophelia cautiously approached, lockpicks in hand, and inserted the tools into the silver restraints. It took her a minute to learn the insides of the lock, but then she released the manacles. Addie gave a glad cry and cast the silver away from her, clutching her ankles and rubbing the mottled, weeping skin. The padding Ophelia had fashioned for her was stained with dark blood and fluid.

Ophelia turned her attention to Salem, and abruptly realized how strangely intimate feet were. One never saw unclothed feet unless you were children going barefoot outdoors, and sometimes not even then. But Salem's pale gray feet were bare, and in worse shape than Addie's—Ophelia hadn't had time to make him padding like she had for Addie. He just had his trouser cuffs and ripped cloth from what was probably his shirttails. She kept her eyes on the keyhole, moving the tumblers with her lockpicks until they clicked open.

She moved on to the locks on the cages.

Addie crept out hesitantly from her enclosure of silver, and Ophelia discovered, with a jolt of surprise, that Addie was actually taller than her by a few inches. She shook the fuzziness from her head. *One more lock.*

After one more long minute that felt like years, the lock opened with a click, and she swung the silver door open wide.

Salem stepped out of the door, and before Ophelia realized it, he handed the lantern off to Addie and swept her off her feet and into his arms. He somehow made her feel like a feather, and she clutched his shoulders in reflexive alarm. "Put me down!"

"No. You're coming with me."

⚜

Once she was in his arms, the wild thing inside him subsided. She was safe. She was safe with him. Salem would make sure nothing ever happened to her again.

"What?" Ophelia gasped, wriggling in his grasp. "No, I'm leaving, and you have to leave too! Put me down."

"You're bleeding," Salem said flatly. "And I can smell infection. That flush didn't just appear. You're sick." He jerked his chin and began to walk through the lab. "Come on, Addie."

Addie followed right on his heels, swinging the light curiously from her fingertips.

"I'll get better at Marie-Claire's," Ophelia insisted. "Let go!"

He stepped through the lab's doorway and inspected the passage and stair out of the cellars before ascending the stair. "A human's house?" He scoffed. "No. They can't protect you there."

"I don't need protection," she protested.

He stopped halfway up the stairs and stared at her. She gulped in the sheen of lantern light when she met his uncompromising gaze. "Clearly you do," he ground out. "Your own brother beat you, and none of them did *anything*." His arms tightened around her unconsciously, and she winced. "What?" he asked immediately, relaxing his grip. "What is it?"

"My ribs. My leg," she said, pressing her lips together.

He bent his head, inhaling the thread of pain and blood, plus encroaching miasma of infection. "We can fix that." He started climbing the stairs again.

She froze in his grasp. "No! I don't want—"

"Breathe. I wasn't suggesting what you're thinking." Salem reached the main floor of the house and glanced around. "Which way is out?"

"You don't understand; I *can't* leave with you! I need to get my animals!"

"Addie can help you get your animals. Which way?"

"At the front of the house. But everyone is having dinner; we have to be *quiet*!"

"We can do that. Addie, shut the lantern."

"How will we see?" Ophelia asked frantically.

"I can see. Just tell me the route." He followed her resigned whispered directions through the west wing to the front of the house through darkened hallways and empty rooms. He and Addie made no sound as they traversed Renwick's halls, moving from the unused portion of the house to the livable great hall. They paced across the large space that had once been the heart of the house in another period and made it to the front door.

Addie pushed open the heavy door easily and descended the steps, and Salem followed.

The dog tied to the hedge against the house looked caught between rushing forward to greet his mistress and growling at their appearance.

"It's all right, Blaze," Ophelia said, reaching out a reassuring hand.

Blaze pressed his muzzle to her hand and whined, but still attempted to put himself between his mistress and danger. But he didn't seem to think that was Salem.

With a glad cry, Addie straightened from where she'd been inspecting the unhappy basket full of cats.

Etienne stepped out of the darkness of the trees with a huge gray wolf at his side.

Addie threw herself at him, wrapping her arms around his neck, and Etienne caught her handily, Salem noted. He nodded to both of them.

Ophelia froze in his arms. "Is that a wolf?" she asked in a thin voice.

"He's with us," Salem said. He could feel the heat under her skin increasing.

"Would you put me down, please?" she hissed through her teeth.

"No."

"Put me *down*, Salem!" She started wriggling in his arms to get free. There was no way in hell she'd ever be able to break his hold, but she'd exhaust herself. Salem sighed and set her down at the bottom of the stairs but kept a hand on her arm. A good thing, too, because she wobbled, even as she tried to bolt away from him.

"You can barely stand," Salem said, "And you want to run out into the dark forest with three vampires and a werewolf behind you?" He snaked an arm around her waist to hold her upright.

"Werewolf?" she gasped.

"Yes. Good to see you, Etienne. Thank you for passing on my message, Faelad. Perfect timing."

The dog weaved in between them and the wolf, pressing himself against Ophelia, and Salem felt her wince.

She stiffened again, staring at the wolf. "You mean that—that our groundskeeper—"

"He would introduce himself, but that would take several minutes, and we are in the presence of ladies," Etienne said, tipping his hat to Ophelia as Addie clung to his arm. "How do you do, *mademoiselle*."

She stared at him, wide-eyed.

"We thought we would have to break you out, *cher ami*," Etienne said. "I am delighted that is not the case." He sent a strongly inquiring glance from Ophelia to Salem, but Salem ignored it.

"Where are we?"

"Not far at all from your abode. We can be there before sunrise."

"I thought you would return to London," Salem said, surprised.

"*Nom de Dieu, non*. Addie needs a good meal—the both of you do, of a certainty, and to rest in safety a while before travel. Besides, did you discover the culprit of this scheme?" Etienne demanded.

"We made progress, but—"

Salem froze, as did the rest of the vampires and Faelad. They all slowly turned to stare at the far side of the house just as Absalom, her scum of a brother, came around the corner and caught sight of them.

He inhaled, his eyes widening in shock. He pushed away from the hedges to run, or sound an alarm.

Your death is mine.

Salem grabbed the pistol he knew Etienne had in his jacket. Pivoted, aimed, and fired.

The man dropped like a tree. They all heard his heart stop.

Bloody-minded men meet a bloody end, Salem thought with satisfaction.

He turned back to Ophelia who was staring at him, face white.

"He wasn't in the house," Salem said with finality.

Chapter Twenty-One

Ophelia swam to wakefulness as someone hummed "I'll Take You Home Again Kathleen," and then segued into "All the Way My Savior Leads Me." The tune sounded sweet and lovely to her ears, and she stretched, her eyes opening. It seemed abnormally dark in her room—had the fire gone out? And the bed felt—different—

She realized three things at once. This was not her bedroom. The humming was coming closer. And her legs didn't hurt anymore.

Her eyes widened but found no light in the darkness. She attempted to push herself up in the narrow bed, reaching for something, anything—

The tune ceased. "Ophelia! You're awake! Oh, I'm so glad!"

Addie?

The events of the night before rushed back. *Was* it the same night? How long had she been asleep?

"Addie? Is there a light?" Ophelia asked in a small voice.

"Oh, that's right, human eyes are different. Let me find the lamp," Addie said.

"I've got it, Addie."

Ophelia started violently at the sound of Salem's voice so close to her. A moment later, a spark caught, and he lit her very own dark lantern and set it on a crate beside her cot. She blinked to adjust, and then peered into the shadows at him. "What are you doing there?" she demanded.

"Looking after you," he said easily.

"In the dark? You didn't have to skulk."

He laughed, his eyes catching the light and sparking gold. He leaned forward on the spindly chair and rested his elbows on his knees, loosely clasping his hands together. "How are you feeling?"

"Fine," Ophelia said, distracted. He had removed his coat and rolled his shirtsleeves up to his elbows, and what's more, he looked...*well*. His face was no longer gaunt to the point of starvation—pale flesh covered his cheekbones and arms the way it should and filled out his frame. He looked *healthy,* his skin no longer gray and decrepit. All signs of burns and wounds had disappeared.

In fact, she thought to herself, heart skipping a beat, *if I met him under the full lights of an evening's ballroom, I might not even be able to tell he was a vampire—except for the constant oddness of his eyes, and the fangs that appear when he speaks.* "You look ...better."

"Thank you, I feel better," Salem said.

After staring at him a moment longer—a *long* moment, Ophelia realized with chagrin, she shook herself and stared around the small chamber. "What is the meaning of this? Where am I?"

"'This'?" he repeated, raising an eyebrow.

"You kidnapped me."

"Did I?"

"You know you did! What else would you call it?"

He spread his hands open idly. "Absconded with?"

She stared at him darkly.

He met her glower without flinching. "Your leg is infected and was sickening you. Your family harmed you, prepared to steal your inheritance, and sold you to their conspirator. Your friend could not have helped you."

"You don't know that."

"As impressive as this century has been, it is still sadly lacking on the subject of women's rights and autonomy outside of their husbands and fathers. You would've had no recourse."

"And so naturally, you abducted me."

He gestured at the room. "Comparatively, your accommodations are much better than the ones we received. Do you see a cage?"

She swallowed.

"I did what was necessary," Salem said with finality.

She lifted her chin. "Was shooting Absalom necessary?"

He stilled, his face hardening into a blank mask. "He hurt you."

"He was my brother."

"That makes it *worse*," he hissed, drawing back from her, his eyes flashing ruby in the shadows.

Ophelia's hands tightened in the bedclothes. "Is he dead?"

"I don't miss," Salem said in a low voice.

She stared down at her hands, unseeing. Absalom had been her tormentor, her bogeyman for years. But he was her oldest brother, too. The strange grief that she felt...it was grief that she could not grieve him properly, could not find the sisterly emotion to miss him.

And guilt, too. Because a small part of her was glad that she wouldn't have to hate and fear him anymore.

"I always thought my limp was from an illness," she whispered. "I didn't remember. Absalom broke my leg."

Salem's face hardened into stone. "He didn't deserve the death I gave him."

Would she be a bad sister if she agreed?

"Ophelia! I made some soup for you!" Addie said, returning to the beam of lamplight carrying a tray. She wore a neat lavender gown and pinafore, and her dark hair was tidied on top of her head in a braided crown. Her face had some color to it—or more color than its prior deathly pallor, and her cheeks were round and smiling. She and Salem had both obviously partaken of some sustenance.

Ophelia shoved that thought away to examine later, as she felt stretched to the limit.

Addie held the tray out. "You fed us, and now we can repay the favor."

Ophelia pressed her lips together before they trembled, swamped by the unexpected emotion. Salem silently helped her sit up and adjusted the pillows behind her as Addie set the tray on her lap. "Did you make this?" Ophelia asked thickly.

"I was a good cook when I was alive. I don't get the chance to do it much now. I hope I got it right," Addie said, twisting her hands in her pinafore. "Etienne helped me set up the tripod over the fire outside."

"You cooked this outside?" Fascinated, Ophelia lifted the spoon and sipped. "It's delicious, Addie," she said, and it was. Despite everything, it was like her stomach had come to life and demanded sustenance.

Addie smiled, pleased. She sat on a low cushion stool while Ophelia slowly ate.

"What happened while I was asleep?" she asked in between bites.

Salem glanced at the dark archway that led from the small chamber. "Faelad went out during daylight and got food for you, and found some herbs for the tea we managed to get down your throat and the compresses we made for your bruises and the infection in your leg."

"It was nasty and smelled," Addie said as she leaned back and waggled her feet in front of her. She wore a pair of slippers that looked worn and too large for her feet.

"Those aren't yours, are they?" Ophelia asked.

"No, they're Salem's. Now that the sun has set, Etienne has gone to get me better shoes."

"Addie," Salem said in a muffled voice.

"What? He offered," Addie said.

Ophelia glanced between them, trying to figure out why Salem was dragging his hand down his face. "Etienne was the other vampire, yes?"

Addie nodded, her expression turning coy.

"You should've seen her," Salem said. "I handed over my slippers—which are *perfectly serviceable*, thank you— because she said it wouldn't be proper to go barefoot. She stared at them with the most woebegone face and said they weren't the right size, and thirty years out of date besides. A perfectly cast lure." He shook his head.

Addie patted her hair. "I did my hair. Does it look all right?"

"You don't have a hand mirror here?" Ophelia asked. "Wherever here is."

Both Salem and Addie looked away from her. "Vampires can't see themselves in mirrors," Salem said in a low voice. "It's the silver in the backing. And having them close by—all silver, really —isn't very comfortable."

Ophelia lifted her hand instinctually to her throat. The small silver cross still hung from her neck. "You mean it hurts, like touching silver burns you?"

"Your necklace is fine," Salem said, his eyes dropping to her throat. "It's not a lot. More like..." he groped for a comparison. "That little itch that means you need to sneeze."

Ophelia's shoulders slumped in relief.

Addie was still chewing at her lip. It struck Ophelia that Addie hadn't been able to see herself as she did her hair. Hadn't been able to see herself for years. "I think you did a wonderful job," Ophelia said. "You look lovely."

Addie brightened and patted her hair again. "Really?"

"Yes, you look wonderfully well. I'm glad you aren't—aren't—"

"Thirsty?" Salem asked sotto voce.

"I am glad you are healed and healthy," Ophelia said firmly, and inserted the spoon—made of tin—into her mouth to change the subject.

As she finished the bowl of soup, Salem disappeared out the dark archway and reappeared with a cup of dubious-smelling tea.

"What is that?" she said, eyeing the chipped china.

"A decidedly potent brew, but you need to keep drinking this. It's to keep the fever down and the infection at bay. We had a devil of a time getting your scrapes clean."

"I did that bit," Addie said. "It wouldn't have been proper for Salem to help."

Salem looked a bit put out at that. "I didn't know saving lives had societal rules around it."

"The scrapes were on her legs," Addie said severely. "Gentlemen can't look at a lady's legs."

"I am sorry to inform you that I am not a gentleman, and do know of the existence of the feminine ankle, and yea, even the feminine knee," Salem said dryly.

"But I had to put her nightie on, and that is definitely not proper," Addie insisted.

Ophelia glanced down at herself. She hadn't even noticed she was wearing the nightgown from her sack of belongings. She took a cautious sip. "Oh!" She made a horrible face. "What *is* this?"

"I have no idea, Ophelia. I expect it's a proper witch's brew, but Faelad assures me that the stuff works, so you have to keep drinking it." Salem shrugged. "Or you could drink a cup of tea with a few drops of blood in it."

She set the cup down on the saucer with a clack. "*Your* blood?"

Salem resumed his previous position, elbows resting indolently on his knees. "It will help you heal. It won't do anything else to you."

"Salem wanted to heal you while you were asleep, but I told him that was a bad idea. So he had to wait," Addie said.

"Tattler," Salem said.

"Thank you for waiting," Ophelia said, taking a bracing gulp of the tea. She really could not pinpoint what on earth was in it, but she'd take it over purposefully drinking blood—and vampire blood at that. She didn't care for the thought. Not unless the occasion was dire enough to warrant it, which this was not.

Salem glared. "Don't thank me. I had to sit here and watch you sweat and thrash as the infection warred with your body without doing anything to help. It was hell."

Ah. Perhaps her injuries had been more troublesome than she thought. "Thank you anyway." She reached out and took his hand. "I don't feel much besides dull aches now."

He stared down at his hand in hers with an intense look on his face, and she felt something inside her flutter.

"Where are my animals?" she said, searching for a new topic.

"The cats are hunting the mice, I think," Addie said. "Faelad took the dog out to do his business and have a walk around. Etienne said it was to get it used to him. They have to establish pack ranking or something."

"Because...he's a werewolf. Right," Ophelia said, her spoon rattling against the dish. She sat up straighter. "You never answered my question. Where are we? The walls look like...."

"Earth," Salem said. "And stone, for support. You're in my dwelling place." He smiled wryly. "It's been a long time since anyone alive has been in it."

Ophelia stared around in shock. "How long was I asleep?"

"Only a day."

"How did we get here so fast?"

"Well, it turns out we're neighbors," he said, pleased. "The locals think it a fairy fort and stay away lest they disappear for a hundred years." Salem increased the lanternlight. In the stronger light, Ophelia could tell the room they were in was roughly round, with stacks of books against the walls, and rugs on the ground. A glance up at the ceiling told her it was corbelled stone and had the mark of ages on it.

"Wait. Is *this* Hob's Howe?" It was a much-avoided area of Yorkshire, twenty miles or so from Renwick, thought to be deeply haunted by a hobgoblin who guarded the door to Fairy and snatched away any who came too close.

Salem nodded, the corner of his mouth turning up.

She stared at him in astonishment. She had been spirited from a gothic novel and into— "You mean to tell me *this* is Fairyland?"

"Fairyland with the glamour stripped away, perhaps," Salem said dryly. "To reveal it's only a barrow mound, the resting place of the dead." He smiled. "Those that walk and those who do not."

"The dead king is in the chamber next door!" Addie said brightly. "He's just bones now. But there is some fairy gold."

Ophelia blinked. She stared down at the tray. "Does this count as having eaten fairy food?"

Salem laughed. "We'll see, won't we?"

She looked up and met his eyes dancing with mischief. It pried a laugh from her in spite of herself. "You're not keeping me for a hundred years."

"You never know," he said lightly. "Some humans found Fairyland so desirable they stayed."

"Or they fell in love with the fairy queen!" Addie said.

Ophelia gulped.

"I don't know why you never invited me before, Salem," Addie continued. "It's nice! Cozy."

"It is cozy, which is a reason why I thought you wouldn't like it. You enjoy the sights."

"I can try new things," Addie objected, collecting the dishes on the empty tray. "Etienne would have brought me."

"Did I hear my name?" The impeccably dressed blond man stepped into the room and doffed his hat.

"Etienne!" Addie bounded over to him. "You're back!"

"Yes, I searched high and low for shoes worthy of our Addie

and lo, I have found them." He produced a box from behind him with a flourish. Addie squealed and immediately dropped to the stool to put on the pair of soft gray boots, very fashionable and probably immensely comfortable.

"Very good to see you awake, mademoiselle," he added, shooting Ophelia a smile that included a wink of fang.

"Thank you," she said. "I'm Ophelia. We met last night, and I—"

"It was a rushed moment, courtesy of your unscheduled departure," he acknowledged.

Were they upset she had disrupted their escape attempt? "I'm sorry—"

"No, no, I am all in favor of your disruption of our friend Salem. He needs this chaos in his afterlife. Allow me to introduce myself. *Je m'appelle Etienne Flambeau*," he said, and bowed to her, colorless eyes shining at her over the pair of pince-nez clipped to his nose. "An ironic name for a vampire, no? *Enchanté, mademoiselle.*"

Salem made a rude noise.

"I should've introduced you before," Addie said, standing and lifting her skirts to peer down at the boots. "Etienne is my friend from London; he helped Salem find me. He's wonderful." She beamed at him and fluttered her eyelashes. "How do the boots look?" She turned in a circle, modeling them.

Etienne turned his attention back to Addie—but Ophelia got the feeling he had always been aware of her as she put on his gift. "Beautiful, *ma chère.*"

Addie lit up like a star.

"What were you speaking of when I arrived?" Etienne said.

"Salem's house. I said you would've brought me to visit if he had invited us. You would've, wouldn't you?" Addie said.

Etienne cast a highly skeptical look around the small room. "Why you would have wanted to visit this hole in the ground, I cannot tell, Addie, but of course I would have escorted you if Salem had bothered to extend an invitation, as is polite."

Salem made another rude noise. "You come into *my* house and insult me?"

"It is not a house," Etienne said flatly, brushing the front of his coat. "It is a hole in the ground. It is made of *dirt*."

"Well, ashes to ashes, dust to dust," Salem shrugged.

"Not *yet*," Etienne said firmly.

Ophelia felt a wave of tiredness wash over her, full of the meal and from perhaps the noxious healing tincture. She covered her mouth and yawned.

It did not escape Etienne's notice. "Come Addie, you should try the fit to see if I guessed right." He extended his arm to her, and she took it. "We will walk along the passage a little."

"You should get some sleep," Salem told Ophelia, standing and taking the tray from her.

"But I want to wait for Blaze," Ophelia said, even as she fought another yawn. "He's going to be confused—I don't want him to be worried...."

Salem's expression clearly said, *you're worried about the* dog? But all he said was, "I'll find Faelad."

Ophelia did not have to wait very long, which was a good thing because her eyelids were fighting against the oncoming tide of sleep, before Salem returned with Blaze and Faelad, who still looked as strange and frowning as the last time she had seen him. As a human, anyway. She did not know whether he had been frowning as a wolf the night before. Faelad held Blaze on his lead, and the dog strained for Ophelia.

She held out her hands to Blaze. The scowling man released the lead and the dog bounded for the cot, wagging his tail madly. Ophelia rubbed his head and ears and cooed to him. "Hello, have you been a good boy, Blaze? Have you? Sit, sit."

The dog obediently sat and rested his head on her leg.

"I'm sorry things have been confusing. Have you been good

for Salem and—Faelad?" she said, realizing she was unsure if that was the man's first or last name.

Blaze thumped his tail on the ground.

"Thank you for looking after Blaze," she said hesitantly. "I'm glad to meet you. Again."

The man gave a curt nod and disappeared with alacrity down the passage.

"I don't know if he likes it down here," Salem said, watching him go with a thoughtful frown.

Blaze whined.

"It's all right," Ophelia assured him, trying to cover a yawn at the same time. "I'm fine." She slumped down against the pillows, and felt Salem adjust them behind her. "Salem?"

He paused. "Yes?"

"How long am I to stay here?"

It was a long moment before he began moving again. "Until you're better. Until...."

"Until what?" she said, her eyelids drooping.

Silence.

Then, "Until I know you'll be safe."

She struggled to open her eyes and stared up at him in shock.

He bent down to her and ran the back of his fingers down her cheek. "I want you safe too," he whispered.

Chapter Twenty-Two

W hen Ophelia was safely asleep, Salem exited the souterrain and found Faelad standing a few paces away from the entrance, staring up at the moon.

"Thank you for your assistance," Salem said. "And for the escort back here. I did not expect... That is, your debt to me is discharged."

"I did naught," Faelad growled. "The lass did that, it seems."

An odd, hot sensation occurred in the vicinity of Salem's chest when he thought of Ophelia descending to the bowels of hell to release them—not once, but twice.

"Still. I appreciate the help. Consider us square."

"And what are you going to do with her?" Faelad asked as Salem turned away.

"Make sure she recovers," Salem said shortly. "When do you return to London?" *And why haven't you already gone?*

"Soon."

"What's keeping you? It can't be the accommodations." Though he had to admit, for the first time in years, he did not view the souterrain as merely a hole in the ground where he stored his books and passed his daylight hours. Ophelia's wonder and delight at being inside a fairy fort had given it a rosier, cozy perspective. Or maybe it was just Ophelia that made the hole feel more like a home.

Faelad pinned him with a warning gaze. "She doesn't belong here with you. Only grief will come of this."

"What—you don't know what you're talking about," Salem snarled.

"You can't keep her here."

Salem's hands clenched into fists. "Don't tell me what I can and can't do, old man."

Faelad shot a dark look at him. "You just remember that I warned you." He stalked off into the underbrush, yanking his shirt over his head. Going to run off his frustration in his fur, no doubt. Damn it, what business was it of his if Ophelia stayed?

Salem went back inside and nearly smacked into Etienne, which did not improve his temper.

"Ah, I was just coming to find you, my friend," Etienne said.

"When do you and Addie return to London?" Salem asked abruptly.

Etienne looked at him and raised a sardonic brow. "Whenever Addie wishes to go. I do not anticipate it will be soon."

"Why?" Salem asked, baffled.

"Because Addie wishes to spend time with you," Etienne said with pitying condescension.

"Oh, right. She mentioned that." Salem frowned.

"You do not have to look so puzzled. You are decent company when you are not trying to push your friends away."

Salem opened his mouth as many thoughts vied for first airing, among them the instinct to refute the statement as ridiculous or urge Etienne to take Addie back to a place more suitable for her. To his shock, what came out was, "I don't deserve friends."

The silence was horribly deafening.

"Ah. Are you more upset about what happened to Addie, or what you did to Renata?" Etienne finally asked.

"Both, most days," Salem choked out.

"I will not speak for Addie. But Salem—your Maker was evil. Renata's destruction was no loss. But you did not have to take that burden on yourself. We would have helped you. We *wanted* to help you."

"I had to take the chance when I saw it," he insisted.

"You mean you did not trust us enough to help you carry out the plan we devised. And now you do not trust us enough to let us in."

"That's not—I don't—"

Etienne eyed him skeptically over his pince-nez.

"Don't give me that look!"

"What look," Etienne said, still giving it.

Salem growled. "Go polish your stupid useless spectacles and leave me alone."

I trust plenty! He thought, stalking away down the tunnel. Weren't they here, in his space? What bigger expression of trust was there? He asked when they were to return to London because they belonged there, didn't they? He wanted what was best for them! And Faelad, having the nerve to tell him Ophelia didn't belong with him! Didn't Salem know that better than anyone?

Mine! The wild thing inside him that only knew hunger howled. *Mine mine mine!*

Yes, keep her here, where you'll be sure to ruin her or drain her dry. What a wonderful plan, his shadow self laughed. *You know you can't be trusted with anything delicate. You destroy everything you touch.*

Salem paused halfway down the hallway and leaned against the wall, passing a hand over his eyes. His hand shook.

He had forgotten how pernicious illness could be. The hours that Ophelia spent sweating out the infection and tossing and turning with fever were the longest he could recall in all his two hundred odd years of existence.

He had been much closer to feeding Ophelia his blood than Addie made it sound. He was prepared to give her as much as he could make her swallow if it would only stop her pain. Only Addie's firm insistence that Ophelia wouldn't like it and he needed to ask first held him back. His shadow voice had bombarded him with the thought that if he didn't, Salem had as good as killed her himself, and waiting was merely torture for her. But she had pulled through. And seeing Ophelia's reaction earlier, he knew Addie had been in the right.

He just hated how near a thing the decision had been.

It wasn't a human thing, drinking blood. It clearly marked the barrier between them. She was not of his world. Indeed, she could never belong with that darkness.

He just wanted to cling to her light for a while longer.

She would never willingly become what he was—God forbid! Who would? But humans, unless stolen as blood thralls and used until they died or were turned, were forbidden knowledge of vampires. Were, in fact, killed for it.

And if Rupert finds out.... his shadow self whispered.

He won't, Salem insisted. *He won't. Addie and Etienne will keep it secret. I will keep it secret. Faelad hates most vampires anyway. And Ophelia, if we make her see the danger to her, will say nothing.*

But her father and brothers were another matter.

Brother.

Salem's lip curled. He could not bring himself to be sorry. He had shown the devil more mercy than he deserved; especially when Salem had longed to have his blood in his teeth and make it last. Make it *slow*.

But the rest...they could not be allowed to return to London and resume hunting for isolated vampires to continue their experiments.

He couldn't return Ophelia before they had been dealt with. He must keep her safe.

But how was he to deal with them *and* keep her safe at the same time?

Plus he still had not found the damned leak.

Salem groaned.

"What's the matter, Salem?" Addie asked, emerging from the chamber where Ophelia slept.

He straightened. "Has she woken?"

"No." Addie laughed. "She just got to sleep, silly." She moved toward him and wrapped her arms around his waist. "You didn't answer my question."

His hands came up to rest on her shoulders. "Nothing's wrong."

"That's a lie. It's always something with you."

"I feel like I should be offended by that."

"Not if it's true," she said sweetly. "What do you think Ophelia would like to eat when she wakes? There's always more soup but maybe it would be better to have something substantial —Etienne said he would get me what I need to cook but you don't have any cookbooks here and my head is better tonight but still fuzzy—"

"I think Ophelia will like whatever you make," Salem said, patting her shoulder. "You are the *artiste*. I bow to your wisdom."

Addie squeezed him again, hard. "Thank you."

The rush of affection took him by surprise. Carried on its wave, he dropped a kiss on her forehead. "Always."

Perhaps it would not be so bad to have Addie here for another night or so after all.

Chapter Twenty-Three

※

Ophelia woke to Blaze's head on her hip and a pressing need. She struggled to sit up.

Blaze got to his feet and whined, his tail whipping excitedly that his mistress was awake again.

Addie walked in the room followed by Salem. "You're awake again! You slept most of the night."

"That's what humans are accustomed to, Addie," Salem said.

Ophelia looked around the small room. "Do I have...my things?"

"Yes, they're here," Salem said, pointing to the sack in the corner. "What do you need?"

"Hm. Yes," she said, looking at her belongings. Then she looked back at Salem and Addie. "I suppose Fairyland doesn't have a necessary, does it?"

"I'll help you!" Addie exclaimed. "Salem, go away," she said imperiously, trying to shove him out of the entrance. "It's not proper to see a lady in dishabille."

"I've seen her in nightgowns multiple times, Addie," he said dryly, but turned anyway.

"Ah, ah! Out!" Addie pointed imperiously, throwing out her

finger towards the darkness. Ophelia put her hand over her face. Salem laughed and went.

❧

"So. Etienne," Ophelia said, as Addie led her back inside the barrow. "He seems nice."

Addie had helped her dress and then assisted in finding a reasonable hedge behind which to attend to personal matters. Ophelia was thankful for Addie's help scouting out the location, because it was pitch black out—a bank of clouds obscured the moon, and she couldn't see anything, though a faint streak of lighter blue had appeared on the horizon to the east.

"*Isn't* he?" Addie clutched her hands together and pressed them to her chest.

"Does he need his spectacles?" Ophelia asked, right before she tripped over a stone at the mouth of the barrow. "Ouch."

"Watch your step," Addie said, entirely too late. "No, he doesn't need them; but they're the height of fashion now, and Etienne hates looking outdated."

"Is that a concern for vampires?" Ophelia asked, feeling her way along the tunnel. The long barrow descended into the earth and then traveled for who-knew-how-many meters.

"Of course! You ignore fashion for a year or two and then one night you emerge at dusk, and everyone points because you're dressed like a dowd and ten years out of date. Or more! Most of us want to *avoid* unnecessary attention. I think the spectacles suit him very well," she added. "He says they're called pince-nez."

"I believe you're right," Ophelia said, and nearly tripped as a furry creature rubbed itself against her leg. "Ah!" She clutched the wall.

"What is it?" Addie said.

"I was nearly murdered by a furry assassin," Ophelia muttered, and lifted the cat wending around her ankles into her arms. By the rocks-in-a-tin-can purr and the weight, she suspected she held Nevada. "*There* you are. I suppose you have no problems seeing in the dark," she murmured, and set the cat on her shoulders, where the claws dug into her dress and the cat balanced with no trouble. "What have you been up to?"

"Oh, kitty," Addie said in a soft voice. "They ran when we let them out of the basket."

"I imagine they were very angry about the hamper. I'll let you pet her when I can see," Ophelia said with a laugh.

"Oh, I forgot again," Addie said regretfully. Her cold hand reached through the dark and clasped Ophelia's. "Can you really not see anything?"

"I can see the spot of light at the end of the tunnel," Ophelia said, "But that doesn't help me see the stones under my feet."

"It gets better further along," Addie assured her. "Less weathering."

They eventually made their way along the tunnel to where the light emanated, and Blaze met them at the edge of the light and pressed against her side. In the small glow, Ophelia could see three openings splitting off into separate chambers, giving the barrow a cruciform shape. The light came from the chamber at the top of the cross.

"Didn't we come out of there...?" Ophelia asked, pointing to the chamber on her right as she patted Blaze absently.

"This chamber has more space in it," Salem said, appearing in the arch. "More chairs as well."

"That is a lie," Etienne said as Addie and Ophelia stepped into the light. "It has more *places to sit*, a thing that is entirely different."

"Semantics," Salem said, waving his hand.

"Ah, no, not when the place you refer to is the stone floor. You are being a poor host."

"I am twisting your tail is what I'm doing," Salem said. "I have the crates the books came in stacked in the king's chamber; you can sit on those."

Etienne heaved a sigh. "You even had available wood and you did not try to make shelves? Benches? Anything?"

"You're welcome to sling a hammer any time you like."

"There's a rug," Addie pointed out.

"Twenty years old and not beaten even once to remove the dirt," Etienne said disgustedly.

"Forgive me for not having the help in to clean," Salem said in a voice as dry as dust.

Ophelia ignored their comfortable squabbling and took in the rounded chamber. Her dark lantern sat on a stack of books and, besides a wax-laden candelabra on a rickety table beside the large armchair in the corner, was the only other source of light in the room. A few stools stood here and there, but they were piled with books. In fact, the whole room was filled with books. The untidy stacks lurched around the room in precarious piles.

"You were here for twenty years," Etienne said. "You could have beaten a rug or two yourself in that time."

"Oh yes," Salem said acidly, "Just take my rugs out and beat them at night, a perfectly normal thing to do if anyone saw me. 'Don't mind me, just beating the rugs for the fairies that live here, carry on. A little while later I'll do some woodworking as well. Ignore the sounds of saws and hammers.'"

"Why not?" Etienne gave a gallic shrug. "Humans are notoriously gullible. No offence, mademoiselle," he said to Ophelia, after a sharp poke from Addie.

Ophelia didn't even care. "How many books do you have?" she asked in wonder. She set Nevada on the ground and slowly turned in place.

"I lost count," Salem said.

"Twenty years in this hole and you didn't make an inventory?" Etienne demanded, clearly horrified. Addie laughed from her place crouched by the cat.

"The point was not adhering to anyone's expectations but my own," Salem said flatly.

"Well maybe you would know how many books you owned if you had *shelves to put them on*," Etienne said, not ceding his point.

Ophelia hardly heard him. She was too busy reading the spines on the books. Volumes of Sir Walter Scott and Jonathan Swift were mixed in with Austen and Anne Radcliffe and Jules Verne. George MacDonald and *Alice in Wonderland* were stacked on top of Wordsworth and Coleridge; *The Decline and Fall of the Roman Empire* supported Keats and Grimm's Fairytales. And through it all were volumes of Shakespeare—so much Shakespeare.

"Do you need—" she counted again "—seven volumes of *Hamlet*?"

"Some volumes are leatherbound," Salem said. "And some I wrote in."

"*You* wrote in a book?" Addie said.

"When I'd come back and read it again, I would read my comments and it was like having a conversation with myself," Salem mused.

Etienne slowly shook his head. "Thank goodness we are here now."

Nevada, unsatisfied with the attention being paid to her, meowed loudly.

"Good gracious, your majesty," Ophelia said. "My apologies. Well, let's have an introduction so everyone can meet you properly." She picked up the cat and put her on a stack of books that looked the most stable. "This is Nevada, everyone. You can pet her," she said, urging Addie to come and stroke her soft fur.

With wide eyes, Addie approached, watching Ophelia scratch the tortoiseshell cat behind her ears. Nevada eyed her warily, her fur starting to hump.

"This is Addie, and she's nice," Ophelia told the cat, taking Addie's hand in hers. "Let her smell you, Addie." She held out Addie's hand to Nevada.

Nevada stared in suspicion for a long moment, but finally unbent enough to sniff Addie's hand. Seeming to find it inoffensive enough to worship at her shrine, the cat leaned forward and rubbed her head against Addie's hand.

"She likes her ears rubbed," Ophelia said.

Salem and Etienne watched intently as Addie gingerly stroked Nevada.

"Do you want to pet her?" She remembered how Salem had acted in her dream, how avidly he had petted the sleeping form of Sheba. "I guess the other cats are around here somewhere…is there food for them? They'll come if there's food. Also, has anyone fed Blaze?"

The dog looked up at the mention of his name.

"We gave the dog some of Addie's soup. He ate it. I believe the cats are eating the mice," Salem said, "but Faelad is bringing more food for the both of you. They can have some of that."

She wouldn't get into the intricacy of an animal's diet versus a human's until Faelad came back with his supplies, she decided. Surely he, being a werewolf (a wolf man. A man who was a wolf. Gracious) would know what sort of things animals could eat. She wasn't sure why she was having such a hard time acclimating to the idea of a wolf man when she was surrounded by vampires.

She cast a dubious glance around the chamber. "It might also be smart to find something we can repurpose as a sandbox. They might go outside, but…they also might not."

Etienne immediately stood up. "If the cats will eat the mice, I will acquire them a sandbox."

Addie laughed as she rubbed Nevada's head. The cat arched her back and preened, then jumped down from the stack of books and began to perambulate about the room, sniffing the various book stacks before meandering past Salem. She didn't look at him, but her tail surreptitiously rubbed against his trouser leg.

Ophelia rubbed Blaze's head as he nosed around her anxiously. "I'm fine."

"But you should sit and take the weight off your injuries," Salem said. Before she could move, he picked her up in his arms.

"I can *walk*," Ophelia said crossly.

"You can, but we want you to get well. Besides," he said, ducking into the side chamber. "It's almost dawn."

"What happens at dawn?" Ophelia asked as he set her down. "And how do you know?"

"I can feel it," he said, his expression going distant. "It's like the tides. We can feel it pulling at us. We all go to sleep. And when we're not in mortal danger of our heads being cut off or our bodies dissected, we sleep very deeply during daylight."

"All except you."

"Yes. All except me. 'Ah, to sleep, perchance to dream. There's the rub.' But I will still rest."

"Well, what am I supposed to do while you're all asleep? *I'm* not tired."

"Faelad will be back soon."

Ophelia did not find this comforting, since Faelad had shown absolutely no indication of spending any time with her at all. Her expression probably showed it, because Salem said, "Wait a moment." He disappeared down the hallway.

It took him a moment to return. She could hear him saying, "go on," in the tunnel.

Salem sighed. "Call the dog, Ophelia; he doesn't want to pass me to get to you."

"Blaze, it's all right." She kissed the air and patted the cot. "Come."

Blaze's toenails clicked against the stones as he came in the room. Salem entered behind him and handed her a green book. "Have you read this? I haven't got any Westerns, I'm afraid."

Ophelia glanced at the cover. *Black Beauty: His Grooms and Companions, the Autobiography of a Horse*. "No, is it new?" She took the book and paged through it.

"In the last few years, yes. Etienne sends all the new books to me. I think you'll like it," he added. "The horse tells the story."

"Really?" She opened it to the first page.

Salem adjusted the pillows behind her and set the lantern on a stool. "Do you need more light?"

"This is fine," Ophelia said distractedly, turning the page.

"Good night, then." Salem said.

Ophelia was already lost within the pages of the book, except for one brief moment of clarity when he dropped a kiss on her hair.

Chapter Twenty-Four

An hour or two later, Ophelia roused from Black Beauty's misfortunes to the quiet scrape of a step along the hall. "Faelad?" she called. "Is that you?"

His visage very reluctantly came into view in the circle of lamplight. He carried no lantern, but he did have a sack with him.

"Hello," she ventured. "The others are asleep."

"I know," he rumbled. "I can smell them."

Wolf man, her brain reminded her. Blaze's head came up and his ears pricked as his tail thumped along the ground.

Faelad murmured something to him in Gaelic, and the dog settled.

"Suppose you'd like breakfast," he said after a minute of silence.

She hadn't thought about it, really, but as soon as he said the words, her stomach growled, loud in the room's quiet.

He grunted. "I'll cook something."

"Outside?" Ophelia asked, turning down the page's corner to hold her spot. "I can help." The promise of sunlight was a tempting lure.

"Don't know that he'd like you leaving here much," Faelad said.

Ophelia said firmly, "He doesn't have to like it. I am not a prisoner. I can go where I like."

He said gruffly, "Come if you're coming, then."

She got to her feet and brushed out her skirts. "Do you not need a lantern?"

"My eyes work like theirs in the dark," he said shortly.

"But it doesn't work like—I mean, you're alive and they're not?"

"Aye, but I'm cursed just the same."

"How so?" she said, lifting the lantern and following slowly behind him.

He exhaled through his teeth.

"I don't mean to pry," she murmured as they emerged into the sunlight. "This is just...new to me."

Faelad built a small fire and made toasted cheese in silence, while Ophelia stared around her at their surroundings. The purple heather covered the hillside along with clumps of bracken. The grasses waved in the breeze as the overcast sky made the light smoky and mysterious. Overhead a flock of birds flew in formation towards the north.

All she could think was, *Salem was wrong. This really is fairyland.*

Cold though. She shivered. She had not thought to bring a blanket.

Faelad's coat dropped over her shoulders.

"Oh, you don't—"

"Keep it." The sun lit his hard, angry expression in an uncompromising light. He handed her a slice of the toasted cheese, and Ophelia devoured it. Something about the simple fare was delicious in the outdoors.

"Have you heard tell of the werewolves of Ossory?" Faelad said abruptly.

Ophelia shook her head and wiped her fingers on her handkerchief.

"It's a legend about Ireland. The werewolves of Ossory, whose warriors go a-wolfing. They take the shape of men or wolves; it gives them an edge in battle. Makes it easy to devour people. I'm descended from them," he said, off-hand.

"It's an inherited trait, then?" she said faintly.

"Some think so, but no. It's a curse. Legend has lost the who or the why—the one I've heard most often is a saint cursing a tribe for their overly-bloodthirsty ways—but a few of us bear the curse for a time for the rest of the clan, and we can pass it on. That's how I got the wolf. My mentor wanted to die, so I took the burden from him, and he passed."

The few carrying the burden for the many, she thought. "You're long-lived, then?"

"The wolf makes us so."

"A lonely life," she said, watching the flames dance.

"Aye," he said shortly, and that was the end of that.

⚜

He was resting when Faelad called him. "Salem. Salem."

It took a time for him to shake off the lethargy. He felt slow and sluggish. The sun was still high above—he could feel it. "What?" he mumbled, feeling as if he was speaking through sand.

"Get up."

"What is it?"

"She's crying."

"What?" he said, already moving, body fighting its way to alertness. *Ophelia, crying?* "Why?"

"Don't know. Not my lookout," Faelad said flatly. "I've told you. Now I'm going out."

The big man retreated from the king's chamber where the rest of them lay. Salem glanced around him. Etienne and Addie had not stirred, and he didn't miss how close they lay next to each other. Addie's doing, no doubt.

Salem hauled himself to his feet, swaying with exhaustion, and listened. He followed the sound of the muffled sobs to Ophelia's chamber, its light dimmer as the lamp oil ran low. He squinted in through the doorway to see her sitting on the cot, the book face down in her lap as she wept into her hands. The dog and the cats lay in a pile by the foot of the cot. Blaze stared at his mistress earnestly, wishing to go to her but weighed down by his furry burdens.

"Ophelia."

Ophelia looked up, her eyes streaming with tears. "Ginger," she blurted in a watery voice, swiping at the tear tracks on her face.

Salem lifted the book from her lap and set it aside. He handed her a handkerchief, and she blew her nose.

"You don't like the book?" he ventured.

"No, it's good—it's wonderful. But *heartbreaking*. Ginger died," she said, a new rush of tears trickling down her cheeks.

"I didn't remember anyone dying; I'm sorry. I can bring you something else to read—"

"No!" She blew her nose again. "I want to finish it. I want to know what happens."

"You can't read like that," he said, "your eyes are red." And swollen. But perhaps she wouldn't like him to mention that.

"It's fine, I can—" she said, reaching for the book.

"I'll read it to you," he offered.

She stared at him. "Really?"

"Really," he said, picking up the book.

"But you're tired," she said. "I woke you up—"

"No, Faelad woke me up, and I'm glad. I don't want you crying alone." He deftly lifted her from the cot, sat down and placed her on his lap. "Are you comfortable?"

She hesitated, and then leaned against his chest, resting her head on his shoulder. She covered her sniff surreptitiously with her hand.

He pulled the quilt up over their legs and held the book with one hand and her with the other. "Where did you stop?"

He read the rest of *Black Beauty* aloud to Ophelia, who listened silently in the candlelit dark. Never mind his tiredness and his increasing hunger—this was worth more than all the rare volumes in his collection. When he reached the end, Ophelia wiped away more tears. "That was wonderful."

"It was a bestseller, if I remember Etienne's letter correctly."

She nodded slowly. "You know, Ben always sends me gothic novels as presents for my birthday and Christmas. Anne Radcliffe's numerous works, Mr. Lewis's *Monk*, *The Castle of Otranto*. And I've liked some of them, certainly, but others scare me or discomfit me. But something like this...." She traced the horse's head on the cover of the book. "He never sent me this, when he should know this is something I would love. But you picked it out of your large library and gave it to me. You *saw* me and knew me. They never did."

"I'd like to say something helpful, but I can't," he said tightly. "Because they don't deserve you."

She looked up at him. "My father killed my dog. Did I tell you that?"

He stilled. "No," he said slowly. "You didn't."

"As a child, I had a lot of animals. I love animals. They love you best, you know. Purely. I had a dog with a lame leg. I loved him so much," she murmured.

"What happened?" he said.

"He disappeared. The way a lot of my animals tended to. But I found him. In the laboratory."

Salem tightened his hold on her. His mouth ached with the urge to bite down on something, to do violence for. To think that her own family had hurt her so badly....

"He was just bones. My father had killed him and stripped him of his flesh just to see how his foot fitted together wrong."

He stroked her hair. "And you went down there again voluntarily?"

"I know how cruel men can be, to animals and people," she said. "I had to do something to stop it."

"I don't understand how you can have so much compassion in you," he said. "But that's how I knew you would like the book. I didn't remember all the separate events, but the story arouses one's compassion. And you make me feel that way too," he confessed, his arm tightening around her reflexively.

Ophelia let out a slow, shaky breath. "What is this?"

"What do you mean?"

"This." She gestured between them. "You. Me. This. You kissed me in my dream, and then everything happened...so we never talked about it."

He stilled. "Do you want me to go?"

"No!" she exclaimed. "No. I just want ...I've spent so much of my life hoping for affection that never came and second guessing myself...I just want to be certain. To know."

His throat tightened, but he had to get the words out. She needed them. "You are precious to me. You vex me and challenge me and scare me and humble me." His arms came around her. "I can never see the sun again, but when I look at you...I remember what it felt like."

She was quiet, then said, " 'I love you with so much of my heart that none is left to protest.'"

A kind of wild joy mingled with terror rose within him. He cradled her head in his hands and kissed her, slowly, lingeringly, savoring her warmth. When he pulled back, he whispered against her lips, "Who do you want me to kill?"

Chapter Twenty-Five

❦

"I am not tired anymore, Salem," Ophelia said firmly, getting to her feet regardless of his hovering. "My leg feels fine, or as fine as it ever does. My bruises are better. I have drunk your nasty tincture once again, and I want out of this room."

When he frowned, she said, "I went outside with Faelad and walked perfectly well. Stop hovering. Why don't you give me a proper tour?" she coaxed. "I need an official guide to Fairyland."

"Will you tell me if your leg starts paining you?"

"Yes," she said patiently. Vampires must not remember what it was like to be human—the aches and pains, yes, but also the resilience. She wasn't a spun glass figurine poised to shatter at any moment.

He sighed and stepped away from the arch so she could enter the tunnel. "It won't be much of a tour." He pointed to the main chamber, the library, as she had begun to think of it. "This was originally the main burial chamber, but I appropriated it because it was the biggest room. I moved the bones and the offerings into this side chamber." He lifted the lantern as he stepped through the dark archway.

"There isn't anything to be frightened of." Salem obligingly let the beam of light cross over the room and illuminate the interior. "His bones are very dry. Unlike some things in here."

Ophelia shot him a look and stepped forward to view the king in state.

There was very little to see. Ancient wrappings covered a yellowed skeleton in a bier, and clustered around him lay weapons and a shield. He wore a torque and a mail shirt, which under the grime may have once been of fine quality. Stacked along the wall lay other anonymous wrapped bones—attendants, perhaps? Or other burials from other times?

"Why do you call him king? Do you know who was laid to rest here?" Ophelia whispered.

Salem shot her an amused look. "No, I don't know. I don't even know when he died. I am from considerably later."

She peered up at him through her lashes, eyes widening.

"Later being 1640, minx," he laughed, fangs sparkling.

"*Sixteen* forty?" she repeated.

"Or thereabouts," he said easily.

"And no one has ever found this place but you?"

"Like I said, the locals believe it to be a portal to Fairy, and thus to be avoided. I have...encouraged this, with Etienne's help. He has a talent for not being seen and can place a similar aura upon a place. A keep-away sensation, if you will. So neither locals nor spade-happy archaeologists have ventured upon my dwelling place."

"Keep away," she whispered. "What—what does it feel like?"

He raised an eyebrow. "It doesn't affect the dead as strongly. But it's a feeling of terror. I have seen many people flee his vicinity when he'd rather not be bothered."

"That...explains some things," she said, thinking furiously. The terror, the spine-tingling fear that had emanated from the family mausoleum—that had been *Etienne*.

"Did I hear my name?" the French-accented voice said from behind her.

Ophelia spun around. "Were you hiding in my family's mausoleum?" she demanded, planting her hands on her hips.

Etienne reared back, eyes widening. "Ah, *oui*."

"*Why* did you feel the need to shoo me away from my own mother's grave? I wasn't going to go *in*," Ophelia said, aggrieved.

"*Désolé*, mademoiselle," Etienne said, spreading his hands in apology. "But *le vaurien* was approaching, and you were having... *un cœur à cœur, n'est-ce pas*? I did not think you would wish him to overhear."

Ophelia blinked. "Oh. *Merci, monsieur*. My apologies."

"No apology is necessary, mademoiselle, only mine for frightening you." He bowed slightly and retreated.

"What were you confessing? That you were conflicted about helping monsters?" Salem asked.

"I was talking to my mother about a number of things," Ophelia said, nettled. "And please pick a complaint."

"What?"

"What *is* a vampire? A leech, a monster, a dead thing, unnatural life, what?"

"All of the above," Salem drawled.

Ophelia slowly shook her head. "I don't think so. I really don't." She turned to stare at the dead king. "I've seen a lot of dead things," she said. "Animals, mostly. But there is a point when you can point at something and say it is dead because you know that the spirit, soul, what have you, has left the body. I saw that with my mother. She was there, and then she was not. I couldn't tell if her breathing had stopped, or her heart had stopped beating, but I looked at her and I knew she was gone." She tilted her head back and stared at him. "And your heart doesn't beat, and you don't have to breathe, but you're *here* in a way that she is not. So what do we mean by 'dead'?"

"We mean *dead* because there is a definitive period of time where vampires are all fully dead," Salem said flatly. "What you describe happens. The part of a person that makes them alive leaves. The body cools. All the horrible uncomfortable things that happen to dead bodies happen. And then the next night, that body sits up and speaks and walks around, and drinks the blood of the living."

"But how is that possible?" Ophelia whispered.

"I don't know," Salem said, laughing a little wildly. "It's…it's some kind of bastardized resurrection. Corrupt and wrong, branding us as damned."

She said slowly, "I don't know what God considers unnatural, or why this has happened to you, but I don't believe it disqualifies you from salvation."

"You don't know what you're talking about," Salem said harshly.

" 'There are more things in heaven and earth, Horatio, than are dreamt of in your philosophy'," she said, and watched his face go blank. "Here is what I know. God forgives thieves and murderers, doesn't he? On the cross, he told the thief that he would be with him in paradise. And aren't we all dead in our sin?"

"You don't know what I've done," Salem said in a low voice.

"You don't know what *I've* done!" she countered. "That's not the point. God *does*."

It was like he couldn't even hear her. "I've drunk blood. Spilled it. Killed. There is *no hope for me, Ophelia*."

Tears sprang to her eyes as she shook her head. "I don't believe that."

His lips peeled back from his teeth as he scowled at her. "When I was a young vampire, my maker wanted me to be a killer. She wanted a trained attack dog she could let loose on her enemies and call to heel, so she set out to break my will. She locked me in a room with a human girl she snatched off the street, and left us in there. And I got hungrier and hungrier. And the girl was frightened and scared."

Ophelia swallowed.

"But I wasn't going to let my maker win. She wasn't going to get the best of me. Typically, a vampire is leashed to their maker via a bond until they are strong enough to make their own children. Making a new vampire weakens or outright dissolves the original bond because it creates a new link. I should've been far too young to make my own children. But it was a chance, and I took it. I knew it was wrong and, in my desperation, I did it anyway. I drank from the bait she had given me, and then forced that girl to drink my blood, and then I killed her. And when she woke the next night, my connection was severed, I was at my full strength, and my maker would never command me the same way again. *But I still did it, and I am still damned.*"

"But don't you remember?" Addie whispered from the archway.

Both Salem and Ophelia jumped and turned to look at her.

Addie watched Salem, a troubled look on her face.

Salem said wretchedly, "Addie—"

"You apologized," she said. "You said you had to kill me, and I begged you not to. But the guards outside the door could hear my heartbeat, and they would know if you tried to bluff. You said that there was no way I could leave the room. Either you would get hungry enough to feed on me enough times to kill me, or I would die from lack of food and water, and you were sorry. But you said I could cheat her too, if I wanted to survive badly enough. I said yes. Don't you remember?"

Salem swallowed, his guilt still visible on his face. "But it was still my fault."

"It wasn't," Addie said, tilting her head sideways. "It was all *her*. I know you regret it. Don't. We were trapped, and I chose. I forgive you."

"But you were hurt," Salem whispered. "Those bastards took your body away and slung it around like a rag doll. You hit your head against the stones before you ever got the chance to rise."

"That wasn't your fault, either," Addie said. She reached for his hands. "I'm sorry you thought you had to carry this guilt around. You don't. Please believe me."

"But I promised to take care of you," Salem said through gritted teeth.

"You have," Addie said. "Don't you think so?" Carefully, she stepped forward and wrapped her arms around him. "You care the most," she whispered into his chest.

Slowly, his arms came up to embrace her, too.

Addie stayed in the circle of his arms for a long moment, and then pulled back and frowned up at him. "Now stop self-sabotaging." She turned to Ophelia. "After a while, vampires get a little stuck in their ways and trains of thought. Just keep pushing back on the topic—it's good for him to get shaken out of his rut." She clasped her hands. "When do you think you'll be hungry again? I made cottage pie to see if I could recall the recipe," she said with a happy smile.

Ophelia cleared her throat and managed to speak on the second try. "I could eat any time. Cottage pie sounds delicious."

"Good!" Addie wrapped her in a spontaneous hug that Ophelia managed to return, just as Etienne reappeared, looking grim. "Salem," he said, staring through his pince-nez, "Someone just pushed through my keep-away glamour. We have a visitor."

⚜

Salem made for the entrance of the barrow. Who was here? A human wouldn't have been able to push aside Etienne's glamour. Very few vampires knew about his dwelling place. If somehow word got out, and Rupert's spies discovered Ophelia here—

He burst into the moonlight, his eyes scanning the area.

"Salem, old friend." The tall blond vampire with wild hair and beard stepped out of the shadows and into the light of the cookfire, a figure he hadn't seen in twenty years.

Salem relaxed. "Kendrick." He held out his hand, and Kendrick approached and clasped his forearm.

"It is good to see you." The big man's face stretched in a grin.

"Good to see you as well. I had heard you were on the continent."

"I was; I just returned. I heard there has been some upheaval involving you and Etienne and came in search of the whole tale." Kendrick fixed him with a keen eye, assessing him.

"You could say that," Salem said inscrutably. "How was the crossing?"

Kendrick laughed, fangs gleaming. "It was miserable. I was stuck in a trunk, and I felt horrible the whole time we passed over the whale road. There wasn't even room to be sick. I was reminded why I only visit the continent every hundred years." He clapped Salem on the shoulder. "Glad I am to be back. Tell me, why does your abode smell like human? And animal? I didn't think you were in the habit of bringing food home."

Salem smiled hard at him. "It's none of your business, Kendrick."

He raised one skeptical eyebrow. "You have a thrall? You?"

Salem growled and knocked his hand away. "Keep your tongue behind your fangs if you know what's good for you."

"It was not my intention to offend," Kendrick said easily. "I will better achieve that end if I know what you have been about."

He cast a glance at the sky, the moon high above. "It's a long tale," Salem warned.

"All the best are," Kendrick mused.

Salem sat with his old friend on the rocks beside the barrow and began to explain what all had occurred, beginning with Etienne's arrival a week before and Addie's disappearance.

"A bad business," Kendrick said after Salem had finally wended to the end. His brows drew low over his eyes as he stared off into the distance. "But I'm not surprised."

"About which part?"

"Rupert's edict. Of course he wouldn't care if a few vampires go missing."

"Well, yes, we already knew he was a bad leader. I assumed he'd be taken out within the first year after Theron's death. I'm surprised he's lasted this long."

"I'm speaking of the population," Kendrick said. "He and his cronies lifted nearly all restriction on turning humans once they gained power. But they didn't realize how much that would strain food resources, living spaces, and endanger discovery." He shrugged a little. "Or maybe they did and didn't care as long as their power base grew. The vampires bound to him are packed into the main hideaways in London, nearly on top of each other."

"What?"

Kendrick lifted an eyebrow. "You didn't know?"

Salem gestured to the barrow, his expression saturnine.

"I thought Etienne wrote you," Kendrick said.

"Etienne sent me books with a few notes about Addie; he wasn't penning me epistles."

"More because he knew you wouldn't respond rather than lack of inclination. He wrote me multiple times when I was in France."

Salem stared at him. "What for?"

"I wanted to know where to eat," Kendrick said, unperturbed.

"You are a vampire, not a connoisseur of patisseries."

"But humans *are*, and you are what you eat, as they say." His fangs gleamed. "And I also asked what art was left over after the Corsican's armies went through, what I should look at and what I shouldn't waste my time on. But my point was, space and food and resources are at a premium now. Renata might've been an evil bitch, but she knew about ruling. She was the mainstay of Theron's power."

"Resources?"

"Those bribes for gravediggers and sextons don't come cheap," Kendrick said.

Something in Salem's brain clicked. He sat straight up, staring unseeing at Kendrick.

"What is it?"

"Do you remember what it was like in the daylight?" he said slowly.

Kendrick said in a low voice, "I'm older than I look."

Salem went on in a dreamlike voice, "Everything lit by the sun's rays, bathed in light. Illuminating your sight. But if you ever tried to look directly at the sun, you couldn't. It was too bright. It hurt even human eyes. And only children really tried. As an adult you...ignored it. You glanced up to tell the time of day and then went on. Only sunrise or sunset caused any pondering of the sun at all."

"I'll take your word for it," Kendrick said sardonically.

"It's the same way with leaders. If they're doing what they should, you don't notice, unless they are on the rise or at their downfall. And we've been ingrained not to question the Master, whoever that happens to be, even though we are no longer bound to him. I've been wracking my brain, trying to think who would do such a thing. Who would sell out their own to the humans? But it's been him, all this time. The whole thing. Selling his own people. For the money."

Kendrick went preternaturally still. "That's a serious accusation."

"But merited," Salem stressed.

"You want to kill another king?"

"I didn't kill the first one. But if the king is corrupt? Absolutely."

"You'll need proof," Kendrick warned.

"And I'll get it. He won't get away with doing this to Addie."

Kendrick smiled, baring his fangs. "It comes from the Cromwellian spirit in you."

"Damn right it does," Salem said. "Divine right of kings only extends so far. And Rupert has never been aligned with the divine."

"I didn't think you were religious."

"...I'm not."

Kendrick smiled again. "It's interesting to see what's changed over the years. You're collecting all manner of foibles and pets, it seems." His glance turned speculative. "I never thought you would have anything to do with humans, but I'm interested to see how I've been proved wrong. Are you going to invite me in?" He gestured to the barrow.

"Are you going to be civil and abide by hospitality laws?"

He laughed and stood up. "Always. Those are my roots, you know. Get the mead cup and we'll drink together."

Salem led him to the barrow's entrance and pushed aside the foliage. "Although if you refer to Ophelia as a pet, I will say you are justified in whatever happens to you."

"So, she is fierce, your human? Good," Kendrick said. "She'll need to be."

Chapter Twenty-Six

O phelia shook out a freshly laundered tablecloth (where had it come from? Had Faelad or Etienne bought that as well?) and laid it over the small table she had cleared of books, deep in thought.

Something had happened in the king's burial chamber, when she was so earnestly trying to explain to Salem what she very firmly believed: as far as she knew, God's love was not barred from him. God earnestly desires all people to come to Him, no matter their sin, no matter their backgrounds. And if Salem wasn't dead in the way that meant his soul was not gone to the hereafter, then was it truly too late? Could he honestly say, "there is no hope for me?"

Vampirism, as far as Salem's interpretation went, seemed to be a separation from humanity, but also from other vampires. Salem had kept himself away from even his friends for nearly twenty years. Ophelia studiously ignored that that was the length of her lifetime. Vampires seemed to gain a different relationship to time. It flowed differently in their minds.

She understood perpetual aloneness. Hadn't it been her state for a good long time, apart from Marie-Claire and her animals and

God? Rattling around in her empty, decaying house, watching the elements and her family peel Renwick away from her bit by bit? She knew what it was like to be cut off, to believe no one would ever love her with a deep, abiding love that made people stay. Some days she had to cling by the very tips of her nails to the truth that God did love her, and that she was worth loving. It was so hard to feel it when everyone who *should* love her had let her down.

But doesn't God reach out across barriers to find us? She thought. *Didn't He defeat the very power of the grave?*

Ophelia did not believe Salem was beyond redemption. Beyond love. But it was hard to accept a truth when you had never felt it.

Ophelia looked up from helping Addie arrange the dishes on the table—not a difficult task, as only she and Faelad would be eating—when Salem stepped into the light. He said, "Ophelia, I'd like you to meet Kendrick. He's a friend. Kendrick, this is Miss Shaw."

The man who stepped into sight behind Salem was built like a warrior and marauder, with roughhewn features that should not merit the amount of attractiveness he held. He wore his hair long, a tawny horsetail bound behind him, and his short beard the same color. He dressed in the clothes of a laborer but carried himself with presence and power.

Kendrick eyed her with keen colorless eyes, his gaze sweeping over her. She felt strangely unsettled, as if he had taken her measure at an instant. He held out his hand to her. "A pleasure, Miss Shaw."

"Please, call me Ophelia," she said, placing her hand in his. "How do you do, sir?"

"Then I must be Kendrick, since I am only a simple man." He bowed over it, his mouth set in an ironic quirk. "I am far better by the pleasure of your company."

If he was a simple man, she'd eat a whole hattery. She flushed as she pulled her hand from his grasp, and she felt sure that he laughed when her heart skittered in response.

Salem wrapped a hand around her waist and tugged her toward him, and she leaned into him gratefully. He said, "I thought you were going to *behave*."

"I never agreed to that," Kendrick said, with a wide grin and flash of fang. He greeted Faelad with a laugh and an outpouring of what sounded like Gaelic, and then turned to Etienne with a salutation in French.

"Kendrick!" Addie exclaimed. She threw her arms around his neck. "You've been away forever."

"Hello, sweet girl. I heard you've had a time of it," Kendrick said, bussing her on the cheek.

"It wasn't too bad." Addie ducked her head. "Would you like to sit down?"

Where that would be, Ophelia had no idea, considering the dearth of chairs and stools or any other surfaces conducive for seating.

"Having dinner, are we?" The man sat on the floor with his back to the wall, entirely at his ease. "No, don't worry about me, my girl. Feed those who need feeding." He waved Addie on.

"Addie's a very good cook," Ophelia said, taking a seat in Salem's large armchair.

"Is she now?"

"It's coming back to me," Addie said, pleased. "Oh, go ahead and eat, before it gets cold."

"Do you want to share the chair? It's large," Ophelia said, scooting over and patting the cushion.

With a bright smile, Addie alighted beside her, their legs pressing against each other through their skirts. Impulsively, Ophelia gave her a hug. "Thank you for cooking, Addie. Isn't it silly I don't know how?"

Addie froze. Then she rested her head on Ophelia's shoulder. "Very silly. You're welcome," she whispered.

Addie's been a vampire for some time, but she was turned younger than me, Ophelia was reminded again. *Only a girl.* She squeezed her cool hand and picked up her fork, savoring the tasty dish.

Etienne alighted on a footstool, and Faelad sat across from Ophelia on a crate he had dragged into the room, silently putting food on his plate.

Salem sat on the floor by Kendrick. He whistled to Blaze, who came, wagging his tail, though it was still held close to his body, and Salem patted him gently, stroking the top of his head and his soft ears.

"And who is this fine fellow?" Kendrick asked, watching the dog intently.

"This is my dog Blaze," Ophelia said after she had swallowed the bite of cottage pie. "My cats are about eradicating the mice population, I think."

"I still cannot believe you voluntarily lived with vermin, Salem," Etienne said in haunted tones.

"It was comforting to hear the things scurrying around," Salem said. "They didn't bother me."

"They didn't try to nibble on your books?" Etienne demanded.

"They didn't like to come in this room." Salem smiled thinly. "Since this is where I normally stay. So a diet of paper was denied them."

Ophelia looked up from her plate, suddenly feeling like her chewing was extremely loud in the small room. Most of the vampires were watching her and Faelad eat. There wasn't anything else to look at. "It feels strange to eat in front of you," Ophelia said, hoping her face wasn't heating.

Faelad seemed to have no problems. He was entirely focused on putting away his plate of food as efficiently as possible.

"As lovely as I believe Addie's cooking is, we cannot eat it. Do not feel put out," Etienne assured her.

Kendrick turned his head. "So, what is there to eat out here, Salem?"

Salem shot him an ironic look. "Sheep."

Etienne shuddered theatrically.

"And the occasional shepherd or farmer that ventures too close," Salem added. "I have to keep up the Fairyland mythos somehow."

Ophelia paused, her fork halfway to her mouth.

"If some people stumble home not remembering how they got there, it adds to the allure." Salem shrugged.

Ophelia forced herself to relax. Vampires drank blood to sustain themselves. She had let Salem drink from her voluntarily, after all, and she was fine. Salem could drink from people without killing them. So could Addie. It was...it wasn't ideal. But no one was dying. No one was being seriously harmed.

An accomplishment her family could not boast of.

"Why sheep?" Kendrick asked. "Aside from their plentiful nature in Yorkshire, of course."

"I didn't want to charm people regularly. I didn't want to be around anyone long enough to bother."

Etienne said knowingly, "I told you killing Renata would have repercussions."

Salem shot him a surly look.

Addie explained, "Salem killed his maker."

"Yes, I know. He told me," Ophelia said.

All the vampires paused. "He did?" Addie said, surprised.

"Yes," Salem said acidly.

"Oh. Well, everyone thought he'd take over afterwards, but he just left," Addie told Ophelia offhand.

"I didn't want to rule." Salem's voice was flat. "I just wanted her dead."

"She's the one who hurt Addie as well?" Ophelia asked.

He slowly nodded. "Yes."

Etienne said, "Well, if you had *waited* for us like the plan we had *agreed* on, maybe you would not have run off to godforsaken *Yorkshire* afterwards."

"Oh, and maybe we wouldn't be in this mess, is that it?" Salem snapped.

"How do you mean?" Etienne said.

Salem ground his teeth together. "Rupert is the one selling his own people."

"What?" Addie whispered.

"He had an overcrowding problem and a shortage of funds. He fixed both problems at the same time. I don't know how yet—probably sent intermediaries to scientists or other speculative buyers to collect payment and share where the younger, isolated vampires resided. But it's him. It has to be."

"*Merde*," Etienne growled. "And he commanded us not to investigate—! I will twist his head off."

"What, no group plan?" Salem muttered.

"How did Salem rope you into this trouble, Faelad?" Kendrick asked, propping his arm on his raised knee.

"I owed him," Faelad said in a voice that brooked no argument.

But Kendrick was not a man daunted by verbal keep-away warnings. "How's that?"

"I let him out of a trap many years ago," Salem said.

Faelad turned to him and raised an eyebrow. "Would've been paid up sooner if you had followed that plan twenty years ago."

Salem leaned back and slowly thumped his head against the wall, a look of martyred resignation on his face.

"That's right, you tell him, Desmond," Kendrick said in a voice full of amusement.

Ophelia's heart stuttered in her chest.

Her eyes flew to Faelad. "Your name is Desmond?' she asked faintly.

He gave a curt nod.

Her mouth went dry.

Many men were named Desmond, it was true. But he had known the land around Renwick well, more than a few days would've given him. And his strange looks at the house—at her—the ones she couldn't explain!

Her mother's journals echoed to her: *Desmond, I am sorry.*

Against her will, hope began to swell in her chest.

"Have you...been to Renwick before?" she asked, eyes wide.

His face hardened. "Once."

Ophelia clasped her hands tightly together to keep them from shaking. "You see, I read my mother's journals, and in them she mentions someone named Desmond, and I didn't know who she was speaking of, because I couldn't place anyone with that name, but—" she rushed ahead before she lost her nerve. "Did you know her? Are—are you my—"

"No," he said harshly, his eyes flashing. His fork clacked against his plate.

She pulled up short, blushing with mortification. "Oh, I'm—yes, it was a very silly question...."

"I *did* know her, aye," Desmond Faelad clarified with crushing finality, "But you are not mine."

As Ophelia's cheeks burned and her hopes crumbled, he swept from the barrow, leaving only ashes and silence in his wake.

❦

With one look at Ophelia's shattered expression, Salem stormed out after the werewolf, reaching him at the barrow's clearing. He grabbed the man by his shoulder and spun him around. "Could you have been more of a bastard about that?" he hissed, only later realizing that Faelad had not resisted.

"Aye, I could've," Faelad growled. "I could've told the girl *she's* a bastard. But it would've been a lie."

Salem frowned. "And you know that for certain?"

"Yes. Wrong smell. She has nothing of me about her."

"Her mother...." Salem said. "She's the one who sent you away?"

Faelad gave one harsh nod, grief and fury etched across his face. "For my sins, yes."

Salem looked away. "I'm sorry."

"It was no great romance," Faelad scoffed suddenly. "Her carriage lost a wheel in a bad part of London. I stopped to help. I thought her a pretty little thing, but that's all." He shook his head. "But she sent a letter to the tavern to thank me for my kind assistance. I wrote back. And we just...never stopped writing."

"Scandalous," Salem murmured.

"Hardly," Faelad snorted. "I went to the big house to try to convince her to leave her husband—miserable wretch that he was —and met her in secret, and we...." He trailed off. "That was the only time. But she changed her mind. Couldn't leave her little boys, she said." His jaw tightened.

"And Ophelia is not your daughter," Salem said, to put the word into the world and give it breath.

"No," Faelad said. "She's not." The words carried the heavy weight of bitterness and regret. "I have discharged my debt to you, Salem. I'm going back to London."

"You have, that's true. Our scales have balanced. I won't ask you to stay. But are you going off without a word of goodbye?"

Faelad hesitated.

"I think she deserves a little more than that," Salem said, eyes hard.

"His bark is worse than his bite," Addie told Ophelia, clasping her hand. "He's not like that usually."

"What dealings have you had with Desmond Faelad, my girl?" Kendrick asked skeptically. "I'd venture to say his bark is exactly like his bite, and both are lethal."

"It's silly," Ophelia said, dredging up a brittle smile for Addie. "What a thing to ask someone you've only had a handful of days' acquaintance with." Her voice trailed off into silence. She had no idea if her cheeks were bright red with embarrassment or pale with misery. Her face and her fingers felt numb. She swallowed and endeavored to gather the tatters of her poise.

So, Desmond Faelad was not her father. She was still a Shaw. Nothing had changed from the past nineteen years. She pushed the nascent and shattered dreams of belonging to a person and a family that would value her down deep, ignoring the way they sliced at her soul. She still carried the stained legacy of the Shaws, a family shadowed by blood and horror.

It didn't matter, truly. Desmond Faelad had still known her mother. He had access to an entirely different facet of her than Ophelia did. It was like that little bit of her was still alive in him; wasn't that what people said? As long as someone kept the memory of a loved one alive, they weren't truly gone?

She opened her eyes wide, blinking away the burning sensation when she heard the whisper of steps along the ground of the barrow's tunnel. She took a deep breath and set her shoulders as the men came back into view, Faelad followed by Salem. Both their faces were set.

"I'm taking my leave," Faelad announced to the barrow at large. "I'm going back to London."

It was like the air disappeared from the room.

"...Oh. Well, I...." Ophelia twisted her hands in her skirt. "I thought...." Obviously, she had been wrong. "It was nice to meet you," she whispered. "I'm glad to...know."

There were so many things she wanted to say—*How did you meet my mother? Did she know you were a werewolf? Did you love her? Why did she stay at Renwick? Did she choose wrong? Don't you want to know how she died?*

Did you know when you agreed to help Salem where you would end up?

Did you have shattered hopes too?

She could see the handsomeness on his features—the attributes that would have attracted her mother.

Do you see her in my face? Ophelia wondered. *Is that why you can't look at me?*

She knew she should summon a polite smile and wish him safe travels, like a stranger one met in passing. But all she could do was stare at him, stricken, as one more hope walked away from her, out of her life.

Addie and Etienne murmured their goodbyes, and Kendrick clasped his hand and said something in Gaelic. Salem shot him a burning glance but said nothing.

With one last scan of the barrow and a nod that seemed to encompass everyone but her, Faelad clapped his hat on his head and walked out without a backward glance.

Ophelia's weak leg trembled, and Salem caught her as she swayed. She never even saw him move across the room.

Sensitive to the moods of others, Etienne took Addie by the hand. "Come on, Addie. Let's go look at the moon."

Kendrick got to his feet in one sinuous movement. "I'll take the dog out, shall I?" He clicked his tongue to Blaze, who was visibly reluctant, but Kendrick's commanding presence called him to heel. The three vampires vanished from the chamber.

Ophelia gripped Salem's waistcoat and bit her lip, vainly trying to keep the tears from her eyes.

"Ophelia," Salem whispered against her hair.

She bent her head. "Why does everyone leave?" she said in a broken voice. "Everyone. I'm not enough for anyone to stay. I'm never enough for anyone to love. What's the matter with me?"

"Nothing," Salem said harshly. "Nothing is the matter with you. You have so much love in you, and they are fools to shun it. Because I am a being incapable of love, and I have never wanted anything so much as to love you." His arms came around her, hard and unyielding.

"Don't say that." She shook her head, pressing her face into his chest. "You *are* capable of love."

"I'm consoling *you* right now," Salem said. "And he's a damned fool. I'm sorry."

"It was a stupid hope."

"No, it wasn't." Salem put his chin on her head and rocked her back and forth.

Ophelia's tears trickled out silently, wetting his shirt. She let them come. She didn't know how long she cried, but he held her up the whole time. She finally sniffed and rubbed at her eyes. "I guess I still have to carry this name around."

"Names are changeable," Salem said. "I should know."

She pulled back and stared at him. "You mean Salem isn't your real name?" she asked, faintly accusatory.

"No. I renamed myself once I knew I was consigned to darkness. It felt more appropriate."

Ophelia pursed her lips. "You do know Salem means 'peace', don't you?"

Salem blinked. "What?"

"Melchizedek, the king of Salem? King of peace? Priesthood in the order of Melchizedek?" Ophelia asked.

Salem stared at her blankly.

Inexplicably, Ophelia found the strength to smile. She patted his chest. "Hoisted by your own petard, *tsk tsk*. You've surely got a Bible in these stacks somewhere, don't you? We'll find it and I'll show you. I suppose names can always surprise you."

Maybe carrying around the Shaw name wouldn't always be such a heavy weight.

Chapter Twenty-Seven

"Ophelia and Addie are talking," Salem said, stepping out of the barrow under the moonlight. "I thought she'd want to sleep, but I guess not."

Etienne's spectacles flashed in the moonlight as he turned. "Highly dangerous, my friend, to leave the women together."

Kendrick leaned back on his elbows, eyeing the sky. "Still many hours before the moon sets."

Salem squinted at the horizon. The corners of his mouth turned down. "Not enough for us to begin anything tonight. But tomorrow...."

"What do you mean 'us'?" Kendrick said idly.

Etienne turned to him and said acidly, "Do not start that. You know he will go to London himself if we do not help. I for one do not want a repeat of twenty years ago."

"I got the job done, didn't I?" Salem groused, laying back in the heather and staring up at the stars.

Etienne leaned over and blocked his view. "*Merde*, it was a blood bath. You almost died."

"Because *she* wouldn't die," he muttered.

Etienne slapped his head. "*Imbécile*. You need to stay on this side of the grave. There is someone who needs you."

Salem batted away his hand. "That's not—it's—it's more complicated than that."

"How so?" Etienne asked implacably.

"She's human. She's—vulnerable. Her family is still a threat. Not just to her, but to us as well." Salem knew that her family's presence and knowledge would be an issue that would have to be dealt with sooner rather than later. Humans were forbidden to know of vampires' existence. He especially didn't want these particular humans free to act on what knowledge they had gleaned from their vampire captives. They could not be allowed to keep that knowledge.

But he had already killed one of her brothers.

The fool had deserved it. However, he knew it would be a different situation for Ophelia if she knew what he contemplated. But he knew no other way to make not just Ophelia, but Addie and any other vulnerable member of his kind safe.

"Ah. That is a problem." Etienne nodded. "However, you do not need to be the one to deal with it."

"You don't understand," Salem said tightly. How could he look Ophelia in the eye and tell her that he had allowed Etienne or anyone else to go and 'take care' of her family for him? She would hate him just as much, if not more. He must be the one to shoulder the guilt. He had to carry it.

"Perhaps I do not," Etienne acknowledged. "But we should prioritize our problems largest to smallest, *n'est-ce pas*? Our largest problem is not one solitary group of humans who held two vampires. It is Rupert."

Salem sobered, considering. "Fine. We cut off the head of the snake first. We need to go to London and deal with the Master."

"At least we would be able to retire 'Draugadróttinn'," Etienne drawled.

Kendrick looked up. "What?"

"What Rupert has renamed the ruling title," Etienne explained. "Did I never write you about it?" He explained the Germanic roots and lofty names. "He even changed his name to Wodan."

"Old Rupert is calling himself Wodan," Kendrick mused, snapping a twig in his hands. "What lofty heights he aspires to. I should pluck out his eye for him. Complete the picture. I suppose it is too much to hope for that he would gain wisdom from it."

"And too late. His time for wisdom has expired," Salem said tightly. "What allies can we count on in London? Who would remember the time before Rupert took over?"

"Mm, many remember the time before Rupert, but we cannot count all of them to back us, because they supported Renata. I do not think they will look kindly on our accusations." Etienne pushed his pince-nez further up the bridge of his nose.

"Because I killed her." Salem made a face. "Rough estimate, then."

"Those that could be swayed by the facts, the need for secrecy...the old guard," Etienne said. "The outliers, perhaps. But Rupert is popular. It will not be easy."

"Who disappeared before Addie? Were they Rupert's enemies? His friends?"

"They were young," Etienne said. "Less than ten years' turning. It went on because we thought they were youths going astray, behaving recklessly."

"No one looked out for them?" Kendrick tilted his head to the side.

"After Rupert lifted the restrictions on turning, the new vampires outnumbered the older ones," Etienne said disgustedly.

"Who was doing the turning?"

"His power base. They gained a massive number of supporters allied to them, but." Etienne gave a gallic shrug.

"Created a problem."

"Several."

"Undisciplined, were they?" Salem snorted.

"I did not stay there in the court." Etienne waved a hand. "That is why I encouraged Addie to stay in her mausoleum. Every time you turned around, your elbows were always knocking someone. So loud. And blood everywhere." He shuddered. "No taste."

"It's going to take a massive effort to bring the society into shape," Kendrick said.

"I'm not concerned with that," Salem said, tone clipped. "I want to reveal Rupert's duplicity and kill him. That's all."

"You tried that once before. It doesn't fix the problem," Kendrick argued.

"I am not interested in holding the reins of the awful gordian knot that is vampire society. I never have. All I want is justice," Salem snapped. "And if the rulers do not recognize it, I will take it for myself. That's all I've ever wanted."

Renata should never have been allowed to torture him the way she did. But she had been Theron's power behind the throne, and she had been the ruler from the shadows. She had been untouchable, enough that she had the authority to lock him up and do everything she could to bind him to her will. And bringing his case to Theron, their previous master, would have served no purpose. She had been his woman, and he derived a significant amount of his power from her.

Salem had killed Renata for revenge, but also to correct the miscarriage of justice.

But with her gone, Rupert had seen the opportunity to take out Theron.

Kendrick pressed, "You want the same situation to arise? What if someone worse rules?"

Salem pinned him with a hard look. "Are we all together on this or not? Because if we are, then what's your excuse, Kendrick?"

The other vampire's brows lowered.

"What, you think I don't know you're older than you appear? I know for a fact you were turned before either Etienne or me. What is *your* reason for not taking on the mantle of leadership? Since you have so many thoughts on what should be done," Salem said bitterly. "Or are you just a coward?"

Kendrick's eyes flashed red as his muscles bunched, preparing to spring.

Salem hissed, his fangs glinting.

"*Chers amis*!" Etienne shouted, holding up his hands. "Be calm. This solves nothing. We are discussing, nothing more."

Slowly, Kendrick unbent, his eyes fading from brilliant ruby to a faint garnet. "I will forgive you the slight on my honor," he said. "This once."

"What does honor demand?" Salem countered.

Etienne groaned and rolled his eyes. "*Bon Dieu*."

"Honor demands I make plans with the both of you and not rise to your prodding," Kendrick said after a time.

Salem watched him for a long time, and then nodded. "We never did drink from the mead cup."

Kendrick raised an eyebrow. "I'm thirsty,"

"Go. I shall stay and watch over your dwelling place," Etienne said.

"When we return, you and Addie can go hunting," Salem said.

Etienne waved them both on.

❦

"What is this place called?" Kendrick said, as they stepped silently through the small village, making their way to the local inn and taproom.

"Burleigh, Burley-on-the...something." Salem shrugged. "Don't remember."

Kendrick turned and inspected him in the moonlight. "The scars on your soul go deeper than I expected," he murmured. "No one was designed to walk through the world alone, Salem."

"Not even monsters in the dark?" Salem joked, raising his head to stare at the waning moon.

"Especially not us," Kendrick said seriously. "When we lose the tethers that hold us to human society, or even our own—then we lose any kind of compass we may have ever had and become completely unmoored. I don't know how you managed to stay sane, frankly."

"Who says I did?"

"I suspect the books had something to do with it," Kendrick went on, as if he hadn't even spoken.

"It was a way to pass the time."

"Don't lie to me. Stories are integral to the soul."

"A thing we don't have."

"Says who?"

Salem stared at him. "I've never known you to be a reader."

"Not all stories are written."

"And so?"

"So. So." Kendrick's eyes flared in the dark. "*Hwæt we Gar-Dena in gear-dagum, þeod-cyninga, þrym gefrunon, hu ða æþelingas ellen fremedon.*"

Salem stared at him as the words rang in the dark.

A moment later, the taproom door swung open and out stepped a pair of stumbling men, cursing through their intoxication at each other.

With a movement of long practice, Kendrick grasped one man by the shoulder who pivoted perfectly to meet his stare. The man opened his bleary eyes wide, and his mouth sucked in a breath.

"Quietly now," was all Kendrick said. The man closed his mouth and stood there docile.

Salem chose instead to tap his quarry on the back of the head and watched, satisfied, as the man folded like a lady's fan.

"You always thump your quarry into submission when hunting?" Kendrick asked mildly.

"I find that the men usually don't respond as well as the ladies when I try sweet talking," Salem said dryly, reaching for the man's wrist.

"You could've just said you're a ladies' man and left it at that," Kendrick laughed, and then sank his teeth into his quarry's neck.

Salem drank deep, but not too deep. He wasn't dangerously thirsty, and he didn't want to get secondhand drunk from the blood. *I'm doing you a favor,* he thought, licking the blood from his fangs. *You'll be a little weak tomorrow, but perhaps with less of a hangover. You're welcome.*

He and Kendrick left the men a little way down a small alley, propped against the wall. They would wake thinking they had drunk too deeply to get home, their memories fuddled as humans always were after a bite from a vampire. For once, Salem didn't walk the small streets of the village whose name he didn't know until the early hours of the morning, staring at shutters closed and doors barred, alone under the sky. Tonight, he returned with a friend.

He returned home to Ophelia.

Chapter Twenty-Eight

"Ophelia."

She looked back over her shoulder at Salem as she struggled to pin up her hair without the aid of a mirror. She should've asked Addie for help, but she was off with Etienne somewhere, and Ophelia didn't want to pull her away. She pulled the excess pins from her mouth and said, "Yes?"

He looked...oddly trepidatious. Salem eased himself down beside her on the cot. "We've decided that we need to go to London. We need to bring a reckoning."

"To your vampire leader," she said.

"Yes. The leader of most bonded vampires in England." He tilted his head to the side, the corner of his mouth twisting. "It sounds pretentious when I say it out loud."

"But he doesn't lead you?" she asked, jabbing in the last few pins, praying that the knot would hold.

"No. I broke the bonds with my maker when I made Addie, and after Rupert killed the previous Master and took his place, I never swore allegiance to Rupert. He doesn't command me, but he does command Etienne and Addie. That's why Etienne had to come to me for help. Rupert had ordered his followers not to investigate the disappearances." Salem's expression hardened.

Ophelia reached out and grabbed his hand. "But you found Addie. You were exactly what she needed."

"I'd say that was you," he said.

She flushed.

He cleared this throat. "Anyway. That's why we have to go to London. To make him pay for his failing, his betrayal."

She nodded. "I've never been to London."

He gave her an odd look. "What does that have to do with anything?"

She stared at him. "Aren't I coming with you?"

"I was going to take you to your friend."

She said blankly, "Marie-Claire?"

"Yes, that's the one."

"But I want to go with you!"

"It's too dangerous," he said tightly. "Humans—Ophelia, humans are forbidden to know about vampires. If anyone saw you in our company, you would be in very grave danger."

"Who would see me in your company?" she countered. "I wouldn't go to your super-secret vampire meetings with you. But I think it would be safer for me anonymous in a huge city rather than vulnerable in Hartley. Isn't that what you said when you refused to take me to Marie-Claire's in the first place?" she challenged.

Truth be told, she didn't want to be parted from him. The thought now gave her an anxious feeling in her stomach. It was irrational, but Ophelia thought that if he left her behind, she would never see him again. And she couldn't fathom never seeing Salem again.

"I'm trying to do the right thing," he hissed.

"Who are you to decide what that is for me?" She crossed her arms over her chest.

Salem reared back, trying not to snap at her. Who was he? He was the man trying to hold hard to his principles. She had no place with him! Even though his base nature wanted to shout in exaltation that she wanted to come with him. Be with him. Stay with him.

She never said that, he reminded himself with gritted teeth. *She wants to go to* London.

"You wished to go to your friend's home before."

"That was before." Ophelia skewered him with a look. "And much as it pains me to say this, you were right."

He was? "About?"

"In Hartley, I would be in the same conundrum. No money, no help, no recourse from my family. No protection should they choose to try to remove me from the Glenwoods' home. In London, even when you are dealing with vampire things, there would be places I could go—to the museums, or the theater. Tea rooms. I would have the safety of crowds and people."

He tried to think of a counterargument. "Wouldn't your friend be worried by your continued absence?"

The look she shot him was full of patent disbelief. Well, it did sound admittedly weak to his own ears. "That all depends on what my family has told them. But I can write to her from London and explain. It might be easier than explaining face to face. Besides," she said, eyeing him, "I need to be on hand to keep you from doing anything stupid this time."

"That won't happen," he said, disgruntled. "Etienne and Kendrick will probably sit on me if I try."

"Addie and I would be first in line for that," she said tartly. "Salem. I want to be with you."

The words shook him to his core in a way that Addie's protestations never had. He had to open his mouth twice to speak the words: "I want that too."

He was greedy, and selfish. He wanted every second with Ophelia. Every moment was stolen from the relentless reality that lay just outside his dwelling, waiting to crash in the moment they left. But he was willing to cheat the world just a little longer. "I will keep you safe, Ophelia."

"I know that, Salem. Is that a yes?" she pressed.

He nodded, resigned.

She smiled, so bright it was like a chip of the sun entered his darkness. Part of him recoiled, fearing the burn, but the rest of him longed for the warmth so long cut off from him. "So, London. And then...." She trailed off.

He understood. There was no guarantee of an "and then." But he would take all the minutes he could get. At least he would have that.

❦

"Are we going to walk the whole way?" Ophelia said to him, closing the clasps on a portmanteau Etienne had magicked from seemingly thin air. "You have neither horse nor carriage."

Addie carefully lowered the cats into a new basket—larger, with a cloth lining—and shut the lid.

"No, we'll go to the village and hire horses and a driver to get us to the train." Salem took the portmanteau from her so she could collect Blaze's lead and offered her his arm.

"And they'll be willing to set out at dusk?" Ophelia asked, adjusting the hat on her head and clucking for Blaze to heel.

"If they're not inspired by the large amount of money we flash them, then I can be very convincing." Kendrick smiled with all his teeth and tipped his hat.

"Everyone have everything?" Addie asked. "Do you need a book to read, Ophelia?"

"I packed one or two. What about you?"

"Reading makes my head ache; I get sick," Addie said.

"Oh, I'm sorry."

"It's all right. Salem reads to me."

"And I will, too," Etienne said, offering her his arm.

Addie's eyes flew open. "Really?" she breathed. She looked as if someone had just handed her a pile of diamonds.

"Of course."

Salem snorted quietly. Ophelia elbowed him in the ribs as he led them out of the barrow.

Salem was never sure exactly how Etienne exercised his talent, but it was as if fog swirled, shrouding the area from view, thickening until it was the consistency of pea soup. Then the small company began to walk, Blaze panting at Ophelia's side.

"Let me know if you need me to carry you," Salem said. "It's not very far to the village, but I don't want your leg paining you."

"You don't have to carry me," Ophelia said. Her cheeks flushed an adorable shade of pink.

"You're as light as a feather."

"I most certainly am *not*."

"You are to me." He smiled in the darkness. "There are one or two advantages to vampirism, after all."

"Gracious," she murmured.

"Don't you remember me carrying you when we left Renwick?"

"I was unconscious for part of it."

He helped her pick her way through the silent woods. "Well, the part you *were* conscious for."

"I suppose I just assumed you were suffering in silence," she muttered.

"If I were suffering in silence or if carrying you was an odious task, I would've thrown you over my shoulder without another thought," he chuckled. "As it was, carrying you was quite—"

"Salem!" Etienne stiffened, his head snapping around, looking for an unseen enemy. "Salem, someone—*many*—coming *fast*—" With a choked curse, he wrapped an arm around Addie, and the two of them became hard to see.

Salem's head snapped around, stretching his senses. Through the trees, he heard the whisper of footfalls—too quick to be human.

And Etienne's talent would not work on all five people plus animals if they were to run.

"Split up," Salem commanded, and swung Ophelia up into his arms. She squeaked. Kendrick grabbed the dog. Salem didn't see Etienne and Addie go, but he felt the air of their passing.

He and Kendrick ran, the trees flashing by as they pushed for speed. Ophelia pressed her face into his neck, and he tightened his hold.

But their pursuers kept pace. There were too many of them. He could sense them in the trees. They would surround them.

Salem cursed silently, viciously. He hoped Etienne and Addie would have an edge due to his talent.

Because their pursuers could only have come from one place.

There's our plan shot to pieces, he thought bitterly.

They came upon a steep hill where the land sloped up at a hard angle, and their pursuers pushed them into it, hemming them in. Salem could see them—recognized them.

He stopped running.

Kendrick stayed at his side and put the dog down as seven vampires encircled them against the hill.

The dog made frightened, high-pitched cries and bolted for a gap between the vampires. A man lunged for it.

Ophelia gasped, fighting Salem's hold, trying to reach for the dog.

A woman stepped out of the circle and backhanded the man, moving too quick to see. "Fool," she bit out as the dog disappeared into the night. "It is an *animal.* We have bigger priorities."

Her gaze swung to them, and she smiled unpleasantly, pushing her black curls away from her face. "Well, well, well. It has been a long time, Salem."

Salem put Ophelia down and stepped in front of her, sandwiching her between him and the hillside. "Not long enough. You are in *my territory* uninvited, Gisela," he snarled.

"I do not need an invitation when I am on the Draugadróttinn's business," she said triumphantly.

"You shouldn't have been able to find it," Kendrick said slowly, his eyes hooded. "Did you follow me here, Gisela?" he asked. His tone was lazy, but Salem could hear the undercurrent of menace in it.

Her lip curled. "And if I did?"

"I dislike those who deal falsely," Kendrick said ominously.

"The Draugadróttinn has called you to appear before him, Salem," Gisela said, dismissing Kendrick.

"Has he? How nice. I've got a few things I'd like to say to him," Salem snarled.

"You will come with us." Her gaze swept the group. "All of you. And your...pet." She licked her lips.

Salem felt Ophelia's hold tighten on his coat.

Through the trees, five more vampires appeared. "They got away," their leader intoned. "We searched his dwelling. No one hiding in his little hole. Just bones." His men snickered.

Salem blazed with outrage. They had stepped foot in his home. They had desecrated his place. Only Ophelia's hand on his back kept him in place.

Gisela's lip curled. "You will answer to the Draugadróttinn for your failure."

"A leader is responsible for the conduct of his men," Kendrick said.

"You, be quiet," Gisela warned. "I don't need to deliver *you* in one piece."

Salem and Kendrick shared a look. Gisela obviously thought herself the strongest vampire of the group. But she had been made by Rupert less than a century ago. Salem and Kendrick could absolutely fight her one on one, but the sheer number was against them here. And Salem was highly conscious of Ophelia at his back, silent and trembling.

The same vampire that had lunged at Blaze took a step forward, his eyes wide and red. "I take charge of pets." He smiled.

Salem heard Ophelia gulp.

He pulled out Etienne's pistol—the one he had kept since Renwick—and faster than the other vampire could move, shot him in the head.

Ophelia hid her face against his back.

All the other vampires hissed and tensed.

Salem looked straight at Gisela. "Let's get one thing straight right now. This is *my* pet. You touch her and you pay the consequences."

The vampire on the ground growled, writhing in pain. He wouldn't die from a lead shot to the head, but it would be a miserable time healing.

"The next one of your boyos who gets a bright idea in his head will get his head twisted off. Permanently. Understood?"

Gisela snarled at him. "You'll answer to the Draugadróttinn for this."

"A declared pet or thrall is exclusive property. Have the rules changed so much since I was gone?"

Gisela looked extremely unhappy, but a man with deep scars in his face stepped forward. "It has not." Salem recognized him. His name was Joseph. They had been contemporaries, of a sort.

"Good." Salem put the pistol away and pulled Ophelia roughly around to his side. He tipped her head back, holding her eyes for a count of three before licking a long stripe up her neck. "Trust me," was all he was able to breathe into her ear, but he felt her squeeze his hand. Her eyes were still ringed with white, and her heart pounded rapidly, but there was nothing he could do about that now.

"Let us go to London, then," Salem said. "I have some things to say before Rupert and all assembled."

Gisela's mouth opened unsettlingly wide as she smiled. "Oh, that's the beauty of it," she said, fangs gleaming. "We're not going to London."

Chapter Twenty-Nine

The journey was interminable. No one spoke.

The strange, frightening vampires wearing a mix of styles from throughout the century had ushered them through the woods to a line of black carriages, curtains drawn shut.

A few looked as though they would've liked to throw their... captives? detainees? bodily into the carriages, but Kendrick gave them all a hard look and warned, "If you place a hand on me, I will take it for my collection."

They kept their distance after that.

The woman, Gisela, had indicated a carriage in the middle of the line, and Kendrick entered it under his own power. Then Salem had urged Ophelia to follow on his heels and got in after her, so she had ended up sandwiched between the two of them on the seat. Gisela and two more men sat on the rear-facing seat, and a silent, white-faced footman lifted the steps and shut the door.

The drivers and footmen on the box hadn't looked at them. Ophelia didn't think they appeared to be looking at *anything*, but the coaches lurched into motion, so they must have been alive, at least.

But with the curtains drawn closed, there was no way to gauge how long or how far they had traveled, and inside the coach, silence reigned.

Ophelia had tried, at the beginning, to whisper to Salem, but he had shaken his head and placed a hand on her knee, and she had subsided. The looks from the vampires across from her had contributed to her silence. They stared at her so oddly, as if she were a dog that had stood on its back legs and begun to recite times tables. Not only unusual and strange, but uncalled for and unwanted.

Ophelia's throat tightened. She hoped Blaze was all right. He must've been so frightened surrounded by predators and danger that he didn't understand. And who knew what the vampires would have done to him if they had caught him! She wouldn't have been able to bear it if they had hurt him.

But it wrenched that he had left her. She had thought that, even if people continuously let her down, her pets' loyalty was something she could always count on.

I didn't account for vampires, I suppose, Ophelia thought, trying to resist despair.

Addie and Etienne had gotten away, at least. Thank goodness for that. Addie would take care of the cats. They would be just fine.

Ophelia couldn't say as much for her own situation. She believed Salem when he promised to take care of her, and she thought Kendrick would help Salem as far as he was able, but it wasn't lost on her that there were only two vampires interested in her well-being, out of at least twelve sent to retrieve them and an unknown number wherever they were going.

Many questions she hadn't asked Salem now seemed extremely pressing, such as, "how many vampires are there, exactly?" and "how did you manage to kill your vampire maker and why was it so difficult?" as well as "besides silver, what *are* vampiric weaknesses?"

And now no one was speaking, and she couldn't ask.

Gisela stared at a point just above all their heads, which made her chin jut into the air. The two men met Salem and Kendrick's stares. The whole space had a threatening air.

Once, when Ophelia moved a little bit to try to gain some room on the seat and flex some of the tight muscles in her legs, the two men's gazes whipped to her. Salem snapped forward in his seat and *growled*. Once they looked away, he leaned back and wrapped his arm around her shoulders, pulling her into him. He only uttered one word. "Sleep."

Ophelia thought it highly unlikely that she would be able to do that in such a tense environment but closing her eyes would at least allow her to shut out their stares. She leaned her head against his shoulder and closed her eyes.

Twice the carriage stopped to change horses, but none of the vampires moved, so Ophelia didn't either. However, after an age, the carriage stopped, and after a few moments, the handle of the door turned.

Gisela's mouth broke into a wide smile. "We have arrived." She and her flunkies disembarked.

Salem handed Ophelia out of the carriage silently, holding hard to her hand. She was glad of it, because her leg was disinclined to support her after who knew how many hours of being confined and cramped. She steadied herself when she reached the ground, leaning heavily on him.

Then she looked up.

She inhaled sharply, clutching Salem's arm as she stared at the oh so familiar façade of Renwick in the gray light of dawn. "No," she whispered.

His arm came around her hard. A support. Protection. A warning.

The door swung inward, and a man stepped out, with long blond hair curling around his shoulders. He wore a cravat and knee breeches and appeared to have stepped from the previous century...except for the red eyes and smear of blood along his jaw. "Ah, this must be the wayward daughter I have heard so much about. The one who consorts with vampires." He smiled, showing all his teeth. "I am eager to make your acquaintance."

Ophelia shook.

"I have explained this to Gisela already, Bacchus," Salem said, sounding bored, "But if you or anyone else lays a finger on my pet, I will assume you wish to leave this plane of existence and will assist you posthaste."

The vampire's lip curled. "You always were a killjoy, Salem. You should learn to share."

"I don't give a damn about you, and I don't share."

Bacchus's flat gaze turned back on Ophelia, and she steeled herself to endure it. He swiped at the blood on his face with a lace handkerchief. "Maybe the Draugadróttinn will teach you some manners."

"Because you won't be able to?" Salem countered.

Kendrick broke in, sounding irritated. "Are we going to stand on the doorstep until the sun rises, or are we going to learn what your Master wants?"

Bacchus glared at him. "Speak of your Draugadróttinn with respect," he hissed.

Kendrick regarded him curiously. "But he's not my Draugadróttinn," he pointed out. "And I thought your name was Cuthbert."

"He decided to do away with subtlety and changed it," Salem said.

Bacchus glared and opened his mouth—

"Inside," Gisela snapped. "Leave this male posturing for another time. I have brought the prisoners for their audience with the Draugadróttinn."

"He is ensconced with Julius and Titus," Bacchus said sulkily. "I cannot disturb him."

"Then let us enter," Gisela said impatiently, and Ophelia could hear the unsaid *Men!* that followed.

The vampire stood aside so that they could enter. "Keep your little pet, Salem," he murmured, as Salem and Ophelia passed the threshold. "After all, we've got a houseful to pick from."

Chapter Thirty

Her house was infested. There was no other way to say it.

All windows were covered, the curtains pulled tight, shutters closed, draped in black. Only a few tapers burned fitfully in their posts. The dark, oppressive atmosphere squeezed Ophelia insistently, feeding her dread.

Bacchus and the other vampires herded them into Renwick's great hall. The large, cavernous space was filled with people. The scene brought new meaning to the word "bacchanal."

The fire was lit and roaring in the massive fireplace that had been able to spit whole animals in centuries past. The floor was streaked with blood smears, the rugs stained. Chairs and sofas from other rooms filled the space higgledy-piggledy, other furniture pushed against the walls. Strangers with colorless or ruby eyes reclined in various styles of dress—and in various stages of *undress*, Ophelia was horrified to see. And in the far corner huddled a small group of people, white-faced and variously locked with terror or horribly blank. They wore various shades of servants' greys and livery. Ophelia's gaze froze on the sight of a black-clad Rivers—*Rivers!*—hunched into a ball, weeping.

She could not hold back her gasp. She could not fathom Rivers, the bastion of emotionless dignity, weeping. What had happened—what horrible things had they seen?

Salem's hand pressed warningly on her arm, but she didn't need the reminder to keep a hold of herself. She was trapped in a room with the embodiment of danger, and it was never wise to bleed around such predators if you could help it.

She shuddered against Salem. Her father opened the door of the house to evil, and evil had taken him up on it.

Where *was* her father? Or Ben? She scanned the group of humans again but didn't see either of them or Lucas Harding. Ophelia gripped Salem's waistcoat as a dull foreboding threatened to overwhelm her.

❧

Worse and worse odds, Salem thought, taking a count of all the vampires in the great hall. Besides the group that had "escorted" them back to Renwick, twice that number had made themselves at home. Salem, with Ophelia plastered to him, stood in a tiny circle of space with Kendrick as vampires began to untangle themselves and approach.

He tried to catch Kendrick's eye, but his friend was too busy examining their surroundings. Kendrick eyed the sword hidden in shadows over the massive burning fireplace meditatively. *Good luck finding an opportunity to swing it,* Salem thought bitterly. *That's if there's any edge left on it at all.*

"Welcome friends!" a man called, dressed only in trousers and a partially unbuttoned shirt, a smear of blood staining one of the cuffs. "Or...are you friends?" One brow lifted in question. Salem knew him but couldn't recall his name.

"That will be determined once the Draugadróttinn makes his ruling," Gisela said severely.

The man possessed himself of her hand and pressed his lips to her wrist. "Gisela, my delight, you look famished. You know an empty stomach makes you tetchy."

"Yes, Orion, the perfect thing to point out to a woman, her mood," Gisela drawled.

"I'm only trying to help, O lady of the night."

"And then you refer to me as a prostitute."

"I cannot win!" Orion threw up his hands. "We fed early in the evening—the stock should still have some good blood in it. I cannot say how long you will be waiting for Wodan."

Gisela rolled her eyes but nodded. "Acceptable. Stop calling me absurd nicknames."

"Of course, my queen of the damned." He smiled with all his teeth.

"If we shall be waiting for an indefinite period, might we have an explanation?" Salem said caustically.

Gisela turned and looked at him derisively, but before she could open her mouth, Ophelia blurted out, "Where is my family? What's happened to them?"

Salem clamped his hand down on her arm, but it was too late.

Gisela and Orion's gazes swung to her, but it was one of the circling vampires who spoke. "No one asked for your thrall to speak," the lurker said, teeth snapping.

"No one asked your opinion," Salem growled. "You are in her house. Answer the question, Gisela."

"We have dealt with them," Gisela said dismissively. Her expression told Salem what that meant, and that Gisela would like very much to deal with Ophelia as well. Only her tenuous status as his thrall kept her safe...for now. Rupert could negate that with a word.

"I should like to know what has been happening," Kendrick said idly. "I should also like a meal if we expect Rupert to be some time. Dawn comes soon."

"Prisoners don't get fed," Gisela sneered.

"We have not been declared prisoners yet," Salem pointed out. "Until that point, we are...forcibly detained guests."

"And so hospitality rules still apply," Ophelia added sweetly.

"Teach that thrall how to act around her betters," the lurker said.

"This is your second warning," Salem said, smiling with all his teeth. "You won't get a third one."

"But it's my house," Ophelia pointed out in the meekest voice possible. "So I am the one who honors the guest right."

"She's right," Orion pointed out with a laugh, as though marveling that a household pet would speak.

Gisela scanned the room. Apparently enough vampires gave off a sated mien for her to click her tongue and sigh, "Fine. Help yourself to one of our...cattle." She shot Ophelia a nasty smile—probably expecting her to react with histrionics.

Kendrick said, "Ophelia, I leave the choice to you."

Ophelia stared at him, wide-eyed.

Kendrick was giving her the choice to place one of the terrified humans nominally under his protection. Salem didn't know if Ophelia would understand—but then she swung her gaze to the huddled group of humans and swallowed. "Thomas," she beckoned, "come here."

Thomas, who seemed to be one of the footmen, stared at her unblinking, his face a queasy green in the firelight.

Kendrick caught the direction of her eyes. "Walk towards me," he said, in a calm, patient voice. The tension in Thomas's face leached away. He stood and stepped forward, even as the others moaned.

The young man stopped in front of Kendrick, who seized him by the back of the neck. "This won't hurt," he said, and the human's eyes became glassy. He would indeed not feel pain. Kendrick sank his teeth into his neck. The footman did not react at all.

"So considerate of you to dull their pain," Orion sneered.

Kendrick pulled back and licked the blood from his lips, his eyes red. "Some of us do not enjoy our meal thrashing like a fish on the end of a line while we are trying to enjoy a long drink." His voice was deeper, edging close to a growl.

Ophelia swallowed, paling a little, and turned towards Salem. She placed a hand on his chest, where his heart would beat if it could. "Master, do you thirst?" she whispered, her hazel eyes wide and luminous.

Like hell would he drink from her in front of all these lecherous degenerates. Everything in him rebelled at allowing Ophelia to show weakness and intimacy in front of a crowd of enemies. "Ophelia—"

She stared at him hard, attempting to send him a message with her eyes. What did she mean? Did she *want* this?

This would be so much easier if I could speak *to her without these fools overhearing*, Salem thought wildly—and then it struck him. That's what she *wanted*.

Her blood would create the connection to allow him to dreamwalk again. And she knew the way to do it, right under all the vampires' noses.

"So, what will it be, Salem? Going to have your own food, or sample the wares?" Orion leered.

Her eyes pleaded at him to understand.

He traced a finger down her face. "You're not too tired after the last time, pet?" he asked, his voice a delicate caress.

She shook her head, relieved that he understood what she had been trying to tell him.

"It's sweet of you to think of my needs ahead of yours." He pressed a kiss to her temple. "Is there food for the humans somewhere in this house as well? We spent all night in that carriage with no sustenance."

Gisela shot a look at Orion. "Go make yourself useful and find something for the cattle to graze on, fool."

Orion moved off reluctantly as Salem grasped Ophelia's arm

and pulled her to the side of the room, as private as he could make it. A vacant chaise lounge that had clearly been brought in from some other room had no suspicious stains on it, so he sat on it and placed Ophelia in his lap. Salem threaded his fingers through her hair and pressed his lips to her neck. He licked the line of her throat, making sure to avoid any of the dangerous arteries.

"Yes," she whispered. "Do it."

He tried to ignore the spike he felt in his blood at her words. His teeth sank into her neck.

She stiffened, gasped. Reflexively clutched him as the blood began to flow and he fed.

He wrapped himself around her, shielding her from view as best he could. This was his and no other's. She pressed her face into his shoulder, and he clutched her tighter.

Salem swallowed. She still tasted of oranges and copper.

The abyss roared in his ears, urging him to drink freely of the blood that was warm and live, to take it into himself, all of it, every last drop. The temptation was a siren's call to fall into sensation, for the fall would be glorious before the crash upon the rocks.

But the control that Salem had forged for himself, made of iron will and conviction, held him back. Never would he hurt Ophelia, and he would never let himself go in a place surrounded by enemies and foes. They would've delighted in his weakness, pounced on any opportunity to wound. So he pulled back after a few short minutes of paradise and licked at the puncture wounds he had made.

He hated them watching. This should not be a thing shared. It was sacred—the fact that she had shared herself with him was sacred. To be forced to do so in this room that stank of blood and fear and pain made him murderous.

But then her hand stole up his chest to cradle the back of his neck, and Salem wouldn't have traded the past two hundred years for anything if he could just have this.

❦

As Salem lapped and sucked at her throat, she inhaled the smell of paper from his neck and pressed closer to him. A few moments ago, she had burned with unspoken questions and fears that she desperately wanted to ask him.

Now she simply burned.

She leaned against him as she felt her heart thump against her ribs, pumping out the blood he drank. It felt so different when he drank from her neck than her wrist. Both were intimate, but this was highly vulnerable with no bars to separate them, his hands around her, pressing her close to him. As the moments lingered on, she did fear if he knew how much to take—and when to stop —but then he paused and pulled back, licking at her neck. His chest vibrated, not with a human heartbeat, but with a subvocal growl. The tension in him worsened. So she lifted a hand and pressed it to his neck.

I'm here, she willed him to know. *I'm safe, for a little while longer.*

Finally, Salem pulled back and pressed his handkerchief to her neck.

Ophelia met his eyes anxiously. When would he be able to talk with her? Soon? Would she have to sleep first, or could he speak to her waking mind, like before?

Salem reached out and snapped his fingers. Orion appeared in her peripheral vision and handed over a hunk of stale bread and cheese. She supposed most vampires didn't have Addie's cooking skills or reason to cultivate them. "Don't look at her," Salem growled.

Ophelia petted his chest and nibbled at the offerings. It was not the most appetizing fare but it was better than nothing, and she'd need her strength...especially after losing blood. Four bites in, she heard Salem's voice in her head.

"You're brilliant, Ophelia. I'm sorry you were subjected to this."

She leaned into him and exhaled shakily. *"I don't care what they think. Can you hear me? Did it work?"*

"Yes, it did. You're amazing. Don't take such a wild chance again; I don't want you catching any more of their attention that necessary."

"Salem, what Gisela said about my family...are they dead?"

Salem's arms tightened around her. *"Most likely."*

The food in her stomach turned to a rock. Dead.

Grief was so strange. She felt such anger towards them...but they were her blood. All she had. All the hurt mixed up with the small crumbs of affection she had received from Ben over the years.

Ophelia pressed her eyes shut. Mourning, and her complicated feelings, could be sorted out later. Right now, she needed to concentrate on those she *could* help. Which included Salem and Kendrick as well as the servants still alive. She had not seen several faces among them, most notably Nancy, but Mrs. Lowell and Rivers and Thomas were still alive. She'd do what she could to keep them that way.

She forced herself to chew, even though she couldn't taste the food anymore. *"Tell me who all these people are. I don't understand the dynamics."*

"Rupert, also known as Wodan, also known as the Draugadróttinn, is the Master of the vampires."

"I haven't met him yet."

"No, he is somewhere else meeting with...Julius and Titus. Gisela, our escort, is trying to be the power behind the throne as Renata once was. I don't think she's quite managed it."

"What about those others? Bacchus? Orion?"

"Hangers on. Toadies. Vastly interested in filling their stomachs and satisfying their base desires. I don't know Orion well enough to know if he carries a torch for Gisela or if he's just an irrepressible flirt."

"And...Julius?" She had not missed the way he had paused at the name, and when he had first heard it, he had gone remote and still.

"He changed his name. I knew him as Andrew."

She inhaled. *"He's the one who—"* Who had been Salem's friend? Who had told their maker the best way to break him?

"Yes."

"He should have changed his name to Judas," she thought fiercely.

"And he didn't even have the decency to get paid thirty pieces of silver for it," Salem said with black amusement. *"He did it purely for the favor of the woman who had killed him. I thought I had seen him in London, before Etienne and I came to Renwick, before I knew who was behind this plot. He's probably the reason Rupert uprooted his court of sycophants and brought them here. He loves to tell tales."*

"What is going to happen when Rupert arrives?"

"Don't worry. I will protect you."

"That's not what I asked," Ophelia thought, but Salem didn't answer. He had stiffened like a hunting dog on point, staring across the room as a man descended the grand stair with liquid grace. From his chest rumbled a low growl.

⛤

Salem stood and pulled Ophelia up with him, stepping in front of her as the threat approached.

Orion swanned up grinning as his glance darted between them. He could probably sense the coming confrontation and wanted front row seats.

"Julius, you remember Salem, of course," Orion said, not bothering to conceal his glee. "And he has a thrall now! He can still turn over new leaves."

Salem stared at his once-friend, still managing to look commonplace even in what Salem knew was a suit of the finest quality. "Andrew. Still crawling after those with power, I see."

Andrew's eyes flashed red. "It's Julius now."

"You can reinvent yourself all you like; I know what you are."

Andrew sniffed. "I never thought you would have brought yourself low for a *human*, Salem. But then...you've always been too soft. Unwilling to do what is necessary."

"And what is that, lick boots? Ask Renata how soft I was when I ripped her heart out."

Andrew snarled, "I should've killed you for that."

"You've had twenty years' worth of opportunity. I never understood why you panted after her. She murdered you."

"You wouldn't understand because you never appreciated the gift she gave us."

"Yes. The gift of fighting to the death and then turning us. What a blessing. I know why she never looked your way, you know. You're a coward at heart."

Andrew lunged at him, an ugly snarl twisting his face.

Ophelia squeaked.

Orion blocked Andrew's grasping fist as Salem thrust Ophelia further behind him.

"No one touches them until Wodan has his say," Orion chided Andrew. "You know that."

Kendrick snorted from his position a few paces away. Rupert's appellation was a little too ridiculous to be believed.

Andrew shook Orion off and straightened his coat. "You just wait until tonight," he warned. "Then you'll finally get your comeuppance, Salem."

"If I do, you won't be the one to give it to me."

"Go and sleep it off," Orion advised. "You, too—one last daydream, Salem. Then Court convenes tonight." He grinned toothily.

They sat on the chaise lounge and feigned sleep as the sun made its pathway through the sky. It went unseen, of course, since the drapes were securely closed, but Salem could feel its movement.

The denizens of the great hall slunk off to other rooms in the house to sleep or collapsed in corners to while away the daylight hours. The guards, vampires who had trained to stay awake during sunup, kept their eyes on them and the human captives as they patrolled.

Salem let his eyes drift to the barest slits and spoke to Ophelia. *"At any chance of escape, you take it. If I tell you to run, you run."*

"You forget that running is not my forté," Ophelia whispered in his mind, her voice carrying a sardonic edge.

"You promise me," he pushed.

"I'm not leaving you. Plus, Kendrick is here—and Addie and Etienne are free. Surely they can do something."

"We can't depend on them."

"You mean you can't. Salem, you've got to trust them. You're not alone. You can't single-handedly engineer our escape and bring down this corrupt ruler."

"I don't care about that anymore. I just want you safe."

"And you'll do what, sacrifice yourself?"

"If you can get out the doors while the sun is up, they can't follow you. If I thought you could make it, I'd smash the windows out right now, but I can't risk you getting cut by the broken glass."

"Then you'd burn!" She stilled against him, her hand wrapping around his wrist hard. *"Do not do that! I do not want that."*

"Then what?"

"We wait. We watch. We have faith."

He didn't have the heart to tell her that was one thing he didn't have.

As the sun wended its way across the sky, Salem caught fragments of thought from Ophelia, half-whispered phrases that were not directed at him. It took him several minutes to realize that she was praying.

Did she think that God would hear her, surrounded by such darkness and evil? He included himself in that group with more than a little bitterness, because he was a selfish fool.

Why appeal to God? You're the one who will save her. Or you won't and you'll fail, his shadow self whispered.

She's the only one that has a hope of reaching him, Salem thought. God had abandoned all of them a long time ago, no matter what Ophelia believed.

His shadow self demanded, *Make her forget her God and love none but you.*

The words hit him like a slap of icy water, chilling him.

No. *No.* To deny her that would be to destroy what made Ophelia, *Ophelia.*

And she would never do it. Asking it of her would be a sure way to drive her from me utterly.

In that moment—in that horrible, soul-revealing clarity—he realized who his shadow self actually sounded like. Not like *Salem*... but Andrew. His so-called friend, who had pushed him and chivvied him and betrayed him. Who had none of his best interests at heart.

I rebuke you, he thought. *Liar. Deceiver. Be gone from me.*

And just like that, the derisive, jeering voice broke and faded, like a fresh breeze dissipates fog or smoke. The only voices that remained were Salem and the irrational, nearly voiceless hunger inside him, which, while Salem wrestled with it and always would, driven by instinct to drink the whole world dry if he let it, was at least *honest.*

For the first time in twenty years—no, for the first time since his turning—Salem felt a weight lift.

He had finally identified the tempter inside himself and banished it.

When night fell, the vampires returned...and with them came Rupert. Andrew followed behind him like an obedient hound.

As the guards prodded the three of them towards the makeshift dais, Salem eyed the vampire he hadn't seen since Theron's end. Courtesy of the vampiric curse, Rupert looked just the same as he had twenty years ago, a middle-aged man of average height and running to gray, with dark, beady eyes and frown lines etched into his face. No wonder he had chosen to borrow the mien of Wodan and not a younger, more attractive pagan deity. Power and nothing else, that was Rupert's motto.

Gisela stepped forward and curtseyed deeply as Rupert seated himself in an opulent armchair positioned in front of the massive fireplace and its heraldry and coat of arms. They must've scoured the house to find the most impressive, thronelike seat possible. Salem hoped it stuck in Gisela's craw that she had to bow and scrape to such a man. He suspected, given ten or twenty more years to gather power, she would seek to supplant him.

Rupert should watch his back.

"Court will convene," Rupert intoned.

"Draugadróttinn, we have retrieved the vampire Salem, as well as Kendrick and this thrall," Gisela said, her lip curling, "to receive your judgment and justice."

"Humans are not permitted in the Court," Andrew said. "They have no place in this."

Rupert's beady eyes took in Ophelia as well as the cluster of horrified servants. "Take them away." He waved an arm.

The guards muscled their way through the crowd.

"If you lay a hand on her, I'll remove every appendage from your body," Salem growled as they approached.

"Be reasonable," Kendrick murmured. "It will be safer for her out of the way. Thomas will look after Ophelia, won't you, Thomas?"

The footman, looking pale but no longer in danger of expiring from fright, nodded and took Ophelia's arm.

"It will be all right," Ophelia said, squeezing his hand. "Just promise—"

He didn't know what she wanted him to promise before the guards shoved them towards the clump of humans.

Salem clenched his fists, fighting the urge to go to her, to put himself between her and danger.

What was it she had wanted him to promise?

It didn't matter.

"I promise," he said.

❧

Ophelia couldn't catch a last glimpse of Salem before the vampire guards forced the sobbing, gasping group of humans down the hallway to the west wing. They passed the music room and continued down the hall to one of the rooms that had been a parlor of some sort twenty years ago. Once all the people had all been stuffed inside, the guards slammed and locked the door.

Ophelia elbowed her way through the throng to shake the doorknob. Well and truly locked, and the wood of the door and frame still seemed sound, though the room smelled like mildew, which indicated some sort of water damage.

If only I had my lockpicks! She thought desperately. *That will teach me not to put them in my pockets.*

The room was nearly full dark, and distraught cries were starting to rise from the throng of people. "Everyone take a breath!" Ophelia commanded. "Hysterics will not serve us. Where are the windows? Opening the drapes may admit a little moonlight."

"I'll go," Thomas's voice said. With a few thumps and muttered curses when he barked his shins on furniture in the darkness, he managed to make his way to the far side of the room and pull back the heavy drapes from the windows. It admitted the bare minimum of light, but it let them pick out shapes and outlines—the room's dimensions, furniture covered with dust and drop cloths, themselves, and—

Mrs. Lowell screamed, a high, thready sound.

Everyone jumped and milled about, trying to see.

"They're dead! They're dead!" she shrieked. Her cries spread to the women. The men swore.

Ophelia unsteadily pushed her way to the front of the crowd, trying to pick out what she had seen.

The shapes tossed into the corner refused to sort themselves out into discernable objects. She kept moving towards the darkness. Then the horror struck her—an arm outflung from a still chest, an unnaturally bent body, heads at the wrong angle.

She picked out the missing servants, as well as the fair head of Mr. Harding...then the slope of a nose, the shape of a forehead too much like her own.

Ophelia swallowed hard as her gorge tried to rise. She pressed a hand to her chest.

I knew they were dead, I knew it...but it's somehow more horrible to see them like this—tossed away like garbage.

"Hush!" she finally cried. It took her two tries to get the words out. "Hush! They're dead. They can't hurt us. Come to the opposite side of the room, near the windows. Uncover some of these settees so we can sit and plan. We have some thinking to do."

Because there are other dead things in this house that can *hurt us,* she thought, *and we need to be ready.*

Chapter Thirty-One

"The Court will now convene," one of the guard vampires intoned. "The accused will stand forth."

No one moved.

"That's you two," Gisela said.

"Oh? What are the charges?" Kendrick asked idly.

"Consorting with humans and revealing our existence to them," Rupert said, his lips twisting up in a smile. "Our most stringent law."

"If I stand accused of such, then I damn you with the same," Salem snapped.

Rupert had the temerity to look bored. "And your claim?"

"You, *Rupert*, sold out members of your own court to humans in exchange for money. You ignored the complaints and sufferings of your people as they disappeared to unknown ends. You have betrayed your oath and your duty to your people."

Rupert leaned forward on his makeshift throne, a snake about to strike. "I am the King, the Draugadróttinn!"

"Do you deny it?" Salem pressed. "The king is not above the law."

Rupert spread his hands. "You are the only one objecting," he pointed out, motioning to his toadies.

"Because you began betraying those you disliked, those on the margins, the vulnerable. But if you are an oathbreaker, your word is empty and void, and whatever promises you have made your followers are like so much ash in the sunlight. Betrayers cannot be trusted."

"Who are you preaching to?" Rupert mocked. "You think someone is going to lift a finger to help you now? I hold all the cards! I hold your death in my hands, and your human's as well!"

Salem stared around at the assembled vampires, who stared back, variously impassive, mocking, and bored. "If you haven't anyone who can speak truth to power, then you are a self-fulfilling prophecy of doom. But if the truth is spoken and no one acts on it, does that make it any less the truth?"

"I've had enough of this," Rupert growled. "How do you plead?"

Salem glared at him. "I don't plead anything."

"Salem, I pronounce you an usurper and an inciter of rebellion. The sentence is death."

"Then I demand trial by combat," Salem said, and a wave of hisses swept the room.

Salem didn't move as the wave of whispers and gasps crashed under the weight of Rupert's rage. "That rule does not apply!" Rupert barked.

"Actually, it does," Kendrick said. "Salem has not committed murder, has not attempted to escape, and the evidence is not heavily damning. He has the right to demand trial by combat."

"And how would you know?" Andrew sneered.

"I helped write the law code, pup," Kendrick rumbled.

"More pitiful attempts to delay the inevitable? Fine. Clear the floor," Rupert snapped. "I call Julius to fight in my place. Bring me his heart!"

Andrew stepped forward, his expression eager.

"You won't even fight me yourself?" Salem asked. "Even that task you'll pass off on your lackeys?"

Anger flashed through Andrew's eyes, burning ruby red. "I'm going to enjoy drinking your thrall dry."

Salem felt fear that was not his own through the bond.

I'm doing what I must, he thought, trying to send the words through the bond. *Don't worry.*

He couldn't see Kendrick anymore.

He and Andrew circled each other as the vampires formed the boundaries of the circle, waiting. Tension filled the air, thickening it like blood. Their audience followed their movements like a shark tracks prey. Smelling who would show a vulnerability first. Who would show first blood. Rupert loomed above them all on the makeshift dais, their tyrant commanding a spectacle.

They had no weapons—or no obvious ones. Salem would not put it past Andrew to pull a knife or a stake from a hidden pocket and jab it in his heart, given half the chance.

"You know, I'm glad it's you, *Andrew*," Salem said, his eyes narrowing on his former friend. "I know what you told Renata to break me. But it didn't work."

"You still carry a grudge about that?" Andrew said, trying to appear nonchalant.

"You sold me out in London, too. You're a creature of betrayal. A crawling sycophant, too eager to sell anything out for your share of silver. And that's all you'll ever be."

Andrew growled.

"What's the matter?" Salem goaded. "Too afraid to face me? I thought you were going to mete out your master's judgment."

With a snarl, Andrew sprang.

Chapter Thirty-Two

Ophelia spent a moment on the windows, but the windows did not open. The panes of glass were small. Smashing them would not provide a wide enough space to escape. They also faced Renwick's courtyard, and that would put them closer to the vampires than safety, especially with the whole night ahead of them.

"Here's what we should do," she told the group of frightened people. "Let's use the furniture to barricade the door. They've locked it so we can't get out? Well, let's make it hard for them to get in. We can break off some of the table and chair legs to use as weapons as well. Does anyone have any silver?"

"No, they took any silver when they arrived," Heloise, the downstairs maid whispered. "They made us take it off and pile it with all the good silver. They locked it away."

"All right. Well, vampires are vulnerable to wooden stakes to the heart, I think—though I daresay most people are. We can be ready." Ophelia made her voice firm and uncompromising, chivvying frightened people into action.

"Why should we listen to you?" Mrs. Lowell demanded, her voice high and thready. "You went off and disappeared—then came back with one of those—those *things*! You were with them! You told them to pick Thomas to *eat*!"

The group hesitated, eyes going back and forth between Ophelia and the cook. Then Thomas cleared his throat. "But I'm not dead. And I might've been if any other monster had picked me."

"We didn't know if they planned to kill anyone else. But if you're a vampire's thrall, none of the others can touch you. I was trying to keep someone alive. And that's what I'm doing now," Ophelia said, voice growing stronger. "I won't try to tell you that Salem and Kendrick are good men because I'm sure you won't believe me. But if they fail in this farce of a court, then we will all probably die. And there are only two of them. So we need to prepare."

Then Ophelia ceded the floor to Thomas and some of the other men as they began to erect a barricade, piling up heavy furniture in the best way to keep the door from being shoved in by supernaturally strong forces.

She sat on a low footstool and closed her eyes, concentrating on her connection to Salem. She listened hard down their bond, trying to follow Salem's conversation and arguments with people she couldn't see. Then she held her breath as he demanded trial by combat. She hadn't even known that was possible. And he would fight Andrew, his old friend...to the death? She pressed her lips together as whispers started building around her.

She lifted her head and hissed. "I am trying to concentrate! Do you *mind*?"

Silence fell.

Guilt oozed forth. Ophelia opened her mouth to apologize, but in the quiet, something rasped.

She froze. So did everyone else.

It came again.

"What is it?" Heloise whimpered.

Lit by a sliver of moonlight, Thomas went rigid, staring into the room's dark corners. "Did something...move?"

⚜

Salem dodged, avoiding Andrew's blow, and lashed out with his own strike to the vampire's knee. But Andrew was fast—more so than he had been twenty years ago. Power had done that much for him.

Salem circled him, looking for weaknesses to the head and heart—the best places for an instant kill if you were a vampire. But Andrew kept his guard up, and stayed light on his feet. He had learned a thing or two in twenty years.

Andrew attacked with a flurry of blows, raining down on Salem faster than any human eye would be able to follow. Salem dodged most of the hits. He too was quick on his feet, but Andrew got in more blows than Salem liked.

Salem backed away and kept circling, but the vampires that made up the throng pressed forward, contracting the fight arena.

"Now who's running?" Andrew said, teeth gleaming. "Call me *coward*, and now you run?"

Salem didn't answer. His eyes locked on Andrew's guard. He lashed out and kicked at Andrew's knee again. As Andrew dodged, Salem made his true strike, seeking Andrew's ribs and the heart that lay beneath. Andrew threw himself out of the way, rolling to the edge of the circle and regaining his feet in one fluid motion. He snarled and attacked again.

Salem only saw the barest flash of metal to signal foul play. He twisted as much as he could. The blade missed his throat but caught his shoulder. He hissed at the harsh burn of silver. Blood splattered his clothes and the floor.

"Not only coward but cheat!" Salem spat.

Andrew's eyes burned red as he attacked again.

The swinging silver blade with a wrapped hilt forced Salem to back up again and again in the confined space. The wall of vampires kept jostling him forward, and he didn't dare treat them with any kind of trust—he didn't know who Andrew's friends were. Any one of them could try to put another silver knife in his back, rules or no.

Salem was outnumbered. He had no idea where Kendrick was, and none of these vampires cared about the rule of law, or Rupert's crimes, or justice. But he had to stay alive. Ophelia's life depended on it. All of the subjects Rupert had exploited and sold —and would continue to do so—depended on it.

If the onlookers didn't care, he had to *make* them care.

Andrew swiped out with the knife again, nicking him. He was bleeding freely now on the varnished wood floor, and their footing was now slick. It was an equal opportunity hazard.

Salem let himself sway a little more.

Andrew crowed, "Who's weak now?"

You're not the one who spent days surrounded by silver, stabbed with it, starved and drained, Salem thought, gritting his teeth, waiting for the smallest sliver of an opening, That's all he'd need. One opening.

"I'm going to skewer you like a pig. Bleed you. You're going to scream, too. And I'll leave you just alive enough to watch what I do to your little thrall."

Salem's muscles bunched, but he didn't take the bait. He would keep Ophelia safe. This scum wouldn't touch her.

"I'm going to have her blood in my teeth before this night is through!" Andrew waggled the knife at Salem, his grin mocking. "No smart comebacks? No words of rage?"

He tossed the knife in his hands and caught it, like a tough in a bar brawl.

He tossed it again.

"No," Salem said, and with a flying kick knocked the knife out of Andrew's hand.

The silver knife spun into the crowd. An onlooker screamed.

Salem was on Andrew before he could react, smashing his fist into the smug vampire's face. He felt a fang break against his knuckles. Salem rained down blow after blow on joints and sensitive areas, hammering his fist into his ribcage, driving a knee into Andrew's groin. Andrew gasped and folded up.

Salem didn't let up, smashing his eye socket until Andrew's face ran with blood. He broke the wrist Andrew brought up to try to block the blows.

Andrew coughed, blood splattering as Salem caught him by the throat.

The crowd hushed.

His shadow self that sounded so much like Andrew would have urged Salem kill him quickly, win the bout.

But there was a higher priority than just winning.

"Cry craven," Salem hissed. "I want to hear it from your lips."

Andrew sneered, his face a bloody mess.

Salem hit him again. "Cry craven, or I rip your throat out. I'll watch you bleed to death, slowly, choking in your own blood. I won't make it quick or clean. You're going to experience every second before your second life is permanently halted." He dug his fingers into Andrew's larynx and artery, knowing just how much force it would take to part the pallid flesh.

"No more!" Andrew choked out. "Leave off, no more!"

"'While you live, tell truth and shame the Devil!'" Salem raised his hand again.

"He wanted the money!" Andrew wailed. "Too many followers to support, not enough respect—Wodan wanted his coffers refilled."

Salem threw him down where Andrew moaned and curled into a ball. "You have heard the truth," he announced to the crowd. "Now what will you do about it?"

The assembled stared at Salem, bloody and covered in gore, swaying as he kept himself upright by force of will.

"Kill him!" Rupert cried, rising from his chair. "Someone kill him, kill—"

Thwack!

Thud.

Rupert's head hit the floor, eyes empty, staring.

Kendrick stood over the body, staring impassively as blood dripped from the ancient longsword in his hand.

The headless corpse slumped in the seat. Kendrick tipped the chair forward so the body slid off in a crumpled heap.

He twirled the sword in his hand and tipped his head in apology to Salem. "I had to find something to give it an edge. It was shamefully dull." He stared over the assembled throng of vampires, frozen in place, staring at their fallen leader.

"The guilt was proved. Justice has been done. The king is dead," he said in a hard voice. "Long live the king."

Just then, the room's windows shattered inward.

Chapter Thirty-Three

Ophelia's pulse echoed in her ears.

Did something move?

For two breaths, there was silence, and her heart-beat began to slow.

Then she heard it—a scrape. Something moving against the floorboards. And then....

A groan.

"One of them's alive!" Rivers exclaimed. "One of them is still alive!" He made an abortive move toward the pile of bodies in the corner.

"No!" Ophelia exclaimed.

Because she suddenly knew what had happened. The servants said that her father and Ben and Mr. Harding had been in the cellar when the vampires were admitted to the house. They had barred themselves in for a few minutes before the vampires broke in and killed them. The blood they drained from Salem was still down there—he hadn't remembered to get it, so concerned was he about her injuries.

They must've drunk the blood, she thought frantically. Known they might die and drunk it and then....

How did Salem say it worked? You drink the blood and then you die for a full day and then...you come back?

"We have to help them!" Rivers insisted. "If the master is alive—"

"Alive is not the word," Ophelia said tightly. "Get back!"

A strange, horrible chuckle filled the air and silenced them all. It rasped, as if someone had scraped a piano wire.

Shivers raced down Ophelia's spine.

One of the grooms swore.

Then all hell broke loose.

"Let us out, let us out!" some began to cry, ripping down the furniture they had barricaded the door with and banging on it. Some of the women began to shriek.

Ophelia tried to think past the blood pounding in her ears, but something in that laugh drove reason away.

It was Thomas whose voice cut through the panic. "Here!" he shouted. "The damp has got into the wall here! Help me break through!"

The men began hacking at the paneling and plaster with the frantic energy of those consumed with terror. Ophelia got out of their way and clutched a broken chair leg, her eyes forced open wide to catch any movement in the dark.

"Ophelia...."

She swallowed a whimper.

"Where are you, Ophelia...I can smell you. I never could smell you before. So lovely. Like an orange. Ripe." The chuckler made a smacking sound. "Ophelia. You were promised to me...and then ran away."

The chuckler was Lucas Harding.

The scraping intensified behind her as the men pried away plaster and boards from the wall. "Make a hole!" Thomas commanded. "Make a hole!"

"Mr. Harding," Ophelia said, hating the tremor in her voice, "Something has happened to you. Let me explain—"

"Yessss, something has ...happened to me." He smacked his lips again. "I am stronger than before. Powerful. My senses are enhanced. I can hear your heartbeat, you know."

"Can you hear the lack of your own?" Ophelia asked.

"It's large enough—go through!" Thomas hissed. "The women first!"

"Hell with that," someone growled.

"Hmmmm," Mr. Harding said through the dark. "Interesting. I don't even need to breathe. What a fascinating scientific discovery."

"Wouldn't you like to take some observations of your condition?" Ophelia asked as people began passing through the space in the wall. She wasn't sure what room it opened onto, but it was something between them and the threat, and if God was good, that door would not be locked.

"Yes, yes...no heartbeat, no breath needed except for speaking. An enhanced sense of smell. And...I can *see you*."

Something hurtled towards Ophelia in the dark.

She shrieked and brought the chair leg she held down.

The stout piece of wood kept Mr. Harding from falling on her neck immediately, but she saw the rictus of his wide mouth far too close, his fangs gleaming. He snarled and wrested the stave away from her with incredible strength, tossing it away.

"Now you will be m—" The words devolved into a long howl as something slammed into his back.

Ophelia staggered back as Mr. Harding fell to his knees, a jagged piece of wood protruding from his back. Rivers stood over him, panting and sheet white.

Mr. Harding measured his length on the floor. A slow pool of blood formed below him.

"Is it dead?" Rivers said.

"I—if you hit him in the heart, then I think—"

"Hello, Rivers." Ben loomed above the butler, smiling. Then he seized him by the hair and sank his teeth into his neck.

Ophelia stuffed her fist against her mouth, stifling her scream.

Rivers screamed and thrashed in her brother's grip. Until Ben pulled back, blood and flesh in his teeth.

Ophelia's gorge rose. *He ripped his throat out!*

She backed away, feeling her way, too afraid to look away from the nightmare in front of her in the dark. The sounds—sucking, slurping, the gurgles of Rivers' death—she would never be able to forget.

"Miss!" Thomas hissed. He reached for her. She took his hand, let him pull her to the hole in the wall, even as her leg trembled. He boosted her up just as Ben's head came up. He swiped his arm over his mouth.

"Ophelia," he said in a sing-song voice.

Ophelia half-fell through the opening and barely got out of the way for Thomas to come through. "Come on!" He seized her hand.

"Where do you go, sister-mine?" Ben called.

I can't run, Ophelia realized. She physically couldn't keep up with Thomas. She would slow him down. "Go," she hissed. "Find Salem or Kendrick! I'll hold him off!"

"How?"

"Talking," she said grimly, and shoved him. "*Go*! That's an order!"

Thomas ran through the darkened doorway of the room. Ophelia limped after him into the hallway.

"Ophelia, are you running from me? From your dearest darling brother?" Ben laughed.

"Ben, I'm so sorry this happened to you," Ophelia said, backing away down the hallway.

Ben's tall form stepped into the hallway, just a smudge in the darkness. "Why are you sorry? I'm the nightmare everyone dreams about." He cackled. "I could kill the whole world if I wanted. Swim in it, all that blood."

"Ben, you don't have to do this. You can control it," she told him.

"I don't want to. I feel powerful. Invincible. *Hungry*."

"Ben, this will never satisfy you."

"How do you know? Oh, that's right. You ran away with monsters." He made a derisive noise in the back of his throat.

He sounded closer. She backed further down the hallway.

"You know what they say about those who lie down with dogs, Ophelia."

"Ben, don't you see? The people you were experimenting on—they were people just like you are now. You can still choose what you do from now on. You don't have to hurt people."

"The way I hurt you? Oh, Ophelia." His low laugh chased her down the hallway. "Ophelia, with her 'woe is me' and her *stupid* letters and her whining about coming to London...like a mosquito in my ear."

"It meant nothing? I don't believe that," she pleaded.

"Nuisance girl," he mused. "I can shut you up now. Swat you. No more buzzing."

"You did care about me. Maybe not as truly and steadfastly as I wanted you to. But you did, even a little bit. That part of you is still in there somewhere. I know it is."

"Monsters care nothing for lesser beings," her brother declared.

"That's not true," she said desperately, trying to feel for something, anything in the hallway. "It's not *true*—"

"I wonder how you'll *taste*...."

A shadow sprang.

Ophelia screamed.

Chapter Thirty-Four

In through the shattered windows poured Etienne, Addie... and *Faelad*. They also had more weapons at their disposal than just their hands and teeth. Addie swung a truly enormous mace, Etienne held a dagger and a dueling rapier, and Faelad had a wickedly sharp axe that gleamed in the candlelight.

The room dissolved into chaos.

Some vampires ran for the doors, some turned on the newcomers with their fangs, some made for Salem and Kendrick as the main threats.

Salem thrust his hand into the ribs of a vampire that came too close and ripped his heart free. The vampire fell in a spray of blood like a collapsed marionette.

"Doing all right?" Etienne said, throwing him a dagger. Salem grabbed it out of the air and severed some else's throat with an arc of blood.

"Well enough. Where did you come from?"

"We went after Faelad for more muscle to help."

"And you were able to find him?" Salem said, twisting a head off. Kendrick was taking out a good number with that huge sword he had appropriated, swinging it in wide arcs with the sense of old familiarity. There was no better way to kill a vampire than a beheading or a stake.

"That's Addie's talent, apparently—she can find anyone." Etienne beamed. "My clever girl."

Salem put a pin in that for later. "And so, you—"

A stream of humans poured from the west wing and created a bottleneck, freezing at the death scene in front of them.

A man elbowed his way to the front of the group. "Help, please!" he panted. It was the footman Kendrick had drunk from. "They came alive! Miss Shaw needs—"

Ophelia screamed in his head, "*Salem!*"

Time slowed.

Salem ran.

He bolted down the passageway, through the darkness, until he saw her crumpled on the ground, her revivified brother bent over her, mouth bloody.

The knife in his hand swung.

Salem didn't bother savoring the look of surprised horror in Benjamin's eyes before he was dust and bone on the floor.

"*Ophelia!*"

Salem was at her side in an instant, teeth cutting into his own wrist to give her blood, his whole being screaming in torment to heal her, *heal her*—But as the blood gushed from her throat, as she struggled for breath, Salem knew with the experience of years it would not be enough.

His blood would try to staunch the bleeding, fix the damage, but it would fail. The rate would not be fast enough. It was not meant for healing. Only fixing those with all the time in the world. The wound was mortal.

Ophelia would die. And if his blood was in her, maybe she would open her eyes again in a night and her eyes, her beautiful hazel eyes, would be devoid of color.

And then she would hate him.

Or maybe she wouldn't open her eyes at all.

He heard his own voice from far away. Begging. "Ophelia, no. No."

But I can't lose her! The monster inside him howled. *She can't leave this world! She can't leave me! I need* her!

How strange, that he should finally admit to his need just when faced with losing everything.

Salem pressed hard on the wound, trying to staunch the blood with cloth, but he had a better chance of holding back the ocean with his hands. He felt the blood soak through, hot and tacky under his fingers.

If you're going to do it, it must be now, the devil in his head warned. *She can't die without your blood in her. Otherwise there's no chance.*

Ophelia choked, her hand spasming. Reaching for him. Still.

"Don't leave me," Salem cried, "I'm sorry. I'm so sorry. Please don't leave me."

She wouldn't want this. The cost would be too high.

But it's the only thing I can do! The only thing I can do to save her!

But it wouldn't save her.

It would only damn her.

Salem didn't have the power to save her in any meaningful way.

"Do you want me to beg? This is me begging!" he shouted to God, though He wasn't listening. He never was. "I'm begging! On my *knees*! Don't do this! Not to her...."

Ophelia's lips formed his name, and Salem felt as if death had come for him, not her. Nothing else could hurt this much. If Ophelia died, what point was left in his existence?

But death would bring no release for him. They were destined for different eternities.

"*I love you, Ophelia*," he forced out, clutching her to him. "Don't go. Please don't go. I can't follow you where you're going."

She was so pale, the blood leaving her. He could hear her heart starting to stutter. A scream built up in him, and he could do nothing to stop it.

God! How can you be this cruel! How can you ask me to live on without her? I can't! I can't; I'm not strong enough.

Tears splattered on her blanching skin. Red. His blood.

He hadn't cried since he lost his humanity.

A hand on his shoulder, forcefully shoving. "Move."

Salem reacted with a monster's snarl, rabid, poised to kill.

But strength met his strike, and he stared back at a monster in Faelad's eyes. "We won't lose her if I have anything to say about it."

The werewolf released him and took Ophelia's hand. He ripped her sleeve, baring her skin. "Lass, if you're willing, I'll give you my last, best gift. Squeeze my hand."

"What are you talking about?" Salem forced the words through the monster's internal howling.

Faelad ignored him.

Ophelia blinked, her eyes attempting to focus on Faelad. Her fingers spasmed around his.

Faster than human movement, Faelad sank sharply elongated teeth into her arm.

She screamed, and her whole body arched, as if given a shock.

Salem instinctively moved to take Faelad's head off, but someone grabbed him in a headlock and held onto him, even as he fought them with everything he had.

"*Attends, imbécile*, and stop trying to pull my arm off," Etienne growled.

Salem stared, dumbfounded, as a rush of—something—flowed from Faelad into Ophelia. She wailed in agony.

He bucked again, fighting to get to her, but Etienne stayed his movement, holding him fast. "Not until it's finished, *mon ami*," he forced out.

"He's hurting her!" Salem didn't sound human anymore, his voice falling into a monstrous register.

"He's giving her something that we can't," Etienne hissed. "Life."

Salem watched Faelad release his teeth from Ophelia's arm and steady her as she shook and thrashed. "Easy, lass, breathe. Breathe through it. The pain will be over soon. The wolf's teeth have to sink into you and grip tight before it eases." He panted as he restrained her, and he looked somehow older to Salem's eyes. Old and tired.

"Wolf?" Salem whispered.

"Aye." Faelad's vitality seemed faded. Worn. The grey in his hair and beard spread, leeching the red color away. "The Ossory wolves' curse is a duty that is passed on. It is a mixed blessing, and a heavy burden—but no damnation. She is not sundered from grace."

Ophelia suddenly relaxed, as if whatever force had taken over her eased.

"There now," Desmond whispered, brushing her hair away from her face and blotting the sweat on her brow. "Forgive me for the hurt I caused you, lass. I wanted you to be mine badly. So badly. When you were not, I forgot that you were still Cornelia's child, and that's enough. Receive this gift, and let it protect and keep you, as I should have and did not."

Faelad sighed and sat back. "You can give her your blood now. It won't turn her."

Salem immediately bit his wrist and held it to her mouth, shaken to the core.

Not gone. She's not gone. He could barely believe it. He had more time with Ophelia.

He could have a *life* with Ophelia, without turning her. Without consigning her to his abject darkness. His chest tightened as her throat slowly knitted itself back together with the aid of his blood. If that was possible...maybe *anything* was possible.

Even grace for the damned.

She had thought it was over. When Ben had torn her throat, Ophelia thought that would be it.

And all she knew was she didn't want to leave Salem. Not yet.

And then Desmond had come, and he'd given her a gift. Life, yes, but as her chest eased and the prickling in her throat strengthened, as the bite on her arm itched and she swallowed Salem's blood, all she could think of were his words.

"You were still Cornelia's child, and that's enough."

She had had her throat torn out by her own brother without remorse...and this man who had no claim on her gave up his gift. Just for her.

She pulled back from Salem's wrist, the sharp, coppery taste registering for the first time, but she didn't recoil as she expected.

"Ophelia?" Salem said.

"Help me sit up?" she whispered. "I'm all right."

When she did, she took Desmond's hand in hers and clutched it tight. He winced, and she looked down in surprise to see that her fingernails had drawn blood in his palms.

"You'll have a bit of that, lass," he said. "But you'll take to it just fine. You're not one to let the wolf rule you."

"I don't feel any different," Ophelia said.

"You just wait until the full moon," Desmond said dryly. Ophelia must've looked startled because he went on, "But don't worry. I'll help you."

"You will?"

"You've got your mother's eyes," he said softly. "Why didn't I see that before?"

Ophelia wrapped her arms around him. "Thank you."

"Etienne, Salem?" Addie's voice called. "I think we should leave. The house is on fire."

All of them looked up.

Ophelia heard a far-off susurration, a crackle that seemed to grow louder and louder as she listened. Salem seized her in his arms and lifted her, taking off for the wing's exit. The rest of them followed close behind.

Once outside, Ophelia stared up at Renwick, the flicker of yellow and orange flames visible through the broken windows.

Addie said, "Some of the fleeing vampires purposefully knocked over candles and lanterns to slow our pursuit. I'm sorry, Ophelia."

"That's all right," Ophelia said. And strangely, that was the truth. She felt a pang—but a dull sadness, not the sharp knife of grief. "That's what happens, isn't it? When a house is too full of darkness, it must be burned down. That's how characters start fresh." The wind blew through the trees, making the flames jump higher.

"Well, that's all right then," Addie said happily. "And don't worry. We hid the cats in the mausoleum. Blaze too! He came and found us," she said. "He's so smart."

"Blaze did?" Ophelia's heart leapt. "Oh I'm so glad!" She threw her arms around Addie.

"Oh!" Addie exclaimed. "You squeezed me."

"Sorry," Ophelia giggled.

"No! You're stronger now!" Addie stared at her wide-eyed.

"This doesn't mean you get to squeeze Ophelia back right away," Etienne put in smoothly. "She is still recovering."

"Fine," Addie said. "I'll just squeeze you!" She threw her arms around his neck.

"Addie, Salem will take my head off," Etienne said, reddening. But Ophelia noticed he didn't let her go.

"No, he won't; I'll protect you," she said, rubbing her cheek against his.

"Should I ask him for your hand, then?"

"Addie is her own person," Salem told him. "As long as you're good to her, I won't need to."

Etienne looked offended. "I will be more than good. I will be the best lover."

As they walked to the mausoleum, Ophelia could hear the barking of a dog. She ran forward and found Blaze straining at the end of his lead to get to her. Then the dog froze and backed up, whining. "Blaze? What is it?"

"He's confused by your scent," Faelad said. "Here, lass." He took her hand and led her forward. "Let him smell you and hear your voice."

"Blaze, everything's all right," she said. "I know you were scared. I'm so glad you're all right," she said, her voice wavering. "You were so good to find Addie and Etienne."

The dog's tail began to wag.

"Do I smell different?" She touched the healing bite on her neck, and the teeth marks on her arm. "I know this must be confusing, but...."

Blaze charged forward, knocking aside her outstretched hand to rub his body against hers, whining and crying.

"Oh, Blaze." Ophelia put her arms around the dog and held him. She petted his ears and told him what a good dog he was. "You're all right. Everyone's all right," she said in a choked voice. "Oh, and the cats." There was the basket, with a lot of upset felines inside. She patted the wicker gently. "We'll find a place to let you out soon."

"We can let them out in the mausoleum," Addie said. "Etienne, help me."

Ophelia sniffed and wiped her nose, standing up. Kendrick was petting her dog as Blaze's tail wagged, looking between the vampires and Faelad and Ophelia to make sure it was all right. But Salem had lingered a few paces away, watching them with a strange look on his face.

Ophelia went over to him. "Salem, what is it?"

His face was bleak. "I thought I lost you. You were dying and there was no choice I could make—nothing I could do. And then Faelad...." Salem swallowed. "I've never been so afraid."

"I'm here," she said, taking his hand. "And I...don't know what the full moon will bring, but we'll figure it out. Together. Won't we?" she asked hesitantly. Then she laughed a little. "'Lord, we know what we are, but not what we may be.'"

Salem pressed a hand to his chest. "I don't deserve this," Salem said. "I don't deserve *you*, Ophelia."

"Isn't that the profound mystery of grace?" Ophelia whispered. "You don't have to."

He closed his eyes, and she saw red tears trail down his cheeks.

"There now," she whispered, wrapping her arms around him, kissing the stains away. "Everything's all right."

"I am not good," he whispered. "But I want to be. I love you, Ophelia. So much more than words could express."

Ophelia smiled. "Even Shakespeare's?"

"Even Shakespeare's, though I'll use his until my own tongue finds its way."

"That's a good place to start."

Salem leaned towards her, hovering over her mouth. Ophelia breathed in the scent of books and paper that was uniquely Salem —as well as the lingering smell of smoke. She closed the distance between them and pressed her lips to his. The pressure of his unwavering frame comforted her even as his hands held her close and his lips...ah, his lips.

Salem whispered in her mind, *You have witchcraft in your lips.*

Ophelia had to break the kiss to laugh.

❧

While Ophelia joined Addie in petting the cats inside the mausoleum, Kendrick carefully wiped the blood and ash off the blade of the sword onto the grass as Salem watched. Then

Kendrick pulled out a handkerchief and carefully ran it over the blade. Finally, Salem couldn't stand the silence any longer. "I'm not going back. I meant what I said."

"I know."

"I won't be the Master. I don't want to be. I'd be bad at the job."

"I know."

"I—what?"

"No one's asking you to," Kendrick said. "You've already done above and beyond what most would do. Now it's my turn."

"Your turn?"

"I think it's time I stopped wandering," he said, his eyes distant. "I stayed gone a few too many centuries."

"Well, I'll say good luck. You'll need it with that snake's nest in London," Salem said grudgingly.

"I think we've winnowed some of the worst already," Kendrick said with a sudden grin. He spun the sword in his hand, testing the weight and the grip, then turned it and offered it to Ophelia, who had come to join them. "Thank you for the use of your sword," he said.

"Oh no, thank you," Ophelia said, blinking up at him. She looked down at the sword, then back at Kendrick. "Do you... would you like it?" She glanced at the burning house in the distance and then down at the sword. "It's never been down from the wall that I know of. I don't know what I'd do with it."

Kendrick bowed to her gravely and kissed her hand. "Thank you."

"You're welcome," Ophelia said, bemused.

"So, what are you going to do, if not go to London?" Kendrick asked Salem.

Salem opened his mouth—then closed it. He looked at Ophelia. "Where do you want to go?"

"What do you mean?"

"I mean I'll go anywhere. Even London. As long as it's with you. I'm not going to leave you. So where does the road lead us?"

She looked up at him and smiled.

❧

Ophelia knocked on the door to Marie-Claire's house, and when the door opened, stepped inside.

"Aren't you coming?" she whispered to Salem.

He smiled crookedly at her, standing on the stoop with Desmond and holding Blaze's lead.

But in that moment Marie-Claire and Owen came down the stairs, tightening their belts of their dressing gowns. "Ophelia!" Marie-Claire gasped. "What are you doing here? Are you all right? We've been worried!" Her eyes traveled over Ophelia's rumpled and dirt-streaked clothes and the basket of unhappy cats and the muddy dog.

"I'll tell you all about it," Ophelia assured her. "May my friends come inside?"

The Glenwoods stared in surprise past Ophelia at the two men on the stoop.

"I promise we mean no harm to you and yours," Salem said quietly.

"Ophelia...who is this?"

"Desmond is an old friend of my mother's, and...this is Salem." Ophelia took Salem's hand.

He looked down at her, and she saw herself reflected in his colorless eyes. She smiled.

"Yes, of course they can come in out of the cold, good grief!" Marie-Claire said. "What has happened, Ophelia?"

She squeezed Marie-Claire's hand. "Don't worry. I'll tell you everything."

❧

Need some more vampires in your life? You can read a FREE short story featuring **Addie and Etienne** if you sign up for my newsletter on my website www.clairetrellahill.com.

And if you enjoyed this story, please consider leaving a review on your preferred book retailer and/or book review site. It really does make a difference. Thank you so much!

Acknowledgments

I've written several books before this one, but this book in particular wouldn't exist without a few things. First, my online group of encouraging writers who have conversations about everything under the sun, and offer their knowledge and wisdom freely about writing and about navigating the world of indie publishing, and ask to beta read and say nice things about my books (and find all my typos). The Things with Feathers are the best. Thank you so much for being my friends.

Thanks to David M. for weekly updates on your Curse of Strahd Dungeons and Dragons game during Covid, and long chats about vampires. It made my disparate, unconnected ideas I've had for years mesh together to form one amazing idea that wouldn't go away. Thanks for listening to all my disjointed vampire rambling, David. You rock.

Ani, thank you for your timely feedback that talked me off a character arc ledge and also for reading this book in TWO DAYS?? Unbelievable. You're the best.

To Mathilda Zeller, you're a trailblazer and a great beta partner. You gave me the courage to take the plunge.

EC Farrell, thanks for quoting the book back to me in such an encouraging way, and also for finding my typos.

Irina, thank you for saving my French and helping me proofread, you're incredible.

Double amount of thanks to Alexandra, number one fan and cheerleader, who called me after she read the draft with all the holes in it and proceeded to yell excitedly over the phone to me.

It means the world, even when I have no idea how to receive praise.

For my writing generally, my college writing group who read all my first drafts—you're the real MVPs. You should've gotten hazard pay. Also, my post-college WriteCreate group—thank you for your encouragement and feedback. Monthly meetups made me persevere.

Thank you to Dr. Strait for my Shakespeare class in college. Something must've stuck, Dr. Strait!! Sorry for all the quotes I pulled out of context for this story. Thanks also to Dr. Gobin for reading us Beowulf in Brit Lit 1—core memory right there, as you can see. Dr. Penner, the Gothic Novel independent study we did together was very formative, if you can believe it!! I wish I could take it again and this time talk about all the texts with a much more knowledgable eye. Dr. Brown and Dr. Hurlow, thank you for encouraging my love of writing and story. Yours were some of my very favorite classes. I will continue to build upon the foundations you gave me.

Heartfelt thanks to Mom and Dad, who don't like vampires, but who do like me. I love you very much.

I never actively set out to write a spiritual subplot. I consider myself a Christian who is a fiction writer, not necessarily a Christian Fiction writer. But sometimes it just shows up because characters need it. When that happens, I tend to panic because I don't know how well it will come across or how it will be received. But the Lord is faithful, and I believe at the end of the day, what Flannery O'Connor said is true: "When a book leaves your hands, it belongs to God. He may use it to save a few souls or to try a few others, but I think that for the writer to worry is to take over God's business."

This book belongs to God. Use it, Lord.

Also by Claire Trella Hill

<u>Bonds of Blood</u>

Black and Deep Desires

Parfit Gentil Knyght: an Addie and Etienne Vignette (Newsletter Exclusive)

Every Longing Heart

<u>The Karneesia Chronicles</u>

The Erlking's Daughters

Mistress of Wardwood and Other Stories (Newsletter Exclusive)

The Flight of the Spellbound

The Heartwood's Choice

<u>Tales from Karneesia</u>

When a Dragon Comes Courting

Come by Water

The Shapeshifter Drives a Bargain

<u>The Lost Treasures of Peredur</u>

Aeronwy's Stolen Child (Newsletter Exclusive)

About the Author

Claire Trella Hill will read anything, but fantasy romance and gothic fiction are her favorites. Born and raised in Houston, Texas, she still lives there because she is impervious to 100 degree weather. She also has a bad habit of making her characters in the Sims and continuing their stories. When Claire isn't writing, she can be found with her nose glued to her library app, assisting with the last tricky pieces of a puzzle, swilling Dr. Pepper, collecting vintage romance covers, or cuddling with her cat.

You can connect with her on social media or sign up for her newsletter on her website ClaireTrellaHill.com.

www.ingramcontent.com/pod-product-compliance
Lightning Source LLC
Chambersburg PA
CBHW030135310726
48970CB00005B/1448